A GRAVE TALENT

A Grave Talent is an exceptional first novel which introduces Casey Martinelli, a newly promoted, female Homicide detective with a secret to conceal, and Alonzo Hawkin, a world-weary cop trying to make a new life for himself in San Francisco.

These two very different detectives are thrown together to solve a particularly ugly crime – the murders of three young girls. All the children are similar in appearance and all are found near a rural colony, home to those who have dropped out of the rat race. Amongst them is one woman, the enigmatic artist Vaun, who is hiding the terrible truth about her past and her real identity.

There is only one obvious suspect, but as they get nearer the solution, Martinelli and Hawkin realize the crimes are not necessarily the sexually motivated killings they had seemed. There is a coldly calculating and tortuous mind at work here which they must outmanoeuvre if they are to prevent both further killing, and the destruction of a shining talent.

This sensitive and absorbing first crime novel was awarded America's highest accolade for a first crime novel and marks the start of an exciting series featuring Casey Martinelli and Alonzo Hawkin.

A GRAVE TALENT

Laurie R. King

HarperCollins*Publishers*

Collins Crime
an imprint of HarperCollins*Publishers*
77–85 Fulham Palace Road, London W6 8JB

Published by HarperCollins*Publishers* 1995

1 3 5 7 9 10 8 6 4 2

First published in the USA by
St Martin's Press 1993

A catalogue record for this book is
available from the British Library

ISBN 0 00 232543 8

Set in ITC Cheltenham

Printed in Great Britain by
HarperCollinsManufacturing Glasgow

for Noel

הֲיֵלְכוּ שְׁנַיִם יַחְדָּו   בִּלְתִּי אִם־נוֹעָדוּ

Other sins only speak;
murder shrieks out.
—John Webster, *The Duchess of Malfi*

———

Men fear death as children fear to go in the dark;
and as that natural fear in children is increased with tales,
so is the other.
—Francis Bacon, "Of Death"

PROLOGUE

The first small body was found by Tommy Chesler one cold and drizzling afternoon two weeks before Christmas.

Before dawn that morning Tommy had left his cabin with his venerable and marginally accurate deer rifle under his arm and a handful of shells in his pocket, his heart set on a supply of illicit venison. He had no license, it was not the season, and hunting was absolutely forbidden where he planned on going, but that did not worry Tommy. Not much, at any rate. However, he did exercise a fair degree of caution, lest a ranger from the park happen upon him, and he stuck to areas where nobody was likely to be that time of the year, particularly in the rain.

Unfortunately, that included the deer.

At one o'clock, wet through, hungry, and in as bad a temper as he was capable of, Tommy turned for home. Two hours later he was pulling himself hand and foot up the greasy, nearly vertical path made by generations of agile hooves toward the telltale clearing in the trees that meant

3

the Road rising atop the hill above him. He shook his head in disgust at the fresh prints and droppings and decided that he'd just have to go to the Newborns and ask for some of the pig they'd slaughtered last week. Trade some firewood, maybe, or split shakes for their addition. Truth to tell, pork was better than venison anyway. Venison you could roast or you could stew, but most of it had to be given away, and you got tired soon enough of what was left. But pork, now. Pork you could roast and stew, and you could fry and mix with apples and eggs, and make bacon, and—.

Tommy's mouth started to water at the thought of cracklings and red-eye gravy, and when he heard a quick scuffling noise and half saw something lying twenty feet from the edge of the Road, his mind was so occupied that it took a minute for his eyes and ears to interrupt.

Tommy stopped dead, his right foot already touching the jumble of scree that the bulldozer had pushed over in the last grading, and an expression of laborious thought came into his normally blank face. Tommy was not, at the best of times, a man who found reflection easy, and now, tired and distracted, he pulled off his hat and rumpled up his hair as if to stimulate his brains. He wasn't stupid; Tyler had reassured him on that point. He was just—careful. Deliberate. Perhaps that explains why Tommy did not immediately turn to the object that had caught his eye but stood for a long moment looking up at the Road. Perhaps there was some other reason. However, turn back he did, deliberately. There was a further scuffle (weasel, Tommy thought automatically) that moved away rapidly through the low shrubs; with care Tommy walked around a tangle of dormant poison oak, and there before him was a foot, the remains of a small, cold, gray, naked foot.

His eyes focused with great concentration on the delicate, round nail of the littlest toe, so as not to have to look at what that toenail was attached to, and the thought came firmly into his mind that he really wished he'd stayed home that morning and worked on the roof instead of coming out here illegally hunting for deer, and when his thoughts marched inexorably on to the idea of ham, Tommy Chesler was suddenly very, very ill.

4

It took some time, but his stomach eventually stopped trying to crawl out of his throat. He rinsed his mouth with the cold water from the little flask he always carried and tried to think what to do. Tommy may have been none too bright, but he was a gentle man, and he loved children. Without looking too closely at why, he knew he did not want to leave this spot to fetch help—from the freshness of some of the spoor (weasel, yes, and fox and—) there might be nothing to come back to. Another man would perhaps have shrugged his shoulders and gone on down the trail, unwilling to display his deer rifle to all and sundry, but not Tommy. As clearly as if she (or was it a he?) had spoken, Tommy knew that this child, what was left of her (it did have longish hair) was his responsibility. It was not often that Tommy was made responsible for another human being, and he was not about to fail this one. Even if she was dead.

A signal was needed, he decided. The nearest houses were about two miles off, so it would have to be a big signal. He stood thinking intensely, oblivious to the bite of the wind and the thick smell, until an idea came trickling up into his mind, the memory of a grainy cowboy movie seen on Tyler's ancient television set. He looked at his gun, and at the handful of ammunition from his pocket. Ten bullets, and one in the gun. They would have to do. He pointed the heavy gun vaguely upward and fired. Paused and fired again. Another pause, and once more. Two minutes later he repeated the three shots and wondered somewhat guiltily where those bullets would come to earth. After another wait he did it again; then, ever tidy, he gathered up the spent shells and wondered what to do next. Perhaps it wasn't necessary to stand quite so close, he decided. He pulled himself back up the slippery hill to the Road, and the response came: three spaced shots. He loaded one of the two remaining bullets and fired it. One shot came in answer. Happy now, he squatted against a tree where he could keep an eye on the hillside below, and waited.

The events that followed were predictable, if unprecedented. The Riddle brothers arrived, and though their reaction to Tommy's find was not as dramatic as his (for they had come expecting to find trouble and had presumably not been thinking of ham), they climbed back onto the Road considerably subdued and swallowing convulsively. Tommy and Ben Riddle set off downhill to the Dodson farm five miles away, and within the hour a pigtailed Amy Dodson was skittering off down the road on her sure-footed little hill pony, Matilda, toward Tyler's Barn and a telephone, four miles further. It was nearly midnight before the police teams arrived at the earthly remains of Tina Merrill, having lost one four-wheel-drive vehicle and its driver (who was flown out with a broken leg) into Tyler's Creek. They did not know the name of the child at first, of course. It took a couple of days to match the dental X rays and the traces of a long-healed fracture of the right arm with the gap-toothed grinning child who looked out from hundreds of bulletin boards and telephone poles throughout the Bay Area, but the identity was certain.

It was not a good Christmas for the Merrill family.

Because Tina's body had been out on the hillside for so long, it was difficult for the pathology people to be certain, but it did not appear that she had been abused in any way before she was strangled. She had vanished in San Francisco on her way home from school, on the Wednesday after Thanksgiving, and was left in the woods not too many days after that. Her murderer had apparently carried her naked body to this spot half a mile down the fire road from where it entered the state reserve, where Tommy Chesler found her ten days later. The overworked detective who was handed her case held out little hope of an immediate arrest. His name was Alonzo Hawkin.

The second child was found six weeks later, fifteen miles away as the crow flies, and in considerably fresher condition. The couple who found her had nothing in common with Tommy Chesler other than the profound wish afterwards that they had done something else on that particular day. It had been a gorgeous morning, a brilliant day following a week of rain, and they had awakened to an impulsive decision to call in sick from their jobs, throw some Brie, sour-

6

dough, and Riesling into the insulated bag, and drive down the coast. Impulse had again called to them from the beach where Tyler's Creek met the ocean, and following their picnic they decided to look for some privacy up the creekside trail. Instead, they found Amanda Bloom.

Amanda, too, was from over the hill in the Bay Area, though her home was across the water from Tina's. There were a number of similarities in the two girls: both of them were in kindergarten, both were white girls with brown hair, both were from upper-middle-class families. And both of them had walked home from their schools.

It was the third death that set off the fireworks, even before the body was found. Samantha Donaldson disappeared from the fenced-in, manicured front garden of her parents' three-and-a-quarter-million-dollar home in the hills above Palo Alto on a sunny Monday in February. She reappeared some hours later, quite dead, on Tyler's Road. Samantha was five years old and had shiny brown hair, and with her disappearance the low-grade fear among Bay Area parents, particularly those with brown-haired, kindergarten-aged daughters, erupted into outright panic. From Napa to Salinas, parents descended on schools, sent delegations to police stations, arranged car pools, and held hundreds of tight-voiced conversations with their frightened children about the dangers of talking with strange people, conversations which brought feelings of deep, inchoate resentment on the part of the adults at this need to frighten kids in order to keep them safe.

The Donaldsons were important people on the peninsula. Mrs. Donaldson, a third-generation San Franciscan, was the moving force behind—and in front of—a number of arts programs and counted the mayor of San Francisco among her personal friends. So it was hardly surprising that within two hours of Samantha's disappearance Alonzo Hawkin's other cases were taken from him and he was put in charge of directing the investigations in all four counties. He was also given an assistant. He was not pleased when he heard the name.

"Who?" His worn features twisted as if he'd smelled something rotten, which in a way he had.

7

"Katarina Cecilia Martinelli, known as Casey. From her initials."

"Christ Almighty, Ted. Some nut is out there killing little girls, I'm about to have half of Northern California come down on my head, and you assign me some Madonna in uniform who was probably writing parking tickets until last week."

"She made inspector a year ago," Lieutenant Patterson said patiently. "She's new here, but she got a first-class degree from Cal, and the people in San Jose say she's competent as hell, gave her a citation to prove it."

" 'Competent' means that she's either impossible to get along with or so nervous she'll shoot her own foot."

"I know she's green, Al, and we probably wouldn't have promoted her to detective yet, but I think she'll work out. Hell, we were all young once, and she'll age fast working with you," he said, trying for camaraderie, but at the lack of reaction on Hawkin's face he sighed and retreated into authority. "Look, Al, we have to have a woman on it, and the only ones I've got better than her are involved, in a cast, or on maternity leave. Take her."

"I'd rather have one of the secretaries from the pool."

"Al, you take Martinelli or I'll give the case to Kitagawa. Look, I want you to take this. I read the reports on the cases you handled in Los Angeles, the two kidnappings, and I like the way you worked them. But I have to have a woman's face on this one—I'm sure you can see that—and I just don't have anyone else free. I'd give you a more experienced woman if I could, but at the moment I don't have one. Believe me, Al, I want this bastard caught, fast, and I wouldn't do this to you if I thought she'd be in the way. Now, will you have her, or do I give it to Kitagawa?"

"No, I want it. I'll take her. But you owe me."

"I owe you. Here's her file. I told her you'd want to see her at six."

ONE

THE
ROAD

*I went to the woods because I wished to live deliberately, to front only
the essential facts of life, and see what it had to teach, and not,
when I came to die, discover that I had not lived.*
—Henry David Thoreau, *Walden*

———

*"Good Heavens," I cried. "Who would associate crime
with these dear old homesteads?"*
*"They always fill me with a certain horror. It is my belief, Watson,
founded upon my experience, that the lowest and vilest alleys in London
do not present a more dreadful record of sin
than does the smiling and beautiful countryside."*
—Arthur Conan Doyle, "The Adventure of the Copper Beeches"

1

San Francisco was still dark when the telephone erupted a
foot from the ear of Katarina Cecilia Martinelli, Casey to her
colleagues, Kate to her few friends. She had it off the hook
before the first ring had ended.

"Yes?"

"Inspector Martinelli?"

"Yes."

"Inspector Hawkin wants you to pick him up at the front
entrance in fifteen minutes. He says to tell you they found
Samantha Donaldson."

"Not alive."

"No."

"Tell the inspector it'll be closer to twenty, unless he
wants me in my pajamas." She hung up without waiting for a
response, flung back the tangle of blankets, and lay for a
moment looking up into the dark room. She was not wearing
pajamas.

A sleep-thick voice came from the next pillow.

"Is this going to be a common occurrence from now on?"

"You married into trouble when you married me," Kate snarled cheerfully.

"I didn't marry you."

"If it's good enough for Harriet Vane, it's good enough for you."

"Oh, God, Lord Peter in my bed at, what is it, five o'clock? I knew this promotion was a mistake."

"Go back to sleep."

"I'll make you some breakfast."

"No time."

"Toast, then. You go shower."

Kate scooped clothes out of various drawers and closets, and then paused with them tucked under her left arm and looked out the window.

Of all views of the bridge that dominated this side of the city, it was this one she loved the best—still dark, but with the early commute beginning to thicken the occasional headlights that passed at what seemed like arm's reach. The Bay Bridge was a more workmanlike structure than the more famous Golden Gate Bridge, but the more beautiful for it. Alcatraz, which lay full ahead of the house, could be seen from this side by leaning a bit. Kate leaned, checked that the defunct island prison still looked as surreal as it always did in the dark, and then stayed leaning against the frame of the window, her nose almost touching the old, undulating glass. She was hit by a brief, fierce surge of passion for the house, for the wood against her right hand—wood which that hand had stripped and sanded and varnished eighteen months before—and for the oak boards beneath her bare feet that she herself had freed of the cloying flowered carpet and filled and sanded and varnished and waxed. She was not yet thirty years old and had lived in eighteen different houses and had never before understood how anyone could feel possessive of a mere set of walls. Now she could. Perhaps you had to put sweat into a house before it was home, she speculated, watching the cars curve past her. Or perhaps it was that she'd never lived in anything but stucco before. Hard to get passionate about a house made of plywood and chicken wire.

This house was about as old as things get in San Francisco, where even the Mission is a reconstructed pretense.

Its walls had smelled the fire of 1906, which had destroyed most of what the earthquake had left. The house had known six births and two deaths, had suffered the indignities of paint and of being crowded by inappropriate high-rises filled with absurdly expensive apartments, which greedily devoured the incomparable view from Russian Hill. The house was a true San Franciscan, fussy and dignified, immensely civilized and politely oblivious of the eccentricities of neighbors. It had several balconies, a great deal of hand-worked wood, heavy beams, crooked floors, and a pocket-handkerchief lawn that was shaded by the upstarts and by a neighbor's tree. Kate hoped that the house was as content with her as she was with it.

"I ought to flick on the lights," said Lee from behind her. "Give the commuters a thrill." Kate dropped a shoe, realized with a spurt of panic that she'd been standing there mesmerized by the lights for a good two minutes, snatched up the shoe and sprinted for the bathroom.

Toast was waiting for her downstairs, and a large thermos of strong coffee and a bag of sandwiches, and Kate pulled up to the curb in twenty-one minutes. Hawkin was standing on the sidewalk in front of the Hall of Justice, a raincoat over his arm, and climbed into the seat beside her. He tossed his hat negligently over his shoulder into the back.

"You know where you're going?" he said by way of greeting.

"Tyler's Road?"

"Yes. Wake me ten minutes before we get there," and so saying he wadded his coat against the door and was limp before they reached the freeway.

Kate drove fast and sure through the empty streets to the freeway entrance, negotiated the twists, merged into the southward lane without mishap. She was grateful for the reprieve from conversation, for although her round face was calm in the gray light and her short, strong fingers lay easily on the wheel, the fingers were icy and elsewhere she was sweating.

She left Highway 280 and pointed the car west over the coastal range, and in the gray light of early morning she made a deliberate effort to relax. She arched her hands in turn, settled herself back in the seat, and reached for the attitude she tried to have before a long run. Pace yourself, Kate, she thought. There's nothing you can't handle here, it's just another small step up the ladder; Hawkin's no ogre, you're going to learn a lot from him. Apprehension is one thing, it's only to be expected—news cameras, everyone's eye on you—but they're not going to see below the surface, nobody's interested in you.

True, it didn't help to know that she was there for a number of reasons that she wouldn't exactly have chosen and did not feel proud of. It amused her to think that she counted as a minority, advanced prematurely (but only by a degree) due to unexpected vacancies and one of those periodic departmental rumblings of concern over Image, Minorities, and the dread Women's Movement, but it was not amusing to think that she had been assigned to this specific case because she was relatively photogenic and a team player known for not making waves, that she was a political statement from the SFPD to critics from women's groups, and, worst of all, that her assignment reflected the incredibly outdated, absurd notion that women, even those without their own, were somehow "better with children." Humiliating reasons, but she was not about to cut her own throat by refusing the dubious honor. She just hoped the people she was going to work with didn't hold it against her. She wasn't sure about Al Hawkin. He had seemed pretty brusque yesterday, but. . . .

Kate had presented herself in his office the evening before at precisely six o'clock with the same nervous symptoms that had stayed with her until this morning, the icy hands, sweating body, dry mouth. He looked up from his paper-strewn desk at her knock, a thickset, graying man in a light blue shirt, sleeves rolled up on hairy forearms, tieless, collar loosened, in need of a shave. He pulled off his glasses and looked at her with patient, detached blue-gray eyes, and she wondered if she had the right room. He hardly seemed to be the terror rumor had him.

"Lieutenant Hawkin?"

"Not any more. Just 'Inspector.' And you're . . . ?"

"Inspector Martinelli, sir. Lieutenant Patterson told me to come here at six o'clock." She heard her voice drift up into a question mark, and kicked herself. You will not be a Miss Wishy-Washy, she ordered herself fiercely.

"Yes. Do you drive?"

"Drive?" she repeated, taken aback. "Yes, I can drive."

"Good. I hate driving. Take an unmarked, if you like, or you can use your own car and bill the department, if you have a radio. Doesn't matter in the least to me. All I ask is that you never let the tank get less than half full. Damned inconvenient to run out of gas twenty miles from nowhere."

"Yes sir. I'll use my own, then, thanks. I have a car phone. Sir."

"The name is Al."

"Okay, Al."

"That stack of folders is for you to take home. I'll expect you to have read through them by tomorrow. See you in the morning."

With that he had put his glasses back on and taken up another file. Trying hard to keep her dignity in the face of the dismissal, she had gathered up the armload of papers and gone home to read into the early hours. First, however, she had filled the tank. And checked the oil.

A generous ten minutes before they arrived Kate spoke his name tentatively, and he immediately woke and looked around him. A few fat drops hit the windshield. She flicked on the wipers and glanced over at him.

"Looks like we'll be needing those raincoats," she offered. He gave no sign of having heard, and she flushed slightly. Damn, was he going to be one of those?

Actually, Alonzo Hawkin was not one of those. Alonzo Hawkin was simply the epitome of the one-track mind, and at that moment his mind was on a very different track from the weather. He missed little, reacted less, and thought incessantly about his work. His wife had found him dismal company, and had immersed herself in their two children—schools, dance lessons, soccer teams. Six months after the younger one left for the university, the presence of a continually distracted husband who worked strange hours and slept stranger ones had proven more than she could bear, and she too had gone. That was a year ago. He had stayed on at his job in Los Angeles, but when he heard of the opening in San Francisco and thought that it might be nice to be able to

15

breathe in the summer, he applied for it and got it. With surprisingly few regrets he had left the city where he had lived all his adult life, packed up his books and his fish tanks, and come here.

Hawkin woke, as he always did outside of his own bed, without disorientation, his thoughts continuing where they had left off. In this case they ran a close parallel with those going through Kate's mind. Hawkin strongly suspected that he, the new boy, had been thrown this very sticky case in order to save the necks of the higher-ups. He was an outsider, easily sacrificed, in the event of failure, on the altar of public opinion. If he failed, well, they would say, he was so highly recommended by his former colleagues, but I guess we were asking too much of a guy who doesn't know the area. If he succeeded, it would, he was sure, be arranged to reflect well on the judgment of those who chose him. Perhaps it wasn't entirely fair to be so suspicious of their motives—after all, the department was short-handed at the moment, and he did have a couple of very successful kidnapping cases to his credit, so he was the logical one to take this one. He knew, however, that there was a certain amount of time-buying going on, and he'd been given the prominence, in the face of a near-hysterical public and the considerable force of Mrs. Donaldson, while the department above him decided what it wanted to do. Disturbing, but he'd probably have done the same. No, he corrected himself, he probably wouldn't. Al Hawkin liked to be in the middle of things. He'd just have to make damn sure he succeeded.

He wondered if this reserved, almost pretty, alarmingly young police inspector at his side might turn out to be as competent as her record and her driving seemed to suggest. He hoped to God she was, for both their sakes. Hawkin squinted up at the heavy sky and sighed, thinking of Los Angeles.

"Looks like you're right," he said aloud, and missed her surprised look as he stretched over the back of the seat for his hat. "Is that coffee?" he asked, spotting the thermos on the back floor.

"Yes, help yourself. There's a cup in the glove compartment."

"No sugar?"

16

"Sorry."

"Oh well, can't be helped," he allowed, and slurped cautiously. "Good coffee. How'd you have time to make it?"

"I didn't. I have a friend."

"Must be a good friend, to make you coffee at five-thirty in the morning."

"Mmm."

"Well, he makes decent coffee, but next time have him throw some packets of sugar in for mine."

Kate opened her mouth, and shut it again firmly. Time enough for that, another day. Other matters pressed.

"About the body—who found it?" she asked.

"One of the women on the Road, Terry something, Allen maybe. She's a nurse, works the odd day in town, always weird hours. She leaves her two dogs at Tyler's place, at the beginning of the Road, and walks home. At two in the morning, can you believe it? Anyway, a couple miles up the Road the dogs started getting jumpy at something down the hill, and at first she thought it was a skunk or a raccoon, but her flashlight caught it, and it was the girl. She woke a neighbor and sent him down to Tyler's to phone while she stayed with the body. That's all I know. We'll interview her at Tyler's later. I told Trujillo—the local man on the case?—to round up everyone on the Road and bring them down. We couldn't possibly do a door-to-door—it'd take us a week."

"The Road is bad? Is that why the woman has to walk home?"

"Wasn't that in the stuff I gave you yesterday? Maybe I never bothered putting it into the case notes. Anyway, the whole area is owned by one John Tyler. Nice fellow, but a bit eccentric even by California standards—he regards himself as some kind of modern-day country squire living on a landed estate, with overtones of an ecological garden of Eden. No electrical lines into the area, no telephones, and cars allowed up the Road only two days a week. More than seventy people up there, some of them nine miles from a telephone, along an old fire road that washes out every third year."

"Sounds fun," said Kate, wondering how her car was expected to tackle that.

"Doesn't it? All the inconveniences of modern life with

17

none of the benefits. It does limit the field considerably, though. There are locked gates at both ends of the Road—locks changed a few months ago, residents have the only keys—and the body was found about two and a half miles up."

"Was yesterday one of the days cars were allowed?"

"Trujillo says yes, and that people who work in town tend to shop for groceries and such those days and drive up at night, so nobody pays much attention to cars on Monday nights."

"Great. Well, if it's a dirt road there should be tracks left, if they get to them soon."

"Depends on what time they were put there. They had rain here after midnight. Yeah," he said, seeing her expression, "it goes like that sometimes."

"Maybe we'll luck out. Do you know if this is the same Tyler who runs a big medieval weekend every year? It seems to me it's held at a place called Tyler's Barn, everyone in costume, archery contests, that kind of thing."

"Sure to be. The place is bristling with lances and broadswords and God knows what. Here we are. And somebody's tipped the press."

2

It was an impressive sight, despite the ominous and growing cluster of press vehicles lined up on the seaward side of the paved road, from beat-up sedans to two shiny vans whose letters proclaimed their channels and whose silver mobile transmitters jutted toward the lowering sky. Tyler's Barn sat on the edge of a twenty-acre clearing, which at this time of year was green enough to be called a meadow. Two huge, pale horses turned their rumps to the human fuss and grazed. Hills covered in redwoods rose dramatically beyond. There actually was a barn, though from here it was nearly hidden behind a big, old wooden house (lodge was the word that came to mind) and a vast, open-sided shed with a rusting, corrugated metal roof draped with leafless vines. The shed seemed to be filled with automobiles and farm machinery, but from the Road it was nearly obscured by the high wire fence, intertwined with more bare vines, that had lined the Road for the last few miles and that continued solidly around the next curve, broken only, Kate saw now, by three gates.

The first gate was a simple, sturdy metal affair wide enough for a truck, and from it the double ruts of a dirt track climbed through the meadow to disappear into the trees. The gate was mounted on a pair of what looked like telephone poles, from which was suspended a tired wooden sign, the width of the gate, which proclaimed this as TYLER'S ROAD. A heavy chain and padlock held the gate shut, and a man with a uniform and regulation rain slickers, sitting in a police car, ensured it stayed that way.

A quarter of a mile down the Road they came to a second gate. This one was simple, low, and wooden, graced by an archway and more vines (some leaves on these—were they roses?), tastefully accompanied by another large uniform and slickers. The third gate was metal like the first, but twice as wide, and opened into the barn's yard. At Hawkin's directions Kate turned into this gate, which was standing open, and held up her ID. The guard waved them through into an acre or more of gravel, a rough triangle edged by the long shed, the house (which was even larger than it had appeared from the Road), and the sprawling barn, to which sheds and lean-tos of various shapes, sizes, and eras had been attached like barnacles to a host shell. She pulled up next to the house, and a slim young man in a beautifully cut gray suit emerged from the door of one of the barn's appendages and trotted across the gravel to greet them.

"Morning, Inspector Hawkin, and you must be Inspector Martinelli. I'm Paul, Paul Trujillo."

"Casey," she offered in return. His handshake was trim like the rest of him, his hands neat, his dark eyes friendly under black, carefully tousled hair. At the moment the wouldn't-you-like-to-run-your-fingers-through-my-hair effect was flattened somewhat by the thousands of tiny pearls of light rain, but Kate could see the intent.

"So, Trujillo, what do we have so far?" Hawkin asked,

and the three of them drifted across to the isolation and shelter of the car shed for Trujillo to give his report. Kate was amused to see him actually squaring his shoulders a fraction as if Hawkin were his superior officer rather than officially his counterpart.

"I just got down from the scene about ten minutes ago myself, but Tyler seems to have things here under control. He's giving us three rooms downstairs to take statements in, and the residents are beginning to come in. He's even doing us a lunch."

"What did you find at the scene?" Hawkin demanded, waving away these housekeeping chores impatiently.

"My preliminary findings are being typed up now, you'll have them before you leave, and I told the Crime Scene people not to move anything until you'd seen her. Basically, though, the Medical Examiner estimates the time of death between one and five yesterday afternoon. Strangled, like the others, by a strong right hand of average size. No mutilation, no signs of sexual . . . no signs of molestation. The Examiner had to leave, but she said she'd be available this afternoon if you want to talk to her. She'll also try to get the autopsy speeded up for us, maybe tomorrow morning. She said to tell you not to expect any surprises."

"Do we have someone who can test for prints on the body?"

"We did that first thing, sir. The Kromekote cards drew a blank, but the Magna brush test gave one very rough partial on the right index finger, from just under her ear."

"More than we got from the other two. Maybe the lab'll get lucky and find some fibers. Have the parents been notified?"

"Yes sir. They'll be at the morgue later to make a positive ID, and they want to talk with you then, they said."

"I'll bet. Tell them I'm occupied up here. No, don't say that, they'll drive up here and we'll have a circus on our hands. Tell Mrs. Donaldson I'll telephone her tonight at her home."

Trujillo pulled a maroon leather pad from his trouser pocket and a gold pen from inside his jacket and made a note.

"Deputy Harris will be at the morgue, too—" he began.

"Who?"

"Harris, the man in charge of investigations from Santa Clara County. If she died there, which the doc thought likely, there's the question of jurisdiction."

"God, you'd think they'd all be wanting to give it away, and instead of that we've got four counties fighting for it. I'm surprised the FBI hasn't grabbed it away from us."

"Well, sir, Agent Pickard has been—"

"Oh, Christ, Pickhead himself is in on it now, is he? Okay, let's see." Hawkin put his thumbs through his belt and drew in a deep breath of air that carried equal parts of salt, evergreen tree, wet rust, and fumes from the van generators across the way. "Right. We'll arrange a meeting with you, Martinelli, and me, and Alameda, Santa Clara, the FBI, Uncle Tom Cobbleigh and all." Trujillo made another note. "Let's just hope we can keep Mrs. Donaldson out of it. Tell them all that I want them to bring complete reports to the meeting, so we're not just making noise. We'll want the postmortem results, the Crime Scene findings, and anything the lab has ready. Also the complete interviews with the families and all the neighbors of all three girls, diagrams of the kidnap sites, and psychological profiles of all three victims."

Trujillo looked up, aghast.

"But, that'll take days."

"So much the better. Now, what can we give Pickhead to keep him out of our hair? Ah, VICAP. Tell him I want a list of every child dead or kidnapped across the country who fits the description of our three. Limit it to the last ten years. I also want a detailed profile of the killer. Have you ever talked to VICAP, Casey?"

"I submitted a case to them last year."

"The Violent Criminal Apprehension Program," he mouthed scornfully. "Submit the completed form to your local Criminal Profile Coordinator, who forwards it to the Behavioral Sciences Investigative Support Unit, who feed it into the Almighty Central Adding Machine. And do you know what the profile will read? 'White male, middle income, above average intelligence, grew up in a dysfunctional family, juvenile record of minor crimes involving fire-setting and cruelty to animals, may or may not be married, all his neighbors find him likeable but quiet.' End quote."

Kate wondered if she was expected to say something

21

along the lines of, "Remarkable, Holmes!" It was just a bit too easy to mock the FBI's profile system, which, give it credit, occasionally pulled off a real coup of identification. Hawkin seemed to realize this, because he shook himself and subsided, and cleared his throat.

"As I was saying. A meeting of all and sundry when we have the paperwork together. Use the word 'brainstorming,' Trujillo," he directed. "They'll like that. Press conference so we can all prove to the taxpayers how busy we are. Find out how long it's going to take them to assemble their reports, and I'll work it in. Thursday or Friday, the early afternoon."

"Great," said Trujillo, and snapped his notepad shut. "Did you want to see Tyler now, or go straight up to the scene?"

"I'd better see him first, it'll only take a minute."

"He's in his workshop, around back of the barn."

"I know where it is," said Hawkin, and walked off across the gravel.

Kate and Trujillo followed him through the door into the little building, where two men looked up from their contemplation of the object on the workbench in front of them. For a wild instant Kate thought it was a dismembered arm, until her eyes took in the metallic gleam and she recognized it as the detached arm of the suit of armor that stood in the corner. The Japanese man remained seated, but the other, older man stood up and, wiping his hands on a white cloth, came around to meet them. He was a small man, barely taller than Kate, about forty years old, and he moved with a heavy, twisting limp. His shoulder length hair, brown streaked with gray, was gathered into a pony tail, and his beard was trimmed low on his jaw. He wore a loose homespun shirt, more nearly a blouse, tucked into faded but ironed blue jeans, and soft leather boot-moccasins on his small feet.

"Hello, Inspector Hawkin," he said. "I cannot say I am exactly glad to see you again, considering the reason you're here, but you are welcome."

"Thank you, Mr. Tyler. This is my assistant, Inspector Casey Martinelli. I appreciate your allowing us to bring half the county to your house."

Tyler waved it aside. "The house is used to it. Some of the residents are setting up the tables Paul asked for. I left it

22

to them; hauling furniture around isn't my specialty, and I had to come out here and get Toshiro started." He looked embarrassed. "I would have asked him to come some other time, but I made the arrangements months ago for him to be here, and I couldn't reach him this morning to cancel them. I hope it doesn't—." He broke off, though Kate could finish the sentence in her head: "—seem callous."

Hawkin spoke calmly. "No, of course not, no reason for everything to come to a halt. You go on with it. I have to go up the Road now, but I'll need to talk with you later."

Tyler looked relieved at this forgiving attitude, and Kate wondered if Hawkin was trying to soften him up. They left the two men and went back into the half-drizzle, and before they were out the door Tyler had resumed his conversation with Toshiro the armorer.

"It's the vambrace, you see, that binds when I raise my sword. . . ."

Hawkin took no notice but spoke unceremoniously to Trujillo.

"What have you got to take us up in?"

Kate was relieved that it was not to be her car that tackled the dirt track and stood with him as he looked past the obviously inadequate cars near the house and toward the shed, with its row upon row of bumpers fronting a mind-boggling collection of rust and dents—two, four, and six wheels, round bodies and square, old school buses, campers, pickups, Volkswagen vans and bugs—and half a dozen shapes covered tightly with dusty canvas shrouds.

"The county cars are all pretty busy but Tyler's loaning us his wagon. It'll go anywhere."

He pointed to an object so large, so old, and so apparently immobile that Kate had assumed it was a display, useful for entertaining children, like the hulls of planes and trains that occasionally grace playgrounds. It looked thoroughly rooted to the ground, resting on cracked tires as high as Kate's waist, doors sagging, windows cloudy with the abrasions of the decades. It had once been red.

"That?" Hawkin stared in disbelief.

"Yes, it's great," said Trujillo with enthusiasm. "It used to be a fire wagon in the thirties, and Tyler keeps it up something great. Of course, parts are hard to get, and it won't

23

go more than forty without the doors flying open, but for getting up the hill there's nothing like it."

Hawkin turned his attention from the vehicle to the man.

"I didn't realize you knew him so well."

"Tyler? Known him for years."

"Maybe they should've put somebody else on this case, then."

Trujillo smiled gently. "Inspector, you'd be hard put to find a cop in the county who doesn't know Tyler and consider him a friend. It's a small place."

"I see. Okay, let's get on with it. Are you going to drive this thing?"

"Good God, no. Tyler wouldn't trust me with his baby. Mark Detweiler's the only one who's allowed to touch it. He'll be driving. Mark?" He went to the door and stuck his head inside. "Mark! Anybody seen Mark?"

After a few minutes of confusion a slow mountain of a man, gray braids reaching to the waist of his ancient jeans, plaid shirt hidden by a beard nearly as long, emerged to plant his heavy boots on the plank steps and survey the yard through a pair of smudged horn-rimmed glasses held together by a twist of wire and dirty duct tape. One gold earring glinted through the foliage.

"I'm coming," he rumbled. "Just hold your horses. Just wanted to use the john. Kinda fun to be able to flush." He grinned merrily at them, revealing a missing front tooth amidst the gray fringe, and climbed up into the driver's seat. Hawkin watched, openmouthed, as the man methodically tied the door shut with a hunk of frayed rope, jerked the window up with a pair of pliers and inserted a wedge to hold it almost shut, and fished around in the mends of his jeans for a pocket, from which he pulled a key.

"What's the matter, Al," murmured Kate as she climbed past him. "Didn't have such classy chauffeurs in Los Angeles?" He shook his head, once, and followed her into the back, Trujillo in front. With a roar and a massive cloud of blue exhaust the starter caught, and they rumbled out onto the road, a leviathan among the minnows.

The reporters would get some fine footage for their pain

24

of turning out so early, thought Kate, and saw a scramble to record the parade of wagon, high-axled coroner's van, and the handful of lesser vehicles that brought up the rear.

Trujillo turned as they went through the gate and saw the expression on Hawkin's face.

"We do have the four-wheel drives, but they're both already up the Road. I didn't think you'd mind this thing, and we needed the others to get the teams up there and to go up notifying people. I hope you don't mind," he repeated, hesitantly.

"Oh, no, it lends the proceedings an air of dignified purpose, evoking the ponderous wheels of justice turning. Don't let me forget to use that for the news cameras, Casey, in case they missed the symbolism. It's quite all right, Trujillo, it serves to remind me of the unswerving support given us by our superiors. So encouraging."

Trujillo did not seem entirely encouraged by this response, thought Kate, straight-faced, but any answer was cut short as the wagon turned a hard corner and juddered to an abrupt halt that had all but the driver off their seats.

"Brakes work fine," was Detweiler's phlegmatic comment. The car face-to-face with their very bumper, filled with white-faced passengers, reversed into a wide spot a hundred yards up the road. It was the county's shiny new four-wheel-drive car, and it contained three women, two men, and a gaggle of excited children, all of whom watched the procession in wonder. The uniform of the man behind the wheel did not look entirely fresh, Kate noticed, and she had a sinking feeling that her own khaki trousers would soon look the same.

"That'll be the second bunch, coming down," said Trujillo. "Like I told you on the phone, I don't know how many of them we'll persuade to come down to Tyler's, but we'll get as many as we can. This third body will shake them, especially the ones with kids, and they'll cooperate more than they might otherwise. Some of them, though, you'll have to just go see. There's six or eight who are real hermits. You'd need a court order to pry them out, and even then they might just walk into the woods for a couple of weeks."

"A nice, straightforward investigation, I can see now."

"It is a bit different from San Francisco. Sir."

"It's a bit different from anywhere."

"That was Tyler's original idea."

"Well, it succeeded."

3

Samantha Donaldson was small for her age, forty-two pounds at her last checkup, but she looked even smaller now, her thin body huddled into the rotten log that had stopped her from rolling down into the creek that ran, at this point, about fifty feet below Tyler's Road. Kate's hands wanted to reach out and brush the leaves from the tumbled hair, wipe the dirt from the surprised little mouth, close the puzzled eyes, but instead she took out her notebook to record Hawkin's remarks and allowed her eyes to avoid the child's neck.

A couple of hours later they stood watching as the lifeless object that had been Samantha Donaldson, hands wrapped in bags against any evidence her nails might be hiding, covered in dirt and leaves, having been prodded, examined, and photographed in ways it never would have been in life, was folded into the anonymity of a body bag. The men moving the tiny burden onto the stretcher were well used to death, but there was none of the customary easy black humor here.

"You okay?" asked Hawkin as the disturbingly small parcel was carried past them.

"I'm not about to faint, Al," she snapped. "I've seen dead bodies before."

"Yes," he said, responding not at all to her tone. "But a dead child is a terrible thing."

"Yes." And because his voice was honest and his own loathing lay openly on his face, she answered in kind. "Yes, it's pretty awful. I probably would feel sick if it didn't make me so angry."

"You wouldn't be the first. The first dead child I had, I couldn't keep anything down for two days. Better to stay angry. Now, tell me where you think the murderer stood to throw her down there."

They found one vague ridge of mud that might or might not have been from the side of a shoe, braced to hurl forty pounds into the air. It was so beaten down by rain that it was impossible to define and could easily have been pushed up by a horse's hoof some days before. Other than that, there was a depressing similarity to the sites where the other two bodies had been found, and by the time the wet, aching team had finished their backbreaking examination of the hillside, they had accumulated a number of rusty tin cans; one broken Coke bottle, old; two buttons, one very old; a handful of odd bits of machinery; a half-buried car tire; a short length of ancient chain with a stub of leather dog collar attached; one cheap ballpoint pen, almost new; and an assortment of paper scraps, including a soggy matchbook from a bar in San Jose.

All that was much later, though. The doors slammed shut on the ill-filled bag that contained what had once been a little girl, the stoic team started down the hillside with their own, smaller, evidence bags, and Kate and Hawkin ducked under the yellow tapes and climbed back into the wagon.

"Back to home base?" inquired Detweiler.

"No, not much point in it yet." A couple with baby, child and dog trudged by, all in bright nylon ponchos. The woman smiled shyly, the child stared from the man's back. "They'll be drifting in for another hour or more. I want to see the Road again, up to the top, if this thing'll make it."

"No question about that," said the driver, sounding hurt. "She may be slow, but she's sure."

"Slow she is. Casey, do you have that map? I want you to make a note of the houses as we pass. It'll make things easier when we get back to Tyler's. Now, whose house is that?" Hawkin pointed past the driver's nose to a shack near the Road, and Kate prepared to mark it on the map with her pen.

"That ain't a house, that's Jenny Cadena's goat shed." Kate wrote in the name. "Only now Harry Gustavson's using it to store the window glass for his house." She crossed out the first name, wrote in the second. "Come to think of it, though, Bob Riddle was staying in it for a while after his brother Ben threw him out. I wonder if he's still there?" He peered incuriously at the blank walls as they passed.

27

Kate looked at the map and sighed. "Anybody have a pencil?"

Slowly they rumbled up the narrow, muddy road, stopping twice to let carloads of residents slip by and once to help change a county car's flat tire. Slowly they reached the upper end of the Road, guarded and heavily gated, and slowly they turned back. Just below the Road's summit Hawkin leaned forward and touched Detweiler's shoulder.

"Stop here for a minute, would you? Come with me, Casey."

The two detectives walked thirty yards back up the Road, rocks prodding the soles of their city shoes, and stood looking down at a tumble of rock and brush.

"That's where Tina Merrill was found. Her father had a heart attack last month, did you know that? Her mother's lost twenty pounds and eats tranquilizers, and her honor-roll brother is failing his last year of high school. The murderer dropped her here on the Road like a sack of garbage, and after a few days something dragged her off down the hill."

The hillside was nearly silent, with only a few birds, the click of the engine, their breathing. The sun came out and Kate began to feel warm, but Hawkin didn't move.

"What is he after?" he muttered, staring hard up the dirt track. He looked as if he were straining to look back three months, to see that day in late fall when a figure had carried its macabre burden down the road. "What is he doing?"

"I'm sorry, I don't understand."

"Neither do I. Neither do I." He suddenly looked at her, as if he had just noticed her presence, and began dutifully to explain.

"The bodies are unmolested; he's not the more obvious kind of pedophile. It isn't money; there's no ransom. He just picks them up, so carefully that so far he's been invisible, and strangles them. After that he removes their clothing and leaves them on or near Tyler's Road. Why here, a hundred miles from where he's picked them up? Why is he doing this?"

He cocked one eyebrow at her and turned back to the waiting behemoth, and though she knew he wasn't expecting an answer, she wished she could give him one. All that came to mind was, "So maybe he's a nut case," and that was so obviously inadequate that she said nothing and followed him meekly back down the rough surface that passed as Tyler's Road.

Five minutes later Detweiler stopped the wagon on a hilltop at a wide, clear area with, incongruously, a picnic table. The temporary, enthusiastic sunshine illuminated glimpses of the Road below them and revealed a wedge of the distant, turgid sea. A scattering of roofs and cleared fields peeped from the vista of dark redwoods. The occasional gleam of solar panels and two high-tech wind-powered generators were the only indicators of the twentieth century.

"Nice, huh?" grunted Detweiler. "Tyler says he's going to build up here when he gets old and gray. I doubt it. He likes to be in the middle of things. Always will." He put the wagon back into gear and they lurched downhill, the engine whining now as it kept the ex–fire truck from flinging itself down to the sea. "Oh, yeah, I forgot old Peterson's place. It's up there, see the flag?" The flag was an old scrap of torn sheeting. "Up along that pathway. No, he doesn't have a drive. When he built the place he carried everything in by foot."

Kate wrote in the name Peterson and reflected that a housing inspector would have a grand time with the violations on this hillside. She said something of the sort to Detweiler, careful to avoid the impression that she was in any way connected with such a low breed of bureaucrat.

"Oh, yeah, well, what they don't know won't hurt them. Actually there's been an ongoing war between Tyler and the county over the building regulations. At first they said that all the houses had to be wired for power, even if there wasn't any for miles. So there's half a dozen places with wall plugs and empty light fixtures, and kerosene lamps. Right now he's trying to get around it by having the whole Road made into an experimental, non-profit organization. Has a state senator on his side; he may do it yet. That's Riddle's place, do you have that?" he asked Kate.

"Yes, Ben Riddle, whose brother Bob may or may not be there or in the Cadena-Gustavson goat shed–storage barn."

"Clear as mud, eh?" He laughed heartily, and Kate wondered if he ever ran out of clichés.

The litany continued to wind with the Road.

"That's Brother Luke's place. He and Maggie've lived there since Tyler first got the idea. He used to be a monk somewhere. Not now, though. They've got five kids. The Dodsons live there, funny place, real dark. Nice clearing in back for the ponies, though. Angie's little girl Amy loves her pony. And I told you about Vaun, way up there? She's an artist, real good one." Visions of castles and maidens with starry-eyed unicorns danced in Kate's head. "The Newborns—those little house things are for the pigs. And Tommy Chesler you know."

Coming down the mountain they stopped to pull the county car out of the creek bed into which its four driven wheels had taken it, and as they continued down, they picked up several parties of chattering hill folk who might easily have been going to a hoedown rather than to a murder interrogation. (What is a hoedown, anyway? wondered Kate.) Kate found herself wedged between Hawkin and a very large, damp young man who smelled of dog, and with an even damper and more fragrant baby on her lap. After ten minutes a high voice from somewhere in the front asked if anyone had Ivanhoe.

"Is that a disease?" wondered Kate aloud.

"It's my baby," the voice answered.

"Is it hairless and wet?"

"Probably."

"Then it's here."

"Oh, good. I just wanted to make sure he got in. You can keep him until we get to Tyler's."

"Thank you," said Kate gravely, and tried to decide whether the bouncing was from the ruts or from Hawkin laughing, and if the latter, what she should do about it. In the end she did nothing.

4

The multicolored crowd that whirled in and out of the rooms in Tyler's house was like something from another world, or perhaps several worlds—part Amish, part Woodstock, part pioneer. Children ran yelling and shrieking among the knees and the furniture, dogs wandered in and were thrown out into the rain, the smells of bread and spaghetti sauce and wood smoke mingled with wet clothing, underwashed bodies, and the occasional aura of stale marijuana. Tyler had given the police three rooms downstairs, furnished with a motley collection of tables and desks, where they prepared to take statements. Kate stood in the main room—the hall—with its fifteen-foot ceilings and the floor space of an average house, and wondered how Hawkin intended to proceed with a murder investigation in this chaos. For the first time she was very grateful that he, not she, was in charge.

As if he had heard her thoughts Hawkin appeared at her elbow.

"As I said, a nice straightforward investigation. I'm going to talk with them, and I want you with me. Over at the fireplace." Within two steps he had disappeared, and Kate pushed through the throng in his wake, wishing that her mother had married a taller man. At the massive stone fireplace, beneath a display of broadswords that fanned out in a sunburst, they stepped up onto the high hearthstones and stood looking out over the sea of heads.

"May I have your attention, please? Please, may I have your attention, there are a few things I need to say." He was not shouting, but he pitched his gravelly voice with a sharp volume that filled the room and reached into the adjoining doorways, and gradually faces turned in their direction and the battering pandemonium began to die down. Children were hushed, kitchen pans stopped crashing, and the assembled residents of Tyler's Road turned to hear what this necessary evil, this representative of oppression, wanted of them.

"Good morning, ladies and gentlemen. My name is Alonzo Hawkin. This is Casey Martinelli. As I'm sure you all know by now, we were sent down from San Francisco to coordinate the investigation into the murders of the three little girls whose bodies have been found in this area. I'd like to thank you all for coming down to Tyler's. I know—I have seen—what an inconvenience it is for some of you to get down here, but it is saving us a great deal of time, and after all, time saved may mean a life saved."

He had their full attention now. A small baby began to whine, and the mother settled it to her breast without taking her eyes off Hawkin.

"We are here to take statements from you in hopes that the pieces of information you give us can be put together and lead us to the killer. I don't need to tell you that the murderer is somehow connected with your Road. You all know that, and I expect that's why a lot of you are here. It is not nice to think that one of your neighbors might be linked to the murder of three children. Might even be that murderer." Eyes dropped, lips smiled nervously, and fear turned a crowded room into a lot of people trying not to edge away from each other.

"We are not here, I will say now, to worry about drugs, housing code violations, or who is sleeping in whose bed, unless of course any of those things are related to the murders. We may ask you about drugs or violations, but it's not what we're after. Any of you are free to choose the police officer you want to take your statement. Because there are so many of you to keep straight we'd like to take your photograph with an instant camera and attach it to your statement. This is only to make things run more smoothly. You will be asked a series of questions, some of which may sound unnecessary or rude or just plain silly. Please answer them. None of us are playing games, and we're every bit as anxious to finish here as you are. From the looks of it," he added with a smile, "perhaps more so."

There was a mild commotion in one corner, and a little voice piped up, "—to have games, Mama? Is that what he said?" Grateful, nervous laughter skittered through the room, and Hawkin's smile broadened.

"That reminds me, you see that little man in the corner

32

over there?" Heads craned, and an enormous man with extremely black skin and an inadequate uniform lifted an identifying hand. More laughter, now uncertain. "That's Sergeant Fischer. Bob Fischer hasn't seen his own kids for two whole days now, and if you want to send your kids to talk to him while you're giving your statements, he'd be absolutely overjoyed. He'll show them all his walkie-talkie and his handcuffs, but, uh, Bob? Try not to lose the keys this time, okay?" Relaxed laughter now, which Hawkin gathered up in his final words.

"One last thing. I know it's a bit late for saying this, but I'd appreciate it if you'd not talk to each other about what you may have seen, or what someone else thinks they saw. Your statement needs to be yours, and yours alone. We'll sift it over, and if we need further information about something, we'll come and find you. There are seven of us here to take your statements, if you would please begin at that end of the room, take one set of forms for each adult. We'd better get started." He held them for a moment with his eyes. "Thank you for your assistance. There's some bastard out there murdering babies. I think you can help us find who it is. Thank you."

"Ever coach a football team, Al?" Kate murmured in his ear as the meeting broke up.

"What do you think I was doing just then?" he replied. "Take a desk. I'll let you know when I'm going to talk with Tyler."

The morning wore on, with the painstaking business of names and numbers, photographs with the instant camera, locations on the map, questions: Where do you work? Have you ever been arrested? Where were you on the Wednesday after Thanksgiving, on the twenty-fourth of January, yesterday afternoon? Did you see anyone yesterday afternoon? Did anyone see you yesterday afternoon? Did you see or hear a car on the Road yesterday evening? Do you smoke anything, use matches, go into bars, own a car, drive a car, have any other pieces of information that might possibly be related? On, and on, and on.

Answers were recorded, reactions to certain questions

33

were noted, voices dropped, and tempers flared. Hawkin moved in and out of the rooms, chatting, encouraging, defusing hot spots, disappearing to walk through the mud to speak with the newsmen. Gallons of coffee and herbal tea were drunk, children were laid down for naps, a hugely pregnant woman began to look pale and was sent off to an upstairs room. At one point a plate of vegetarian spaghetti and hot bread appeared in front of Kate, and she and her interviewee slurped at each other and got sauce on the forms.

At one o'clock Kate found herself in one of the more difficult interviews of the day. Not that Flower Underwood wasn't cooperative—she was, and friendly and intelligent besides. It was her child who created the problems.

The child was a boy, or at least Kate assumed it was a boy, for the woman didn't correct her when she asked how old he was. He was an utterly irrepressible two-year-old who took her pens apart, ate one of the forms, emptied her purse three times (wallet and keys went into her pocket after she pried them from his inquisitive fingers), and climbed up onto his mother's lap to nurse five times, the last time squirting Kate with milk from the unoccupied breast. Deliberately. Into this stepped Hawkin, who put his hand on her shoulder as she was writing.

"Pardon me, Casey, but when you're finished you might like to join Tyler and me upstairs. All the way to the top of the stairs, third door on your left."

Kate nodded her agreement and looked up to catch the tail end of an extremely odd expression on the woman's face.

"What is it?"

"Nothing, really." She was stifling amusement.

"Something about upstairs? Was that it?"

Flower Underwood's lips twitched, and finally she burst out laughing, which caused her son to pull back and stare at her, milky mouth agape.

"Well, you know," she said helpfully, "the downstairs of this place is pretty public. Everyone on the Road uses it like a living room."

"And upstairs—the top floor—is not public, you mean? Quite private, in fact?" The woman's eyes were sparkling, those of her son drooping as she caressed his back. "By private invitation only, that sort of thing, yes?"

34

"That sort of thing," she agreed.

"Have you been up there, to the top of the stairs?"

"Not in quite a while, though I don't imagine it's changed much. Or Tyler either, for that matter." It seemed a good memory, thought Kate, judging from the face across from her.

"Would you say that many of the women on the Road have 'been upstairs'?"

"A fair number. Probably most of the single women at one time or another, maybe, oh, a third of the attached ones."

"I would have thought that would cause a lot of trouble."

"Not here. In suburbia, perhaps, but not here. And Tyler's very careful not to get too close if there's another man involved who would object. He's a good man, very caring, very generous."

"With money?"

"With everything." Again the amused, fond smile crossed her face.

"He only invites women upstairs?"

"Oh, no, men too. Not to bed, of course." She giggled at the absurdity of the thought, and Kate was struck dumb by this outcrop of conventionality. "He takes guys up there to play chess, I know, or just to have a drink or a smoke if something's happening down here and he wants some quiet."

"But you're sure it's no more than that?" Kate persisted.

That gave her pause, and Kate had her turn to be amused, to see that Flower Underwood was troubled by this idea, whereas Tyler's wholesale hetero relationships had fazed her not at all.

"No, he invites a lot of people up to his rooms, not just to sleep with them. I've never heard of him sleeping with a man. I'm sure I would have. There's no hiding anything on the Road, not for long. No, I'm sure Tyler's a normal man," she said, firmly rejecting the possibility.

" 'Normal.' "

"Well, straight, anyway. At any rate, he is very sweet. In bed, I mean."

This interview is getting out of hand, thought Kate, and tried to pull it back to earth.

"Does he have any children?"

"A couple for sure. He has a wife, or an ex-wife, I guess, who lives in L.A. with their daughter, who's ten or eleven. There's also a little boy here on the Road who's probably his, though it's hard to be sure because he's only three. There's a couple other possibilities, but the mothers aren't sure."

Kate's eyes involuntarily strayed to the sleeping blond terror, and the mother's eyes followed.

"No, not this one. You'd only have to see my old man to be sure about that. She looks just like him. Say, if you want to know what the men do. . . ." Her voice faltered as a thought struck her and strengthened again as she pushed it away. "If you want to hear about Tyler's rooms from a man, you could talk to Charlie. Charlie Waters is my old man. He's down here all the time, playing chess with Tyler." Her voice trailed off and her eyes rose to search the room beyond, and Kate thought it a good time to call the session to a halt.

"Thank you very much for your time, Ms. Underwood. I really appreciate your coming down today," but the woman had already risen with her groggy burden and headed for the hallway.

Kate scribbled her signature and dropped the papers on the next table—where Bob Fischer was talking to a man, with three peaceful children distributed over their two laps—and sprinted for the stairs.

5

The stairway was lined with odd bits of old weaponry, a small tapestry, a cloak pinned out fully to show off its thick embroidery, several framed photographs of castles and people in colorful medieval costume, and similar elements of Tyler's passion. At the top landing a full set of armor, with both arms and its helm in place, stood guard over a locked glass case that held numerous small objects, bottles and combs and such, which Kate did not pause to examine. Voices came from the third door on the left, so she knocked lightly and opened it.

". . . decided on a maximum of a hundred and fifty. Ah, come in, Inspector Martinelli. We were just getting started. What will you have to drink?" Tyler stood up and moved to a tall, glossy cabinet made of several kinds of wood, and Kate allowed herself to be talked into a glass of soda water. Tyler presented it with a flourish and went to stand by the open fire, his back to the stones and the heavy mantelpiece.

His air of jovial goodwill seemed somewhat strained, and Kate soon diagnosed that the source of his nervousness was Hawkin, who was sitting comfortably back into a leather chair with a somnolent expression on his face and a glass of amber liquid on his knee. Tyler's eyes kept glancing off the relaxed figure, as if by avoiding eye contact he might escape a blow. It was a reaction Kate had seen many times before, but she was a bit surprised to see it in Tyler.

Hawkin picked up the conversation again, continuing where it had been left, and with half an ear Kate listened to Tyler's plans for his land, proposals for a grant and tax-free status, the balance between convenience and freedom from gadgets. She listened, but she also studied the man's surroundings, the room at the top of the house.

The room was magnificent, wrapped in glass on three sides, with the tiers of hills soaring up at one end and the fields across the Road flowing down to the sea at the other; from the middle the owner could survey the graveled triangle and the comings and goings of his tenants. From the fourth wall jutted an open-sided granite fireplace, dividing the space in half visually. This was a lordly tower, and even if Flower Underwood had not said as much, Kate would have known immediately that this was where Tyler lived, not in the casual funk of the ground floor or in the relatively impersonal hallways Kate had glimpsed from the middle landing. Here Tyler had no need to bolt a broadsword down for fear of accident or theft, no need to limit the furnishings to sturdy dark chairs that would neither intimidate the residents nor show the effects of their children's heels. Here John Tyler could be what he was: the sole heir to three generations of money. In California, three generations is a long time.

The room was not flagrant in its opulence. The walls

were smooth redwood, the floor polished oak with an inlaid pattern of some darker wood running around the edges. The intricate carpet underfoot was wool, not silk; the buttery leather of the chairs and sofa showed signs of long use; the beams and mantelpiece were of the same unadorned redwood as the walls. The solid wall to Kate's left held a cluster of watercolors on this side of the fireplace. The other wall was hidden from where Kate sat, but she could see another group of chairs at the other end of the room around a low table with a chess set. Her attention was caught by a change in Tyler's voice.

". . . wine, Inspector Martinelli? No? Very abstemious of you. Inspector Hawkin? You don't mind if I do?" He limped over to the cabinet again and poured more of the amber liquid into his squat glass, then put the bottle with the unpronounceable name back on the shelf. A smoky fume rose from the glass, and he returned to put his back to the fireplace before he sipped from it. At bay, thought Kate, though Hawkin looked less like a pursuer than he did an old, well-fed hound drowsing in front of the fire. It was an odd way to question someone, she thought, and waited impatiently for him to get on with it. Soft voices drifted up the stairs, distant pans rattled, a child cried, and raised voices from the road outside reminded her of the gathered media. Finally she couldn't stand it.

"When you say 'we decided,' Mr. Tyler, just who do you mean?"

Tyler looked relieved at the question, and Hawkin shot her a quick glance.

"You're looking at him. I get in the habit of saying 'we' because I do consult the people who live here, and my various money men, but ultimately I decide. I still find it faintly ludicrous to think of one person 'owning' a stretch of forest, but it's mine in the eyes of the law. I prefer to think of myself as the landlord, keeping out undesirables and maintaining the road. If anything it owns me, not I it."

"The land lord," said Hawkin, making it two words. "A nice feudal concept."

The oblique accusation seemed only to relax Tyler, as if he were settling into an old, familiar argument.

"There's nothing wrong with a feudal system," he began,

"not if it retains the key element of responsibility. It's popular to think of the lord of the manor as a parasite who drained the peasants of their hard-earned products and spent all his time drinking and hunting deer—"

"And screwing wenches," contributed Kate unexpectedly. Tyler looked at her cautiously until he decided that she didn't mean anything by it. Hawkin raised an eyebrow.

"Yes, that too, but it was his responsibility to protect the people from invaders, to make judgment in a dispute, to provide for the old and widows and orphans, so they wouldn't go hungry. The deer hunting and the riding to hounds were not just sport—deer ate crops, and foxes killed farm animals if they weren't kept down. The whole idea of hierarchy and authority is bound up, in the feudal system, with responsibility. The peasant had few rights and privileges, but then he was only responsible for producing a certain amount more than his family needed. The greater the rank, the greater the accountability. Why, do you know," he said, warming to his argument and the whiskey, "in ancient days the king was seen as being responsible for the life of the land itself? He was cheered and begrudged nothing when food was plentiful and the people healthy, but if the crops failed or there was a drought or a plague, he was seen to be the cause of it, and the people would slit his throat to restore the land to fresh life. That's the real origin of 'The king is dead; long live the king.' "

He was totally caught up in the thought of this anachronistic threat to himself, and his eyes gleamed with the relish of it.

Without raising his eyes from the contemplation of his glass, Hawkin placed a gentle question into the room.

"What do you think of human sacrifice, Mr. Tyler?"

Kate felt the hairs on her arms rise and her head snapped around, but Tyler had not yet realized that the old hound was no longer drowsing.

"Human sacrifice—any sacrifice, for that matter—is a means of feeling in control of one's fate by giving the gods what they want before they can take it. By offering them the best, the purest, the newest—" The words strangled in his throat as he saw what he had been led to say. His eyes flew to Hawkin, who looked back at him with the patient air of an old hunter waiting for his prey to panic, watching neither in triumph nor in glee, but certain of the outcome. Tyler's face drained bloodless above the dark fringe of his beard, his knuckles showed white around the glass he held. The room's only movement was the slow dip and rise of the whiskey in Hawkin's glass as he swirled it around and around and around, waiting.

"I . . . You don't . . . You can't think. . . ." Kate thought the man would not look much worse if one of his jeweled daggers had been pushed into his belly.

"Yes?" coaxed Hawkin.

"You can't think I had anything to do with it?" He spoke in a hoarse whisper.

"Can't I?"

"You can't be serious."

"No?"

"Why would I do something like that?"

"Why would anyone, Mr. Tyler? You've just given me what could be construed as a motive, have you not? You would be physically capable of it, would you not? This is your land, and you know the comings and goings of the people here better than anyone, do you not? So can you tell me, Mr. Tyler, why I should not consider the possibility that you, as you say, had 'something to do with it'?"

Tyler stared at Hawkin, searching his face for anything other than the polite curiosity with its hint of steel that it now presented. He looked to Kate, found no help there, and lurched about to face his fire. A minute passed, then two, while the two of them sat and watched his back and the movement of muscles along his jaw.

Suddenly his arm shot out and the glass exploded into the fire with a billow of blue flames. His voice began low and the words bitten off in rage.

"Why did he have to come here with his filth? This is my land. My land! Bringing his sickness here and defiling us like this. I'll never be able to go up the Road without seeing this last child, never go up to the top without thinking of the first one, the smell—" He broke off, one hand gripping the mantelpiece. They waited.

Steps came in the hall, a tap at the door. A flash of anger crossed Hawkin's face, and after a moment Tyler turned, his

40

color high but his anger gone, looking both annoyed and relieved at the interruption.

"Yes?"

"John?" The door opened and the tall, gentle-faced woman with corn-silk braids wrapped about her head who had brought Kate lunch looked in. "I'm sorry to break in like this, but Jenny Cadena's going into labor. Her water broke, so she'll go too fast to get her home. What room do you want her in?"

"But she isn't due yet, is she?"

"Only two weeks early."

"How about the green room?"

"That bed's too soft. I thought either the quilt room or Alice's room."

"The quilt room is better; there's nobody downstairs at that end. Strip the bed first, though, would you? Did you call the midwife?"

"She'll be here in an hour, and Terry's with her now. Sorry to bother you."

"S'okay, hon, I'll poke my head in when we're finished here and see how you're doing. It'll be nice to have another baby born in the house—it's been a long time."

She smiled affectionately at him and nodded vaguely to Hawkin and Kate, and the door closed.

"Shouldn't you get her to the hospital?" asked Hawkin.

"Oh no, she'll be fine. This is her fourth, and she's never had any problems. Quite a few of the women come down here to give birth. The midwives don't have to go up the Road, and there's the insurance of the phone and the highway if something goes wrong. Never has so far, touch wood," and he flicked a fingernail lightly against the mantel, "but it goes easier when they know help is available." He was calm now, and met Hawkin's eyes steadily. The interruption had firmly restored him to his position of mastery, and Hawkin reluctantly accepted that nothing would be gained by pressing on that day. Still, his main goal had been achieved; he'd have to settle for that. He started again on a different tack.

"Can you tell me who is not down here today?"

"Offhand I can name a half a dozen. Old Peterson, of course. He comes out of the hills once a year at Christmas, to visit his mother in Santa Barbara, and stays until the end of January. Never other than that."

"His full name?" asked Kate, pen poised.

"Something like Bernie. I'd have to look it up, to tell you the truth."

"That would be helpful. Who else?"

"Vaun Adams. Tommy would've told her, but she's probably busy painting. Ben Riddle is in San Francisco for a few days. I think Tony Dodson is off on a job somewhere, probably be back tonight or tomorrow. Susanna Canani is in Florida with her kids. Hari Bensen I haven't seen, or his lady Ursula." He thought for a moment, then shrugged. "There might be one or two others. If I think of them I'll let you know."

"Do you keep close records of the residents?" Kate asked. He laughed.

"Are you kidding? Half of the kids here don't have birth certificates, and a few of the adults. A lot of them make a point of having no bank account, social security number, driver's license, voter's registration card—not all of them, by any means, but there's a handful of residents who are greater purists—fanatics, if you prefer—than I can afford to be."

"Strikes me you've laid yourself right open for some not very nice people to come in."

"I don't know that keeping track of people's past is any insurance against that. We don't let just anyone in, you see. It's the one place where everyone over the age of twelve has an equal say, whether or not to allow a specific individual in after a four-month trial period. Three-fourths of them have to approve a residency application, or the person goes. I can veto someone, but I can't override their negative. So far it's worked fine. In fact, one time we voted out a couple, and a few weeks later I found out that they'd been arrested for some knifing that had happened the year before in Arizona. There was something wrong with them, and after four months we knew it."

"Don't you have problems with the county and the tax man and all?" asked Kate.

"I pay two full-time lawyers to keep my affairs sorted out. I tell them what I want to do, they tell me how to do it."

42

"Their names, please," asked Kate, and added them to the growing list.

Hawkin scowled at his glass for a moment.

"It remains to be seen if your method of weeding out the twisted ones has been one hundred percent effective, Mr. Tyler. Tell me, why do you think the bodies were brought here to your Road? Who do you think it is, this person who has 'brought his filth here'?"

"I wish to God I knew. It feels . . . I feel like someone is doing this to me personally. I know that's ridiculous, and I would certainly never say such a thing to the parents of those little girls, but it is how I feel. Like someone's got it in for me, laying dead children on my doorstep, and yes I'm aware of how absurd and egocentric it is, but I can't help it. And no, I can't think of anyone who would want to do that to me. God knows I've thought about it."

"Mr. Tyler, there's something else that's been puzzling me. Maybe you can shed some light on it. If the murderer didn't want the bodies found, he could have chosen a thousand better places between here and the Bay Area. If he did want them found, his method seems a bit chancy. Any ideas?"

"Not so very chancy. Certainly this last one would have been found within a day or two. It's a relatively built-up part of the Road, and that patch of ground is pretty open. And the one they found along the creek, even that would have been discovered before too long. It's a public footpath, up from a public beach, and even at this time of year people use it regularly. I had to put in a fence along the creek to keep people out. She could have gone longer if the weather had been bad, I suppose." His face twisted in a parody of humor and he gave a short bark of desperate laughter. "Christ, what a macabre conversation."

"Yes. You were having a meeting that night, the night Amanda Bloom was left here, weren't you?"

"Yes, from eight until about one in the morning. It was impromptu, or anyway it wasn't supposed to be here, but the place we were supposed to meet, one of their kids came down with the chicken pox, so we met here instead."

"A political meeting, wasn't it?"

"Sort of. A group of us coastal landowners who oppose

43

oil drilling off the coast. I gave their names to Trujillo at the time."

"And nobody saw anything."

"He must be invisible; nobody sees him anywhere."

It was an opinion that Kate had heard before.

"And the first one? Tina Merrill? It was quite some time before Tommy Chesler happened across her."

Tyler pushed himself abruptly away from the fireplace and went to pour a fresh glass of the smoky drink. Kate and Hawkin watched him patiently. It took two swallows and a circuit of the room before he spoke.

"I would have found her on the first of December if I'd been here. I always ride to the top of the Road on the first and then come back and put on a party for the residents, but I wasn't here. I had to fly to Seattle very suddenly on the thirtieth; my uncle was in an accident, and I didn't get back until the third."

"You told me that, yes," said Hawkin. "And you drove up the following day, was it?" Kate saw he was puzzled—wondering why this should so trouble Tyler.

"Rode, on horseback. On the fourth. And she wasn't there. Not on the Road, anyway, though she must have been just over the edge. She didn't . . . it had been cold," he ended, and took another swallow.

Hawkin's face took on a look of polite incredulity, and after a moment Kate realized that in spite of the weeks of evidence and despite Hawkin's fairly explicit words to the general assembly downstairs, the man Tyler was only now allowing himself to face the inevitable conclusion: that someone on his Road was responsible for the deaths of the three girls.

"And everyone on the road knew it was your habit to be on that stretch of the Road on the first of December. So there's a fairly good chance that whoever put her there meant for you to find her."

"I . . . think so. Which means whoever is doing this didn't just pick the Road off a map."

"No, Mr. Tyler, I think that is a pretty safe bet." Hawkin drained the last drops from his glass into his mouth and set the glass lovingly on the table. It took just a few minutes to wrap up the interview, arrange for access keys and a room

44

for Trujillo and one other for the night, and make a list from Kate's notebook of the information they needed. They walked down the stairs together, and Tyler left them on the second floor landing to survey his private obstetrical ward. Hawkin leaned against the wall and lit a cigarette.

"Give me your reactions so far."

"To Tyler?"

"To everything."

Kate thought for a moment.

"Did you notice that the only person here who wears a watch is Tyler's lady friend with the blond hausfrau braids?"

Hawkin looked surprised and then began softly to laugh. His face was transformed, and he looked considerably younger.

"Very good, Casey. No, I hadn't consciously seen it. The chatelaine with the watch and the keys to the storehouse, eh?"

"I only noticed it because I thought my watch was running slow, and when I went to check it I couldn't find anyone who had one. After that I began to study wrists. They may all have pocket watches, but no wristwatches."

"Interesting."

"About Tyler. He really was horrified that you connected him with the murders, but it didn't look like guilt or fear. His anger was real, too, though I wish I could have seen his face."

"Mmm," was Hawkin's only response. After a minute they descended from Tyler's ivory tower to rejoin the fray.

6

Two hours and several residents later Kate pushed back her chair, scrubbed at her face with both hands, and went to join the line outside the toilet. As she walked back towards her desk, a hand from the kitchen thrust a steaming mug at her, and she buried her nose in the life-giving smell of fresh coffee. She carried it through the much-peopled living room and beyond to the long covered porch, where the clean air smelled of salt and trees and the rain that dribbled off the roof. A pile of wet dogs thumped their tails at her, and when she ignored them, tucked their noses back into each other's flanks.

Some thoughtful soul had draped a piece of canvas over the rose bower, and the guard, hearing the front door close, peered out at her, raised his own steaming cup in greeting, and stepped back under the shelter. Beyond his casual canopy she could see that the newsmen had arranged a series of more elaborate tents and marquees, some in bright colors, so that the space across the Road was beginning to resemble a high-class gypsy encampment. She could hear a mutter of voices and after a moment pushed her lethargy aside long enough to move to the far end of the veranda for an unobstructed view of the tent city.

Hawkin was there, talking with the newsmen. He looked every bit the proper police investigator, in a belted trench coat with the requisite crumpled fedora in his hand. He was facing away from her, but she could see that his feet were planted squarely, his back was straight, his gestures few and controlled. He turned his head slightly to listen to a question, and Kate saw him respond with a sharp shake and could see his mouth move in a "no" before he turned away again for the next question. There was the slightest sag to his shoulders now as they moved with a gesture of his unseen hands. In another few seconds the hat was clapped onto his head, and he turned back to the house with an air of getting back to his job. The reporters lingered until he reached the gate and then began to disperse.

The sag to his shoulders was more pronounced when he appeared on the stone walk. He reached the shelter of the porch and fumbled with belt and buttons until he extracted a large, limp handkerchief, which he proceeded to rub like a towel over face and hands. He shoved it back into its pocket and began to shrug off the wet coat when he saw Kate in her silent corner and grinned.

"I hope to God that's coffee and not some herbal concoction that tastes like dirty straw," he said.

"Coffee, just made, and strong enough to bite back. Want me to get you a cup?"

"No, it's too cold out here to stand around in wet shoes,

46

thanks." Still, he made no immediate move for the door. "How's it going?"

"Nothing yet, if that's what you're asking."

"It's early still."

"Can I ask you something, Al?"

"Of course."

"How much of your method of talking to the media is deliberate?"

"Deliberate? A performance, you mean? Oh, it's all a game. They want the truth, but more than that they want a good story; you want them to shove off, but not completely— they can be useful. And they're not a bad bunch, most of them, just doing their jobs. If you keep them fed, make them feel included, put on a show from time to time, they're not too much trouble. Especially in weather like this. I go out every hour or two and churn out all kinds of exciting non-sense they can work up into a story—keeps them happy. They're having loads of fun with that Cadena woman and her baby. One of them wanted me to tell her that if she could make his deadline there'd be a hundred dollars in it for her."

"What did you say?"

"I told him that she was trying her best. I also said that you'd come out and talk to them in a while. It'll give my shoes a chance to dry out."

"Throwing me to the wolves?"

"Propitiating the gods, Tyler would say."

"How do you feel, really? About the case?"

"It's too early to feel anything, but I don't feel good. And my feet are damned cold. Back to work, Martinelli."

At four thirty-seven the midwife guided little Amanda Saman-tha Christina Cadena-Panopoulos into the world, and all the honorary aunts, uncles, and cousins downstairs cheered and kissed and clapped one another's backs when the short, indignant yell trickled down to their ears. At four-fifty Kate and Bob Fischer went out to present a grainy photograph of mother and daughter to the waiting reporters (and collect the new mother's hundred-dollar check), and two sets of grandparents saw their newest granddaughter's wet, squashed features on the six o'clock news. At six-thirty the last question was asked of the last resident. At nine-thirty Kate dropped Hawkin at the station and drove on to the pool for twenty minutes' hard swim. At ten-thirty she walked back into the office, clearheaded, and they worked for two hours at sorting out the mountain of papers. At one o'clock Kate finally fell into bed, and at five forty-five the telephone rang.

She hit the receiver, fumbled and dropped it, retrieved it from the floor, and squinted to see the luminous hands of the bedside clock. She had to clear her throat before any intelligible sound would come.

"Yeah."

"Casey, pick up some doughnuts on your way in this morning, would you? I've got the coffee on, but the place wasn't open when I came by."

"Doughnuts."

"Chocolate glazed, if they have them."

"God."

"What?"

"Chocolate glazed doughnuts."

"Yes, or whatever looks good. See you," he said cheerily, and the line went dead.

Kate replaced the telephone with the gentle care of a hangover victim, turned to the single eye that scowled up at her from the next pillow, and pronounced the words again.

"Chocolate. Glazed. Doughnuts."

The eye cringed, closed, and retreated beneath the blankets. Kate made her own toast that morning.

It was a day given over to the computers, those electronic busybodies into whose impersonal clutches fall the bits and pieces of the personal histories of criminal, victim, and Jane Q. Public. Kate's feet echoed in the still quiet hallways, and a thick fug of cigarettes and rancid coffee greeted her when she entered Hawkin's office. She dumped the greasy white bag on the desk next to him, pushed open a window, and went over to inspect the coffeepot. It held a strangely greenish liquid that seemed an inauspicious start to the day, so she started another pot, politely refused the kind offer of a doughnut, and sat at the console. Her mind itself felt not unlike a cold, greasy wad of cooked dough when she looked at the stack of yesterday's papers.

"Where do you want me to begin?" she asked.

"Up to you," he said around a mouthful of crumbs. "Alphabetical, geographical, the pin-prick approach, or you can follow hunches. They're all equally bad."

"In that case I'll proceed with some semblance of logic—start from Tyler's place and work my way up the Road."

"Why not the other way around?"

"From the far end down? Why?"

He shrugged. "Look at the farthest point from civilization to find the biggest misfit?"

Kate looked at him closely, but she couldn't tell if he was joking.

"I'll compromise, five from the top, five from the bottom."

Throughout the long day Kate worked to pull together the information contained in the electronic network on the fifty-seven adults and nineteen (now twenty) minors who lived on Tyler's Road.

Hawkin spent much of the day with the telephone tucked under his chin, and when that failed he read through the assembled reports and printouts with a fierce concentration, made notes, and stared blankly out the window. He disappeared in the early afternoon and came back three hours later looking rested and shaven, and wearing a clean shirt.

At five-thirty Trujillo called in with the statements from three of the residents who had not been at Tyler's and names of the remaining eight. Hawkin shouted at him.

"What the hell have you been doing down there? You should have had all eleven before noon, even if you had to walk up the road to get them! You've got what? Oh, Christ, yes I did hear about it, but I didn't know they'd called you in on it. All right, sorry for shouting. Yes, give them to me now, the rough outlines anyway." For ten minutes Hawkin grunted and scribbled notes; he finally dropped the phone and sat back.

"Half of Trujillo's men are down in San Benito county with that gunman who wants his kids." An irate father with a rifle was holed up in an office building demanding that his ex-wife give him their two sons—the kind of situation that

49

eats up a lot of hours and manpower. "Well, at least it's put off that damn meeting with the FBI and half the cops in northern California. Throw these names into the machine and go home." Hawkin picked up a stack of papers and settled down at his desk with his nineteenth cup of coffee that day. "Go home, Martinelli. We'll go down ourselves tomorrow."

Thursday morning the telephone allowed her to sleep until after six before jerking her from a luxurious dream in which she was sitting on the deck of a cruise ship eating spaghetti and watching a child play with a windmill. The child began suddenly to wail, and it took a long moment for Kate to realize that the wail was the telephone.

"Yes!"

"Martinelli, I need you down here. Ten minutes ago."

"Piss off," she snarled, but he had already hung up.

"I knew we should have gone to bed rather than watching the late show." The muffled voice was not even accompanied by an eye this morning; it was simply an untidy lump in the blankets.

"See you on TV," Kate replied.

"You did look cute."

"Scared stiff."

"So adorable, showing off that baby's picture."

"Shut up."

"What is it, Al? What happened?" she asked as she walked into his office.

"Nothing happened. I'm going home for two hours, and I need you to sit on the phone in case something comes up. If Trujillo calls, we'll be there by noon." He stood up and reached for his jacket.

For that you woke me up and made me run down here? she wanted to say. Why couldn't you sleep ordinary hours? Haven't you heard that telephone calls can be forwarded, for God's sake? But she bit it back, and asked simply, "Don't you ever go home?"

"When I don't have this kind of case, yes."

50

Kate squashed her own guilt feelings at having gotten six whole hours of sleep and turned resentfully to the console. She worked away for slightly over an hour and a quarter before a series of words came onto the screen that made her back go straight and her heart thump. She looked at the telephone and couldn't help the malicious grin that spread onto her face.

At the fifth ring the telephone was taken off the hook. Long seconds passed before the sound of heavy breath told of the passage up to his ear. His voice was coarse with sleep, but Kate pushed away another twinge of guilt.

"Hawkin here."

"Al? This is Casey. Something's come up I think you should see. Right away." She hung up gently. Revenge was sweet.

She was on the phone when he came in. He had stopped to shave, she noted. She handed him the thick sheaf of computer printout. Out of the corner of her eye she saw him pour a cup of coffee and settle to the continuous pages, eyes moving swiftly. She hung up and turned in her chair.

"Sorry to wake you."

"S'okay. Bunch of misfits, aren't they? Marijuana, LSD, peyote possession, arrest at Diablo Canyon, defacing a public building, army desertion and dishonorable discharge, mental hospital. What a place."

"Very few violent crimes, though. Number fourteen, there, six months as a juvenile for assulting a teacher, and number twenty-seven, who shot up a billboard while under the influence. But it's number fifty-four I called you about; it just came in."

He flipped over the pages until he reached the name of Siobhan Adams, unmarried Caucasian female; he skimmed the first few lines, and then his eyes slowed abruptly. Kate watched his lips move slightly as he read the words. He closed his eyes.

"God in heaven, why didn't we have this twenty-four hours ago?"

"It was one of the names Trujillo gave us last night. There was some confusion over it, and I got the correct name from Tyler's lawyer only an hour ago. Everyone knows her as Vaun, but I drew a blank on that."

"Vaun. Vaun Adams. Detweiler mentioned her. An artist, he said. Maidens in castles and metaphysical trees, no doubt. How do you get Vaun from Siobhan?" He gave it three syllables.

"It's pronounced Zhi-von, an old Irish name. I told Trujillo to have his people stop her if she tries to leave, but not to approach her otherwise. Was that okay?"

"On the nose. Let's get out of here."

He threw the printout onto his desk, and Kate snatched up her gun and her jacket and hurried down the hall after him. The paper lay face up, the lines of impersonal dot-matrix print telling of one Siobhan Adams, age thirty-six, unmarried Caucasian female, arrested at the age of eighteen and charged with the murder by strangulation of six-year-old Jemima Brand. She was convicted, served nine and a half years, and had been paroled seven years before. Her house was less than two miles from where Samantha Donaldson had been found.

7

Vaun Adams lived in one of the few houses on the Road that looked like a place to live in rather than an experiment or a fantasy, despite the gleam of photovoltaic panels on the roof and its almost unreal air of perfect simplicity. It lay on top of a hill half a mile up from the Road. A footpath wound through redwoods and opened up on a broad acre or two of vegetable beds and fruit trees, surrounded by a high wire fence. Some of the beds had a few straggly lettuce heads, beets, and broccoli growing in them, and one tree showed a handful of premature white dots on its branches, but the rest was neatly mulched over for the winter.

The house looked more at home on the site than the garden did, as if it had grown from the ground under the supervision of the wise trees. Simple, long, wood and glass, its back set actually down into the earth so that its two stories appeared low, it was a structure both distinctive and totally unobtrusive. Kate wondered where Adams had found an architect who did not insist on a splashy signature and wondered, too, if in houses as in clothing the simple and well-made were the most expensive.

There was a face looking down at them from the stretch of upstairs window.

"She's seen us," Hawkin noted.

"She could hardly miss the sound of that truck."

"Looks almost Japanese, doesn't it?"

"The house? It does, now that you mention it. I was thinking it looked deceptively simple."

Hawkin nodded. "Solid. It sure wasn't built by the guy who did the leaky dome or that place with the turrets and gargoyles."

The entrance was tucked under an upstairs deck. A small, mesh-covered pond with a few bright koi swimming in it lay next to the front door. Hawkin reached for the bell rope, but the door opened first.

Christ, she's gorgeous, was Kate's first thought, followed immediately by, She looks like one of those living dead looking blankly into the camera outside Dachau or Buchenwald. Her glossy black curls were slightly too long and tumbled onto her shoulders and around a pair of startling, icy blue eyes that revealed nothing whatsoever of the thoughts behind them. Her cheekbones were high and thin, her skin pale, her mouth a fraction too wide for the rest of the face. A heavy, loose, brown sweater with flecks of color spun into it and a smear of blue paint on one sleeve emphasized the slimness of the body it covered and revealed long hands with short, square nails. She had soft, dark brown corduroy trousers on her long legs, cloth shoes on her feet, and a deep, even voice as she stood back from the door.

"I wondered when you would come for me."

"Miss Adams?" Hawkin, too, seemed taken aback by her appearance and words.

"Yes. Come in."

"You were expecting us, then?"

She shut the door and turned to face him. Her eyes were

as calm and as vulnerable as those of a dead woman, but there was a slight smile at the corners of her mouth.

"Come now, Inspector Hawkin. If three dead girls are found within a few miles of a woman who was convicted of murdering a little girl, she'd have to be a considerable fool to expect that the police would ignore her. I've been expecting you for weeks."

"You know my name."

"And Inspector Martinelli's. Tommy Chesler was here last night and told me all about you. I was about to stir up the fire and make myself some coffee, but when I heard you coming I thought I'd better wait to see if you planned on taking me in, 'for questioning,' as they say. I don't like to leave the house with a fire going," she added simply.

"No, go ahead," said Hawkin. "Unless, of course, you're planning on confessing to the murders." Kate thought it a joke in very poor taste, if it was a joke. Vaun Adams did not react, other than smiling the half-smile and turning to lead them through a dark hallway and out into a spacious, high-ceilinged living room.

"That's not too likely. I don't suppose you want any coffee?"

"That would be nice, thank you."

"Breaking bread with a convicted murderess?" She smiled wryly and knelt down to load two split logs into the large, freestanding iron fireplace. A wide-bottomed black kettle sat on the flat top.

"You have paid your dues, Miss Adams."

She paused and studied him from under the hair, a log forgotten in one hand.

" 'Paid my dues.' I haven't heard that phrase in years. Nearly ten years of my life gone as dues for the privilege of rejoining a society that neither wants nor trusts me. Rather high membership fees." Her mildly amused voice might have been discussing a slight inconsistency in the plot of a play.

"High compared with the price paid by Jemima Brand?" Hawkin smiled gently, but his eyes were hard. Vaun Adams looked down at the log in her hand and finished the job, opened the stove vent, stood up, and brushed off her hands.

"No, I would not consider the price high, if it had been I who killed her. But then I realize that nearly all felons claim that they were falsely accused, so I won't bore you with that. This will be a few minutes," she gestured toward the kettle, "and I'm sure you want to ferret about in my things. I give you my permission. I won't even ask you for a warrant. Just don't touch the wet paint on the canvases upstairs, or the charcoal. There are a couple of drawings I haven't sprayed yet." She disappeared through a swinging door, which revealed a glimpse of kitchen sink and cabinetry before it shut. Kate and Hawkin looked at each other and shrugged.

"Do you want to 'ferret'?" Kate asked him.

"Not much point, I shouldn't think. I would like to see the house, though."

The house was well worth looking at, regardless of any evidence it might contain. The room they were in was a space of immense calm and simplicity, open to the rough, beamed ceiling two stories above their heads, its sides made of smooth redwood boards laid vertically, with large, uneven quarry tiles underfoot. One wall, to Kate's left, was glass. Its opposite, behind the free-standing wood stove (now radiating a comfortable antidote to the gray day outside) was an expanse twenty-two feet high entirely of redwood, broken only by the rectangular outline of the kitchen's swinging door and by one wide painting. A couple of thick, subtle Oriental carpets, a cluster of soft chairs and matching sofa, two low tables and a small cabinet were the only furniture, although the house's end wall ahead of them had built-in cabinets running the length of it, ending at a door that led (judging from a glimpse through its window) to a wood pile. Kate walked a few steps into the room and turned around to look up above the doorway through which they had come. To her surprise it appeared that the entire space above the rest of the house was one large, open room, divided from the living room below by a simple, waist-high railing, on the other side of which stood a pair of heavy easels. Various people along Tyler's Road had mentioned that Vaun Adams painted, but Kate had hardly expected to find her studio taking up one third of the floor space of a generously sized house.

As she turned back to Hawkin her eye caught on the painting above the wood stove. It was actually a triptych, three panels depicting a mossy stream bed in which a minimum of brush strokes and a nearly monochromatic palette of grays and greens managed to convey an air of mystery and anticipation. Kate drew it to Hawkin's attention with a dry comment.

"Unicorns and starry maidens it ain't. If that's her work, she's very good."

There were three other rooms on the lower floor. On the right-hand side of the hall as it went to the front door was Vaun's bedroom. A subtly colored patchwork quilt made of hundreds of tiny squares lay on the double bed, its corners knife-sharp. The top of the bedside table held an electric lamp and a clock; a small gray vase with a sprig of dried flowers and grasses sat atop the narrow, chest-high dresser. All else, even the walls, was bare, polished wood, with the exception of one small, very old-looking painting on the wall above the bed, a Virgin and Child. Kate forced herself to open drawers and closets, a thing she always disliked, but inside things were equally neat—not with the recent tidiness of the nervous housekeeper faced with an unwelcome and judgmental guest. Kate was familiar with the rapid neatening of strewn magazines and the quick dusting of obvious surfaces. This was a compulsive order, the obsessive tidiness of a woman who could not go to bed at night knowing there was disorder in the house, lest she be whipped away during the night and other eyes see the evidence of her debauched way of life. Looking at the straight line of shoes on the closet floor, Kate would have bet that Vaun Adams never wore a safety pin in her brassiere. Had she always been this way, or was it only recent? Since December? Kate closed the closet door and went across the hall to the bathroom.

After the austere bedroom, this room seemed positively flamboyant, tiled in warm oranges and browns with a brilliant batik shower curtain and mat in the same colors. The furnishings here were also minimal: two towels and a face cloth, hairbrush, comb, toothbrush, toothpaste, soap, one bottle of shampoo, and nailbrush, all precisely aligned. No water spots or rust stains in the bath tub; no soap smears on the taps or porcelain. The only profligacy was a cupboard startlingly full of medications, both prescription and over-the-counter: vials at the top, three kinds of antibiotics; aspirin, Tylenol, Bufferin, and a codeine-and-Tylenol mix; cough syrups; half a dozen antihistamines with their fluorescent caution stickers (do not operate heavy machinery; do not take with alcohol), a handful of nasal sprays and drops; antacids, both liquid and chewable tablets, and a liquid laxative; nine bottles of assorted vitamins; a snakebite kit; wart removal drops; three small bottles of liquid charcoal and one of syrup of ipecac, for accidental poisoning; and on the lower shelf tubes of antiseptic cream and ointments for sore muscles, for burns, bites, stings, and sunburn, for yeast infections and athlete's foot; and an unspecified cortisone preparation. Nothing illegal; nothing more narcotic than the mild codeine prescription, six months old and less than half gone. No tranquilizers. Kate closed the cupboard door with a smile. That Vaun Adams was a hypochondriac was the most human side of the artist that she'd seen yet.

She opened the doors under the sink and rummaged through the pharmacopoeia there, mostly outdated, raising her eyebrows at a pair of disposable hypodermic syringes, still in their wrappers, each with a glass ampoule taped to it. Kate squinted thoughtfully at the printing on the glass and put them back.

She spent a few minutes writing the names of various doctors and pharmacies in her notebook, closed up the drawers and doors, and went back out into the hallway. A noise came from the room to her left, on the side away from the living room, so she followed that and came upon Hawkin, hands in his pockets jingling the coins, running his eyes over the walls of the combination office and library.

One corner of the room was chewed off by the overhead stairs, and below that was an oddly angled window. It probably gave a brief flood of light in the early morning, but now, the other window being a narrow, chest-high strip the length of the room but barely above the grasses that grew on the hillside cradling the back of the house, the room was inadequately lit for any serious reading. Nonetheless, the walls were solid bookshelves, broken only by the door, the windows, a small oak rolltop desk, and its matching filing cabinet.

Hawkin signaled Kate to close the door, and asked her what she had found.

"Very precise lady, not even any hairs in her comb," she

commented. "One area of nerves, though. She's got a small pharmacy in her bathroom, everything from headache to ingrown toenails, with a concentration on sinus and lungs. Nothing hard, nothing illegal. Couple of needles, but they seem to be for allergic reaction to bee stings. How about you?"

"A very precise taste in music," he reflected. "Clearly divided, at any rate. Sing-along stuff, folk music from the sixties and the stuff they put on the radio and call mellow rock—muzak for yuppies—lots of fiddly instrumentals, Vivaldi, some Haydn, all the Mozart piano concertos, both of Glenn Gould's Goldberg recordings, that kind of thing." Kate nodded, catching the drift if not the specifics. "And then music to be overwhelmed by—huge, pounding stuff that doesn't leave you any room to breathe. Four different versions of Verdi's *Requiem,* no less, and three of Mozart's. Great stuff to sublimate depression and keep the mind off of suicide. Three separate shelves, all in alphabetical order. What about the books?"

Wondering uneasily how much of Hawkin's last comments had been rooted in personal experience, Kate turned to the shelves. Here, too, order prevailed: general art history books here, volumes on specific artists (alphabetized) there; psychology there, novels here. The art world took up at least two-thirds of the shelves and represented a massive investment of money. Oversized books with many color plates ran the gamut from Egyptian and primitive to Frankenthaler and de Kooning, with a heavy emphasis on the European masters of the sixteenth and seventeenth centuries. Slick, expensive, serious books, not something Kate would have expected to find on Tyler's Road. She leafed through a few of them and found two with writing on the flyleaf: *Art in the Making: Rembrandt* was signed, "With love from Gerry," and a very worn copy of *The Art Spirit* by Robert Henri was inscribed, "To my dear niece on her seventeenth birthday, with love from Uncle Red."

Second in number were works on psychology, ranging from college textbooks (two of them familiar to Kate from her own shelves) to popularized pseudopsychology to abstruse academic tomes with multisyllabic Latinate titles that seemed to deal with the more obscure varieties of madness.

Running a poor third, and placed on shelves behind the door, was an eclectic gathering of fiction: Doris Lessing and Dorothy L. Sayers, Elie Wiesel and Isak Dinesen, a few Updikes, some Steinbeck, a couple of early Steven Kings. Some of them were old friends, some Kate had never heard of, and she could see no particular method in the selection.

She had now circled the room and stood near Hawkin, who was looking at one of a series of worn legal reference books. She eyed the adjoining shelf, filled with delicate volumes with arty titles—poetry by, apparently, modern women poets, a closed field to Kate.

There was a pile of books on the table in front of one of the room's comfortable chairs, and Kate glanced through those. Books on Titian, Poussin, Bellini, and Michelangelo, and three volumes of Christian symbolism, bristling with strips of paper marking depictions of women and children, some classical, most of them Madonnas with child or Pietàs. Under the circumstances, Kate thought, a strange topic to research. She said as much to Hawkin.

He glanced at the books, put the legal volume back on the shelf, and moved to the desk. A search through drawers and pigeonholes revealed nothing of immediate interest, and he moved to the two-drawer wooden filing cabinet beside it. It was unlocked, but before he could do more than run a thumb over the manila folders it contained, there was a gentle rattle of silver in crockery outside the door. He drew back his hand.

"I'm taking this upstairs," came Vaun's voice. "It's warmer up there."

"We'll come back," he said to Kate. "No point in letting the coffee get cold."

They followed her up the stairs to the enormous studio. Even on this gray day, three glass walls and a skylight filled it with light. Around the perimeter and down the middle ran long, high worktables, but the immediate impression was of a large space entirely open to the elements—except for one corner, where a room sat above the downstairs kitchen. Its door was slightly ajar, and Hawkin walked over to peer curiously inside, into a storage room for completed paintings, with built-in slots of various sizes along the outside wall. From the looks of it, she was a busy lady. He closed the door and glanced out the window at the hilltop, which dropped off again just beyond the house into a sharp canyon of oak and scrub, the dominant redwood for some reason keeping its distance. Several easels stood waiting in one corner, and the two at the end of the room, backs to the railing that separated the studio from the living room below, seemed slightly reproachful under their stained canvas drapes.

Vaun had put the tray on a battered table that stood between two grimy armchairs and a paint-splattered sofa. She poured the coffee into three rough mugs.

"There's usually a lot more stuff lying about," she said. "I tend to have several pieces going on at a time, but I've put everything on hold until you're finished with—" She sneezed into a hastily retrieved handkerchief, smiled apologetically. "—with me. Sorry, I'm getting a cold. Honey? I haven't any sugar, I'm afraid."

Hawkin looked resigned. "Just cream, thanks."

"It's goat's milk, this time of year. Inspector Martinelli?"

"Black's fine, thanks," she said hastily.

"I didn't know if you'd be hungry, but I haven't eaten yet. Help yourself."

Hawkin took a thick roll with ham in it and wandered unerringly to the work surface below the window.

"Haven't put quite everything on hold, I see," he said around a mouthful. Kate went to see what had captured his attention.

It was a simple, quick charcoal sketch of the view down the hill from this window a short time earlier, black lines on the thick white paper of a spiral-bound pad. The trees that rose up on either side of the page should have dwarfed into insignificance the two central figures walking up the path, but they did not. They towered above the two, certainly, but at the same time seemed to twist slightly away from them, as if flinching from a source of power and threat, and the final impression was of the two humans looming large and ominous at the end of a tunnel or the nucleus of a whirlpool. The woman was turned slightly toward her companion, saying something. He, however, faced directly ahead, and the quick marks that were Hawkin's eyes seemed to look straight into the eyes of the viewer. Kate leaned forward, fascinated, to see the drawing dissolve into a mere swirl of lines and dots.

Vaun spoke up from the chair behind them.

"There's something slightly wrong with the perspective."

"I don't think so," contradicted Hawkin. "No, I think the artist's perspective is very clear indeed."

"I meant technically."

"So did I." He put down his cup and turned abruptly. "Miss Adams, where were you on Monday afternoon and evening?"

Her smile was crooked, but for the first time it touched her eyes.

"So, the truce is not even to last through the meal. You know, there are still some people on earth who feel that when you have shared bread with another, that person cannot be an enemy. Think what havoc that would wreak on our society. Yes, yes, Inspector Hawkin, I shall answer your question." She put her cup carefully down and leaned forward, studying her long hands.

"When I moved here five years ago, it was chiefly because of the solitude. A person in prison has no privacy, ever. It is . . . I found it very nearly intolerable. After my house was finished, I put a sign out on the Road asking people to keep away, and I saw no one, not a single human being, for a solid month. I took the sign down eventually, but even now I often go three or four days without meeting another soul.

"Since the second body was found, however, it's been different. It's not just me, of course. The whole timbre of the Road has changed, and everyone seems to go out of his or her way to say hello if you're walking past, or drop by for a chat or to borrow something. It's fear, Inspector; I don't have to tell you that. And I have a special reason to be afraid, don't I? Since that second child was found, I've begun to take my walks along the Road rather than away from it. I call out when I hear someone go by down on the Road. I make fires even when it's not absolutely necessary, so people can see my smoke. At first I didn't realize what I was doing, but when I did, I made it a conscious habit. I didn't know if they'd find another body, but if they did, I wanted to have some sort of alibi. An innocent person doesn't think of alibis, I know, but my innocence was taken from me years ago. As I said before, I'm not a fool.

61

"On Monday afternoon I was here working, as I usually am. In the morning I sketched in a canvas, and I started painting in the afternoon. I also finished another one I had been working on. They're over there." She waved at the two draped easels.

"May we see them, please, Miss Adams?" Hawkin asked.

"Certainly. It's dusty here, even in winter, so I keep them covered. I also don't want my neighbors to see them." She went over to the right one and folded back the cloth, revealing a canvas covered in a light wash of intense blue with several large areas of color roughly brushed on. The underlying outlines seemed to be of a figure on a chair, with a tree overhead, but the lines were mere suggestions at this point. Still, something vaguely familiar stirred in the back of Kate's mind.

Vaun moved to the larger canvas on the left and carefully rolled the cover up and back. "It's still wet," she commented, and stood away from it.

Kate gasped. A woman with brown hair and a blue dress was holding a naked child to her breast. The child was dead. The woman, the mother, had just realized that her daughter's blue, limp sprawl was final, forever. The finish was exquisite, the background detailed, the texture of hair and fabric palpable, and the overall effect on the viewer was of a knife in the heart.

"But that's—my God, you're Eva Vaughn!"

Vaun turned with a surprised look, the first real emotion that had crossed her face since they had arrived.

"You didn't know?"

"I saw your show in New York last year. Al, you know—"

"Yes, I know who Eva Vaughn is. In fact, I helped out when the painting was stolen in Los Angeles a couple of years ago. It wasn't my case, but I remember the painting."

"I owe you thanks, then, Inspector," said Vaun, one eyebrow arched in amusement at the turn of events. "It no longer belonged to me, of course, but the owner is fond of it."

"And here we thought you were some hippie painter who sold magical unicorns at the flea market," Hawkin mused, and turned to eye the door to the storage room. "Doesn't it worry you just a bit having them all sitting there?"

Vaun actually laughed, warm and much amused.

"Very few of my paintings are worth what that one in Los Angeles was, particularly if they were stolen, and they're probably safer here with the doors unlocked than in a gallery in New York with burglar alarms. Besides, so far—touch wood—none of my neighbors know that I'm Eva Vaughn when I'm 'out there.' That's the main reason why I keep the paintings under wraps until I send them off," she added, and lowered the covers again. She turned back to face the two detectives. It was an awkward moment, which she herself broke.

"But all of that has little to do with your investigation, doesn't it?" She went back and sat on the couch to pour herself another cup of coffee with steady hands. "In fact, considering the sorts of things Eva Vaughn is known for, it may even make your pointed questions that much more necessary. You were asking about Monday, I believe, three days ago. Amy Dodson came up on her pony just before lunchtime with some bread her mother had baked. Angie usually bakes Mondays and Thursdays, and she always sends me some of whatever she's made. I let her use my hillside for her garden, and she feels she owes me for it." Which explained the incongruity of the pale face and hands with the considerable garden outside the door. "She doesn't owe me, but when it comes to her bread, I don't argue. Have you talked with Amy yet?"

"Not yet, no."

"You'll find her a sensible child, very bright. She's had home schooling, like most of the kids here, since she was seven, and her test scores are high-school level by now. Anyway, she was here a bit before one. I also saw her father later, it must've been almost six, because the light was changing too much to paint any more so I went for a walk along the road. He makes a trip to town most Mondays and he was—" She sneezed again, blew her nose, coughed. "He was just getting back. I stopped him to ask if he could take some canvases into San Francisco for me next week, which he's done half a dozen times."

"Did you see anyone else?"

"Did anyone else see me, you mean. I don't think so. It started to rain, so I cut it short and came back here. Someone else went by a few minutes later, but I was already off the

63

Road so I didn't see who it was. It sounded like Bob Riddle's truck, but I can't be sure."

"What did you do after that?"

"The same thing I do every evening. Stirred up the fire, had a drink, read for a while, ate some soup and the bread. After dinner I usually write and sketch. The sketches were lousy, so I used them to start my fire the next morning. The letters Tommy Chesler took down to Tyler's for me on Tuesday, for Anna to stamp and mail. I had a bath, dried my hair, and went to bed, about ten-thirty. And slept until about five the following morning."

"Alone?"

Her smile was ironic, and acknowledged his peculiar right to intrude on her.

"Yes."

"Every evening?"

There was a pause while she studied him, her smile deepening.

"No."

"Who?"

"I think, Inspector Hawkin, we are nearing the point at which I am going to ask you to put this interrogation on a more formal basis."

"Tyler?"

Kate thought she wouldn't answer, but it came eventually.

"Occasionally."

"Why didn't you come down to Tyler's Tuesday morning?"

She must have been expecting the question, for she answered without hesitating.

"These people are my friends." She weighted the word heavily. "I never had friends before, and I found myself reluctant to have you accuse me and peel apart my life in front of them. No one here knows who I am, other than that I'm Vaun the painter. There's no Eva Vaughn on Tyler's Road, and no felon either. Just 'Vaun'."

"Nobody knows?"

"Tyler knows that I've been in prison; I'm not sure if he knows the reason. I offered to tell him, but he said he didn't want to know. He may have found out since then, but he won't have told anyone else."

"You sound very sure of that."

"He didn't tell you," she pointed out. "Tyler is famous for his stubborn refusal to talk about anyone else. The Road gossips find him enormously frustrating."

"Who are the Road gossips?"

She hesitated for a moment.

"You really should ask someone else about that. I'm not fully a part of the Road society. Angie Dodson could tell you. She isn't what I would call a gossip, but she lives closer to the Road and knows better than I do what goes on."

It sounded a feeble excuse for avoiding an answer, but perhaps to respond to the question would have felt too much like informing for a convicted felon's taste.

To Kate's surprise, Hawkin stood up abruptly.

"That'll be all for the moment, Miss Adams. We'll be back if we need to finish 'ferreting about.' You won't leave the area without informing us, please."

"Of course." She too seemed at a loss. "Will you . . . that is, I suppose I'll need to leave my work as it is for a while. On hold." Her voice came perilously close to pleading.

Hawkin looked down at her for a long minute and finally relented into something close to sympathy.

"That would probably be for the best, Miss Adams."

Kate watched the deadness creep back into the remarkable ice-blue eyes and was annoyed to feel a twinge of sorrow. She's a suspect, Martinelli, she told herself harshly, and ignored the little voice that protested, But not Eva Vaughn!

Outside the house Hawkin set a fast pace down the slippery path, muttering to himself.

"What did you say?"

"I said, what's the world coming to, drinking coffee with goat's milk and honey, that's what I said. It's the most disgusting thing I've ever heard of."

"It wasn't bad black. And those ham sandwiches were great."

"The sandwiches were good. The coffee was disgusting. Can you run in those shoes?"

"Run?"

"Yes, run. To cover ground in a rapid manner. You're supposed to be the athlete here. Would those shoes do for running, or would you need your Nikes or Adidas or whatever they are?"

She looked down at her feet, which were covered with a pair of relatively soft, low-heeled leather shoes, chosen that morning for walking in the wet hills.

"Sure I could run in them. I wouldn't want to do a marathon, but—"

"How far could you go?"

"Well, I'd hate to go more than ten miles."

"Will they slow you down much?"

"After the first five, yes."

"That's all right, then; it's only four to Tyler's."

"You want me to run to Tyler's Barn?"

"For Christ's sake, Martinelli, wake up. You heard her; she was seen at one and at some time before six. We have to know if she could have made it on foot to Tyler's to pick up a car, driven by car to the Donaldson house in Palo Alto, snatched Samantha Donaldson between three and three-fifteen, and made it back here to see Dodson by six."

"Leaving the body in the car, or carrying it with her?"

Hawkin's shriveling look went a long way to explain his ferocious reputation among his colleagues. Kate felt three feet tall.

"In broad daylight?"

"Good," she said gamely. "It saves me from having to carry forty pounds back up the hill with me. Where will I find you?"

"Probably at Tyler's. I'll cheer for you as you go past."

"Thanks. You can buy me a pizza afterwards, to replace the calories."

"And a big glass of goat's milk."

"Come to think of it, I'm busy tonight, very busy. Here, take my jacket and stick it in the truck, would you? I'll drop it in the mud if I try to carry it. And the shoulder holster too, it'll kill me to run in it." She took off the restricting leather harness, retrieved her gun. "I'll take this in my bag. You going to talk to the Dodsons?"

"First on my list. Also, I'll get Trujillo started on the cars, see if we can find who was up here that day, have a chat with Mr. Tommy Chesler and maybe another talk with Tyler."

"Have fun." Casey slung the shoulder strap of her heavy bag across her chest, aware that it made her look like an advertisement for bras, and did a few leg stretches before setting the chronometer on her Christmas watch (alarm clock, the time in London, Sydney, and New Delhi, and an unreadable face, just like Dick Tracy), and then set off carefully down the rough and slippery track.

In the house on the hill Vaun Adams heard the old fire wagon cough into life and lumber off. In another minute or two she moved at last. She opened her eyes, took her hand away from her mouth, scrubbed the palms of her hands slowly up and down her trouser legs, and finally stood up, deliberately, as if her body ached all over. Inevitably, she moved to the two easels, touched the smooth handle of a squirrel-hair brush lightly in a gesture of taking bearings, and stood before the nearly finished figure of the agonized mother. The artist's face was without expression, but the tendons in her neck seemed exaggerated, and when her right hand reached out automatically to mix the drying paints on the glass slab, the fingers were unsteady against the handle of the palette knife.

She drew back her hand and held it up in front of her face, fingers spread and still trembling. Her eyes studied the hand curiously, examining in minute detail the back of it, then the palm and the softness of the wrist, then the back of it again, the webs, the knuckles, before they looked through the fingers and focused on the painting behind. The hand dropped and as of its own volition, without the eyes looking down, reached out for the tube of cadmium red. She flicked off the cap with her thumb and squeezed a huge dollop out on top of a blue that had taken her half an hour to mix. She dropped the tube and, still without looking, seized a random brush, a large one, and scooped up the blood-colored pigment. She carried it to the face in front of her and stopped, holding it a fraction of an inch from the canvas. Her hand was rock steady now, but the sound of her breathing was suddenly harsh in the room. Thirty seconds, a minute, and abruptly she straightened and put the brush down onto the

67

palette. She scrubbed her palms again down the front of her thighs and glanced at the table next to her, grimaced at the pool of red, and set about carefully to rescue what she could of the laboriously achieved blue tint.

When her face came up again it had changed. Her eyes went to the unfinished woman, and her hand, no longer disconnected but as a part of her, went again to the bundle of brushes and chose one. She rubbed the white bristles into the edge of one of the globules of paint, rose up onto her toes, and reached out for the painting.

8

Al Hawkin stood watching until Casey Martinelli's nice firm backside disappeared behind some trees, and then he turned to the wide spot up the Road where Detweiler waited in the muddy wagon. Thank God she's not my type, he thought—no strains there on Hawkin's Rules of Order, Law One: Thou shalt not get involved with a female colleague. Two, no, three years ago in Los Angeles he'd been assigned a lady whose long legs and blond curls had been painfully distracting to work next to. He'd finally gone to the man in charge, and a few weeks later, when she was transferred with a promotion, he was freed from Law One and had found her distractions a source of pleasure rather than discomfort. This one, though, would be no problem—no chemistry. Too short, too dark, too well muscled. Wonder if she lifts weights? He climbed up into the car.

"You can take me to the Dodsons now."

"Where'd she go?" asked Detweiler, puzzled.

Hawkin looked at him blandly.

"Downhill. The Dodsons?"

"Just up the Road, about half a mile." He ground the engine into life and coaxed it into the lowest gear, and the vehicle set off phlegmatically up the pitted road. "Great thing, this old gal. Just point her in the right direction and she'll climb right over everything, feels like. Ever see that

Star Wars movie with those walking transports? Too unstable, of course, but that's what driving one of these feels like, just plodding along, sure and steady wins the race."

Worse than a taxi driver, thought Hawkin morosely as the man chattered away. That's another thing about Martinelli—she doesn't chatter. A person can think around her. Perhaps she wouldn't be such a burden as he'd originally thought. He pictured her setting off down the Road with her bag strap slung between her breasts, muddy water flying at every step, and wondered how she would get on.

Kate was getting on slowly but not steadily and with increasing annoyance. The Road seemed to be crawling with people, all of whom wanted to know what she was doing, what had happened, where was her car, or, in the case of the various police, if she wanted a ride to Tyler's. She shut off her ticking chronometer three times in the first mile, until finally she just decided to give a cheery wave and keep running. Her shoes were totally inappropriate to the job and would probably be ruined, her pant legs clung up to her knees, and after threatening all day it finally started raining, gently, a mile before the gate. When she hit the final quarter-mile straightaway where the road dropped through the meadow, she stopped abruptly. She had totally forgotten about the press. There must have been thirty cars camped across the Road from Tyler's Barn and even more cameras waiting to capture her bedraggled, sweaty, filthy self on film for all the Bay Area to feast their eyes upon. One of Trujillo's county cars was just edging through the gate. She ducked back around the corner, switched off her timer, and greeted it wetly when it appeared. Trujillo himself was at the wheel, with Tyler beside him. Trujillo wound down the window.

"What happened to the fire wagon?" Tyler asked, echoing the cry that had followed Kate for the last four miles, and from Trujillo came its mate, "Where's Hawkin?"

"Paul, can I talk with you for a minute?" He hadn't spent the morning sloshing around in the mud, she thought in disgust as he joined her beneath a sheltering tree, though with the slick soles on those shoes it's only a matter of time before that nice gray suit ends up in the mud. The thought cheered her considerably, and she smiled sweetly through the drips that ran down her face.

"If you don't have any urgent business up the hill would you mind going back to Tyler's so I can pick up my car? Hawkin's got me doing a timing test, round trip to the Donaldson house, but I really don't want my mother to open her newspaper and see her little girl looking like a mud slide survivor."

"Sure, no problem. We were just checking on a couple of my people, it can wait five minutes more."

"Look, I should tell you, Hawkin's going to want to know every car that was out of Tyler's shed on Monday, and then he's going to have every one of them gone over for traces. If you haven't started on the cars yet, you'd better do so."

"Thanks for the tip." They turned back to the car.

"Hello, Mr. Tyler. No, I'll sit in the back, it's all right. Mr. Tyler, I hope you don't mind turning back to the barn for a minute? I really couldn't face those reporters like this."

"Happy to. How—"

She interrupted firmly. "Why are the press staying behind the fence? I'd have expected to see them crawling all over the hill by now."

"That was Tyler's doing," laughed Trujillo. "He went around nailing up all these signs that say Trespassers Will Be Shot, and told them that it was private property and that everyone who lives here owns a loaded shotgun. When one of the television guys didn't seem to believe him, he gave them a little demonstration—for which he will probably be fined—and then, when he had their attention, said very nicely that if they're well behaved he'll come and talk to them every two hours. So far it's worked."

"Threats, bribes, and a disgustingly wet day. Very clever."

"I've had some practice in crowd control," said Tyler. "Besides, Hawkin authorized some money to come my way, and I've got two of the residents down in the kitchen turning out regular batches of hot soup and brownies."

"And looking photogenic," Trujillo said, grinning.

"They won't charge Hawkin for that. I think I saw a towel back there, if you want to dry your hair or something," he added. "You can put it over your head if you want to hide."

70

"Don't need to hide if it makes a poor enough picture for them." She toweled her hair with enthusiasm for the next few minutes as Trujillo threaded his way through the questions and cameras and into the privacy of the compound. Kate's little white box stood between someone's silver BMW and an ancient John Deere tractor with half its guts on the ground under a plastic tarpaulin. To the left stretched the roofed-over car storage shed. Kate eyed the vehicles speculatively as she ran a comb through her hair.

"Where is Miss Adams's car?"

Tyler seemed unsurprised at the question, which struck Kate as a bit odd.

"You heard about it, did you? It's the one there, with the blue cover." He pointed to a long, low shroud. "Want to see it?"

"Yes, I would." The rain had let up for the moment, and the damp gravel scrunched underfoot. Tyler peeled back the cover, and there stood a diamond among the hunks of everyday rock: a proud, gleaming maroon Jaguar, at least thirty years old, but in mint condition.

"Would you look at that!" exclaimed Trujillo, and they did.

"You haven't seen it before?" Tyler asked. "It's a beauty, isn't it?"

"Does she let anyone else drive it?" asked Kate.

"Oh, yes, I take it out every week or two. Doesn't do to let a nice car sit, not good for it. She pays me to keep it up, but I always tell her I'd do it for nothing."

"Nobody else, though?"

"No. Well, come to think of it, she let Angie Dodson use it to take Amy in to the doctor's one day when Tony had the truck, but that was, oh, October maybe. Yes, the middle of October, just before the harvest fest. She was scared to drive it, I remember, but I had both of mine apart and it was either that or the old truck, which would've been worse. Of course, I could have let her use someone else's, but I hate to do that without permission. It's asking for problems, with insurance and all that."

"But you could have, you said. Do you have some of the keys for these?" Kate waved her hand at the ranks of bumpers.

"Oh, yes," he said in all innocence. "There's keys for all of them on the board just inside the door. We have to be able to move them, to get at other cars or in case of a fire or something."

Kate met Trujillo's eyes as Tyler turned back to cover the Jag lovingly. She tipped her head toward the car, and he nodded in understanding. The Jag would be the first under scrutiny.

Her own car seemed small and tinny as she fished her dry clothes from the trunk, and the sound it made closing had all the expensive thunk of a child's toy.

"I need to get out of these wet things. Can I use the house?" she asked Tyler.

"Sure, go ahead. You know where the bathroom is. Have a shower if you want; there's a stack of towels in the thing that looks like a garbage can."

As Kate stripped off her clammy clothes she was amused to see that it *was* a garbage can—a plain, galvanized metal garbage can filled with thick, multicolored towels. A man who sits on a piece of property worth millions, with a leaky faucet and towels in a garbage can. Could he really have been innocently unaware of the drift of her questions about the cars? Or was his open admission that all the keys were in his possession just a bit too blithe? Was Tyler protecting Vaun Adams, his sometime lover, or using her as camouflage? Or did he not know enough to put her together with the murders? She shook her head at all these speculations, pulled on her rumpled sweats, combed her hair again, and went back out into the yard.

She threw her sodden clothes into the trunk of her car, unlocked the driver's door and tossed her weighty handbag onto the passenger seat, and remembered to switch on the chronometer before settling herself comfortably behind the wheel and starting the engine. She ran the windshield a couple of times against the accumulated drops, backed out into the gravel, nodded to the uniformed cop who now stood watch over the cars, and turned out onto the main road going north through the crowd. One of the television vans seemed to be having some problems with the transmitter on its roof. Two men were up working on it, but it didn't seem very likely that their efforts to revive it would succeed. It looked as if it had been swatted sideways by a giant hand. Kate slowed and peered curiously up at it; then she noticed the spray of small dents and lines in the paint, up along the edge of the van. She laughed and accelerated. Tyler's demonstration to the media on privacy rights.

There were three cars parked at the public park where Tyler's Creek met the sea. No, four—one pulled up among the trees where the creek path led towards the state reserve up in the hills. Probably curious citizens wanting to see where the body of Amanda Bloom had been found. If it were summer they'd be running a bus from town.

It was not raining just at the moment, but out over the ocean the clouds were massing, a black, lowering Pacific storm gathering its forces. Kate shivered and turned up the heater. Maybe she'd be lucky and it would come in slowly.

Traffic was light going over the hill into the Bay Area, and an impatient Audi rode her back bumper for half a mile before passing on a blind corner. She stifled the urge to violence and glanced at the time. Had traffic been this light on Monday? Once she'd successfully negotiated the downhill curves and entered the freeway in the direction of Palo Alto, she reached for her car phone and identified herself to the familiar voice of the dispatcher, a tough, middle-aged Japanese woman whom everyone called Marge, for reasons long forgotten, though her name was Yuki.

"Marge, can you ask around concerning traffic conditions over the pass on 92, Monday afternoon? I'm most interested in twelve-thirty to three eastbound, and, say, three to four westbound."

"I can give you instant service on part of that," her voice crackled over the receiver. "There was a spill there just after two-thirty on the downhill side. A lumber truck went over and blocked both lanes. My brother-in-law got caught behind it, for nearly an hour. Do you want me to check further?"

"Very interesting. Yes, I'll check with the highway patrol later, but keep your ears open."

"I always do." Her voice was prim behind the static.

Two-thirty. A very close thing, but if she'd left immediately after Amy, if she'd run fairly fast, if she'd driven just marginally above the speed limit, she could have slipped over the hill before the Road was buried in two-by-fours.

Kate pulled off the freeway toward the Donaldson's exclusive neighborhood and wound up the smooth, narrow road through fragrant bay and live oaks and madronas, and from a rise she saw the garden where Samantha had been playing seventy-two hours before. The area was immediately visible, just for an instant, but quite clearly, before the trees closed in again. The Road dipped back down among oaks and high walls before rising to curve around the Donaldson property and continue on into ever higher reaches of elevation and income. Kate pulled over on the far side of the Donaldson hedge and put her chin on the wheel. Ahead of her lay the heavily treed drive to the neighboring house, where faint marks in the grassy shoulder had been found Tuesday morning, nothing more definite than the hint of a hidden car.

"Why the hell can't we be having a drought this winter?" she said sourly into the silent car. She sat for several minutes, thinking thoughts that were not pleasant about a woman she wanted very much to be innocent. Finally she twisted the key, slammed the car into gear, and headed back to Tyler's Barn.

9

The rain began again an hour later, with that slow steadiness and determination that makes the natives of the Pacific coast check their supplies of candles and firewood. A good night to be in bed, thought Kate. I wonder if I'm forever doomed to drive into rain as I approach this place.

There were no cars at the creekside park, and the group of vehicles perched near Tyler's Barn had thinned considerably. Two more cars skulked away as she drove up and pulled into the fenced compound. Trujillo's men were busy with the Jaguar and a couple of others, and the corrugated metal roof of the great shed rang with the heavy drops. Trujillo looked up at her approaching headlights, waved in recognition, and then put his head back inside the car. Even in the dim after-noon light his gray suit no longer seemed fresh. She laced on the old running shoes she always carried in the car, zipped on a hooded rain parka, and set off down the main road, ignoring the amazed looks of the two uniforms, and dodging the unenthusiastic reporters with ease.

The man keeping guard beneath the Tyler's Road sign rolled down the window of his marked cruiser.

"Inspector Hawkin was just asking if you'd shown up yet. He's still up there." He looked across the metal gate at the gradually disappearing dirt road.

"Maybe you should call back and tell him I'm on my way up. I should be there in forty minutes or so."

"He said to tell you that if it was raining you didn't have to do it."

"No, I'd better, just to finish it. The surface won't be too wet." But *I* will, said a protesting voice, I'll be wet and damned cold. Shut up and get on with it, she said, and she did.

The surface was actually better than it had been that morning, but the trees looked very large and dark, and they swayed and creaked gothically in the rising wind. In a minute they swallowed her up, and she jogged steadily uphill on the narrow, rocky road, very much alone, with the huge trees bending and groaning on all sides, the big drops splatting onto her face and clothes, the occasional lighted house, glimpsed through tossing branches, serving only to increase her sense of isolation. It was getting darker, and she ran faster now to shake the eerie shadows and fought off the feeling that someone was behind her by pushing herself physically. Her shoes chuffed rhythmically and she had to concentrate on the road surface to avoid ruts and stones. She was sweating freely now despite the chill drops that worked their way down the neck and through the seams of her parka, and her breath was coming in great gulps as she fought toward the fast-fading point where the pale road disap-peared between the dark walls of the woods. She passed the Adams house on the left—not far now.

Without warning the world exploded into light and for a moment Kate, completely disoriented, braced herself for the clap of thunder. Instead she heard a welcome voice shouting angrily.

"Turn that thing away, for Christ's sake, you're blinding her." The light shifted, and through the dazzle in her eyes she was aware of figures, a car, a lighted house beyond. She automatically reached down and switched off her timer, and then stood, hands on knees, gulping in air.

"You all right?" Hawkin's voice again. She bobbed her head, and spoke as best she could.

"Yeah, just wanted, to make it, before dark, couldn't run, by flashlight, could use, a drink, of water, though."

"I'd have thought you had enough on the outside to make you happy, but come on in the house and catch your breath."

Kate ducked into the log cabin after him and accepted a chair and a drink, and as her heart slowed she was grateful for the glow of the wood stove at her side. Angie Dodson was a tiny, thin woman with a thick tumble of dark blond hair held determinedly in place by numerous inadequate hairpins, and she had filled the low room with bright pillows and tapestries and the smell of good food, with a large loom in one corner and a spinning wheel behind a chair. A serious, freckled child of about twelve brought Kate a big cup of hot, oniony soup and a warm, seed-filled roll.

"You're Amy, aren't you? I remember you from the other day."

"Yes. Why did you run up from Tyler's in the rain when you could use a car?"

"Because it's there, I guess. Did you make this soup?"

"I helped Mom."

"Thank you, you may have saved my life with it." Seeing the serious consideration of this, Kate smiled. "It's just a saying, but I do thank you very much for it."

"You're welcome."

"Ready, Martinelli?" Hawkin stood at the door with the jacket she had left with him several lifetimes before.

"Ready. Thank you, Mrs. Dodson, it really hit the spot."

"Please, the name is Angie."

"Good night, Angie," called Hawkin. "I hope your husband makes it home okay."

Kate looked more carefully at the narrow face of the

woman who seemed scarcely older than her daughter, and noticed then the tension of worry in her face.

"I expect he'll stay in town with friends, if it's raining too hard. It's happened before." She lifted the bright kerosene lamp and led the way to the door. "Feel free to come tomorrow, if you need a hot drink."

"That's very good of you, Angie," said Hawkin. "We'll try not to bother you too much."

"It's no bother, really it isn't. It—" She stopped, and looked faintly embarrassed and something else. Defiant? "I shouldn't say this, I suppose, considering the reason you're here, but it's actually been a treat, seeing all these new faces. I've had fun."

Yes, thought Hawkin, he could imagine that fun was a rare commodity up here this time of year, in a tiny dark house with no electricity and a child. His face relaxed into a smile, the smile that tended to fluster women like Angie Dodson.

"Fine, then. You keep the kettle on for us."

The wind blew the rain into them as they stepped from the warmth and ran for the shelter of the wagon. Detweiler folded down his spotlight and picked up the portable radio Trujillo had provided. The crackling and whining were bad, but he eventually got the message across that they, the last car, were starting down.

"Sorry about the shouting," he said, and pulled into the road. "There's something wrong with the aerial."

"Can you turn on the heater?" The man must be from Alaska, thought Kate.

"Sorry, it's gone too. There's a blanket back there somewhere. Are you cold?"

"For God's sake, man," Hawkin burst out, "she's soaked through; of course she's cold. Here, Casey, put this around you. Oh, Christ, don't tell me the wipers have gone out again."

"They'll be fine as soon as the engine's warmed up," the driver said desperately.

"Jesus, Mary, and Joseph," said Hawkin in a soft voice. Kate did not think it was a prayer.

It was fully dark, and the headlights, which did work, picked out no press cars through the rain at the bottom of the hill. Kate clamped her jaws shut against the shudders of cold that threatened to take possession. The electricity seemed to be out at Tyler's, but lamps shone in several windows. Hawkin was out of the wagon before the brake was set. He reached into the back door, pulled Kate out, steered her with one firm hand into the house and thrust her toward the bathroom. A kerosene lamp burned on the back of the toilet.

"Hot shower," he ordered in a hard voice, and shut the door. A few minutes later Kate, under a stream of blessedly scalding water, heard the door open.

"Don't put those wet things on again," came another order, and the door slammed. She pulled the curtain to one side and saw jeans, sweatshirt, and thick gray socks folded next to the sink. The urge to shudder subsided, the water began to run cool, and she dressed. When she came out of the steam-dripping room she heard a now-familiar voice shouting in monologue.

"—when it ought to be hauling cantaloupes in the Coachella Valley. You get me a decent four-wheel-drive vehicle in here tomorrow or I'm going to have to make some major waves about the lack of backup here for my people. No, I don't want to hear about your problems. I don't care if you have to break into the goddamn Jeep dealership and steal something. I can't have my partner getting pneumonia because you people don't maintain your equipment, and I'm too old and too ill-tempered to walk. Have I made myself sufficiently clear? Good. Have a nice evening," he added maliciously, and hung up. He rapidly wiped the grin from his face when he saw Kate standing in the doorway, but it crept back in twitches. She was grinning too, in her cuffed and belted jeans and the sweatshirt that reached to her thighs. She felt ridiculously pleased at his use of the word "partner."

"Warmer now?" he asked.

"I should ask the same of you," she said mildly, with a glance at the telephone.

"Yes, well, if they think they're all going to hide behind me, they're very much mistaken. You want something to eat before we go?"

"A cup of coffee would be great, but that's all."

78

"I gave Tyler's lady your thermos. Anna. She said she'd fill it. I'll just tell Trujillo we're leaving—he's staying here again tonight."

They found Trujillo in the dimly lit great hall with his feet up on a table in front of the huge fireplace, talking to Tyler and sitting next to a woman who was apparently not a stranger. He had a glass in one hand and no tie on, and he jerked upright as they entered.

"Christ Jesus, Trujillo, you seem to think this is some kind of holiday arranged for your entertainment. You're on duty here, mister, or had you forgotten? Maybe you think the people of this county pay you for sitting and drinking whiskey while some bastard is out there murdering children? I don't expect you to stay up all night, I told you that. I don't even expect you to sleep alone. I do expect you to stay sober enough to answer the phone if I feel like having a chat at three in the morning." He snatched up the glass and took it over to the fireplace, paused at the sight of the bottle on the mantelpiece, and looked at Kate. "You driving?"

"Sure."

"Not too tired? Good, it'd be a shame to waste this. I'll bring back your glass tomorrow, Tyler, and from now on put the good stuff away or I'll have to charge you with attempted bribery." He took a small sip and rolled it around his tongue. "We'll overlook it tonight, though. Good night, all."

They detoured through the kitchen and retrieved the thermos from Anna.

"Sorry I didn't have anything smaller," she said, smiling at Kate's attire.

"I did wonder if Tyler went in for lavender," replied Kate. "I'll bring them back tomorrow."

"No hurry. Drive carefully. They're predicting gale-force winds by midnight, I heard on the radio before the power went out."

"A cheery thought."

In the car Kate slipped off her sodden shoes, the second pair for the day, and drove in her stocking feet. Hawkin poured her some coffee and slumped back, nursing the glass.

"You like whiskey?" he asked.

"Not especially."

"White wine." From the scorn in his voice he might have said "soda pop."

"Sometimes. I prefer a red. When I drink, it's usually beer."

He was surprised, and said so.

"It has character," she commented. "And if you want the results of the afternoon, I've written it on that pad in the glove compartment. The final figure should be"—she looked at the glowing figures on her wrist—"four hours, twenty-eight minutes door to door. I didn't run very fast going down, but I doubt she could have done it as fast going up. We'll have to ask Dodson if she seemed out of breath at all. Where is he, by the way?"

"He borrowed Tyler's pickup to go to Sacramento to pick up an engine. His truck has a cracked block, and a friend had one that he was going to sell him cheap. Trujillo checked, too. His engine really is shot." He threw the notebook back into the glove compartment and slapped it shut.

"What else turned up today?" she asked.

"One little lock of brown hair in the back of the Jaguar, one child's ring under the seat."

Kate frowned.

"There was no mention of a ring on any of the girls, was there?"

"No, there wasn't. One of Trujillo's men is going to do the rounds with it tomorrow. Parents sometimes forget just what a kid walked out the door wearing. One of them might recognize it. It was too small for an adult."

"You said a lock of hair. Cut off?"

"No, caught in a door handle, a little twist of twenty, thirty hairs. Brown, straight, about six inches long."

The rain sheeted down the windshield, and even on high speed the wipers managed to clear only brief glimpses of the black roadway and the drops that fell and bounced back up in the headlights. When Kate broke the noisy silence, her voice was flat.

"It doesn't look good for Vaun Adams, does it?"

"No, it does not."

"Do you think she did it?"

"We're not allowed to play favorites, Casey."

"I just want to know what you think."

Hawkin took a minute to answer.

"You know, all day I've been thinking about a case I had, oh, fifteen years ago, maybe. This little, quiet mouse of a woman whose kids and husband disappeared. She came in to report that he'd taken them, filled out missing persons forms, we put out their descriptions. His car was found a few days later near a bus stop, so we went back to talk with her. She was just what you'd expect—teary, worried, furious at her husband, but completely rational. She showed us the kids' rooms, and there was this teddy bear, no eyes, one ear chewed off, all the fuzz gone—you know how a toy looks when it's been loved to pieces. Anyway, this teddy bear was sitting there on the table next to the bed, leaning up against the lamp, and it just struck me that it looked, I don't know, lonely. It stuck in my mind, and later that night I got to thinking about it, and I got to thinking that really there were kind of a lot of clothes in the closets, that he would at least have taken coats or shoes. The next morning we went and got a search warrant, and found them in the basement, buried deep. And she was such a nice, gentle lady, with absolutely no guilt in her eyes."

"But you can't think that Vaun Adams is stupid, and to bring the bodies to her own backyard, as she put it, would be stupid. Suicidal."

"Maybe that's it. She wouldn't be the first psychopath who arranged to be caught. 'Stop me before I do it again,' that sort of thing."

"Do you honestly think so?"

He squinted out the side window, but saw only the reflection of the dashboard lights and his own unhappy face.

"No, I don't. She looked like a badly beaten ex-con who's trying to decide whether or not to stand up on her feet, not like a murderer who's half afraid of being caught and half afraid of not being caught. She didn't look afraid at all, for that matter. Maybe she really is crazy. I dunno, we'll have to find out what Dodson says tomorrow and see the results from the lab and the prints boys. Oh, hell, I shouldn't have had that Scotch on an empty stomach, it's making me all weepy. Next thing you know I'll be telling you about my ex-wife. I'm tired. Do you need me to keep you awake?"

"No, I'm fine," she lied. "Will it disturb you if I listen to the radio?"

"Nothing disturbs me when I'm asleep," he snorted, and soon proved it.

10

Kate reached for the car radio and pushed various selector buttons until the muttering of voices filled the car. For a long and tiresome drive a severe irritant is called for, and there is nothing, but nothing more irritating than listening to one of those twenty-four-hour talk shows, particularly at night, when the callers are regulars who glory in their moments of authority, commanding the airwaves and the attention of hundreds, even thousands, of ears. The current caller was working himself into a rant about oil drillers and water wells, with brief excursions into the weight of concrete and the encroachment of fill into the Bay. It wasn't until the moderator cut him off that Kate learned the topic for the evening, which was earthquakes, the prediction of and how to prepare for. Floods might be more appropriate, she thought. The little car suddenly slowed and veered as it hit a deep wash of water from a blocked drain. The noisy burst of spray from below and the sharp change of speed half woke Hawkin, who looked around blankly and went back to sleep.

Kate carefully poured herself a cup of coffee from the thermos, barely taking her eyes from the road. She drove with her left hand on the wheel, sipping, listening to the radio with half an ear, enjoying the sensation of being a warm, dry speck pushing through a cold and nasty universe.

After a few miles a pair of headlights came blurring at her, fellow travelers in the storm. She glanced at Hawkin as the lights passed and had etched onto her inner eye the brief, clear image of a younger man, the lines and hardness of the face softened, vulnerable. Innocent.

It was a disturbing view of an already disturbing man. Kate did not want to see the vulnerable side of Al Hawkin, no more than she wanted to be emotionally intimate with any of the people she worked with. She had labored long and hard on the defenses around her life, defenses all the more efficient for being nearly invisible, and did not wish to see them breached now.

It is no easy job, being a police officer. For a woman it is an impossible job, fitting into the masculine world of the station while retaining her identity as a woman. For a woman to be a street cop she must, from the first day in police academy, create a clear picture of what is required of her, and stick to it without wavering: she must be tough but not coarse, friendly but not obsequious, unaggressive but ready without a moment's hesitation to hurl into a violent confrontation. Impossible, but women do it. Kate had done it. She had also pushed and scrambled and sweated the books to work herself into an early promotion off the streets, knowing the resentment and mistrust her single-minded ambition would cause.

Those feelings and the tensions they had created had undoubtedly contributed to the willingness San Jose had shown in giving her to San Francisco, but once there she had made it her business to play down her urge to competitiveness. For once, she would just fit in, as much as her private self would allow. The men and women she worked with found her friendly and easygoing, to a point. Everyone knew that she ran and worked out at the gym, that she liked pasta and baseball and spicy little carnations, that she had an ongoing feud with the plumber. Everyone knew that Casey could be counted on for donations to shower gifts, for trading shifts so you could get to your sister's wedding or your aunt's funeral, for a wicked accuracy with the bat on the departmental team, for being a good cop to have at your side in a tight place. Yet not one of them had been inside her home, knew what she did in her off hours, knew how or with whom she lived. Her intensely private home life she concealed by the very openness of her work life. It was a somewhat schizophrenic way to live, she knew, but she had found that the only way she could continue as a cop was to preserve a place totally apart where she could retreat. No work came home, no colleagues came inside. Most of them didn't even realize that they hadn't been invited.

Hawkin, though. She had a feeling that Al Hawkin's eyes missed very little. Not that he would push her—she'd had to deal with a number of people, men and women, who wanted to be buddies, who felt the presence of a hidden Kate and wanted to pick at it, like fingers on a scab. She could deal with these—it had become almost a game a couple of times—but Al Hawkin was different.

Al Hawkin, she knew by now, was totally involved with whatever case he was on. He would eat, sleep, and drink the case, and be eaten by it, until it ended. Any partner of his who wanted to be more than an assistant would have to follow him at least part of the way down that road. It was something Kate had always resisted, but she felt the threat of it now, radiating from this sleeping man at her side.

The ease with which he plunged into an all-revealing, vulnerable state of unconsciousness was perhaps the most troubling thing of all. Kate herself never slept in the presence of strangers, on a plane, with a half-known man she'd taken to her bed. Exhausting hours later she would invariably get off the plane, out of the bed, red-eyed, unable to let go and sleep until she was by herself.

Except for Lee, of course. With Lee, at home, for the last four years, she had let go entirely, utterly. With Lee, and with no one else, she was absolutely vulnerable, freely open to crushing criticism or heart-filling communion. With Lee. Alone.

How could a person sleep with a stranger watching?

Another image came from out of the long, busy day, that of Vaun Adams at the door of her house: the beauty of the fairy-tale princess—blackest hair, palest skin, red lips, ethereal eyes—and the flat expression of a person dragged out from the gates of hell.

That expression—all her expressions, with the exception of that one moment of surprise at their ignorance of her identity—was not a normal reaction to a police questioning. The only people Kate had known who did not respond to the police with nervously exaggerated emotions, of politeness, aggression, humor, or whatever, were old lawyers and young punks convinced of their own invulnerability, and even in the latter there was always a slight air of disdain to give them away. In Vaun Adams, though, there had been no nervous

84

exaggeration whatsoever. Watchful caution, yes, and a vague amusement, but, as Hawkin had said, there had been no fear, which in a woman who had spent over nine years in prison was a very strange thing.

She had seemed, now that Kate thought about it, open, honest, even trusting, amazing as that might be. Childlike in her confidence that the world would not hurt her. Less guarded, in fact, than twelve-year-old Amy Dodson had been.

Yet, this was a murderer who had spent a quarter of her life in prison.

Vaun Adams had claimed that her innocence had been taken from her. Certainly her paintings were not innocent. They were powerful, raw, subtle, moving, beautiful, sordid, pain-filled, and joyous, sometimes all at once, but innocence was not a word that came immediately to mind.

What is innocence, though? Kate wondered. There's the legal definition, but isn't innocence the absence of wickedness, of sin—that old word? "One of the world's innocents." An innocent was someone untouched by the wickedness of the world, whose simplicity was a highly polished surface where the dirt of the ugly world could not cling. (Oh, come now, Martinelli, the Scotch fumes are getting to you!) Nonetheless, she had met one or two of them, who would have been called saints in other times.

Is that what Vaun Adams is, truly: an innocent? A mirror who has seen considerable evil, in herself as well as others, and reflects it back, along with the good, becoming ever brighter in the process? How else to explain the lack of fear, or anger, or joy, or any strong emotion in the eyes of the painter, yet the tumultuous presence of all of them in the canvases she painted?

Can an innocent commit murder?

The muttering radio was forgotten as Kate's mind reached back to a hot afternoon in New York the summer before, and the series of paintings that leapt from the white walls of the gallery. She and Lee stood long in front of the one entitled *Strawberry Fields (Forever)*. It was a single figure of a man, a middle-aged Mexican farm worker, standing in the center of a vast field, row after row of strawberries, radiating endlessly, hypnotically, out from the horizon. He was leaning on a hoe, and the viewer's eyes met his with a shock, for in

85

his face and stance lay a total and uncomplaining acceptance of the miles of grueling work that lay around him and the knowledge that he would never finish, he could never really stop, would never get the dirt from under his thick fingernails or the ache from his back.

Many painters would have left it at that, glad enough to disturb the wealthy elite who would see the work and for a few hours feel ennobled by their guilt. Eva Vaughn, however, had gone one step further. As one studied the farm worker, the huge flat field, the hot blue sky, and came back to his face, gradually the feeling grew that this man was deeply, sublimely happy, in a way that someone with a choice could never be. "Well done, thou good and faithful servant" came to mind, and Kate had left the gallery much shaken. Strawberries had never tasted quite the same ever since.

Afterward she and Lee had gone to a nearly empty coffeehouse, and for an hour they had talked about Eva Vaughn and women in the world of art.

"Why do you think there are so few great women artists?" Kate had mused.

"Didn't you even look at that Germaine Greer book I gave you?" Lee chided. "Yes, I know, anything that doesn't have the word 'forensic' in the title gets pushed to the back. You do remember what the title of this one was, don't you? *The Obstacle Race,* right. That should tell you what her thesis is. Men start off on a flat track, half the time with the proper shoes, starting blocks, and coaches. Women have to climb and struggle the whole way, mostly against the circular argument that women artists are minor artists, and therefore if a painting is by a woman it is a minor painting. Training of techniques, not just of art but of the craftsmanship that makes a painting last, the apprentice system, patronage—" Lee was launched on a monologue that left Kate far behind, catching the occasional familiar name—Rosa Bonheur, Berthe Morisot, Mary Cassatt, Suzanne Valadon—and a flood of others. "There've been any number of extremely competent, even brilliant women artists. Look at Artemesia Gentileschi—an infinitely superior painter than her more famous father. Or Mary Cassatt: some of her stuff is every bit as good as some of the male artists who were—and still are—better known than she was. Maybe if she'd had less of an emphasis

86

on mothers and babies . . . I don't know. I'm afraid that women have to be ten times as good as men to overcome their early training. Little girls are raised to be cautious and sensible. Even tomboys like you are too busy fighting their upbringing to leave it behind, and it's the complete, passionate absorption in one single thing, like painting, that allows genius to produce. If you have to worry about folding clothes and constipated babies—if you have to worry about having babies at all—you can't concentrate on one important thing. Geniuses of any kind are always impossibly bloody, single-minded bastards, and women have never had that option, not as a class, not until very recently."

"What about Eva Vaughn? Or wouldn't you count her as first rate?"

"Oh, God, yes, especially considering that she's only in her thirties and getting better all the time. I don't know about her, why she doesn't fit the mold, except that maybe her genius is just so exceptionally great that it rules her. Nobody knows much about her. Even that article in *Time* said that she wouldn't meet with the person who wrote it, although they talked on the phone a couple of times. Remember the rumor that Eva Vaughn was actually a man? That one's still around, by the way. I heard a couple talking about it in the gallery."

"You don't think it's possible, though?"

"There'd be no point in it. The work is so good it makes no difference if it was done by a man or a woman. No, I'm sure she's a woman, a woman who's somehow managed to break away from caution." Lee tapped the photograph of *Strawberry Fields* that lay on the table, and looked wistful. "I'd love to meet her, to know how she's done it, how she was raised to be that free."

And now Kate knew how it had happened. Eva Vaughn would have been a fine painter any time, any place, but nearly a decade in a tough women's prison, convicted of a crime intolerable even to the other inmates, had flayed her of her caution, had cut her loose from any of the expected possibilities. A normal woman would have gone mad, or retreated into the anonymity of ordinariness, or died. Instead, Vaun Adams, Eva Vaughn, had become empty of herself, had become a pair of all-seeing eyes and a pair of hands that held a brush, and she had channeled the pain and the beauty of life into her canvases. She was a murderer who had strangled a small girl, a child who would now be a woman of twenty-four had she lived. Nothing Vaun could be or do would make up for that, and deep down Kate could never finally forgive her. Painful as it was, she knew that her own work, her own humanity, demanded that she pit herself against the woman who had painted those magnificent visions of the human spirit. It was a bitter thought, as filthy and oppressive as the night outside.

On the outskirts of the city Hawkin woke and reached for the thermos.

"Not letting up any, is it?"

Kate pulled her thoughts back into polite normality with roughly the effort of pulling a boot from deep mud.

"No," she said. "No, if anything it's worse. The wind certainly is, even on this side of the hills."

"Ah, well, it'll blow over soon." He seemed almost cheery, disgustingly so considering the night and the thoughts that had been in possession of Kate's mind.

"Do you always wake up so cheerful after a nap?"

"Always, if it's a nap. Sleep is a fine thing. You should try it sometime." Kate hadn't had a nap since she was five years old.

"Not while I'm driving, thanks."

"You're probably right. What's that line about Brother Sleep?"

"Something from Saint Francis, no doubt."

"No, it's Shelley. 'How wonderful is Death, Death and his brother Sleep.' "

"A comforting thought," she said drily.

"Isn't it? Isn't it just?" He took a swallow of the coffee and made a disgusted noise. "Goddamn goat's milk again. What's that you're listening to?"

She reached over and switched off the mumble of voices.

"A discussion of how to prepare for a catastrophe."

"Appropriate. Drop me at the station, would you? Then go home and get some sleep. You've done well today."

She tried to find the words patronizing, but in the end succumbed to the little glow of warmth they started up in her.

"We aim to please."

"Wish I thought the same of Trujillo. Christ, what a miserable night."

The garage was empty, which gave Kate a moment's pause until she remembered that this was a third Thursday, Lee's night working at the med center. Hell. The automatic door rumbled shut behind her, and she gathered up an armload of debris from the car—sodden clothing, sandwich bags, thermos and two cups, handbag, shoulder holster, jacket. Plodding up the stairs she thought, I have been on duty or reading files for fifty hours out of the last seventy-six, since six o'clock Monday night. I am tired.

With that thought came another, something that had occurred to her as she drove home. She glanced down at the boxes of newspapers and magazines piled at the back of the garage awaiting recycling, and then shook her head firmly and went on. Nope. Not even for Al Hawkin. It would wait. She needed to sit still, think of nothing, eat something. One word of praise from the man was not going to turn her into a fanatic.

At the top of the stairs she unlocked the door, stepped into the house, dropped the armload in an untidy heap on the floor, turned, and walked back down the stairs.

The magazine she was looking for wasn't in the recycling bins, so she turned to the doors under the stairs and began a haphazard search: intuition, past experience had taught her, was the best tool to use in breaking Lee's idiosyncratic filing system.

It took another twenty minutes, about average. She shoved the rest of the journals, magazines, and photocopied abstracts back into place, wrestled the doors shut, and returned to the house.

She tossed the magazine onto the kitchen table and went to investigate the refrigerator, whose contents sat complacent in the knowledge that in her present state they were quite safe. She took out the cheese bin and broke off some knobs of a hard orange cheddar, dumped half a box of crackers into a big bowl with the cheese and a couple of pears, poured some dark, heady Pinot Noir into a stubby French glass, and took the lot back to the table, where she sat with her elbows on either side of the magazine, emptying bowl and glass and reading the article.

It was even longer than she remembered, a fair chunk of the glossy art journal's hundred and fifty pages, and actually comprised separate articles by three different people, two men and a woman. She looked at the three photographs, two of them older and aristocratic faces, one aggressively blue-collar, and glanced through their biographical sketches, filled with vaguely familiar names of galleries, museums, and art schools, before turning to the articles themselves.

The woman, an editor of the journal, had written a very helpful if noncommittal review of the known history of Eva Vaughn, from the first, almost unheard-of one-woman show twelve years before, which had set the art world to talking and had sold out within a week, to the recent New York show that Kate had seen with Lee. Noncommittal was not the word, Kate decided. Frustrated, perhaps. Baffled, even. The woman was certainly torn and had retreated into the safety of facts. That Eva Vaughn was a difficult person to contact, and quite impossible for a mere journalist to meet face-to-face. That her oeuvre of paintings and sketches represented the first real threat to the supremacy of Abstract Expressionism since it had conquered the art world beginning in the forties. That her approach to art, painstaking and painfully traditional, had already begun to make people think about the role of art and about "painterly" paintings (a derogatory description, Kate was surprised and amused to find). That, most amazing of all, it was a woman who had swept in like a Vandal through Rome, a barbarian with power on her side against the civilized art establishment; a woman, an outsider, a source of absolutely maddening frustration.

The introductory article came to an abrupt end, through poor editing or a fear on the part of the author that her objectivity was about to fail her. The other two essays, by the men, were a pro and con, which began side by side before setting off to leapfrog through the advertisements for galleries, liquors, and jewelers. After trying to keep both going at once, Kate gave it up and read the anti–Eva Vaughn first, written by the man who looked like a bricklayer, beginning it at the kitchen table and ending up in the bath.

90

It was like reading a technical piece in a foreign language: the words looked familiar, but she found it almost impossible to hang on to the train of thought. Individual phrases stood out, though, and the cumulative effect was one of scathing, vituperative condescension. Eva Vaughn's vision was compared with flea-market seascapes, "Wyeth with a social conscience," "Grandma Moses naiveté combined with Rembrandtesque chiaroscuro," whatever that meant. As the writer became more insistent his obscurant terminology fell away like an acquired accent, until he seemed to be holding off Anglo-Saxon monosyllables with an effort.

Miss Vaughn [he wrote] has proven highly popular with the masses, those who grumble that they know what they like, that their five-year-old can do as well, those who like their bodies three-dimensional and their emotions simple. Eva Vaughn has legitimized classical forms for the twentieth-century proletariat. That the forms are empty of anything but nostalgia matters not.

Ouch. The writer went back to another bout of technical language, which Kate skimmed in self-defense, although some passages stood out:

In *The Creek* Vaughn achieves a level of sensual sentimentality that would render a male painter suspect of pedophilia. *Quiet* belongs in the pages of a specialist journal of female erotica. The derivative *Troll Bridge* looks as though Bouguereau had set out to finish Munch's *Scream:* horror prettied up.

Finally, he concluded:

Miss Vaughn's refusal to see and be seen makes her highly suspect in the world of art, where dialogue and criticism are the only things that save an artist from drowning in her own vision. Instead of learning from her century, she seems determined to turn her back on it, to the extent of an eremitical existence somewhere, apparently, in California, judging from the recurrence of redwood trees, Hispanic farm workers, and unreconstructed flower children gone somewhat to seed. Her motto seems to be 'Eva Vaughn, mystery lady of the brush,' as carefully nurtured an idiosyncrasy as we have seen for a long time, on a par with Dali's moustache and Warhol's collections. The public is beginning to know her by her characteristic absence. Perhaps the walls of certain galleries should follow suit, and recognize Miss Vaughn for the absent, imitative would-be that she is.

Scalpel and bludgeon. Kate wondered if Vaun had seen it, and if so whether she had difficulties picking up her brushes the next day. She took herself and her reading to bed, and tackled the third writer.

The aristocratic gentleman's style was more accessible than the anti's, but his enthusiasm was cautious. It would have been easy, Kate realized, for the editor to have chosen for this section an author whose effusiveness undermined his case but, despite her own reservations, the editor had not done so. His praise was unstinting, but he was sternly prepared to demonstrate the flaws and inadequacies of Miss Vaughn's work.

The names that come to mind [he wrote] are not those of the moderns, not Rauschenberg or Picasso or even Monet, but the noble and formal names of centuries past and styles no longer taught, or taught only as a dead language, for the purpose of translation. For Eva Vaughn has taken an outmoded, classical, dead style, imbued it with the idiom of the twentieth century, and restored it scintillating to life.

Her images are classically simple: a man, a woman, some children, a kitchen. Landscape is background, allegorical in its overtones but secondary to the humans who dominate all her work. The figures are generally unposed, or informally so, and so intimately known as to embarrass the viewer.

Aside from that, it is difficult to reduce the Eva Vaughn style to mere description, even to say that she belongs to one school or another. The lesbian lovers of *Quiet* are caught in a shaft of light from a window, two fresh bodies pinned into the still, silent moment of a

Vermeer, a suspension of movement before life sweeps in again to animate and discomfit. Her farm laborers—*Strawberry Fields, Three P.M.,* and *Green Beans*—rival Van Gogh for lumpen grittiness. The surface beauty (how seldom does a critic use that word in a review!) of *Cas, Asleep* could have come from Bouguereau's brush, and the voluptuous pleasure of the woman's sprawl could be an early Renoir, but whence comes the vague sense of unease? Is there menace in the shadow that falls across the bed, or is it merely the drapes? Is that a man's shoe in the corner, or the arm of a chair? Is the scarlet stain a part of the multicolored bed cover, or something more sinister? Is Cas actually asleep? Or does she lie there, murdered in her bed?

This is not an isolated fling of imagination in viewing Eva Vaughn's work, for emotions are her forte, particularly the dark and disconcerting ones. It is no accident that the structure of *Troll Bridge* echoes Edvard Munch's *The Scream,* but in this case the androgynous figure is caught in an innocuous, sunny stretch of bridge, with a normal couple approaching along an everyday bit of roadway. The woman/man has obviously been seized by a fit of insanity. Or is there something dark lurking under the bridge, something the couple has yet to see? Or, worse yet, that they are a part of?

Is there any style this painter has not mastered, any field she will not enter? Well, yes. She will have nothing to do with Abstract Expressionism; and she is not a Romantic. Romanticism is emotion for its own sake, and leads nowhere outside the frame that surrounds the canvas. Eva Vaughn fascinates, disconcerts, lays a hand on the hearts and minds of her viewers. That, after all, is what art is meant to do. She employs the light of Vermeer, the vigor of Caravaggio, the massive, sculptural drama of Michelangelo, and the eyes—no one since Rembrandt has painted eyes like this, eyes the depth and breadth and fullness of the human soul, of devastating honesty.

Objections to her art abound, and valid objections they are. She *is* naive, and she *does* largely ignore everything art has said over the past century. She is a painter of immense power, yet she is curiously passive. The agony and passion she paints, the menace she evokes, the madness and the sheer impossibility of life belong to others. She sees agony; she paints passion; whether she lives them or not cannot even be guessed.

It is this sense of distance, of noninvolvement, that may keep Eva Vaughn from joining the ranks of the truly great. She is young, true, but inhibitions and formalities have a way of becoming more ingrained with age, not less. A great artist leaves one with no doubt—he (and the pronoun is used advisedly) has borne the sufferings and ecstasies of his subject, himself, alone and without relief. When Eva Vaughn finally decides to paint herself with her pigments, then we shall see if we have here the greatest artist of the post-Picasso age. Even—say it quietly—of the century.

Tired as she was, this man's personal and authoritative analysis of the woman she had met as Vaun Adams kept Kate from sleep, kept her from noticing the storm building outside her window until she closed the magazine, when she suddenly noticed the rattling windows and gushing downspouts. She fell asleep as soon as she heard Lee come in, and her dreams were of strawberries.

11

Across town Hawkin worked late in his office and eventually had himself driven home. He poured himself a drink and sat in the darkened living room of his rented house, watching the rain slant down in buckets like some B film of a storm at sea. At eleven o'clock the streetlights flickered, dimmed, and strengthened again, and the low hum of the aquarium pumps behind him hesitated, then clicked back on. In San Jose a huge area of the grid went abruptly black, and a thousand newcomers to Silicon Valley cursed and cracked their shins on the furniture as they searched blindly for flashlights and the stubs of Christmas candles. Old-timers just went to bed and told each other that it would be all over in the morning.

The storm center massed from Eureka to Santa Barbara, and the force of it was immense, incomprehensible. At one o'clock a homeless woman in an alleyway off Market Street died of exposure. At one-thirty another seven thousand homes across the Bay were suddenly without power; electric blankets went cold, and seldom-used fireplaces were stuffed with paper and lit. At two o'clock fire crews fought to save a burning house for its shivering owners, winds gusted to nearly a hundred miles per hour, and the bridges across the Bay were shut down. The gale ripped up trees by their roots, threw satellite dishes about like Frisbees, blew out the windows of office buildings. Before the night was out the storm would kill five people in the Bay counties: the woman in the alley; an old man whose heart stopped when a garbage can lid sailed through his bedroom window; a young mother who was standing in the wrong place when the wind plucked the neighbor's badly mounted solar panels from the roof; and two young men who were returning early from a liquid party, swerved to miss a falling branch, and went off the road into a madly swollen river.

At two-thirty a redwood tree died. One of hundreds that went down that night, this was a youngster, barely two centuries old, and its characteristic lack of a taproot made it vulnerable to the combination of near-liquid soil and hard gusts from the Pacific. Six of its cousins already lay across Tyler's Road, but this one fell directly upstream of one of the junctions of road and creek, washed top-first downstream, and inserted itself like a cork into one culvert with its roots blocking the mouth of the second. Watery fingers pried at the road bed.

At three o'clock the pent-up waters lifted the two four-foot-deep, fifteen-foot-long iron drainage pipes like a couple of straws and hurled them downhill, madly gobbling up huge pieces of the road and hillside as it passed. At three-thirty the winds faltered, very slightly. At four-ten the sodden hillside above the spot where Tina Merrill had been found abruptly let go and dumped several hundred thousand tons of mud and rock onto the upper end of Tyler's Road. At four-thirty the storm suddenly gave up and moved on to see

95

what it could do with real mountains. By five o'clock silence descended, broken only by the pervasive sound of running water.

Light seemed to come earlier than usual that morning, as if the sun were anxious to see what its clever child had accomplished during the night. All over Northern California life slowly dug itself out and ventured into the changed world. For hundreds of miles the ground was carpeted with branches and trees, broken glass, tangled wires, drowned birds, billboards, mudslides, roof shingles. Anything and everything that could be lifted and moved by wind or water had been. The world took a shaky breath, grateful birds began to sing, and the sun rose in clear blue skies to give its blessing to this humbling of creation.

At six-thirty Kate jerked awake and wondered why the telephone had not yet rung. Then she came fully awake and laughed to realize that she had come to assume, after only three days, that the day began with a call from Hawkin. She stretched hard like a cat and turned over to kiss the sleep-soft mouth next to her. The phone rang.

"Martinelli," she answered through clenched jaws.

"Look, Trujillo just called to say the Road's out, and it'll be some time before anyone can even walk up it, so I thought we'd spend the morning here, trying to put a few things together."

"Good morning, Inspector Hawkin."

"What? Oh, good morning. Is this too early to call?"

"What time do you get up, anyway?"

"I don't. Get here when you can."

"Seven-thirty." She dropped the receiver down hard onto the base and hoped it hurt his ear.

At seven-fifteen she found him in his office, and at first glance she thought the wind had gotten in during the night. She pushed aside the drift of scraps, set a white paper bag on the corner of the desk, and drew out a whole-wheat croissant. Hawkin looked up from the pages he was pinning on the wall.

"What's that?"

"Breakfast. There's one for you, if you want it."

96

"Did you bring me a coffee?" He eyed the foamy top of her double cappuccino.

"You have a machine."

"I'm out."

She sighed, and poured some off for him into a chipped white mug with a thick brown glaze in the bottom.

"Al, I should tell you that these are the days when even the lowly secretary takes her boss to court when he expects her to make him coffee."

"Aren't you glad you're not a secretary? No sugar?"

"Aren't you glad it's not goat's milk? No sugar."

She took her roll over to the wall and studied his handi-work. Her original map had been replaced by a contiguous series of large-scale topographical maps, taped together and tacked to the wall. Houses and buildings were drawn in with small blue squares (even the octagonal, circular, and rhom-boidal ones), some of which had red check marks in them. Scraps of paper, mostly pieces of computer printout, but also handwritten notes, a few Xeroxed newspaper clippings, and several photographs, were taped and pinned in clusters, with a line leading from each collection to a blue square. On a number of the papers Kate saw green frames around words or paragraphs.

"Why?"

"Why what?" Hawkin grunted, trimming a length of paper and pinning it up to the wall.

"Why all this fuss? I've got all of it in the computer, if you want to retrieve it."

"I hate computers," he said absently. "Glorified filing cabinets that are always locking themselves up just when you need them. Computers don't think, they just suck up information and tyrannize the people using them into think-ing the way they do: yes, no; A, B. It's limiting, and it's no way to catch a murderer."

"Is that—" Kate bit her tongue.

"Speak, Martinelli."

"Well, you have to admit it's unusual for someone to make lieutenant and then willingly take another job that means a reduction in rank. I was just wondering if being allergic to computers had something to do with it."

"It had nothing to do with it, Martinelli, and don't be so

damned superior. My mistrust of computers isn't a phobia, it's common sense. I am in the vanguard of a new age, the post-computer age, when our race turns from the worship of silicon idols and recognizes anew the superiority of the human brain. As for the other," he said, stabbing up a note in green ink, "I dumped the job because I was too damned good at it. There was no challenge. Now, if you're not going to help me with this you can go buy some coffee."

"What are the red check marks?" she asked, peering at his wall collage.

"When I'm satisfied that we have relatively complete information on each person in the house, no large gaps, I put a check."

"And the green looks like it marks evidence." She was looking here at the first name attached to the farthest-left blue square, which was Tyler's. His pieces of paper included a note of two years' residence in the same town as Amanda Bloom's mother and the fact that Anna grew up less than ten miles from Samantha Donaldson's neighborhood. Both of those facts were marked in green ink, along with the word *keys,* circled in green, and the note *Jag—hairs,* similarly colored.

As the morning wore on, the leaves of paper on the wall multiplied and fluttered like aspen leaves whenever the door opened. The red checks gradually progressed in from both ends, a few green marks were added, and Kate's back began to ache. The telephone rang steadily throughout the morning with names to add, alibis checked, information received. Shortly after noon Kate picked it up to hear Trujillo's indistinct voice.

"That you, Casey? Sorry this line is so bad. It's actually down across the road, but it still works, if I can keep the press from driving over it too much. I wanted to tell you that I've been up the Road to the washout, and we probably won't be able to bridge it until tomorrow at the earliest. They're working on it from both sides, but the water in the creek is still pretty hairy. What's that? I couldn't hear you."

"I said," she shouted, "what about from the upper side, through the reserve?"

"Even worse, apparently. There's a lot of big trees gone down, and a major slide across the Road. Sounds like an ungodly mess. Look, this line is getting pretty bad. If you want to reach me you'll need to use the radio. I'll call you in a couple of hours. Ciao."

Ciao? she thought, looking at the phone. The man's up to his nicely tailored behind in mud and reporters, and he still manages to be trendy?

"That Trujillo?" Hawkin had been running his hands through his hair while he stood staring at his map, and he looked very rumpled.

"None other. The Road's out until at least tomorrow."

"Thought it would be. Christ, what a mess. At least there aren't any brown-haired six-year-old girls living on the Road, or I'd have to have somebody go in and haul *her* out." By the way he said *her,* Kate knew he meant Vaun Adams. "Let's take a break, I'm seeing contour lines in front of my eyes. Time for lunch."

Lunch was two beers and a hamburger for Hawkin, one beer and a chicken salad for Kate. After that it was back to the computer screen and the wall, and standing and thinking and half waiting for *the* telephone call, which finally came at two-forty. Kate took it, listened for a minute, and then interrupted.

"Hang on just a sec. Al? I think you should hear this." She waited until he picked up the other extension. "Go ahead, start again."

The words tumbled out over the telephone in a rush, as if the speaker did not want to stop and consider too closely what he was saying.

"Jim Marsh. Trujillo sent me to try and track down the owner of that ring we found in the Jaguar yesterday, and I think I've got it. I'm sorry it took me so long, but the roads are pretty bad all over. I started with the Donaldsons, but nobody there or at her school recognized it, and the same story with the Blooms. I went to the Merrill house, then to the child's school, and her teacher, who was just leaving, said she thought it might belong to the girl who was Tina's best friend. She gave me the address, and the child's mother said it looked like one her daughter had been given for her birthday last November, but she thought the kid had lost it. So we talked to the girl—she was scared, thought I was going to arrest her I guess—and she finally told me that she'd given

99

it to Tina on her last day in school. Tina told her that it was a magic ring and that she was going to use it to fly to Never-Never-land—their teacher had been reading them Peter Pan, you see—and this kid was convinced that's where Tina was, in Neverland. She wanted—" His voice broke, and Kate realized how young he sounded. "She wanted to know when Tina was coming back. If you talk to Trujillo tell him I'm home getting drunk." The line went dead, and Kate slowly hung up, watching Hawkin do an imitation of a stone.

"That's it, then." He hung up his receiver.

"Are you going to have Trujillo pick her up?"

"No, damn it, I'm not. If she hasn't made a run for it by now, she's not going to, and I want to see her face when she hears about the ring."

"If you go like that, you'll ruin a nice suit," Kate noted mildly.

"Hell, you're right. We'll have to go by my place on the way. What about you?"

"Al, the last few days have turned me back into a Girl Scout, always prepared. I have a bag in the car."

12

Tyler's Creek runs year-round. Ten months out of the year it is a tidy, attractive, well-behaved little stream where salamanders creep and damselflies skip. On a lazy August afternoon, when the kids laugh and haul rocks for a dam and the deepest pools are barely waist-high to an adult, it is very difficult to visualize the process by which that snarl of tree roots ten feet up the bank came to be wedged there or to imagine the force that caused the convenient sunning spot of a flat granite boulder to come to rest half a mile downstream from the nearest granite outcropping. Moss turns sere and brown, tadpoles become frogs, water bugs dimple the surface on a hot August afternoon.

Kate stood well back from the gaping edge of Tyler's Creek and realized that living in San Francisco, with the occasional power outage and blocked storm drain, did not fully prepare one for this. The image that had come to mind with the phrase "the road is out" combined a deeper degree of rutting, a lot of mud, and a bit of a gap across which some boards could be put; certainly nothing like this.

Tyler's Creek was a ravening, greasy gray monstrosity, thirty feet of grasping, hungry, primal power. It thundered like Niagara, pulling bits of the hillside, roadway, and vegetation into itself with its strong greedy fingers and eying its human audience hungrily. Kate swallowed, mute, as a piece of the opposite bank the size of a small car suddenly broke away and slithered down into the muddy torrent. A good-sized tree came washing around the turn, its naked roots twelve feet across. The waters rammed the roots into the soil. They stuck for a long moment before the bank gave and tossed the tree back into the center of the flood, where it whirled around crosswise in a fast, ponderous spin before being caught on a cluster of boulders, snapping instantly with a crack that momentarily silenced the constant roar, and folded itself in a streamlined fashion for the flume to run it to sea. All in barely thirty seconds.

She turned to Hawkin and raised her voice.

"We'll never get across that, not for days."

He shook his head, thin-lipped, his eyes on the boiling, white-capped demon that was Tyler's Creek.

"Any chance of a chopper?" she asked.

"Not until these gusts die down."

"Which won't be until after dark, if then. Al, I want to go around, find a place to cross."

"No, Casey, we'll just have to wait until they can rig a sling across."

"Tomorrow? Look, we've got an hour and a half of light, maybe more, and I can cover a lot of ground in that time. The creek isn't that long, according to the map. Let me try it. Please?"

He looked at her, at the waters, at the small group of people who stood well back from the opposite bank. His eyes traveled back to her, to Mark Detweiler and Tyler where they stood talking, and on to Tommy Chesler, who sat on a rock and watched the waves go past like a kid at a space movie.

"Tyler?" He had to shout, but the man looked up and limped over to them.

"Inspector Martinelli is thinking of taking a walk upstream to visit a friend on the other side. Is that practical?"

Tyler looked astonished, then even more so.

"You mean—?"

"I mean we should have someone over there to keep an eye on things. Can she get over there before dark?"

"It'd be a near thing, but it wouldn't be the first time someone's gone around—this section's been washed out before. There's even a sort of a bridge about a mile up, if it hasn't gone. It's hard to find, though," he said doubtfully.

"Could someone go with her, as far as the bridge?"

"I know where it is, but I'm not the fastest thing on two feet. Mark might, or, no, what about Tommy? He knows these hills better than anybody."

"Tommy Chesler?"

"Yes. I'm sure he'd jump at the chance to help."

"Casey?"

"Fine with me. I'll need a flashlight and a walkie-talkie. And a plastic bag if they're not waterproof."

The flashlight was waterproof and clipped onto her belt. The radio was not, and went into a pocket of her jacket, inside a doubled-over garbage bag from one of the cars. She settled her gun under her arm, zipped up the front of the jacket, and turned to Tommy, who was looking self-important and a bit nervous at his assignment.

"Let's go, Tommy."

A light hand touched her shoulder, and Al murmured into her ear.

"You don't have to put her under arrest unless you think it's best. Just keep an eye on her. And, Casey? Watch yourself."

"Thanks, I'll try. I'll give you a buzz on the radio from her house."

It was nearly impossible to make any kind of speed, but they tried. Kate was faster than Tommy, but he knew where to put his feet, which leaves were most slippery, what branches most likely to drench a passerby. Kate went down three times in the first half mile, once gouging her thigh badly on the exposed end of a broken branch. Tommy led, Kate

102

scrambling in his wake, along the ridge of the hills over Tyler's Creek. Once when Kate looked up, she caught sight of a house on the opposite ridge, a mile off, that looked like that of Vaun Adams. She peered through the wet trees, trying to see if there was any movement, and her foot hit a slick smear of leaf-covered clay that threw her ten feet down the hill to fetch up hard against a tree trunk. She lay on her back for a moment, eyes closed, chest heaving, until the stab of the flashlight into her spine forced her to sit up. Tommy stood looking down at her, a worried expression on his young face.

"You okay, Inspector Martinelli?"

"Oh great . . . and to think . . . some people . . . do this . . . for fun."

"You're bleeding, Inspector Martinelli."

"Not much. . . . Call me . . . Casey."

She accepted his hand to be pulled back onto her feet, clapped him on the back, and gestured that he should lead on.

What are you trying to prove, Martinelli? she berated herself. Trying to prove they didn't make a mistake, choosing you for the wrong reasons; watch that slippery bit, that's better, you're learning. Wonder if the damn bridge is there, what'll we do if it isn't? I don't much care for the idea of coming back this way by flashlight, but if the other choice is sitting under a tree with Tommy Chesler until morning, well, I hope the bridge is there. How could she have done it? How *could* she have done it, my God, with talent like that—could she have thrown it away, of course she could if she's crazy, that's what it all comes down to, doesn't it? All artists are a bit crazy, but no, please God no, don't make me have to arrest That One for strangling little girls. Oh come on, Martinelli, isn't that what you're fighting your way across this goddamn hillside for the privilege of doing, hurrying to arrest her because of a ring and an alibi that isn't, and what—oh Christ, nearly lost it that time, pay attention, Martinelli, a broken leg won't do anyone any good. Damn it, my leg hurts, probably get a fine infection in it, please God hold the sun up for a while, I can't get across that vicious bastard of a creek— "creek"? ha!—in the dark, how much farther, couldn't be too much, we've been going downhill for a long time, and it sounds loud now, there's Tommy, can we stop for two minutes, for one, just one. . . .

They could, and did, but though the rest allowed them to catch their breath, it also allowed Kate's bangs, bruises, and cuts to catch up with her and make her all too aware of how wet and muddy she was. She forced herself to her feet.

"How much farther to the bridge?"

Tommy looked in the direction of the roar and seemed to be counting.

"Not far. If it's there. The water's going down, but whooee! it was higher this morning than I've ever seen it."

Wild thoughts of Tarzan swings from the redwoods flashed through Kate's mind, and a knot began to form in her stomach.

"Are you sure, Inspector—Casey, that you don't want to do something about your leg?"

"Let's get across first." The leg hurt, and the muscle quivered when she first stood up, but it would hold. They set off down the slippery hill toward the noise.

The bridge, such as it was, was there. Barely.

Kate and Tommy stood between two sturdy trees, the water lapping at their toes. Before them lay fifteen feet of fast, dangerous, dirty water, and three logs, twenty feet long and ten to twelve inches thick, that bobbled and fretted in the wash of water spilling over them.

Tommy squatted down onto his boots, a slow, calculating look on his face. Kate felt nearly paralyzed, the knot in her stomach reaching now from bowels to throat, and thought that really she'd better turn back fast, before the light was gone completely, because she couldn't think of a single thing in her training that mentioned how to avoid being swept away into the clutches of several million tons of water and rock. It was a long way from learning how to get a knife from a wacko junkie, and all in all she'd rather face a wacko junkie than this—two junkies, armed with guns even—and really the bridge could hardly be said to be "in," now could it? And Christ, she hadn't even brought a rope to do a Tarzan swing. There'd be no failure in turning back now, no cowardice;

even a man would say that pile of floating sticks was no bridge, certainly not passable. . . .

She tore her eyes away from the creek and looked at Tommy, his face calm, deliberate, still calculating slowly.

"Is it passable?" she asked. Her voice, she was pleased to note, was steady, though shouting helped.

He pursed his lips and seemed to come to a decision. He straightened and shouted back at her.

"I think so. There used to be four logs, but if those three haven't gone, they probably won't now."

Probably.

Probably was very little protection against that hungry-looking water. Probably was no help at all if the extra joggling of her weight caused a log to slip out from its wedged mooring and toss her gaily into the torrent that—

She pushed the thought into a closed room, shut the door hard, and set her mind to the job.

"Thanks, Tommy, I couldn't have found it without your help. I won't have any problems finding the Road—"

"Oh, no, I'm not going to leave you now," he said, and before she could grab him, he was into the muddy water. The three logs settled obediently under his weight, bound together somehow, and although his feet disappeared under the water, he walked surely across and up onto the other side and turned in the loose tangle of branches to wait for her.

Kate took a step into the water and stopped as a chilling little thought bubbled up into her mind. Tommy Chesler is a suspect, said the little singsong voice. Tommy is not completely right between the ears, said the voice, and Tommy found the first body, and, yes, it made him sick but what if he himself did put it there, and what if he's waiting to give those logs a nudge when you're out on them? She looked across at the darkening hillside, less than twenty feet away. Was that a shadow across his face, or was he smirking at her?

She took another step into the icy water, and another, until the toes of her shoes hit the rough end of one of the logs, and she looked up at Tommy, who stood, waiting, in the water at the other end. Half consciously she lowered the zipper of her jacket, and she stepped onto the logs.

It actually was a bridge—uneven and very wet, but it was thirty inches wide, and the logs did hold together as a unit.

Tommy didn't move, and she took another step, and another, and now she could feel the water tug at her feet, and she walked with bent knees, her arms outstretched. Tommy didn't move, and she took three more steps into the grasping torrent, and three more, and she was four feet from the far end when her shoes betrayed her and she went down.

Her right arm caught around the top log, and she clung desperately as the full force of the water sucked her body into the middle of the stream and pulled. Her muscles fought to get one leg up, around the logs, to sit up, and she might have made it, might have won, but for the shifting of her body on the tenuous balance of the wood in the water. She felt the whole bridge shift violently and cried out, tried to scramble to the bank, so close, and a wave slapped her face as the bridge became a raft, and she flung her left hand hopelessly toward solid ground, and it connected with flesh, a hard, warm human hand that gripped her wrist like a vise and held her gasping and blind in the water as the logs scraped and slithered across her body, struck her hip a glancing blow and began their brief journey to the sea.

She was buried in water, but the hand was still there, one solid reality in the tumbling, shocking, cold universe. She worked her other hand up to the bony wrist above her and clung. Something touched her side, and again, and then a third time, and she realized that she was among the tangle of branches that dragged into the water and that the rush of the stream was slightly less powerful here. She got her face to the surface, gulped a wet breath and coughed violently, but managed to catch a glimpse of the bare branches that surrounded her. The grip on her wrist held, though it must be costing him a lot to hang on, she knew, and she raised her head again to look for a branch big enough to take her weight. There were none this far out, but she forced her free hand to let go of his wrist, slowly, and plunged her arm up into the tangle, pulling herself deeper into the thicket, and then her legs found a submerged purchase and, half lying on her back, she shoved and pulled and scrabbled up and out of the current, which seemed to gibber its disappointment as she cleared the branches and collapsed on the bank beyond, coughing and retching.

It was some time before she could speak.

"You can let go of my wrist now, Tommy."

"I can't."

She turned her head and looked at him where he lay, arms fully outstretched between the anchoring tree and her hand, his feet in the water, a distressed look on his face. She started to giggle, then, in relief and the dregs of terror and the absurdity of their position.

"Well, you'll have to, damn it, or my hand will fall off."

He started laughing too, then, and the two drenched and filthy creatures lay guffawing helplessly on the edge of the mindless creek, until Kate finally crawled to her knees and pried his grip, finger by finger, from her wrist. She rubbed her hand to bring back the circulation and watched Tommy slowly flex the abused muscles of his arms and chest and try to move his hands.

"You're going to be damn sore tomorrow, Tommy."

He thought for a moment. "Not as sore as you'd be if I'd let you go."

"No," she agreed, and started to laugh again until sensation came back to her fingers. She staggered to her feet, moved away from the water, and sat down on a log to begin the necessary process of removing several gallons of water from shoes and clothing. The weakness in her hands was terrible, and she concentrated on squeezing out the sodden jacket until she looked up to see Tommy seriously pouring about a quart of water from a boot, and she started laughing again, weakly, until she needed to go behind the bushes, but the thought of peeling off her wet, clinging trousers was too much for her, so she just lay back and laughed until the tears came, and then the telephone rang.

It was the walkie-talkie, crackling and muffled by the water-sogged heap of cloth and its plastic covering. It squawked angrily for quite some time before Kate uncovered and unwrapped it.

"Good evening, Al, at least I assume this is Al—who else would call at such a totally inconvenient time? Remind me to tell you sometime what I think of your telephone calls, Al. What can I do for you? Over."

His voice came blasting tinnily out from the machine.

"Thank God you're all right, are you all right, and what

about Chesler? Tyler saw what he said looked like the bridge wash by a minute ago. Over."

"It was the bridge. We're both wet but thanks to Tommy unhurt, just bangs and a mild case of hysterics, but if I sit here and chat with you we'll both freeze to death, so I think I'll sign off if it's all the same to you." And she did so.

All four feet squished as they walked, but despite the wind the effort of movement kept the cold from becoming seriously threatening, and the path back to the Road was both shorter and less strenuous than it had been on the other side. It was nearly full dark when they reached the deserted road.

"Where are we now, Tommy?"

"About a half a mile up from the washout."

"Then it's about a mile to the Dodsons?"

"Is that where we're going?"

"No, you're going home. It shouldn't take you more than ten minutes and it's not that dark. I'm going on up."

Tommy stood for a long minute, his face screwed up with the effort of thought. Then he shook his head and turned decisively uphill.

"I suppose you can threaten me with your gun, or hand-cuff me to a tree, but short of that you won't get rid of me. Tyler told me to guide you, and that's what I'm going to do. Sorry, Casey, you're stuck with me." She saw his teeth flash white in the dark and heard him move off. She fell in beside him and unclipped the flashlight from her belt.

"All right, and thank you, Tommy. I'll take you, but on one condition: you have to promise me that if I tell you to do something, you'll do it, immediately, no questions. Even if you think I'm in danger. You've saved my life once tonight, but remember, I'm a cop, and it's what I'm paid to do. Promise me? No hesitations?"

"Okay. We're going to the Dodsons', then?"

"No, we're not. We're going to see Vaun Adams."

Something in her voice stopped him dead. She kept walking.

"Vaunie? But you don't . . . you can't think . . . Vaun? But, she's . . ."

"I think it would be best if you went home, Tommy, I really do."

"But you're not going to arrest her? She couldn't have killed those girls, she couldn't have."

"Tommy, do you know anything you haven't told us about?"

"No, but—"

"She couldn't have done it because you like her, is that it?"

"Yes, but—"

"I like her too, Tommy, but there's a lot of things we've found that make us want to ask her some more questions, to see what she knows."

Euphemisms for the truth, but Tommy was just simple enough to half believe them and trust in her official status. His agitation lessened, though he remained dissatisfied. At the foot of Vaun's hill he looked up to where a soft glow illuminated the windows of the big room.

"I'll go up, but I won't go in."

"You can go now, if you want. You've been a tremendous help, Tommy. I can't even begin to thank you."

"No, I'll take you to the door." Tommy had accepted the responsibility and was no more about to abandon her than he would have left Tina Merrill, although just then he'd have been hard put to decide which task was the more unpleasant.

13

Kate pulled at the bell rope and listened as the deep, gonglike sound reverberated through the still house and died away. She heard no vibrations of walking (or running) feet, no sound of response. She tried the door, and was surprised to find it locked. Apprehension stirred in her. She pushed past Tommy and moved around the front of the house to the big expanse of windows. She could see the back of the sofa, the wood stove with a low fire flickering in its glass front and a squat black pot on top, a single electric light shining above the sofa, a low glossy cabinet with its door slightly ajar and a nearly empty bottle on top. No glass.

Moving faster now, Kate continued around, tried the side door, found it locked, and moved up around the house past the woodpile to the back, where the house dug itself into the hillside. Narrow windows, below knee level, were all that appeared of the lower story. A shaft of light from the swinging door that joined the kitchen and living room, propped open now, angled across the kitchen table, set with one plate, one bowl, silver. She went down on her knees, trying to see into the living room from this side.

"What's wrong, Casey? Isn't she—"

"Oh, God, oh God, I knew it," Kate moaned, and tugged impotently at the window frame. The damn woman would choose tonight to start locking her doors!

"What's the matter?"

"Damn it all, man, get out of my way," she swore and pushed him aside, ran back to the neat stack of firewood next to the side door, and snatched up a sturdy branch. At the window she ordered Tommy back out of the way, yanked off her jacket and held it up across her face, and slammed the piece of wood into the window. She ran the branch hard along all four edges, and shards of glass exploded onto the tile floor, the chairs, and the potted plants with a violent sound that shocked the night. Kate swept the splinters from the ledge with the stick, threw her jacket across the bottom of the frame, scooped the flashlight up from the ground and thrust it at Tommy, and rolled herself into the room.

"You stay there," she ordered, and crunched rapidly across the glass into the living room.

Vaun Adams lay neatly tucked up on the sofa that faced the fireplace, her face slack, one hand limp over the edge of the pillows. A small, stubby glass and a paperback novel lay on the floor beneath the hand. The tumbled black curls gleamed even in the dull lamplight, and her face was the pallor of death.

But alive, still alive, though her heart was slow and erratic.

"Tommy!" Kate yelled, "I need the nurse. Go find her, fast."

"You mean Terry Allen? Yes, I think she's up here today, though she usually works—"

"Go!" she screamed, and he took off, the flashlight skittering its beam across the ground as he ran heavily past the windows. Kate found a bowl in the kitchen and got to work on Vaun. It took an agonizingly long time before Vaun roused enough to vomit, and she sank immediately back into her deadly lethargy. Kate left her lying on her side and retrieved the walkie-talkie. Her back twinged, for some reason, as well as her thigh. She ignored them.

"Hawkin, Hawkin, c'mon Al, I need you."

"Hawkin here, Casey, what's up?"

"Vaun Adams has taken some kind of overdose. I emptied her out, but I need medical support right now. Tommy's gone to get the nurse, but this lady needs a hospital. Is there any chance of getting a medicopter in?"

"The wind's died down a lot. If you can get a lighted clear area, they should do it. Any chance of that?"

"I can't leave her now, but when Tommy gets back we'll do something. This may be him now, gotta go."

If anything Vaun looked worse, her breathing slow and rasping. The bob and swirl of lights coming up the hill had caught Kate's eye, and she went to open the front door to Angie and Amy Dodson and a hairy man whom she took to be the absent Tony, returned from Sacramento. She spoke quickly.

"Vaun's sick. She needs a doctor. There's a medical helicopter that'll be here in twenty minutes, but they need a big, flat, clear area with lights around it to land in. Can you do it?"

Angie recovered first.

"The pony's field, that's the best place. We'll make bonfires at the four corners. Would that do it?"

"Ideal, but hurry."

Angie pulled Amy away, and Tony followed, slower. Her rapid voice came to Kate's ears. "You take Matilda and ride as fast as you can to the Newborns and to Bobby's place. Get them up here, tell them to bring some kerosene. . . ."

Kate stirred up the fire and watched Vaun's chest rise slowly, struggling against whatever it was in her bloodstream. No sign of pills in the basin—they must have been dissolved in something. The whiskey? The woman's pale face turned slowly bluer, her breath more ragged. Kate laid two fingers against Vaun's carotid artery and picked up the walkie-talkie with the other hand.

111

"Al? Look, I'm not going to be able to respond for a while. I'm going to have to start CPR in a minute. She's losing it."

"Seven minutes, Casey. Are the lights going?"

"I just saw the first one start, Al. There she goes. Martinelli out."

The walkie-talkie crashed to the floor. Kate pulled Vaun onto the carpet and started the rhythmic breathing and heartbeat. Fifteen heartbeats, two quick breaths; fifteen heartbeats, two quick breaths. In two minutes Terry Allen came running in with a small bag in her hand, out of breath, and dropped next to Kate to take over the chest compression. Kate turned gratefully to the easier breathing assist, and the two women worked in silence until they felt the distant, subaudible thud of the helicopter beneath the gentle crackle from the stove and their own sounds. It came closer, and when it was directly overhead they felt the pounding of it take over their rhythm, and still they worked, until finally the uniformed paramedics clattered in with what seemed like a crowd of escorts and onlookers. One of them kneeled next to Terry and took over, the other gently pulled Kate to one side and set to work with tanks and masks. Kate knelt there, dully overcome by their competence, aware of Terry stretching her arms and clenching her hands a few times. She walked over to Kate and put a hand on her shoulder.

"Come and sit down until they can look at your cuts."

Confused, Kate looked down at her thigh, which was still oozing red through her trousers, and her arm, which had stopped bleeding.

"They're not that bad." She just wanted to sleep, for a week.

"No, I suppose you could go on leaking all over everything until you collapsed, if you like."

"It's just a gash," she protested.

"I mean the ones on your back, or hadn't you noticed that there's blood clear down your leg?"

Kate reached back with her hand, and drew it back red. She felt suddenly weak.

"No, I hadn't. It must've been from the window. Can't you do something? Just put a butterfly bandage on it or something?"

"That really should be seen by a doctor," the nurse

hedged, in a tone of voice that said she often had done things of the sort without a doctor's supervision.

"I sure as hell am not going to report you to the AMA, and these two are too busy to notice. Just do something to keep it from getting any worse."

She allowed Terry to push her onto a stool, where she sat, vaguely aware of a male voice ordering the room cleared, of Terry preparing a hypodermic with novocaine, of scissors on cloth and the needle prick and spreading patches of numbness on her back, of the sure hands and the tug of stitches. All the time, though, she was fully aware only of the body on the floor, the pale chest with its small breasts and blue veins beneath the strong dark hands of the medical technicians who fought hard, impersonally, for her life. At one point she heard a distant voice that she realized had been hers.

"You're working on another Cézanne," she told them, "a female Renoir." The less occupied of the pair glanced up at her curiously. "That's Eva Vaughn."

It obviously meant nothing to him, but the other one glanced up, startled, to meet her eyes for an instant. The wide mouth remained slack, the eyes stayed rolled up under the pale lids. Behind her Terry stitched and clipped and bandaged, and disappeared for a few minutes before returning with a soft flannel shirt, slightly too long in the sleeves. She fumbled with the unfamiliar apparatus of the shoulder holster, and eased it off Kate along with the shreds of her shirt, then gently dressed Kate again. Kate never took her eyes off of Vaun.

The hand that had painted *Strawberry Fields* lay forgotten on the floor like a crushed flower. Kate sat and stared at the slightly curled fingers, the short fingernail edged with blue paint, and knew that she had not been fast enough. When one of the men sat back on his heels, she closed her eyes at the words to come.

"We have a heartbeat."

It took a second to sink home. Kate's eyes flared open to see the man's expression, of faint hope and satisfaction.

"She's not—she'll make it?"

"Her heart's beating. There's no telling yet what damage there's been, or when she'll breathe, but the heart's going.

113

Let's get her on the stretcher," he said to his partner, and to Kate, "You'd better come too, you're not looking too hot."

"No."

"Casey, you need to see a doctor," Terry protested.

"No. I'm staying here until I'm relieved."

"Your choice." The paramedic shrugged. "She'll be at the General in town." He secured a blanket and the straps around Vaun. She looked white now, not blue. Terry fretted around Kate until the man suggested that if she would carry some equipment it would save them a trip back up. Kate followed them to the door and stood watching the men navigate their burden down the hillside to the helicopter, whose spotlights overcame the dim remains of the bonfires. She closed Vaun's front door and turned the key. How long would it be before the anesthetic wore off? she wondered. Better take a look at the place now, while I can still move.

Kate walked like an automaton through each of the downstairs rooms, checking windows, comparing the rooms with what she had seen the day before. Upstairs the studio looked much as it had, tidy, on hold but for the two brooding easels. The slab of glass that the artist used as a palette had moved and grown a smear of brilliant orange-red, and there was a large, white-bristled brush she didn't remember seeing. The figure on the undraped canvas had evolved into a woman, unidentifiable as yet. The spiral-bound drawing pad which Hawkin had left on the top of the cabinet under the south window was now on the long table. When Kate lifted the cover, the only drawing was the quick charcoal sketch of her and Hawkin coming up the hill, the tall trees still seeming to flinch away from the ominous challenge of Hawkin's gaze. She touched it lightly, and found that it had been sprayed with fixative. In the spiral binding there was an edge of perforated paper behind the drawing. Vaun had done at least one other, and torn it out—or, she corrected herself, it had been torn out. No point in looking in the fireplace for it now. She straightened, wincing, and went to check the studio windows, which had sliding metal frames. Each one was firmly caught in its latch until the second to last one next to the storage room, which flew open unexpectedly at her tug and caused her to curse with the awakened pain from a hundred sites down her back and legs and arm and—. She stood still for a long moment until the worst of it had passed, then let out her breath in a hiss and turned back to the window. She wished for her flashlight as she examined the frame and the track, slid the window shut again, pulled at it tentatively. It had latched. She looked more closely at the windowsill and picked up a tiny sliver that lay there, pursed her lips in thought, put it back down where she had found it, and went downstairs to the walkie-talkie. She swore again as she tried to bend down to where it had been kicked, just under the edge of the sofa, but gave that motion up quickly and settled for a sort of sit-and-slump to the floor. The casing looked a bit squashed; she wondered if it still worked.

"Al? Anyone home?"

"Hawkin here."

"They're taking her now. They managed to get her heart started again."

"Thank God. Are you going with them?"

"No, I'm staying here."

"Tommy Chesler was down at the washout a few minutes ago. He said you'd been hurt."

"Scrapes and cuts, that's all."

"Go with the helicopter, Casey, somebody should stay with her."

The shots were definitely wearing off, and a wave of weakness and pain and heavy exhaustion washed over her.

"Oh, Christ, Al, she's not about to take off on us, not for a long time. Damn it, she may be a vegetable the rest of her life."

"I want you out of there."

"No."

"Why the hell not, Martinelli?"

His anger sparked her own, and the truth tumbled out of her.

"I don't know why not, Al. I have a bad feeling about this, but I hurt and I've lost some blood and I know my brain isn't functioning properly. I can't think straight, but there's something here that smells rotten, and if I stay here I'll be able to see it more clearly in the morning. It's too late to argue, Al, they've already left, and I'm going to sleep for a few hours. And if you call me on this damn thing before seven tomorrow morning I will not be held responsible for your eardrums."

It was very comfortable, leaning against the sofa in front of the fire, but the upholstery and the carpet were spattered with her own blood and stank sourly of vomit and Kate couldn't bear to think of sleeping there, or on Vaun's bed for that matter. She walked across the carpet on her knees to load a few logs into the stove, crawled upright against the armchair, and stumbled upstairs again. The studio sofa was so stained and battered already, a bit of blood and dirt would pass unnoticed. She eased herself down face first, with the walkie-talkie and the probably useless gun close at hand, and fell gratefully into darkness.

The crunch of shoes on glass brought her awake some hours later. She reached for her gun, but the sudden movement of her back muscles lit the flames of the two deep cuts and the thirty-odd needle punctures from the stitches, to say nothing of the bruises. She must have made a noise, because the feet stopped.

"Casey?"

"Al? Is that you? I'm upstairs."

It was ridiculous, but without adrenaline she could only inch off the couch like an old rheumatic cripple. The anesthetic had most emphatically worn off, and the burn of the glass cuts added to the torn thigh, gouged arm, scraped hip, and several square feet of bruises made her stand very still and wish she could get by with just moving her eyes.

Even in the dim lamplight she must have been a sight. Hawkin stopped abruptly.

"God in heaven, what happened to you?"

"Just a nice hike in the woods, Al. Hey, don't look like that. It's mostly mud and bruises. They'll scare children for a few days but won't bother me by tomorrow. Really. I'm just stiff."

"Nearly a stiff, by the looks of it. Let me see your back."

"Al, I'm fine."

"That's an order, Martinelli."

She started to shrug, thought better of it, and turned to let the dim lamp shine on her back. He lifted the long tail of Vaun's shirt, peeled back the tape, looked and gently touched one or two spots, and let it fall.

116

"No internal bleeding? No ribs gone?"

"None. I wouldn't even have the cuts if I had taken more care with the window."

"You were in a hurry."

"I was. Any news of her?"

"The same."

"How did you get here?"

"Helicopter."

"I didn't—" She stopped. "I guess I did hear it, but I thought I was dreaming. You could have left it until morning."

"And if the wind comes up again? You'd be here for days. Show me what made you want to stick around."

"A lot of little things. No note, though of course not all suicides leave one. No pills—whatever she took was dissolved. The whiskey bottle looks like it was wiped clean. There's about an inch in the bottom for the lab to check. She also set the table for dinner and had a pot of some kind of stew on top of the stove, which got pretty scorched before Terry Allen pulled it off. The book she was reading did not strike me as the sort of thing I personally would want to have as my last conscious awareness, while it would be ideal as a way of taking the mind off an unpleasant day. Light and undemanding. Her painting's not finished, but she worked on it during the day. Then there was this, in the only window that was not securely latched, though it was closed."

Hawkin picked up the sliver of wood and took it to the light.

"Shaped with a knife," he commented.

"It looked like it."

He turned the sliver around thoughtfully between thumb and fingers, and studied her face. She was obviously fighting a losing battle to keep fatigue and pain at bay, but there remained a stubborn set to her mouth and defiance in her eyes. She was tough, this one.

"You don't want to think she's guilty, do you, Casey?"

"What I want has very little to do with it at this point," she said stiffly.

"I wouldn't say that."

"Al—"

"But you're right, of course. It does smell wrong." He

117

turned away, ignoring the astonished relief that flooded into her face, and spoke into the walkie-talkie.

"Trujillo?"

"Trujillo here."

"I'll be leaving your man here tonight, if you'll tell his wife. Also, I need you to get through to my people and tell them I want Thompson and his crew down here first thing tomorrow, and that it has to be Thompson. I'll be leaving here in a little while with Casey. I'll see you at the hospital in the morning. Got that?"

"All clear. How's Casey?"

"She looks like hell and no doubt feels worse, but she'll live. Hawkin out."

Hawkin retrieved Kate's equipment and found a wool blanket in Vaun's bedroom to wrap around her shoulders. They left the warmly dressed sheriff's deputy on guard and walked slowly down toward the glare of lights in back of the Dodson house. Movement helped sore muscles not to stiffen, Kate told herself fiercely, a number of times.

"Several questions come to mind, do they not?" Hawkin mused. "If this is not a suicide attempt, and I think we can safely rule out accident, who would want her dead, and why?"

"Someone here, on the Road."

"Who knew her habit of a drink before dinner, assuming the lab finds something in the bottle, and who had access to the bottle since last night. I suppose he planned on planting a suicide note and clearing up anomalies like the pot on the stove when he came back. Or she. Or maybe he just wanted to make sure it worked. Maybe he realized that a drug is an uncertain means of killing someone."

"It must be related to the other murders."

"Two unrelated murderers in one small area is unlikely, I agree. Revenge? Fear? Or somebody who knew the woman's past decided to use it to explain her suicide, just taking advantage of an unrelated situation, like he took advantage of the storm, which would have delayed anyone finding her until it was far too late, had it not been for a stubborn police-woman. Woman murderer commits remorseful suicide, case closed."

"And if the killings didn't stop?" It was hard to think

against the jolting pain of walking on uneven ground, but Kate tried.

"Ah, there's the prize question, which leads us into a very . . . interesting possibility. A whole different ball game." His voice was distant, but when Kate stumbled on the rough track in the bobbing flashlight beam, his free hand was there on her elbow, steadying her.

"You sure you're okay walking? I can get a stretcher."

"No, I'm fine, just tired."

"You realize, of course," he continued as if the interruption had not occurred, "that one possibility, a small one, I admit, but worthy of consideration, is that Vaun Adams has been the target of all this, that those three little girls gave their lives to set her up for suicide."

"Oh, come on, Al, that's . . ."

"Farfetched? Yes. The work of a madman? That too."

Kate began to shiver. "But why? Why would someone hate her so much? Why not just bang her over the head on one of her walks and make it look like an accident?"

"You find who, I'll tell you why. Or vice versa. I agree it's a crazy idea, but it does fit better than the theory of Vaun Adams as a psychopath wanting to be caught."

They had come up to the Dodson cabin now, the helicopter just beyond. Eight or nine residents stood in an uncertain group near a pile of brush and wood.

"Good evening, Angie," Hawkin greeted her, "and Miss Amy. Thank you for your help this evening."

"Is Vaun going to be all right?"

"I don't know. If anything comes through I'll send word by Trujillo. I'm glad your husband made it back before the road went out. Is he here?"

"He and Tommy went up the Road to let people know what's happening. Everyone will have heard the helicopters."

"Right. Look, Angie, tell him to go down to the washout tomorrow and give someone his statement. If the wind stays down we'll be around here, but he and old Peterson and a couple of others are missing from the records."

"I'll tell him."

"Thanks. 'Night, everyone, you can let the fires go out.

119

Maybe you should leave Matilda in her stall tonight, though. We'd hate to land on her head in the morning."

The cold and the pain and the loss of blood had Kate trembling by the time they reached the copter, and Hawkin and one of the paramedics had to help her climb in. The man wrapped her in more blankets, strapped her in with Hawkin at her side, closed the door, took his own seat. She had seen his face before. Why was thinking becoming so laborious? His face, bent over Vaun's still body with the mask. What was wrong there, what was so terribly stupid? The copter lifted off, Hawkin leaned into her, and she knew what it was.

"Al, these two paramedics? They know. Who she is, I mean. I said something to them—"

"It's all right. They told me what happened, and I had a talk with them. They understand, and they won't blab. You done good, kid. Have a rest now."

Her body hurt all over, but in her mind the words brought relief, sweet relief. She leaned against Hawkin's broad shoulder and surrendered to the darkness.

TWO

THE
PAST

The past is but the beginning of a beginning.
—H. G. Wells, *The Discovery of the Future*

————

It was all so long ago; so closely encompassed and complete;
so cut off as by swords from the bitter years that lay between. . . .
And afterwards, the stark shadow of the gallows
had fallen between her and that sun-drenched quadrangle of grey and green.
But now—?
—Dorothy L. Sayers, *Gaudy Night*

14

California spent the weekend at the task, familiar to her assorted generations, of digging herself out from under mounds of debris and rubble. The whine of chain saws filled the air; the scrape and slop of shovels moving mud, the taps and bangs of hammers replacing shingles and panes of glass were heard in every corner. There was a belated run on candles and purified water, "for next time." The repair trucks from the gas and electric company and the telephone companies and the cable television companies pushed gradually farther out from the centers into the hills, and deep-freezes hummed back to life, telephones rang, televisions brought pictures of the other storm victims. Power at Tyler's Barn was reestablished on Monday, and the first thing Tyler's lady Anna did was to put Vivaldi's *Gloria* on the stereo and blast the joyous chorus up into the hills, startling the pale horses. She found the house exceedingly dreary without lights and refrigeration, and had it not been for all the extra residents who needed feeding she would have escaped the close surveillance and the noise and tension with all the others who were now visiting friends and family.

The Sunday papers all ran full-page photographic spreads of the storm, freak incidents and bizarre incongruities next to close-ups of mud-smeared faces caught in attitudes of fear or exhaustion or agonized relief. The events on Tyler's Road rated a small paragraph, and Kate wondered how long it would be before some enterprising reporter discovered that the unconscious woman being treated for a drug overdose was also an artist whose last show had brought well over a million dollars in sales.

Tyler's Road reemerged in its entirety over the next few days, as Tyler, with Hawkin glaring over his shoulder, arranged for an unprecedented amount of huge machinery to invade the bucolic hills and lay two larger culvert pipes and scrape the mudslide from the Road's upper end. Kate spent two days lying uncomfortably on her side, reading a ridiculously thick stack of files and trying to urge her back and leg to heal. Al Hawkin spent sixteen hours a day on the case—up at Vaun's house, meeting with the representatives of three counties, the FBI, and the press, talking to three sets of parents, staring out of various windows—and began to show it.

And in her hospital bed, Vaun Adams slept on.

On the Monday following Thursday night's storm, Kate's little white car turned off the street and stopped in front of a garage door that was sternly marked No Parking. Kate got laboriously out of her car, left it blocking the driveway, and climbed the steps to Hawkin's bell. The door opened an instant after she took her finger from the little lighted circle, and Hawkin stood there with his venerable briefcase, shaven, in a clean, open-necked shirt, with dark circles under his eyes.

"Morning, Casey, you look nice. I'd forgotten you had legs."

"Come on, Al, it's not even a week since you saw me in a skirt."

"Ah, yes, shiny-clean Miss Martinelli wondering if Alonzo Hawkin would bite. God, only a week?"

"Seven days."

"How're you feeling?"

"Fine. A bit stiff, but that's because I haven't been able to run or swim since Friday."

"Sure."

"Really. The leg cut is healing cleanly, and one of the ones on my back has reached the itching stage already."

"And the other one?"

"It's deeper," she admitted, "and the middle of it bleeds if I jump around much, but it's coming along."

"You okay for driving? What does the doctor say?"

"The doctor says I'm not to do racing sprints in the pool or lift weights. A nice quiet drive and some nice calm interviews are no problem."

"All right, but if you want me to drive, just say the word."

"I will."

Hawkin removed his jacket, opened the back door of the car, tossed the objects already on the seat to one side, and threw the jacket in.

"That's for you," commented Kate, cautiously folding herself into the front.

"Thank you very much, but I don't think your coat will fit me."

"The pillow, the pillow. I get tired of hearing your head thump on the door every time the car moves."

"All the comforts."

To Kate's surprise, though, he didn't immediately curl up to sleep. As she dodged her way across town to the freeway he was reviewing the files from the case at his feet. He did not read the pages so much as glance at each one, as if to remind himself of the contents.

The worst of the morning commute was over, and the traffic moved smoothly across the Bay Bridge. On the east end, however, the inevitable snarl was compounded by a spill—a garbage bag filled with crushed aluminum cans that had fallen from the back of a pickup truck. Cars crawled past the trivial barrier of flattened metallic bits and then immediately accelerated to the speed limit once past it. Kate shook her head at the mysterious ways of automobile drivers and turned to Hawkin with a comment.

He was asleep, heavily unconscious of the freeway, the fluttering papers sprawled across his lap, the hard door's jamb against his head, the glasses crooked on his nose. He looked like he could sleep for a week, thought Kate, exasperated. With one hand on the wheel and both eyes on the cars ahead she gritted her teeth and stretched gingerly back for the pillow, which she inserted between skull and metal. She then reached over and drew the file from under his limp hand and pushed it, closed, between the seats. Three or four pages had slipped down onto the floor, and she retrieved those too. She took her eyes from the road for an instant to aim the loose sheets between the file's covers, and as she did she recognized what he had been reviewing: the transcript of Vaun Adam's testimony during her murder trial.

Kate knew those pages well. Some of it she could recite from memory. All day Sunday she had spent collating the myriad fragments into a coherent whole, working toward a portrait of the woman who lay unconscious in a hospital room a hundred miles to the south. The portrait, though voluminous, was oddly dissatisfying, incomplete. She could only hope that by the end of the day it would be less so.

Vaun Adams had been thirteen when she lost both her parents in an accident. She had, even by that early age, a history of considerable talent and considerable mental instability, and to be thrown into orphanhood at the inevitably tumultuous age of puberty was a shock she apparently never completely overcame. She was sent to live with her aunt and uncle. Her mother's half brother was a stolid farmer with two children, a large mortgage, and now a problem niece. Eventually Vaun settled into a state of equilibrium there, although she never really fit in, never made any close friends. Until her last year of high school.

A few months before her eighteenth birthday Vaun began to go around with a young man who had come back to finish his degree after a two-year absence from school. Andy Lewis was something of an enigma at school, and rumors grew up around him. The most popular was that he had been in the Army, slaughtering small brown people, having lied about his age to enlist. Needless to say, the army had never heard of Andrew C. Lewis, though the records from the draft board showed that he had been issued a deferment on the grounds of chronic back pain, an injury that did not keep him from the high school football team.

This mysterious, slightly sinister figure came to school a grown man among children, a blooded killer (or so rumor had it) among the sheep, at a time when across the country students wore peace pins and burned their draft cards—or at least talked about it. While the other seniors experimented with hair down to their collars and the occasional marijuana cigarette to complement their illicit beer, Andy Lewis looked down on their thrills as childish, and, it was later discovered, patronizingly allowed these lesser mortals to accrue merit and sophistication by purchasing their recreational drugs through him.

He came to school in September. In October he discovered Vaun, a withdrawn, friendless, virginal outsider. By Christmas vacation they were, in the eyes of the school, "going together," despite (or perhaps because of) strenuous opposition from her aunt and uncle. Some time in December Vaun first tried LSD. During that winter her schoolwork, which had been solid B's with a few A's and C's, fell to near failure. She began acting even stranger than usual. In mid-March she dropped a second dose of LSD and launched herself straight into an eight-hour screaming frenzy which ended under hospital restraints and was followed, according to her own testimony during the trial, by weeks of gradually diminishing flashbacks and disorientation. Only her uncle's standing in the community prevented her arrest for possession of an illegal substance. She refused to say who had given it to her.

Then suddenly in early May, just before her eighteenth birthday, things changed again. Homework assignments began to come back complete and correct, and absences dropped off. She started joining the family again at meal times, trimmed her hair, and stopped seeing Andy Lewis. For her birthday she asked her aunt for a trip to San Francisco, and the two of them spent the day in museums and galleries and stayed the night at the Saint Francis. Her aunt later testified that Vaun had seemed happy, somehow slightly shy, but relaxed for the first time in months.

Two weeks later Vaun Adams was arrested for the murder of a six-year-old girl whom she was baby-sitting. She was

127

accused of strangling Jemima Louise Brand (known to all as Jemma), removing Jemma's clothes, and then casually going into the next room to work on a painting of the child's naked, dead body transposed onto a hillside. The jury saw the painting, heard the testimony, and after five hours' deliberation found her guilty. She was sent to prison.

A little more than three years into her sentence Vaun was discovered by her psychiatrist. More than that: she was saved by him. Dr. Gerry Bruckner was called in when Vaun went into a catatonic state during a spell in solitary confinement, where she had been put during an outbreak of prison unrest. He succeeded in prying her out of it, gave her the art materials her soul craved, recognized the stunning power of her work, and sent several pieces to a friend in New York who owned a gallery. Under the name Eva Vaughn she was an overnight success.

After serving nine years and three months, she was released. She spent a year of parole near Gerry Bruckner, then a year traveling in Europe and the United States. She met Tyler two and a half years after she was released from prison, and six months later she was building her house on Tyler's Road. That was five years ago, and she had lived there ever since, aside from occasional trips to New York, where she kept an apartment.

Such was the outline of the life of Vaun Adams, built up from the stack of papers, nearly a foot thick, that sat on Kate's desk at home. From birth certificate to passport to Friday night's hospital admission forms, the papers included prison reports, psychiatric evaluations, pale copies of copies of letters, signed statements, the trial transcript, photographs, pathologists' reports, and hundreds of mind-numbing pages, each presenting in microscopic detail a segment of the life of Vaun Adams.

And yet, when Kate should have felt that she knew this woman better than her own sister, better than Hawkin, better than Lee even, she simply could not connect these segments into a whole; she simply could not match the avalanche of words with the woman in the brown corduroy trousers who had served her a ham sandwich, who had sketched in a few lines the threat in a pair of approaching police investigators, and who had lain blue and still under Kate's hands and lips.

Kate's mind could not make the most tenuous of links between the woman and the girl she had been.

Even the trial itself seemed disjointed and incomplete and left some very perplexing questions unanswered. Why had Andy Lewis been allowed back into school, rather than pursuing the more normal course of enrolling in the local junior college for a high school certificate? Why was his role in the trial so perfunctory? Neither the prosecuting attorney nor Vaun's court-appointed defender had pressed him, but had on the contrary treated him with wary respect. He had a solid alibi for the night, playing cards with no fewer than eight friends, but he had apparently graduated and was allowed to go free, without prosecution for the drugs he had almost certainly supplied to Vaun. Why? And where had he gone after the trial? He had disappeared with only the sparsest of a trail left behind: driver's license renewal two years later, one job in California and one in Alaska on his Social Security records, then—nothing. Ten years ago Andrew Lewis had disappeared, completely.

Hawkin slept like a dead man for the next three hours, until Kate pulled into a gas station in the small town nearest the Jameson farm. She told the pimply young man who came out what she wanted and walked around the back of the station to the door marked Ladies. When she came out the car was empty. She paid the attendant and fished two cups and the thermos from the back seat. Hawkin reappeared in his jacket and a tie. The circles under his eyes had lightened several shades, she noticed, and his walk had a spring to it. She handed him a cup.

"Oh, good," he said. "Chamomile tea with goat's milk and honey."

"Sorry, all out, you'll have to settle for Ethiopian mocha. Sugar's in the glove compartment."

He raised an eyebrow at that but said nothing aside from an appreciative sigh after the first swallow. Three miles down the road he drained the cup and placed it in the back seat.

"A good sleep and a cup of fine coffee always takes ten years off of me. Your housemate make the coffee again?"

"This morning I made it. Lee buys it from this crazy little

129

hundred-and-fifty-year-old Chinese woman who cooks it up in a two-hundred-and-fifty-year-old coffee roaster. It's a great honor to be taken on as one of her trusted customers. The turnoff is up here somewhere," she added. "Could you check the map, Al? It's in the glove compartment."

Although he was fairly certain that she had been looking at the hand-drawn map back at the gas station, Hawkin obediently fished it out and read off the landmarks. If she didn't want to talk about her home life—and her reticence was well known to her colleagues—it was her business. He suspected that few of the others had even been given the man's name.

15

The house was slightly more ornate than Kate had anticipated, a bit larger, its landscaping somewhat more elaborate than what she imagined commonplace for a farmhouse. From meeting Vaun's aunt at the hospital and having seen the amount of money that was transferred monthly from Vaun's account, she had expected it to be well maintained, and indeed it was: bright white rail fencing that stretched out into the distance, three nicely blending colors of paint that brought out the house's gingerbread details, a flawless acre or so of lawn encircled by wide flower beds and at the moment edged by several hundred tentative daffodils, slightly flattened by the recent rains. A small pond sparkled through the bare branches of a curve of trees. Kate switched off the engine, and she and Hawkin got out to sounds of rural life: quacks and honks from the pond, the rumble of distant machinery, the sharp snarl of a far-off chain saw, then the evocative, nostalgic screak of a screen door, followed by a familiar voice.

"You didn't have any trouble finding us, then?" said Vaun's aunt, in what sounded to Kate like a common greeting. She turned and smiled at the grandmotherly figure and was struck, as she had been at the hospital in the small hours of

Saturday, by how precisely the woman fit the image of a farm wife, with graying hair, round figure, full cheeks, and calm brown eyes.

"Not at all, Mrs. Jameson. Your directions were clear, even to a city girl."

"Good. You're looking considerably better. How is your back?"

"Doing very well, thanks."

"I must say I hadn't expected to see you up and around so soon, after how you looked the other day."

Kate grinned. "We old San Franciscans are made tough."

"So I see. I didn't get a chance to thank you, then."

"Not necessary."

"Not for you, perhaps. I have a feeling that your job is thankless often enough, that's no reason for me to add to it. Would you like some coffee? I was just about to put it on." She moved easily from the honest gratitude into the role of hostess, and Kate shifted with her.

"Thank you, that would be nice."

Hawkin had stood oblivious to the exchange, looking out over the distant fields. Turning back from the top of the porch steps, Kate could see a red tractor making its way through a green field, pulling after itself an unrolling ribbon of rich brown.

"You have a beautiful place here," she offered.

Rebecca Jameson looked faintly surprised, and half turned to survey her vista with the new eyes of a stranger. A small, worried frown came between her eyebrows at the sight of the tractor, and she shook her head slightly and turned back to Kate with a smile.

"It is beautiful, isn't it? A person forgets to look at it, somehow, when she's so wrapped up in day-to-day things." She looked again, as if to fix the memory of it in her mind, and then she led Kate and Hawkin through the screen door, which slapped shut behind them, across the throw rugs and gleaming wood floor of the hallway, and back into the big, warm kitchen. A cat slept on a chair in the sun, a clock ticked on the wall, faint smells of breakfast bacon hung in the air, and a man's voice came in monologue from somewhere in the house. The farm wife took a brightly enameled electric coffee percolator and ran water into it, filled its basket with grounds from a green can, and plugged it in. She reached for cups, and paused.

"Did you have breakfast?"

"We did, thank you," Kate replied firmly. Hawkin was still silent, exploring the view from the window, the whatnots on a shelf, a display of trophies and ribbons, the cat on the window seat.

"Then you won't want more than something to go with the coffee for the moment. We'll eat at one," she added. "You wanted to talk with Ned and Joanna too—they'll come then. Meanwhile you've got me and Red to talk to. Red's my husband," she explained unnecessarily, and came to the table with a large bowl of thick oatmeal-and-raisin cookies that instantly transported Kate back into childhood, when she'd lived next door to the neighborhood grandmother. "Did you see her this morning?" she asked abruptly. Hawkin put a small gold baseball trophy back on its shelf.

"Your niece? No, not since last night," he said.

"I talked to the hospital an hour ago. They said there was no change. 'No change.'" She chewed at her upper lip, staring down at the bowl. Kate looked for something to say, but Mrs. Jameson just shook her head and tried to smile. "I think Red's off the phone now. I'll just go get him."

The percolator chuffed and gurgled, Hawkin prowled around, and Kate ate a cookie. Voices from upstairs grew closer, followed by the hum of machinery and then the whisper of tires on the wood floor. Mrs. Jameson came back into the room, followed by her husband.

Red Jameson had once been a big man, and even now his wide shoulders filled the chair, his back was straight, his big hands powerful. Only his legs were small, wasted, and inert on the footrests. His thinning hair hinted at the shade that had given him the obligatory nickname, and though his skin had probably not been pale and freckled since babyhood, it remained finely textured under the weathering, like well-cured deerskin. He was younger than Kate had expected, in his middle fifties. The only heavy lines in his face were those next to his mouth, and they spoke not of age but of an intimate familiarity with pain.

"Red, this is Miss Martinelli, and Alonzo Hawkin."

Jameson's handshake was gentle for such a large man,

132

though the skin was hard with callus. His eyes looked over Kate, then met Hawkin's.

"Becky tells me you've come about my niece," he said. His voice was low and pleasant, and Kate had a brief image of him reading aloud to a group of children. "Are you investigating the murders of those three little girls, or Vaun's . . . what Vaun tried to do to herself?"

The words were too direct for his wife, who moved off abruptly toward the kitchen. Hawkin met his gaze and gave him an equally blunt answer.

"At present we are working under the assumption that they are related, Mr. Jameson."

The man nodded, and allowed himself to be distracted by his wife putting the pot of coffee and a jug of cream on the table. They sat down at a round pine table set with gingham placemats. Hawkin pulled out the chair next to Kate's and lowered himself into it, fussed with the coffee, refused a cookie, and waited for the social necessities to subside. When they did he continued with his thought.

"For lack of an alternative, as I said, we are forced to assume that what appears to be a suicide attempt on the part of your niece is related to the deaths of Tina Merrill, Amanda Bloom, and Samantha Donaldson. I am convinced that the relationship is there, although I am far from certain about its nature. There are too many uncertainties, most of which have their roots here, in your niece's past."

Red Jameson's blue eyes narrowed at Hawkin's careful choice of words. The inevitable suspicion and mistrust of police investigators he must have had was put aside as he opened his mouth to speak, glanced at his wife, and looked back at an imperturbable Hawkin.

"Are you—what sort of a 'relationship' are you talking about?" he asked cautiously.

"Mr. Jameson, we are beginning to think that she did not try to kill herself."

Kate watched as a series of emotions borne on a wind blew through the room, settling first on the husband's face, then on the wife's, to be replaced by another on his. First puzzlement, as the words sank in, then speculation as he and then she reviewed Hawkin's words and realized that he had not been suggesting an accident, then an instant of relief before the thud of fear hit, and two pinched faces stared at Hawkin, tight with apprehension and battered by the brief storm that had just passed through. The husband found his voice first.

"You think somebody . . . But who?"

"Yes, Mr. Jameson, I think there's a strong possibility that someone tried to kill Vaun. I don't know who yet— whoever it was is a very clever person. And before you ask, there's a guard on her at all times, and the hospital is exaggerating her condition to anyone who asks. As far as anyone else knows, she's on the edge of dying. You may see it in the papers. It's not true. It's just a way of protecting her."

"You think someone would try again?" Mrs. Jameson sounded appalled.

"If it was an attempt at murder, it was no spur-of-the-moment thing. It was carefully planned, and yes, that sort of person would indeed try again."

"But why?"

It was a cry of pain, and Hawkin responded by allowing his own frustration and exhaustion to show through.

"I don't know, Mrs. Jameson. Not yet. I do intend to find out. With your help."

The room rippled with the effect of his last phrase. Red Jameson sat slowly up in his chair, shoulders straightening, chin up. His wife grabbed at the idea as if it were a life ring in a stormy sea, and Hawkin her rescuer, about to tell her what to do. Five minutes earlier they had both been closed, wary, and would have parted with information grudgingly, if at all. Now they saw Hawkin and Kate as their champions in the cause and would withhold nothing.

Kate reached for her coffee and swallowed deeply to hide her face. Pray God these two would never know how thin was the evidence supporting Hawkin's declaration: a sliver of wood, the lack of pills, a pot of stew. Pray God they would not have to be faced with a future Hawkin who had withdrawn from the confident opinion that had just won their support, an opinion that she knew he only half held, but which was very, very useful in opening up this vital source of information. Manipulating people without an outright lie was never easy, but Hawkin was a clever man. The coffee tasted suddenly sour, but she drank it all.

"How can we help?" the hostess asked eagerly.

"Just tell us about her," Hawkin said simply. "What was she like as a child, how did she change as an adolescent, her friends, her painting. Anything that comes to mind."

"You should see her studio, then—the shed where she painted," she offered. "And I have photograph albums, if you like? Is that what you want?"

"Exactly right. However, I'm also hoping to see one or two of her teachers at the high school this afternoon, which leaves us short of time. Casey, why don't you go have a look at the studio with Mr. Jameson while Mrs. Jameson and I go through the albums."

Kate was mildly surprised at his division of labor, and Mrs. Jameson began to protest that the ground was too muddy, but her husband growled at her and she subsided. Kate held the kitchen door for him as he pulled on a billed cap with "Samuels Feed n' Seed" stitched on the front. He rolled down the ramp onto the concrete path that wound around the house and spidered off in various directions, pointing his chair towards the older, wooden barn. Kate walked beside him in the clear spring sun.

16

The small shed had three steps leading up to it, and Kate had to push the chair up the rough boards that had been nailed down as a ramp. She felt a sharp pain in her back as the stitches pulled, and she cursed silently, hoping that the double gauze pads she'd had Lee tape on that morning would absorb the blood.

It was an unlikely place to have nurtured such a talent, she thought as she followed Jameson through the narrow door: white paint on coarse plank walls and ceiling, a bare bulb on a wire, ancient linoleum with odd tacked-down seams, salvaged from somewhere else; a narrow metal-framed bed in one corner, once painted dark green but chipped now, still laid with a lumpy mattress with blue ticking and loose buttons, three blankets folded neatly at the foot.

Three things made it the home of an artist. One was the massive storage cabinet that almost hid the south wall, a cruder version of the storeroom in Vaun's house on Tyler's Road. This one was built of various thicknesses and qualities of plywood, painted white, and its two tiers of slotted racks still held a number of paintings. Then on the opposite wall the rough planks had been cut away for three large, metal-framed sliding windows that opened up the shed and made it a place of clear, even light. They were almost identical with the window from which Kate had taken a sliver of redwood three days before. Below the expanse of windows lay the third and unmistakable sign of this structure's most recent life: a midden of drops, dribbles, and smears that obscured the faded linoleum entirely near the windows and trailed off to a thinner layer of footsteps and drops as it reached the middle of the room. Jameson saw her looking at the motley surface.

"Becky wanted to clean it up, but I told her not to bother. We've left it like it was. We don't need the space, not really, and I think Vaun likes to see it when she comes. She sleeps here sometimes, though we kept her old room for her in the house. Becky comes in every month or so to make sure the mice aren't moving in, and she does a quick dust and a mop once or twice a year. Silly, I suppose, not to use the space, but somehow we couldn't bring ourselves to clear it out after—when Vaun left, and after a while it just got to be habit. Silly, I guess," he repeated, but he didn't sound embarrassed by this tangible evidence of sentimentality, and his face was relaxed in the silent air that smelled faintly of ancient paint (or was that imagination?) and of the sun-soaked farmyard breeze that moved through the open door behind them. Kate realized that a comment was not necessary.

"Did you put these windows in for her?" she asked.

"I helped her. She paid for them herself—her first sale, it was. She was sixteen. She used to paint some of the kids in school, and one time she did a really nice one of the daughter of the fellow who owns the lumberyard in town. A few weeks later she started asking me if she could have some of the money from her parents' insurance settlement to make this shed more usable for painting in—Becky wasn't too happy about Vaun's getting all that on the floor of her bedroom, as you can imagine." He gestured at the floor and chuckled. "I hated to see her eat into the money, even for that, so I said why didn't she take the painting over to Ed—Ed Parker, his name is—and see if he'd trade it for some glass. She liked that picture, but she liked the idea of windows even more, so she thought about it for a couple of days and then wrapped the picture up in one of Becky's old tablecloths and went down to see him. She came back two hours later, riding proud in his delivery truck with those three windows. She helped me put them in, and when we finished, she looked at them for the longest time and went over and slid them open and shut a few times, and then she just stood there with her back to me and said 'thank you,' real quiet. My own daughter would have hugged me or jumped up and down, but Vaunie was always different. It was okay, though. It was enough, that 'thank you.' She really meant it. Not just putting in the glass for her, but everything attached to those windows." A lost past echoed in his voice, gone.

"She hasn't changed much, has she?" mused Kate, thinking of her own experience of the woman's understated intensity.

"She hasn't changed at all. A little bit quieter, but everything she's been through has only made her more of herself. The only time she's been at all different was when she was hanging around with that Andy Lewis."

"What happened to him, do you know?" Kate asked it in as offhanded a manner as possible and was not prepared for the violence of his response.

"Don't know, don't care. He was a slimy little bastard, pardon my French, and I told him that if I caught him on my land I'd empty a load of buckshot into him."

"When was that?"

"The week Vaun was sent to prison. I saw him in town, standing around with some of the kids who used to kiss his—who used to look up to him. His father died when Andy was small, I think, and his mother was a weak little woman who never said no to him, so I guess it's not surprising he turned out the way he did. He went away not too long after that, I remember. Took all the money he could find in the house and disappeared. Broke his mother's heart, wouldn't you know? She died the next year."

"He gave Vaun drugs, didn't he? Marijuana, LSD? Why was he never prosecuted for that?"

Jameson sat staring out the window. The red tractor had come into sight, still far off, the black-brown trail unfurling in its wake. He muttered something under his breath.

"I beg your pardon?"

"I said, It's too wet. I told Ned this morning he'd just make a mess of it, but off he went."

Kate, bewildered, followed his gaze for a clue, and then realized that Ned was the son, and he must be referring to a disagreement over the wetness of the soil. She waited for a long moment while they both watched the tractor pull (struggle?) up a rise and then disappear down the far side.

"Mr. Jameson . . ."

"Yes, I heard your question, Miss Martinelli. He wasn't prosecuted because there was no evidence, and nobody would squeal on him. They were all either in love with him or scared to death of him, and the sheriff couldn't get anything on him. Yes, I think he gave her drugs. I know that for the five months she was hanging around with him, from December to the end of April, she was not herself." He circled abruptly away from the window wall to the stored paintings and without hesitation pulled out one from near the right side, set it upright, and fished out another, smaller one from a few slots down. He set it to the left of the first and pushed his chair around next to Kate.

"The one on the left is dated October; the one on the right is from the following March, when she was still involved with him. She always dated her paintings when she finished them, on the back. Still does, I think."

The smaller painting was a deceptively simple study of a girl, almost a young woman, sitting with her back against a tree trunk, one knee up, a gaudy paperback in one hand. She was dressed in shorts and a white cotton shirt. Her right hand was absently fiddling with a lock of her light brown hair, and her eyes were both on the book and far away. Simple, unassuming, intimately personal, it was the work of a mature artist.

The larger one was still technically superb for the work

138

of such a young painter. Its subject was another young woman, this one seated at a mirror, grimacing open-mouthed as she applied a wand of makeup to her eye. She wore a tight, sleeveless knit shirt, and a bra strap peeked from the edge of it. The colors of the palette were harder, the brush work slightly coarser, but it was a finished painting that many artists would have been proud of. The difference appeared when the two were put side by side.

The earlier painting was a gently humorous glimpse of a girl on the edge of womanhood, a look at the potential, the choices, the dreams that lay before her. Her back slumped with the unself-conscious grace of a child into the curve of the tree, and though her legs were brown and a Band-Aid could be glimpsed on one shin, their positioning was somehow deliberate, an experiment with seduction. The indication of as yet unnoticed breasts lay under the fabric of her grubby T-shirt. In different hands, adult ones, male ones, it would have edged into nostalgia, cuteness, even verged on pornography. This painting, however, was too utterly honest, and could only have been made by someone who was painting a self-portrait, though the face was not her own.

The larger one was the vision of another set of eyes altogether. Where the first girl was growing into her womanhood, this one was grabbing it by the handful. The nubs on her chest pushed against the too-snug shirt; the viewer suspected padding. Too much makeup, inexpertly applied, served not to enhance her womanliness but rather to underscore her denial of what she was, and her carefully disarranged hair brought to mind snarls and tangles rather than evoking a bedroom scene. It was graceless, hard, a nonetheless powerful statement of political and sexual rebellion. The first painting revealed the complexity of a life from within, a loving, accepting vision of an individual and the stage she was passing through. It was not particularly profound, but very human. The second painting called harsh judgment on a life from without, a sarcastic condemnation of someone who was trying to be something she was not. The first was confident, sure, and open; the second angry, pitiless, and completely without empathy for the human being depicted.

"I see what you mean," she said drily. "You'd say, then, that these two are representative of her state of mind at those two times?" She sounded like a prosecuting attorney, she thought, annoyed. Still, it was risky to place too much emphasis on two paintings, and after all, didn't every teenager go through that period of scornful rebellion? True, few had the ability to express the state so eloquently, but the talent and the temperament that had produced the March painting did not necessarily depend on chemicals to see the vision. Her own eyes were not sufficiently trained in either art or psychology for her to feel confident in judging the potential imbalance in that later painting, but the madness in it seemed more anger than psychosis. She wished Lee were here to advise her.

"Representative?" Jameson was saying thoughtfully. "You mean was all of her stuff like that," he pointed at the larger one, "during those months? I guess so. She didn't do all that much then—started a lot and then scraped them off the canvas, mostly. There's only that and a couple others."

"Any unfinished ones?"

"Vaun never left anything unfinished. If she didn't like it she'd scrape it off or throw the canvas into the incinerator, but once she was satisfied she'd put her name on it and never touch it again." He paused, thinking, and Kate held still, though she ached to sit on the bed.

"It was like her eyes changed during that time. Not how they looked, though that too, but it was like there was someone else behind them. She was always kind of strange, the way she'd look at you. Put a lot of people off, especially when she was small. You ever had your portrait painted, or drawn?"

"Once, yes."

"Well, you know how it feels to have someone staring at you, while you're sitting there frozen, and then they get up and look at your nose for a while, like it's some troublesome piece of machinery they're trying to figure out, and then they go back to the easel, and a few minutes later they're standing over you staring at your eye, but they're only seeing the shape and the color of it, and you're not there at all, not looking out of that eye, you're just buried underneath the cornea and the iris or whatever, wondering where to look and feeling like a damned fool?"

140

Kate burst out laughing, and went to sit on the edge of the bed. It was surprisingly firm.

"Vaunie was a bit like that all the time. You always had the feeling that at least part of her was studying your face and the wrinkles in your skin and the hair that came out of the end of your nose and the way your mouth moved when you made words, and it was very off-putting sometimes. I'm sure it was one of the reasons she had so few friends. But at times it was even more than that, and it would seem like she was still studying your face and your hands and the way you walked, and you'd feel self-conscious, and then you'd begin to get the feeling that she was also looking through your eyes right into your brain, that she was studying the way you looked on the inside too. Not physically, though she could do that too. I remember one night she sat with her sketchbook and drew the bones of my hand, and then she attached the muscles to the bones, and then the skin, and ended up with my hand, perfect—it was eerie. But I mean that she seemed to be memorizing the inner things that make a person work as well as the outer way he looks, and how the two come together, like the bones and the muscles and the skin. There were times, even when she was little, when you'd catch her studying you so seriously and you'd wonder if she knew about how a barn full of hay made you feel, or how it felt to be in bed with your wife, or how deep-down angry the thought of your wife's old beau made you. Not even *if* she knew, but *how* she could know those things. Like you were being taken apart, a little impersonally but with respect, and affection. Does that make any sense at all?" he asked somewhat desperately.

"Oh, yes," she said emphatically. He seemed encouraged, and went on.

"Well, that was how Vaun was. Odd, but I never worried too much about her. I mean, anyone who could see people like that," he gestured at the small painting, "she might get hurt herself, but she'd never deliberately hurt another person. I didn't think it so clearly at the time, but I've spent a lot of time mulling it over since then, and I can put it into words now, but it was how I thought then.

"And then around Christmas she began to change. Christmas is a big thing with us, and we always have a lot of

141

relatives and noise and fun. Vaun was always quiet, but she seemed to enjoy it, the excitement of the little kids and all. She did a couple of nice paintings about Christmas, in earlier years. But that year—I remember it like it was yesterday—it was such a shock. We were sitting around in the morning with the presents and the wrapping strewn around, Ned helping a cousin set up his train, the girls with a new tea set, and I looked over at Vaun and she was just sitting like a statue, looking at everyone, so cold, it made my guts turn to ice. Not scornful, like teenagers do—it was different. I've had two teenagers of my own, and I taught wood shop in the junior high for years, so I know all about scornful looks. This was something else altogether. Cold, and far away, like she was taking notes on the habits of human beings for a bunch of Martians. It scared the hell out of me, and it put the whole day off balance, for everyone.

"I saw that look a lot over the next few months, and I didn't know what to do about it. I'd get angry with her, and she'd just look at me. I told her she couldn't have Lewis over any more, and she just said, 'Okay,' and looked at me like I was an interesting kind of insect. I couldn't take her out of school—it was her last semester—and I couldn't force Lewis to stay away from her just because I didn't like the way she looked at me, could I? I should have done something, but I was very busy, we didn't have enough money, and I thought she'd go away to college in the fall, and I couldn't imagine that he would follow her. I should have done something, but I couldn't think what to do, couldn't threaten or bribe her. She had no close friends I could turn to, and I couldn't—God forgive me, I just couldn't reach her."

His voice broke, and he suddenly whirled the chair around and sat staring out the window, his jaws working tightly. In the silence Kate heard a faint sound from outside the door, but no one appeared. In a minute he resumed, his voice calm to the point of dullness.

"I don't believe now that there was anything I could have done. She had to work it out herself, whatever she was doing with him, but I tell you it was like sunshine breaking through when Vaunie began to reappear in April. I'm not a religious man, but Becky went down to church and prayed her thanks, and I knew how she felt. I wanted to sing the first time I saw

142

funny little Vaunie looking out at me again, curious and half smiling and not cold any more. We had three or four weeks of her, before she was arrested."

"Do you think she killed Jemima Brand?" The bald question made him wince, but he turned the chair's wheels to meet her eyes and did not hesitate.

"I did then. I was sure she had. Nothing would have surprised me out of that other Vaun, not even, I had to admit, murder. She just wasn't anyone I knew, and when they said she'd had a flashback of the LSD and done that, I could believe it. I'd seen her in the hospital, when she was going crazy and attacking the nurses and trying to hurt herself. Vaun said she couldn't remember anything but painting that night the child was killed, but she agreed that she must have done it. I was convinced she had."

"And now?"

"Now, I don't know. I've had a lot of time to read and think in the last ten years, since my accident, and I have to admit, I'm no longer so sure of it. If I'd felt then the way I do now, I'd have fought for her a lot harder than I did. It would have meant losing the farm—we nearly did, anyway—but I would have done it, no matter what evidence they had. But that was eighteen years ago, and I was a different man. I have regrets, but I can't change what happened."

"Do you blame her state of mind during those months on the drugs she was taking?"

"No, I blame Andy Lewis. I'm no expert on how the human mind works, or the brain itself, for that matter, but smoking marijuana, and even taking that other poison, doesn't turn a person like Vaun into what she was. It was Lewis. He had control of her, somehow, like some filthy virus that infected everything she did. He was such a big man, claimed to have killed men in Vietnam, you know? He probably spent the time mugging old ladies in Los Angeles. God knows why, but Vaun was susceptible to him. I know he was good-looking and he chose her out of the whole school and she was no longer a leftover but the big man's girl, but it was more than that. Something in him latched onto her and wouldn't let go. Hypnotized her, if that doesn't sound too melodramatic. I think she was breaking free, but whether or not she killed Jemma, and if she did whether it was the

143

chemical in her brain or his hold over her that made her do it, I do not know. I wish to God I did."

Jameson had come to an end, and he stopped and let the silence settle over them. Kate felt drained, and the thought of rousing herself for the next set of questions raised by this extraordinary interview made her residual aches, which were considerably greater than she'd let on to Hawkin, take possession of her will. There were more questions to be asked, but she needed a pause, and Jameson seemed content.

There was a sound of stirring outside, followed by the hollow thump of feet on the wooden steps next to the ramp, and the shed darkened. Kate looked up to see Hawkin outlined dramatically in the light that came streaming in the door, and Vaun's charcoal sketch flashed vividly into her mind.

"Mrs. Jameson asked me to check and see if everything was all right, and to say that lunch would be in half an hour." His eyes took in the room, paused to consider Kate's face, smiled at the metal windows, and went to the pair of paintings resting on the floor. He stepped forward to look at them, and the room brightened.

"Interesting," he said after a few minutes. "I take it that the larger one was done during the time she was with Andrew Lewis?"

"In March," Kate confirmed. "The other one is from the previous October."

"Yes, very interesting," he repeated, his eyes flicking from one to the other. "Do you mind if I take a look at these other ones, Mr. Jameson?"

"Of course not, help yourself. Just so they go back into the same slots. Vaun has them in order."

"Right, we'll keep track of them. I'll put these two out of the way," and he laid them on the bed next to Kate. "No, don't get up, Casey. I just want to have a peep. I spent part of the day yesterday looking at the ones in her studio." And the rest of the day recovering, he added to himself. He walked over to the far end and slid the first of the canvases from its berth. He checked the back before he set it up against the wall, and stepped back.

144

"Done four months after her parents died. She was thirteen."

The order was chronological, the cumulative effect shattering, an intense, intimate portrait of the artist as a very young woman. There were a few paintings of animals and two landscapes, but most of the forty-odd canvases were Vaun's vision of her neighbors and her family. Three images of a younger, whole Red Jameson jumped out at them, and two of his wife. Jameson kept up a commentary, identifying each figure and most of the locations. Finally there were two canvases left. Hawkin pulled them out together and stood them next to each other.

They formed a pair like the two on the bed behind Kate, though not so striking. The earlier one here, dated early November, was of a young, ginger-haired boy-man of about fourteen, identified by Jameson as his son Ned, Vaun's cousin. He was splitting logs with his shirt off, and she had caught an expression half embarrassed, half proud, on his young face. The second of the pair, dated February, was of a slightly older boy. He was dressed in jeans and an army jacket, and was sprawled back on a bench with an utterly expressionless face. It was a disturbing painting, with that utter blankness, and Kate found herself trying to put some emotion into it—insolence, contempt, disgust—anything human to fill it in.

"That's Timothy Bauer, lived down the road. He was one of Lewis's followers. He died a couple years later, higher'n a kite on something and ran his car off the levee into the canal."

"No paintings of Lewis, then?" asked Hawkin.

"Isn't there one?" Jameson sounded very surprised, and wheeled himself forward to look. "There isn't, is there? Used to be one. Vaun must have taken it," he said doubtfully. Hawkin shot a glance at Kate, who felt her tiredness abruptly leave her.

"Was it in here, Mr. Jameson?" asked Hawkin, sounding only slightly curious.

"Yes, between the one you took out and the one over there. I know, because I used to look at these sometimes, and I used to avoid that slot—I didn't like to see his sleazy face. Maybe Vaun didn't either and finally burned it." He sounded

145

as if he found that a more likely possibility than his niece wanting it. Hawkin knelt down to replace the two he had removed and looked closely at the adjoining two slots. The odd bits of carpet that lined the bottom of the case were indented wherever a painting had rested over the years. The pile was notched clearly in the slot from which he had taken the young man and in the one where the young woman putting on her makeup had rested. Between them was a gap, one of several in the storage wall, and an indentation showed that a canvas had indeed rested here, although a thin layer of dust had had time to drift across the matted pile.

"Pity it's not here, said Hawkin easily. "I'd have liked to see his face, and how she saw it."

"You didn't see it in her studio, then?" asked Jameson.

"Do you remember what it looked like?"

"I sure do. He was sitting in a turned-around chair, his arms along the back of it, his chin on his forearms. Shirtless. He had a tattoo, I remember, on his upper arm, a snake or something. He looked sweaty, and when I first saw it all I could think was, Thank God he put his pants back on before she painted it."

"It had sexual overtones, then?"

"Yes. I don't know why, something in his face, I guess. It was awful. But it wasn't there, then? In her house?"

"I may have missed it; there's a lot of paintings. When did you see it last?"

"Years. It's years since I actually looked at it—like I told you, I didn't like to see him. I think it was here last summer, but I couldn't swear to it."

"No problem—just curiosity. Mr. Jameson, I'd like to borrow a few of these paintings, if I may."

"Which ones?"

"The two final ones, and two or three of the earlier ones. I'd be interested in having someone more knowledgeable than myself look at them and tell me about her state of mind when they were done. It could be very helpful," he added.

"Oh, well, sure, if it'd help you. You'll have to be careful of them."

"We will. I'll get them back to you as soon as I can," he said. He retrieved the last pair, rested them next to the first pair that Jameson had shown Kate, and then went back and unerringly pulled out the second one of Jameson, squinting into the sun from the seat of a tractor. He put it next to the other four, and Jameson turned away, looking slightly embarrassed.

"Write him out a receipt of some kind, would you, Casey?" he asked, but she already had her notebook in her hand. As she finished, a thought occurred to her.

"Mr. Jameson, that painting of the lumberman's daughter? And any others people around here might have—does anyone know what it is they have? An early Eva Vaughn would be a pretty valuable thing, I would have thought."

"Nobody but the family knows. We don't talk about her. She wanted it that way."

Kate could well imagine that. This family's ability to keep their mouths closed was probably the only thing that had stood between Eva Vaughn and a massive influx of vultures, disguised as reporters, onto the dirt of Tyler's Road.

Hawkin moved towards the paintings, but Jameson stopped him.

"Leave them here," he ordered. "You can bring your car over for them later. If we make Becky hold lunch for us, she won't be happy." He turned to the door and then drifted the wheels to a halt against his callused palms. Something else was on his mind. "It's not good," he said finally. "I don't like not knowing just how she is. I want you to have them tell us the truth. You can do that."

Hawkin took out a small notebook and pen, wrote a few words, and then handed the sheet to Jameson.

"This doctor can tell you whatever you want. I'll let him know you'll be calling."

"Thank you." He folded the sheet carefully and buttoned it into a shirt pocket. He took a last look at the studio and shook his head. "I often wonder what Vaun would have been like if she didn't have this . . . 'gift.' Curse is more like it. It's made her life hell; it tortured her mother. God forgive me, I can't help but think it was also at the back of Jemma's death and now these three—" He stopped, took a long and shaky breath, exhaled carefully, took off his cap and ran a hand across his hair, and put control back on along with the hat. "I remember an essay she wrote once in high school, an English assignment. Becky still has it somewhere. They were supposed to write on a word, any word, to research it and say what it meant to them, that kind of thing. Vaun chose the word *talent*. She started out talking about a talent as a kind of Roman coin and then went on to say that money was a form of energy, neither good nor bad in itself, just energy. 'It's how the talent is spent that makes the difference,' that's how the paper ended. Clever, it was, better than most of her schoolwork. But sad. At that time, she thought she was in charge. She never has been. Her talent has eaten her up, from the time she was a bitty little girl. She can never be normal, never be free and happy, not while this 'gift' has her. I think she knows it, too, now. I'm sure she does. It's a terrible thing to say, but I wasn't all that surprised when I heard she'd tried to kill herself. She's a sad girl, is my Vaunie. Not just sad, I don't mean to say that, but she has very few dreams left. All she has is her 'gift' and the world she paints. All she has is her eyes and her hands, and if one of them fails, that will be the end of her." He turned his head and looked straight up at Kate, and she was shocked to see tears brimming into his tough eyes. "I love Vaun like a daughter, and this talent of hers is not a happy thing. I wouldn't wish it on an enemy."

He blinked, gave the paintings a final glance, and yanked hard at his wheels, disappearing down the ramp at a heart-stopping speed. He was halfway to the house before Kate and Hawkin caught up with him.

17

The house smelled of onions and hot cheese and nutmeg. Kate excused herself and ducked into the small bathroom just inside the back door. She was relieved to find that the blood had only reached as far as the lining of her jacket. She took off her blouse, pulled off the soaked bandages, and replaced them with two sterile pads and a plastic-backed six-inch square, held down with lengths of tape. It was awkward, but she got it on. She sponged off her blouse, one chosen that morning for the dark colors and all-over pattern,

148

dried it with toilet paper, and got dressed again. Wrapping the gory evidence in more toilet paper, she thrust it into the waste basket, used the toilet, washed her hands, opened the door, and nearly collided with a tall man with red hair whom she had last seen as a boy on canvas, splitting wood.

His arrogant blue eyes probed lazily over her body from hair to ankles before rising slowly to her own eyes. She felt herself stiffen and blocked it immediately, but she could never do much about the impersonal smile that came to her lips when this happened, the civilized version of the raised-hackle snarl.

"Well, well," he said. "I must say that when Mom told me a police lady was coming today, I didn't expect someone like you. I'm Ned Jameson, and I'll shake your hand when I'm a bit cleaner."

"Casey Martinelli. Isn't the ground a bit wet for turning today?" she asked innocently, and she was unprofessionally gratified to see a flush of anger start up, before he decided that it was the simple question of a female nonfarmer.

"A bit. Not too bad." He turned to put the black rubber boots he carried onto a sheet of newspaper near the door, and she glanced at his clothes. Mud from knee to hips and fingertip to shoulders was probably not normal. She turned away to conceal her smile.

The cat had disappeared from the window seat, Kate noticed, replaced by Hawkin, who was seriously discussing a multicolored, much-jutting Lego construction with a small brown-haired boy in patched jeans, while a toddler with a head of the most stunning red curls Kate had ever seen sat glued to Hawkin's other side, her little round body twisted forward to watch their faces as she followed the conversation with serious concentration.

Kate exchanged an amused look with Red Jameson and moved to one side to let pass a slim woman with darker red curls and a heavy casserole in her hands. She plunked the pot on the table, wiped her hands unnecessarily on her apron, and held out her hand to Kate.

"Joanna Olsen. The two monsters are mine, Teddy and Marta. My neighbor was going to watch them for me but one of hers is coming down with something, so we'll just have to shout over them."

149

"They'll be fine, Joanna," said her mother's voice from behind Kate. "Let's sit down now, Miss Martinelli there, and Alonzo, you can sit there."

"It's Casey, Mrs. Jameson."

"Then I'm Becky. What's wrong, Teddy? Oh, all right, you can move your chair next to him. Where's Ned?"

"Upstairs changing. He was kind of muddy."

"I told him . . ." began his father.

"Now, Red, we know you told him not to, but he was anxious to do something and he's gone next week, so he had to try. You'd have done the same thing when you were thirty. We won't wait for him, though. Some salad, Casey?" Her voice was almost sharp and she thrust the bowl to her guest in an emphatic change of topic. "I hope you like tomatoes. Ned grows them year-round in his greenhouse."

Lunch was a full farmhouse meal, a hot dish of chicken and herbed rice, hot mixed vegetables and a salad, two kinds of bread rolls, three jams, and bottled spiced peaches for dessert. Kate ate more than she usually ate in an entire day, and when after the meal Joanna carried a heavy-lidded Marta off upstairs, she wished she could join the child, thumb in mouth and all.

Ned Jameson had come in halfway through the meal and dug into the food with great concentration, answering direct questions without looking up from his plate. The conversation eddied around him, his sister juggling admonitions to her offspring with tales of her cousin Vaun, of whom she was obviously very fond and very proud. Red and Becky Jameson contributed, and even Teddy piped up.

"Auntie Vaun is teaching me to paint. She said that if I like it I can have my own paints maybe for Christmas. She painted a picture of me. I had to sit very still, and she gave me a Lego space cruiser to put together so I'd sit still enough, but Matty's too little to do that, so she just makes drawings of her."

"I've seen that painting," said Hawkin. "It looks just like you."

"Was that in her studio?" asked Kate.

"When I was there yesterday," he said, nodding.

"Did you see Auntie Vaun?" Teddy asked quickly. "She's sick, isn't she? Is she going to be all right?"

150

Spoons around the table stopped in midair. Ned Jameson's jaws went still as he awaited Hawkin's pronouncement, oddly intent.

"You like your Auntie Vaun, don't you?" Hawkin asked the child.

"I love her," he said simply. "And she loves me."

"I could see that in the painting. I hope she'll be okay. I'm not a doctor, but some good doctors are taking care of her."

"She's in the hospital."

"I know. I've seen her."

"I can't visit her, I'm too young," he said, disgusted.

"Maybe you could make her a drawing, so she knows you were thinking about her." It was the suggestion of an experienced father, Kate realized, and wondered why she always forgot that side of him.

The child tipped his head, thinking.

"She likes my drawings. May I be excused, Mommy, so I can make a picture for her?"

"You don't want the rest of your peaches? Okay, you come up with me and we'll find your crayons."

Becky Jameson brought in coffee and began to clear the dishes, refusing any help. Kate and Hawkin were left alone with Red and his son, who had not yet spoken to each other. Hawkin stirred sugar into his cup and opened a polite topic of conversation.

"You grow hothouse tomatoes, Ned?"

"Not commercially, it's too expensive, but it's nice to have a few of the summer vegetables in winter."

"What do you do, then?"

"Farm this place, some experimental stuff I'm doing with the local organic farmers' organization. Fruit mostly, but the last year or so I've been growing those tiny vegetables that fancy restaurants like. Inch-long carrots, beets the size of marbles, that kind of thing. I don't think they have much flavor, myself, but people buy 'em, so I grow 'em."

"Can you make a living out of that? You hear a lot about farms closing down these days."

Kate wondered where Hawkin's sudden interest in agriculture came from, or was going to. Ned seemed reluctant to answer.

"Oh, yes. Well, not a great living. Farmers don't drive

151

Rolls Royces, but the bills get paid. Course, a lot of us have other jobs, too, just to help out, during the slack times."

"What do you do? Your other job?"

"I make deliveries." Red was looking oddly at his son.

"Truck driving, then? Long distance?"

"Sometimes."

"Yes, I think your mother mentioned that you were going away next week. Must be hard on your wife."

"Oh, she doesn't mind; it doesn't happen that often." Here Red interrupted with a snort, and when his son shot him a look of barely controlled rage, Kate realized what Hawkin was after, though she was not at all sure how he had known it was there.

"It doesn't," he insisted. "And the money's damn good."

Teddy came back into the room, crayons and paper in hand, and climbed into the chair next to Hawkin, who helped him clear a place for the pad, automatically placing a half-full glass of milk to one side without taking his interested gaze from the young man across the table.

"The money's not the reason—" began Red, but Hawkin seemed not to hear him and talked over his words.

"I've always been fascinated by those big rigs—an eighteen wheeler, is it? A refrigerator truck?"

"Usually. It's owned by the local co-op of organic farmers. Three of us have licenses, so we take turns with deliveries. Usually the truck's only half full, so we fill up with stuff for the other growers." The young man spoke easily, but he seemed to be warmer than the room's temperature would account for.

"Mostly California?"

"Yeah, some Oregon."

"And Nevada, and Utah, and Texas," broke in his father. "It's a crazy thing to mix with trying to grow crops."

Several things happened at once. Ned shoved his chair back with a crash just as his mother entered, and the oblivious Teddy reached for a crayon just as Hawkin put his own arm out to place his napkin on the table. The anger from one end of the table and the maternal consternation from the doorway were both drowned by a child's horrified shriek as the contents of the glass shot across the drawing, over the edge of the table and all over the front of the young artist.

Only Kate, seated directly across from them, saw that it was Hawkin's hand rather than Teddy's arm that had propelled the glass, and by the time it had been cleared and wiped and the child taken upstairs for dry clothes, the air had cleared.

Hawkin accepted another cup of coffee and sat back, meeting Ned's wary glances with the same benign, almost drowsy look Kate had seen him wear in Tyler's upstairs room, just before the coup de grâce.

"Tell me, Ned," he said in the same conversational tone he had started with. "Do *you* think your cousin killed those little girls?"

Ned froze, but with what emotion Kate could not tell. When he spoke he looked slightly ill, nothing more.

"It looks like it, doesn't it? She killed one already, and she's always been a little crazy."

"Ned!" his mother said, horrified.

"Well, it's true, you know it's true, even if you won't say so. Sure she could have killed those girls. Who else would be doing it? Why ask me, anyway?"

"I've already asked your parents about her. I wondered what you had to say. After all, you must have been fairly close as children."

"Vaun was never close to anyone besides herself."

"Not even Andy Lewis?"

"She used Andy and dumped him." He stood up again, this time more gently but with greater finality, and deposited his napkin in his place. "Look, I have work to do this afternoon. If you're through questioning me maybe you'll let me get back to work."

Hawkin smiled up at him, and the smile held the younger man like shackles.

"I wasn't 'questioning' you, Ned," he said gently. "Just talking. If I wanted to question you, you would know you were being questioned. It's been nice talking with you, Ned. Hope to see you again."

He stood up and held his hand out in front of the man, and waited. Ned reached out with reluctance, clasped it briefly, and without another word crashed out through the back door.

Becky Jameson shook her head.

"He's so funny about Vaun. They used to be such good

153

friends, when they were kids, but they had a falling out about something, and before they could patch it up she got involved with Andy Lewis, and then, well, there was never a chance. Sad, really."

"What did you say their age difference was?" asked Hawkin.

"He's three and a half years younger than Vaun, and Joanna's three and a half years younger than he is."

"Kids are funny," he said, as if to himself. "I have two, both in college now, and they're just starting to talk to each other civilly again. Maybe if Vaun comes out of this okay, they'll start to work it out again."

"Maybe," she agreed, "though if anything it's been getting worse lately. They had some kind of a fight about a year ago, but neither of them would say what it was about. The last time she was here, he wouldn't come over until she'd left."

Hawkin shook his head in sympathy.

"Kids are funny," he repeated. He finished his coffee and stood up again. "We must go. I told the principal we'd be there at two-thirty."

"You know how to get there?"

"Yes, no problem. Thank you for lunch, Becky. Good to meet you, Red. I'll be in touch, and feel free to call if I can help with anything."

Mrs. Jameson followed them to the studio and helped them load the canvases into the back of the car. She gave Hawkin an old curtain to cover them and stood watching as they drove off. She looked small, and tired.

18

"That's one angry young man," commented Kate a few minutes later.

"Isn't he though? Look, pull up at that wide spot. I need to think for a minute."

He got out and went to lean against a neat white fence.

A single black cow lay ruminating, and watched him watch her. Kate joined them.

"What did Jameson tell you before I came in?" he asked.

She told him about the installation of the windows, Red Jameson's feelings about Andrew Lewis, what he had told her about the changes in his niece from December to April, the uncertainty he felt concerning her guilt.

"Yes, I heard from then on. Interesting about the missing picture, isn't it?"

"It wasn't in her studio, then?"

"It was not. Even more interesting is the fact that last November the Jamesons had a break-in. A few valuables missing, some money, and assorted odds and ends—including one of the photograph albums. Not the family one, but one in Vaun's room."

"You're saying that someone has made sure we have no pictures of Andrew Lewis?"

"Odd coincidence, isn't it?"

"Could be," she said doubtfully. "What made you go after Ned like you did?"

"I wanted to confirm a suspicion I got from talking with his mother. Ned was fourteen when Vaun took up with Lewis, remember, a boy proud of his new muscles, with a not unattractive young woman living close enough to be always there, but far enough away—both emotionally, and physically often away in her studio—to take away the taint of incest. She was never a sister, after all."

"Becky Jameson told you this?"

"Of course not. If she even thought of such a thing she'd clam up immediately. Just my cynical mind, putting two and two together and getting eight."

"And they had another confrontation, of some kind, last year."

"I wish someone had overheard it." He flipped his cigarette over the fence. "When we get to the school I want you to find yourself a nice quiet office and track down that farmers' co-op. We need to know if any of his trips coincided with the three dates or with the other night's attempt on Vaun."

"You sound decided, then, that it was not a suicide attempt."

"Oh, no. No proof, of course, but nobody who can fill a

studio with what I saw yesterday could lie down in front of a fire with a bad novel and a Mickey Finn to commit suicide. It's wishy-washy and uncertain, which she is not. Besides, she'd never endanger her life's work by leaving a pot of beans on the fire. No, it wasn't suicide."

"Does Ned Jameson strike you as being clever enough to do all this elaborate business? And I just can't see a farmer with another job on the side having the time to plan it out and kidnap and murder three children and put their bodies so they'd point to her, and then find her when she's most vulnerable, just when she's cut off by the storm, and somehow get to her and stage a suicide—I'm sorry, Al, but the whole thing seems ridiculous. It would have to be the work of a totally fixated person who has all the time in the world and is within reach of her even when the road's out."

"One of her neighbors, in fact."

"But who?"

"That's why I want a picture of Andy Lewis."

"So you're not looking at Ned Jameson?" She tried not to sound petulant, but her back was hurting.

"Of course we're looking at him. We can't very well leave a loose end like that dangling, not with his attitude and motive."

"The fact that she turned him down nearly twenty years ago? That's a motive?"

"That, plus the fact that his father obviously worships her, and the fact that he got trapped into marriage two months after he graduated from high school by a woman who pretended to be pregnant but who has since proven to be infertile."

"Becky Jameson said that?"

"She said, and I quote, 'Yes, it's such a pity they've never had any children, though she had a miscarriage two months after they were married.' "

"Two plus two. . . ."

"Sounds like eight to me. But I think the thing that galls Ned the most is the money. They live off Eva Vaughn. She keeps the roofs over their heads and the bank paid, and to know that and yet to accept each month's subsidy, from a woman who probably laughed at his overtures—well, it wouldn't be too surprising if he were to wish her dead and have her estate come to them."

"Assuming her will is written that way."

"It is. There was a copy of it in her desk."

"But you still see him as a loose end rather than a prime suspect."

"I do. Don't you? Yes. Why?"

"All the reasons I just gave you."

"And . . . ?"

"And . . . personal reactions to the man, which I don't think are valid reasons."

"Why not? You have to be wary of personal reactions, but that doesn't mean ignore them."

"Well, all right. It's the way he looked at me. A few years ago I began to realize that every time I met a man who looked me over like I was a piece of prime breeding stock, and he the blue-ribbon bull, he would turn out to be the same kind of person—an empty-headed incompetent who was so taken with his own sense of magnificence that he couldn't see that the only prick he had was between his ears. If you'll pardon my French, as Red Jameson would say. Ned is just too stupid not only to pull this off but to see Vaun as any kind of a threat. In fact, I'd doubt he's very troubled by the money. You would be, but he very probably thinks it's his due."

"You got all that from a look?"

"From a lot of looks over the years, Al."

He started to laugh, and as before it changed him into someone she could begin to like a great deal.

"Casey, I think I'm going to like working with you," he chuckled, and as he moved to the car he reached out and slapped her shoulder with a large hand, and then his face collapsed at her reaction.

"Oh, God, I'm sorry, I forgot. Are you okay?"

It took her a minute to catch her breath.

"Oh, yeah," she finally gasped, "just great. I always stand around with watering eyes, gritting my teeth. Makes me look tough."

At the high school the final bell had just rung, and Kate steered toward the visitor's parking against a surge of yellow buses, overladen cars, and clusters of long-legged students with the bodies of adults and the clamor of second-graders. Nothing like a high school to make a person feel short, clumsy, staid, and totally conspicuous. It seemed to affect Hawkin the same way.

"I never feel so much a cop as when I come to a high school," he muttered.

"Flat feet and a truncheon," Kate agreed.

"Just the facts, ma'am." He raised his voice. "Pardon me, ladies, can you tell me where I'd find the principal's office?"

The answer came as multiple giggles and a flurry of vague waves as the collective of females fluttered away. At the next junction he directed the same question to a group of males, and got vague thumb gestures and deeper guffaws, and the same mass sideways movement. He was drawing breath for a third inquiry when Kate nudged him and pointed to a sign saying Office. They pushed slowly inside to the desk.

The harassed secretary gradually realized that Hawkin was not a student and turned her stubby nose and small eyes in their direction. Her piercing voice cut across the din and caused it to slip several notches as the student bodies took note of the nature of these two intruders.

"Are you Detective Hawking? Mr. Zawalski said that you and Officer Martini would be here and that he'd be back in ten minutes if you'd like to wait in his office."

The waters parted and the two of them moved meekly under the speculative eyes and the beginning of whispers into the inner sanctum marked Principal. A burst of voices was set off by the closing of the door, and Kate grinned at Hawkin.

"Well, Detective Hawking, what do you bet there's a scramble for lockers and many flushings of toilets in about two minutes?"

"Sorry for the janitor tomorrow when they're all backed up."

The office was large and cluttered, the lair of a proponent of hearty camaraderie and school spirit. Plaques and group photographs of bulky young men in shoulder pads, cheerful young men in baseball hats, and unnaturally tall young men in basketball shorts crowded every inch of wall space. Bookshelves held trophies, a dusty, much-autographed football on a stand, a shelf and a half of multi-colored and multisized yearbooks, and several generations of the school mascot, a bear. On the wall behind the door was a yellowed list of scholarship students, three years old. Three small photos of a women's basketball team huddled together in the corner.

Hawkin moved directly to the bookshelves, pulled out an old yearbook, and took it to the cluttered table. After flipping through it for a moment he opened it flat at the formal portraits of the senior class.

The third photograph was of Vaun. To her left smirked a pair of sun-bleached twins named Aaronson; to her right another blond face looked out, a chubby boy with the euphonic name of Alexander Alarzo. Framed by the blond, tan, smiling faces, Vaun's hair seemed immensely dark and her startling eyes were a luminous near-white on the page. The photographer had caught the hint of amusement in her still face, and she looked an exotic creature set down inexplicably amongst the oblivious natives. Down the page the pattern of black and white rectangles of near-adults was broken by a famous, or perhaps infamous, picture of Richard Nixon gesturing a V-for-victory sign. Beneath that picture it said, "Marie Cabrera," and under that, "Escaped our Camera."

An uncomfortable premonition stirred in Kate. Hawkin turned the page. Marcia Givens to Richard Larson. One more page, and again the presidential visage grinned up at them. "Andrew Lewis. Escaped our Camera."

"Damnation." Hawk slammed the book shut.

On cue, the door opened, and the flustered pink face looked in. The upturned little nose twitched.

"Would either of you like a cup of coffee?" She spoke in a more normal voice, the masses in the outer office having miraculously departed. (To their lockers? wondered Kate. Surely not all of them!)

"Not right now, thanks," said Hawkin. "Maybe later. We do need a telephone, though. Is there a direct outside line, one that doesn't have any other extensions?"

"Oh!" The pink face got pinker, and she sidled into the room and planted her solid backside against the closed door. She looked so like some television caricature of a blue-rinsed lady thrilled at the chance to assist a professional sleuth that

159

Kate had to bite down a giggle. The secretary spoke in a whisper that could be heard in the hallway.

"Oh, yes, Mr. Zawalski has a private outside line, right in his phone. You just punch the last button, number nine, on the bottom, and he's the only one that has access to it. I mean, his phone is the only one. I mean, it's perfectly private."

She grew so pink during this speech that Kate began to worry that something internal was about to burst, and was relieved when Hawkin gravely thanked the woman and gently pushed her out the door, closing it firmly behind her.

"You go ahead," he said to Kate. "When Zawalski shows up I'll have him take me to see the art teacher and then head for the playing fields."

"I don't see a phone book."

"Start with Trujillo, then. I'll get you one."

Kate sat at the large desk and began punching numbers. She heard Hawkin's jovial voice calling, "Hey, beautiful—" before the door cut it off. She had barely finished giving the code of her billing number when he reappeared, laughing, giggles spilling through the door behind him, and tossed the thin book onto the desk. "So long, schweetheart." He sneered, and disappeared.

She shook her head. What an odd man was Alonzo Hawkin.

She met Hawkin on his way back to the office, walking with a man who looked more like a retired accountant than the force behind that massive display of homage to physical prowess. This little white crow of a man hopped along next to Hawkin (who looked, she realized, as if he had played football at one time) bobbing his head and flapping his hands energetically. His birdlike quality extended even to his handshake, feathery skin over frail bones, and he fluttered on to the office while Hawkin and Kate spoke quietly.

"Trujillo says there's no change, but she's stabilized enough that they're talking about taking her off the machines tomorrow. The lab results are in—it was chloral hydrate in the whiskey. Your classic Mickey Finn, plenty to put her to sleep after one drink, and she had two large ones, on a totally empty stomach. The stomach contents also show remnants of some kind of cold pills, which may have contributed to it. The doctor Trujillo talked to says the reaction was 'unexpectedly profound,' but not unheard of. Funny she didn't taste it."

"You ever had Laphroaig whiskey?"

"Isn't that what Tyler was drinking?"

"And Vaun Adams. It would mask the taste of pretty much anything. What else did you find?"

"I reached the co-op, but the woman who keeps track of their delivery schedule is off for the day, though the man I talked to thought she might stop in again at five. I didn't tell him what I wanted, only that it was urgent. Did you have any luck?"

"The art teacher is a sixty-two-year-old lady with thick black shoes and a white bun who remembers Vaun Adams well, tried to encourage her to paint more watercolors and still lifes, and thinks it's a pity Vaun never made a name for herself in the art world after she got out of prison, she seemed such a talented child. The coach is new, never heard of Andy Lewis. Zawalski's only been here twelve years. He's going to check Lewis's records to see who his teachers were."

In the office they found the principal fluttering, the pink-faced secretary giggling, and neither of them proceeding with any efficiency. Kate wondered in despair how long this was going to take. It involved a trip into the back room and a search through a cabinet, but eventually the secretary came up with the right year's microfiches clutched in her hands and led them all to the reader. Zawalski fussed with the various switches and knobs until Kate finally commandeered the chair, slipped the proper sheet under its glass plate, and whizzed the transcripts across the screen until she zeroed in on Lewis, Andrew C. No photograph in these transcripts. The grades listed were unexceptional: in addition to the required senior courses of English 4 (for which he had received the grade of C), History 3 (C), and a foreign language (Spanish, a B +), he had taken wood shop (C +), Art 1 (C −), and a study hall. He had also been on the football team, but a search on the walls of Zawalski's office had already proven fruitless.

Two of his teachers had moved, two had retired, and the

English teacher had died in a plane crash three years ago. The coach had also retired, but lived nearby and came to all the games, to contribute his expertise to the efforts of the current coach. The secretary, whose name most horribly turned out to be Piggott, found the telephone numbers of the retired coach and teachers, and got from the district offices the last addresses of the two who had moved. Kate went back to the telephone. Ten minutes later she hung up with the information that of the local people one teacher had died, one was recovering from a stroke and could not be disturbed until at the earliest next week, and the coach would be delighted to see them any time that afternoon, and what would they drink?

Hawkin stood up.

"I'll go see him. You see what you can scrape up here, about Vaun and Lewis. You might glance at Ned Jameson's records too, out of curiosity. But first, why don't you call, what's his name, the police chief here? Webster?"

"Walker."

"Right. See if he remembers anything funny about Lewis. I know he was never arrested, but there might have been rumors. Follow your nose. 'Ferret about,' in fact. I'll see you in an hour or so."

19

To Hawkin's surprise the principal seemed eager to go along, so the two of them drove off to a very solid hour of football talk, home brewed beer that tasted of plastic, and a heavy-handed determination on the part of Hawkin to fight the tide and keep the talk on Andrew Lewis.

At first wizened little Coach Shapiro could remember no Andrew Lewis, eighteen years before.

"There was a Tommy Lewis, ten years ago."

"That would be his cousin. Andy Lewis was only here for one year. You might remember him because he was older than most of your kids, came back after a couple years to finish his degree."

"We had two or three of those—wait a minute. Lewis. Yes, oh yes, Lewis, good arm, fast on his feet, but not much of a team player, wanted to stick out too much. Had to bench him a couple of times. He'd insist on trying for an impossible run instead of making a pass. Quit before the end of the season, I think."

"That sounds like him."

"There was something else, too. What was it? Never had any problem with my memory before I retired," he complained. "Now it's like running in mud. There was something he was involved in, later, some kind of trouble. Ah, got it! That girl. It was that girl, the one who killed the little Brand child and went to prison. She was Lewis's girlfriend for a while, wasn't she? Is that why you're here? It was a long time ago. Wait a minute. Where did you say you were from?"

"San Francisco," Hawkin admitted, and the coach was on it in a flash.

"Those little girls they've been finding in the mountains? Is that why you're here? You think she's done it again, and you're trying to find her through Lewis? You're wasting your time, I'd say. He's been gone for a long time."

"Yes, Mr. Shapiro, I know that." He neither confirmed nor denied the man's assumption, but retreated into a convenient, if true, formula. "We have some questions we'd like to ask Mr. Lewis; we think he can help us clear up a case we're working on. One of the problems we're having at the moment is that we don't know what he looks like, other than vague descriptions. We're trying to find a photograph of him. Would you by any chance have one?"

The old man burst into cackles, slapped his knee, and pushed himself to his feet. He gestured for Hawkin to follow him and shuffled into the next room, which had once been designed as a bedroom but was now what might be called a study, or a storage room, or a segment of primordial chaos. Filing cabinets with overflowing, unclosable drawers sat on top of dressers and chests; storage shelves, floor to ceiling, towered along the walls, in front of the window, as an island in the middle of the room. Every flat surface was laden with

163

precarious, bulging cartons and grocery bags filled with papers, books, ribbons, trophies, and just plain debris.

"Memorabilia of forty years' teaching and coaching. Always told myself that when I retired I'd spend happy days sorting it out, but somehow I never seem to find time for it. Can't think where to begin, for one thing. My wife wouldn't even come in here, terrified something would fall on her. I used to bring a chair in here to have a smoke. Damn fool of a doctor told my wife I had to give them up, but she'd never come in here." He surveyed the incredible room with the complacent pride of a grandfather, and Hawkin's blood ran cold at the thought of what an errant spark could do. "Anyway, to answer your question, there's probably a picture of your Andy Lewis in here somewhere, but God alone knows where."

He led them back into his living room, which seemed in retrospect a paragon of tidiness and order. Hawkin drew a deep breath and prepared to spend a chunk of taxpayers' money.

"Mr. Shapiro, if I arranged some help for you, would you be willing to go through your . . . memorabilia . . . and see if you can find any photographs of Andrew Lewis?"

Chief Walker listened, screamed, and agreed to send a man the next day. Hawkin suggested three or four additional sorters—unemployed housewives?—and some muscular teenagers to carry and load. Walker screamed again, and Hawkin spoke the soothing words of financial responsibility and reminded him not so gently of the murdered children, to say nothing of the fire hazard. They parted, if not friends, at least colleagues.

Shapiro seemed thrilled with the arrangement, and they left him a-babbling of a show at the local historical society and pulling at Zawalski's coattails for a display of his prizes at the high school's next homecoming game.

Hawkin rode back to the school brooding darkly over the possibility of a conspiracy that reached back eighteen years, and the very absurdity of it put him into a foul mood. Kate, on the other hand, was positively bubbling over with news and had some color in her face for the first time that day.

"Al, you'll never guess what I found out."

"Oh, Christ, Martinelli, let's not play guessing games, huh?"

Her face went blank and her chin went up, and Hawkin kicked himself for a clumsy fool.

"Yes, sir. Would you like to hear the results of my—"

"Casey, stop. I'm sorry, I've been drinking bad beer, thinking bad thoughts, and I need a toilet. I'll be back in a minute, and we'll start again." He went out, and a while later there was a dim rumor of rushing water and he came back.

"Okay, now, what have you come up with?"

She eyed him cautiously, but retreated from formality.

"Walker couldn't find anything, but the town Lewis came here from is about sixty miles north of here, and Walker knows the man who was sheriff at the time. He's retired, but he still lives there. I phoned around and finally tracked him down at his daughter's house, and I explained who I was and asked him if there was a possibility that the name Andrew Lewis meant anything to him. He didn't answer at first, so I started to explain that it would have been twenty years ago and he had no record so he'd probably never even been arrested as a juvenile, but he cut me off and said in this very quiet voice that there was no need, he remembered Andrew Lewis very well, what did I want to know? I left it general, that we were looking for him for information he might have concerning a murder, but he cut me off again, and said—shall I read it to you? I got most of it." She held up her notebook, and at his nod went on.

"He said, 'I wondered how long it would take before he got caught with something.' I started to say that we were only trying to find him, but he said, 'I knew twenty-five years ago that Andy Lewis was rotten, and I knew eighteen years ago that he had something to do with that little girl's death."

"What?" said Hawkin, incredulous.

"That's what he said."

"You mean he thinks Lewis did it?"

"He didn't say that. He was very careful not to. Just that Lewis was involved in some way. Shall I read the rest of this?"

165

Hawkin ran a hand through his hair, took out his cigarettes, and nodded for her to continue.

"I asked him if maybe he could explain that statement. He asked me if I had a few minutes, and I assured him that I had all the time in the world."

Kate looked back at her notes, remembering that at this point in their conversation the retired sheriff had excused himself and laid down the receiver. She had heard footsteps going across a room, followed by an unintelligible mumble, and a door closing to shut out the sounds of children. Footsteps again, the scrape of a chair, and then his voice had come again. She found her place on the page.

" 'First of all,' he said, 'I want you to know that I'm not the kind of person who sees bogeymen in the woodwork and criminal psychoses in every kid who cracks somebody over the head. I'm sure that anyone who's ever worked with me would tell you the same thing that's on my first academy evaluation: I don't have a lot of imagination, and I tend to give everyone the benefit of the doubt.' He sounded like that, too," Kate added. "Slow and thoughtful.

" 'Andy Lewis and his mother moved here when he was nine. It's a small town, and I live here, so I'd always hear when people came in or out, you know? Well, a couple of weeks later I had a phone call from the sheriff where they used to live, down near Fresno, a guy I'd met a couple of times. He told me, just casually you understand, that if people started reporting dead pets, I should keep an eye on the Lewis kid. Yeah, I know, I thought it sounded kind of crazy too, and I told him so, and he kind of laughed and agreed with me, and that was the end of it.

" 'Then about four or five months later an old lady found her poodle strangled. She'd thrown some kids out of her yard the week before. Four months later a cat and its kittens were found strangled, two days after their owner had shouted to a gang of kids to leave them alone. That time I remembered the phone call. Andy Lewis was in the gang, he had scratches on his arms, but what kid doesn't? And his mother said he'd been home all night. About two or three times a year, after that, somebody would make Andy Lewis mad, and one morning they'd find their dog or cat dead or their bird cage opened. No sign of a break-in, but in the country people are

166

careless about locking doors and windows. I even began checking for fingerprints, on the collars and stuff, but nothing. Never anything I could prove, and never a valuable animal or livestock, but it made me nervous, especially the way he wasn't in a hurry about it. Nothing pointed to him, there was always a gap between the insult, if that's how he saw it, and the revenge. If it hadn't been for the phone call, I don't know how long it would have taken me to put it together. As I said, it made me nervous. And when I found that he didn't go bragging to his friends, well, that made me *very* nervous.

" 'He was cool, he was patient, and he was smart. Except for once, once that I caught him, I should say. You'll understand when I say that by the time he was a teenager I was getting more than a bit concerned about him and keeping my ears flapping and my eyes open for anything concerned with Andy Lewis. That's why I was onto him so fast when he finally stepped out of line. Only once did he just let fly without planning, and that was the end of him in this town. Tell me, have you met him?'

"I said I didn't know if I had or not and explained about the pictures.

" 'Well,' he said, 'Andy Lewis was a charmer. He'd have made a great con man. He was a con man, come to think of it, only not for money, not directly. He wanted power over other people, always moved with a group of worshippers to admire him. When he was sixteen the local preacher's daughter caught his eye, a pretty, overly protected little thing, very bright.

" 'He got her pregnant. She was fourteen, almost fifteen. She wanted him to marry her, some dream she had, but when he pushed her off she started talking about turning him in for statutory rape. He blew up, beat her so badly she nearly died, lost the baby of course and half her teeth, ruptured her insides so she couldn't have any more children. And, you know, damned if she didn't refuse to press charges against him. Partly she was scared to, but she was more than half convinced that he really loved her and hadn't meant to do it.

" 'I did something then I've never done before or since and I'll only admit to it now because I'm an old man and my deputy's dead. I took my deputy out, and we picked up the Lewis kid, and we took him out to the quarry and beat the

167

shit out of him. Still makes me sick to think about it, the two of us and this sixteen-year-old kid, but I knew it was the only way he'd listen to me. I didn't hurt him, nowhere near what he'd done to the girl, but when I finished I told him I wanted him gone, never to set foot in my county again, or next time I wouldn't stop. The next morning he was gone. A few months later his mother moved to the town you're in now to be with her sister. The next I heard of Lewis was three, four years later, when his name came up in connection with the Adams girl. I have no idea where he was during those years. He was supposed to have been in the army, but I find it hard to imagine.

" 'Anyway, the other thing you should know is that he always had to be in control of any situation, any group. The only time he faded into the background was when something was about to happen. Now, as I understand it, the Adams girl was a brilliant artist. The whole school knew her, knew that she was going somewhere, a very large and exotic fish plunked down temporarily in their little pond. She doesn't seem to have been aware of how others looked at her, but when Lewis walked into that school—God knows why or how he did—he saw immediately that she was one of the power points of the school and he set out to take her over. And, as I said, he was a charmer.

" 'For a few months he rode around on her shoulders, making everybody think that he was dangling her, rather than she carrying him. And then she wised up. From what she said at the trial, she decided he was getting in the way of her painting, so she told him to leave and went back to her brushes. He couldn't have that—not only the rejection, but the public humiliation. She didn't bother to hide it, and apparently some of the other students saw what had happened and laughed at him.

" 'A month later the child given into her care was found dead. Strangled. With no sign of a break-in. Apparently by a girl who had just made Andy Lewis angry. And I knew that Andy Lewis was a kid with a thirst for revenge, the ability to be patient and quiet, and bright enough to keep his temper under control, most of the time.

" 'I did what I could. I went to the police there. I put it all in front of them, and they tried, but none of us could find the smallest chink in his armor. A week or two after the trial ended I went to talk with him. I guess I thought that I could threaten him into not doing anything else by letting him know that we were all watching him. He laughed at me. Laughed right in my face, and turned his back on me and walked away. I went home and I thought about it, and I realized that I had two choices: I could shoot him like I would a dog with rabies, or I could sit tight and wait until he stepped into someone else's hands and see what I could do.

" 'There was really no choice in the matter. I couldn't shoot him. I never even seriously considered it, although I knew that I might very well save innocent lives if I did. So I sat and waited, and I've been waiting eighteen years. I know who you are, and I know why you're calling, and all I can say is, if there's anything an old, retired sheriff with a bad conscience can do to help, I'm yours.'

"I told him that he'd been more help than I could have dreamed of and that the only thing we were missing was the photograph. He said that he'd try to think of someone who might have one, and if we had no luck he'd be more than happy to come down and try to make an ID. I thanked him and said we'd be in touch."

Hawkin had sat and listened quietly to her narration, his face growing more strained with every sentence. He now took a cigarette out of its soft package, tapped the end of it squarely on the principal's desk, twice, put it to his mouth, lit it precisely with one match, shook the match out and put it carefully into the ashtray he'd found in a drawer, his movements those of a technician defusing a bomb.

"Classic," he commented, then, "damn, damn, damn. How many other people have made Andy Lewis angry over the last eighteen years? Get a hold of Trujillo——"

"I talked with him again after the sheriff's news and told him to increase the guard on the road as much as he could and stop every male of about thirty-five to forty who wanted to leave."

"Good."

"I take it the coach didn't have a photo?"

"If he does, it'll take days to unearth. Eighteen years ago Lewis was a bit over five ten, one seventy-five, brown hair

169

and eyes, no marks but a tattoo on his upper left arm, something snaky."

"Except for the tattoo it'd fit half the men on Tyler's Road. Maybe more than half."

"Christ, what I'd give for a fingerprint or a fuzzy picture."

"I just may be able to oblige you," she said with ill-concealed glee. "Andy Lewis had a driver's license."

"Hot damn, you don't mean we're going to get a break with this?"

"Trujillo tracked it down. They'll send the photo to the office. I wouldn't count on much, though. DMV photos aren't exactly the greatest."

"I won't cancel the search through the Shapiro archives, then."

"The what?"

"Never mind. Anything else?"

"Not much. There's nothing of interest about Ned Jameson. Average grades, some trouble as a kid but nothing nasty, just paint on walls and a shoplifting charge when he was fifteen. I was just going to try the co-op again when you came in."

"Your ear must be falling off," he said by way of praise. "Do you have their address? Let's go by and play nasty cops. I need to growl at somebody. Call Trujillo once more and let him know where we're going. Tell him I'll call him from home tonight, and have him start inquiries on the Road for a man with a tattoo."

Hawkin did not growl at the blushing Mrs. Piggott, nor at Mr. Zawalski, who fluttered them to the car. He did not even growl when the trio of hippie farmers at the co-op produced a hand-scribbled list of drivers that seemed to put Ned in the clear for at least two of the killings. It was not until the new-age farmers responded to his query about restaurants with the name of a vegetarian health-food place that he finally exploded, cursed tofu, beans, and goat's milk violently, and only subsided when, cowering, they threw him the name of an Italian place that they vowed had no tofu, ferns, or posters of Venice on the walls and was responsible in its choice of veal calves.

It wasn't a bad dinner. They parked immediately outside the windows so as to keep an eye and ear on the car. Hawkin talked about his childhood in the San Fernando Valley and about his kids, and asked nothing in return. Neither of them drank wine; both of them ate meat. The zabaglione was followed by thick demitasse cups of espresso romano.

Outside the restaurant it was almost dark, the air cool. Hawkin stood and lit a cigarette.

"Look, Al, I don't mind if you smoke in the car."

"It's a filthy habit," he said.

Kate was anxious to go while the coffee still surged in her veins, but Hawkin seemed in no hurry. He took his time and snuffed the end out thoroughly in the planter box.

"You look tired, Casey. Do you want me to drive?"

"It's all right. I don't mind driving."

"I'm quite competent behind the wheel. I got in the habit of letting my partner drive some years ago, and as you know I catch up on my sleep, but I am perfectly able to get us home in one piece."

"Really, Al, I'm fine."

He looked at her, then shrugged and walked toward the car. She unlocked the passenger door, and held the key in her hand. The exhaustion rolled up like waves and beat against the wall of her determination. Why do this? She knew she could make it home. Hawkin knew she could. So what was the point?

She handed him the keys.

"You drive for a while, please, Al."

Where some men might have shown triumph, Hawkin's eyes held only approval and warmth. He nodded, took the keys, and drove with easy concentration towards the freeway.

20

Kate drowsed as the white lights sailed past and the red ones blurred and swam into each other. The car was warm and smelled of coffee and, not unpleasantly, of tobacco. She punched up the pillow and settled her head back into it.

"You awake?" said Hawkin softly, without taking his eyes from the road.

"Yes."

"Can I ask you something?"

"You can try," she said, rousing herself slightly.

"Are you a lesbian?"

Kate examined her reaction to the question. Nothing. Mild surprise perhaps, which was very interesting. "Are you asking as a cop, as a man, or as a friend?" she wondered.

"Mmm. Let's say, as a friend."

"Al, as a friend, I hope you won't be offended if I say that I don't think we know each other well enough for you to ask me that question. Try it again in a couple of months." She settled back and closed her eyes.

"And as a man?"

"You didn't ask me as a man."

"And if I had?"

"If you had, my answer would have been somewhat different."

Neither of them mentioned the third possibility.

"A couple of months, huh?"

"Maybe more. Maybe less if we have another case like this."

"God forbid!"

"Not offended?"

"Of course not."

Hawkin drove in silence for several miles, thinking. He was not all that concerned with her answer to his question and had asked it only because he thought it might be necessary to provide an opening for her to talk about herself. She had not chosen to take the opening, but it hardly mattered. The initial move away from the strictly professional had been made, and that was what he had been after.

The road cleared at a well-lit junction of sweeping concrete roadways, and he looked over at his partner. She was asleep, her full lips curled in some secret amusement. The precise nature of the joke, if joke it was, he could not know, but it made her look very young and wise, and made his own mouth curl into a smile as well.

Kate slept for an hour and took the wheel to drive across the lighted bridge into the city. She waited in the car while Hawkin went up to get the DMV photo from the office, and when he came out onto the street she could see from his face that it was even worse than she had anticipated.

"The picture's bad?" she asked as he climbed in.

"In a very good light you can see that he has two eyes, a nose, a mouth, and brownish hair. Do you know where Susan Chin lives?"

"Our artist? No."

He gave her an address.

Susan came to the door of her small apartment. She had obviously been in bed when Hawkin called and did not invite them in. She squinted at the photograph and looked at him dubiously.

"You did say it wasn't very good, but this is ridiculous."

"Can you do it?"

"You want me to use this to make a series of sketches, one of which might remind somebody on that Road of one of their neighbors? To extrapolate out from it, intuitively?"

"Exactly. Can you do it?"

"Haven't the faintest," she said cheerfully. "Well, it's an interesting problem. Makes a change from computer-generated IdentiKit drawings."

"Good luck."

They left the young artist standing in her doorway peering at the photo in the light of the bulb over her door. Kate dropped Hawkin off at his house and drove home.

The garage door rattled down behind her. She leaned forward and turned off the ignition, and felt the strength that had kept her moving throughout the long day ebb away into the silent garage. She sat at the wheel and thought about the motions of moving her right arm down to push the button and disengage her seat belt and moving her left arm down to pull the door handle and drawing first her left foot and then her right out and onto the concrete floor and standing up, but somehow sitting and breathing were about all she could manage at the moment.

The sound of a door opening, feet on a wooden staircase,

slight scuffs on the slab floor, the click and pull of the car door coming open, Lee's voice, dark and restful.

"Sweet Kate, you look all done in."

"Hello, love. God, it's nice to sit still."

"I started a hot bath when I heard you come in, and the oil's warming for a massage."

"You will kill me with pleasure."

"I do hope not."

A light finger brushed the back of Kate's neck, and then the scuffs and steps retreated upstairs. In a minute Kate followed.

There was a bath that was almost too hot for comfort, and a large mug of something that tasted of chicken and celery, and thick warm towels, and then strong fingers probing at locked muscles and easing the tension from neck and back and legs until Kate lay groaning with the sweet agony of it, and when she was totally limp and the hands had moved on to wide, firm, integrating sweeps, she spoke, halfway to sleep.

"Hawkin asked me tonight if I was a lesbian."

The sweeping hands checked only slightly.

"And what did you say?"

Odd, thought Kate muzzily, how hands can be amused when a voice isn't.

"I told him to ask me again when we knew each other better."

This time Lee laughed outright, and then the towel began to wipe the last of the oil from Kate's skin.

"How utterly un-Californian of you, Kate."

"Wasn't it?"

The hands finished and soft sheets and warm blankets were pulled up to Kate's neck.

"I have some work to do. Give me a shout if you need anything. Now, go to sleep."

"I'll work at it."

Kate's breathing slowed and thickened, and a few minutes later the bed shifted and then the room clicked into darkness. Lee's soft curls formed a halo against the hall light, and she closed the door gently and went downstairs, an expression of fond exasperation on her face.

174

Several miles away Alonzo Hawkin lay on the sofa in his living room, a glass balanced on his stomach, his eyes on the large, delicate fish that performed their glides and pirouettes for his amusement, his mind on the events and the texture of the day. He was, for once, satisfied.

It was almost magical the way one day's work could on occasion, on very rare occasion, transform a case entirely and bring its whole setting and landscape into focus. That morning—yesterday morning, now—he had walked down the stairs with a huge sheaf of unrelated papers and more questions than he could begin to even ask, and Andrew C. Lewis was just one name in a hundred others. Sixteen hours later he had trudged back up those stairs, bone weary, with two things: a name and a direction. His weariness he bore like a badge of accomplishment, and he felt himself a fortunate man. A break.

The police artist Susan Chin was not the only one he had disturbed that night. First was Chief Walker, from whom he had asked two things: the whereabouts of Andy Lewis's aunt and her family, and further information concerning the reliability of Lewis's alibi the night of the murder eighteen years ago. Hawkin would have preferred to do that himself, but as it was not strictly his case, it would be hard to justify another couple of days up there. Next week, maybe, but not now.

Then he reported in. The man listened, concealed three yawns, grunted approval, and went back to bed.

Then the hospital: no change. Hawkin heard the first prickle of worry in the back of the doctor's voice, but as there was nothing he could do in that department, he pushed the thoughts away and called Trujillo.

That young man sounded older than he had a week before. He confirmed that a guard was now installed next to Vaun's bed instead of in the corridor, with orders not to step outside the door, and not even to close the bathroom door when he needed to use the room's toilet. She was not to be out of his sight.

Trujillo was disappointed that the photo was bad, though not surprised, and agreed to set Susan's drawings up in the main room to guarantee the most contact.

He then told Hawkin that he was not sure how much longer he could keep control. The Road's uneasiness was nearly to the breaking point. He'd had to let two families with children leave during the day (one of the men was black, the other in his late fifties) to take refuge with suburban friends, and the efficient bush telegraph had spread the news clear up to old Peterson's place that Vaun's near death was not being treated as a suicide. Trujillo had spent the day going up and down the Road—Tyler had been forced to suspend the anticar rule—reassuring people and reminding them to inquire first before they let fly with buckshot or bullet. The bedrooms at Tyler's were full tonight with nervous residents (peasants come to the castle during a siege, thought Hawkin with amusement, right down Tyler's alley), and he, Trujillo, would be staying there too. Sharp-nosed newsmen were back to camping outside, and it was only a matter of time. . . .

There had been no immediate response that afternoon to the tattoo inquiry, although only a couple of dozen people had been asked. Hawkin told him in all honesty that he was doing a fine job. The younger man responded to the confidence in Hawkin's voice, and after a few minutes Hawkin told him to go to bed.

After that he went and took a long, mindless shower, wrapped his stocky body in his favorite soft and threadbare kimono, and settled down with a glass.

The time with the Jamesons had proven a gold mine. He now *had* Vaun Adams; he could now see her walking the halls of that unremarkable high school, an extraordinary teenager with an aura of untouchability and genius to keep the world at bay. And her short liaison with clever, nasty, sophisticated Andy Lewis—even that was not as completely unlikely as it had first seemed.

But what to do about the maddening shadow figure of Andrew C. Lewis? Hawkin's eyes were caught by the enthusiastic rooting of the eel-like loach in the gravel, and his mind wandered into a side track. What, he mused, does that C stand for? Charles? Clifford? Coleoptera? The father's name on the transcript had been Edward, or Edmund . . . He caught himself angrily and dragged his wayward thoughts back to the problem at hand. Lewis was on Tyler's Road; Hawkin knew it in his very bones. If he had not made a break for it

176

by now, he wouldn't, not until he knew for certain that Vaun was not about to die. Perhaps not even then, if he felt sure enough that he had covered his tracks. Andy Lewis was not a man to panic blindly. How best to find him? And, once found, how to tie him to the wispy bits of circumstance, how to weave his involvement into a fabric strong enough to hold up in court? How to spin a sliver of wood, a hypothetical tattoo, and a deliberate concealment of identity into a rope strong enough to hang a man? Best would be if Lewis could be forced into an incriminating bolt—that would help to solve both problems at once. Hawkin lay there considering and discarding options and ideas, building up a plan around the geography and the psychological makeup of his prey and the people he had to work with.

The level in his glass went down very slowly, but eventually it was dry, and he sat up.

Twenty-four hours, he thought. If nothing's happened in twenty-four hours—no photograph has appeared, no description has clicked—I'll bring down the retired sheriff and Coach Shapiro and anyone else I can find and drive them up and down Tyler's Road in Trujillo's shiny new wagon until one of them says, "Say, wait a minute. . . ." Tomorrow night I'll decide whether or not to turn Tyler's Road inside out. The thought of that possibility gave him a moment of pleasurable anticipation, seventy-four long-haired adults and twenty minors dragged in and printed and grilled until something gave under the pressure.

(I wonder what that C stands for? he thought in irritation.)

Yes, something will happen. If not tomorrow (today!) then Wednesday for certain. As for Monday, he could end it content that he had done all he could.

He put his glass on the table, said good night to the fish, and went to bed.

He was not to know until the sun rose that succumbing to the day's all-too-rare glow of satisfaction had been a mistake.

Two hours to the south a woman with black curls lay in a hospital bed, her hands tucked neatly beneath the crisp cov-

177

ers, her remarkable ice-blue eyes staring, unblinking, up into the dim room. The hour was very late, or very early, but a disturbance down the hall and the rapid departure of a much-attended gurney had brought her eyes open some minutes before. One could not say that she was awake, exactly; only that her eyes were currently open, where before they had been closed.

The room's machinery had been edged back from the bed, save for the tall pole with the intravenous drip and the rolling cart with the monitor, whose wires were connected to little round sensors taped onto the woman's chest. The tracery of the heartbeat was slow but regular, and the cart would be removed later that day.

The woman did not know that, though. There was considerable debate over what she did, or would, know. The bruised puffiness of her mouth had subsided, the marks of her resurrection were fading, but Vaun Adams had given no sign of anything other than a mere physical presence. The words "brain damage" and "oxygen deprivation" had slid into the room and been carried away again, but they waited just outside her door and would return.

The room was lit solely by the corner reading lamp that sent its beam across the guard's paperback novel and laid a stretched circle of light along the wall and across a corner of Vaun's bed. She gazed passively up at the reflection of her face in a bit of polished metal overhead, distorted but familiar. One tiny part of Vaun saw it and recognized it, but that part was disconnected from her now, in abeyance, hiding.

The brain of the woman who had been Vaun Adams and Eva Vaughn was not physically damaged, not badly at any rate. Her mind, however, and her spirit—those had been severely wounded. The spark of being that was Vaun Adams, the spark that had flamed into being as Eva Vaughn, lay smothered beneath a burden that had finally proven intolerable. Vaun was covered by a blanket of despair, a thick, gray blanket that was crushing her, stifling her will to move and create and live, a thick gray blanket that said, "Enough."

Enough.

Enough was the ruling principle that governed what there was left of this life. Enough. I can no more. Since I was two years old I have fought for the right to be what I am, and

I can fight no longer. I yield. I give up. I can no more. Enough.
I choose to die.

The blue eyes were still open when a nurse came in ten minutes later to check the drip. Vaun's ears registered sound waves, and some dim hidden part of her automatically deciphered them as words, but they did not connect, did not penetrate the thick gray blanket. The nurse leaned over her eyes, and behind the white shoulder appeared the face of a man above a dark uniform. More sounds came, a few squawks and a rumble, and the male face withdrew.

The nurse addressed Vaun with professional cheeriness, though even the guard could hear the uneasiness in her voice. Vaun was a problem, a VIP who was in an unclear state of either arrest or protection, or both. She was also, to all appearances, a vegetable. This mysterious black-haired woman with the unseeing, crystalline eyes gave a number of people the creeps, and the night nurse was one of them. She left after servicing the body in the bed, and eventually the eyes drifted shut again.

In the dark hills between Vaun Adams's hospital bed and the city where two detectives slept, a shadow moved onto Tyler's Road. The man who had been Andy Lewis closed the door on its oiled hinges and slipped silently away from the house he had thought of as home these last years. He felt no regret at leaving the woman who slept behind him in the bed he had built from a single oak tree, and only slight regret at leaving the child in the room his hands had made. There was no room for any feeling other than the white-hot, piercing-cold, all-consuming rage that trembled and bubbled throughout his body like dry ice furious in a bucket of water. In his mind's eye the leaves scorched and blackened overhead, small animals dropped down dead with his passing, the road cringed from his boots—and Vaun Adams woke screaming from her hospital bed to feel the approach of his terrible hate.

None of these things happened, of course. The muted beep of Vaun's monitor kept its hypnotic rhythm, small night animals rustled leaves, a dog barked once, the breeze from the ocean stirred the fragrant needles.

By dawn he had crossed the mud slide's remnants, avoided the guards posted at the upper end of Tyler's Road, and entered the adjoining state park. At eight a neatly dressed man with a mustache, carrying a thick briefcase, caught a ride with a computer programmer who worked over the hill. The driver's daughter was with him in the front seat, going to spend the day with her grandmother. The child was six years old and had shiny brown hair and one loose front tooth, which she delighted in wiggling precariously with her tongue. The man who had been Andy Lewis smiled at her with his charming smile, chatted easily with her about kindergarten and with her father about computers and the problems of remote automobile breakdowns, and thanked them both when they got to San Jose. By noon he was in Berkeley, completely invisible.

Long before that—shortly after he left the park, in fact—Angie Dodson woke to find that her husband was gone.

21

Angie's pounding echoed through the house and roused the sleepers, Trujillo among them. He wrapped himself in a borrowed bathrobe and walked yawning down to the kitchen. Angie's face was tight with worry despite her deliberately casual words, and Trujillo was far from sleepy as he unobtrusively left the room and sprinted for the upstairs telephone.

Hawkin cursed viciously, Kate cursed with less imagination and opened her back again, and two hours later they burst into Tyler's kitchen.

"Where's Angie?"

The huddled group all busied themselves with their cups or studied their hangnails. Blond-braided Anna told them that she was upstairs with Trujillo. Hawkin took the stairs two at a time, Kate on his heels, and when they got to Tyler's door he threw the door back without knocking.

Angie Dodson looked up from where she sat crouched in front of the fire. She had passed through tears and now

180

looked old and beaten and utterly without hope. Hawkin walked over to her and put his arms around her, and she clung to him and began to moan in a breathless, high-pitched animal noise. Trujillo turned to look out the window. Tyler smiled sickly at Kate and lurched through the door, muttering something about coffee. Kate studied the watercolors and gradually she realized that Angie's moans had resolved themselves into a monotonously repeating phrase.

"She was my friend. She was my friend. She was my friend."

"You mean Vaun," said Hawkin in a gentler voice than Kate would have thought possible.

"Yes. She was my friend. She was—"

"Where's Amy?"

That got to her. She took a deep and shaky breath and sat up. Hawkin's arms fell away, but he sat close to her and bent his head to her.

"She's with the Newborns. I told Rob to watch her every minute, and not let her go off anywhere, not even with—Oh God . . ." She collapsed again. "She was my friend, and they say he killed her. Is it true? You must tell me."

"She isn't dead, Angie."

"She might as well be. Did he do it?"

"Does the man you know as Tony have a tattoo on his arm?"

His non sequitur caught her full attention.

"What?"

"A tattoo," he repeated. "Does Tony have a tattoo?"

"How did you know?" She straightened and blew her nose. "He never let anyone see it; he was embarrassed by it. He'd had it put on when he was real young. Not even Amy knew he had it. He always wore a T-shirt, even when he went swimming."

"What was it?"

"A dragon."

"A dragon? Not a snake?"

"No, it was one of those long, skinny dragons. I suppose it looked a bit like a snake, but it had little legs. It was on his left arm, up high. I only saw it clearly two or three times myself. He'd usually only take his shirt off in the dark. What does his tattoo have to do with it?"

181

So he told her. Tyler came in with a tray of coffee, and Hawkin broke off until he had gone; then he resumed and told her all, or nearly all.

"So you see, Angie, at this point the only positive identification we have is that tattoo."

"He always was funny about having his picture taken, I know. Even at our wedding." She giggled softly and sighed, dazed with the impossibility of what her life had become in a few short hours.

"Angie, I have to ask you some questions now."

"I won't testify against him," she threw out at him. "I'll talk to you, but I won't testify against him."

(Andy . . . he was a real charmer . . . she wouldn't press charges. . . .)

"Just talk to me, then. Tell me how you met."

They had met at one of the Road's yearly Medieval Faires, three years ago come June. He had come as a visitor, not in costume, and though he had bought his ticket from her early in the morning, it was not until afternoon that he had reappeared and made her teach him the steps to a pavane, and they'd danced and drunk and laughed on into the evening, and on the Sunday he'd been back first thing and spent the whole day with her and with Amy, and that night he'd gone up the Road with them and slept on her couch. Two weeks later he moved his few belongings into the small house, and in November they married. Not a church ceremony, but one they wrote, and Tyler conducted. It wasn't a legal marriage, because Angie's husband had neither divorced her nor been in touch since he deserted her, but it had not mattered.

"What is he like, Tony? With you and Amy?"

"Very good with Amy. I don't think he'd ever been around kids much, before he moved in with us, but he was a good father to her. Quiet, polite. Private, but not like he was hiding anything. A gentleman, I guess."

"Always?"

"With Amy, yes. And almost always with me. He . . . he has a temper. Had. He never hit me, I don't mean that, but once he got really mad at me—for something small, too, I was just teasing him about a stupid mistake he'd made when he was building the addition onto the cabin. He didn't like it."

182

"What did he do, Angie?"

"He chopped up my loom." Her face remembered frightened bewilderment as she studied her clasped hands. "He got really quiet, and his eyes . . . He went out to the woodshed and got the big ax and came back with it and chopped my loom up into little pieces, and then he hauled it off and burned it. Afterwards he was sorry, he kissed me, and the next day we went to Berkeley and he bought me another one, a better one, too, an eight harness I'd been wanting for a long time. We never talked about it again, but, well, I never teased him again."

"And with the other people on the Road? How did he get along with them?"

"Really well, with most of them. As far as I know he never lost his temper with anyone else, not that I heard of. He's never been tremendous buddies with anyone, he likes to keep to himself, but when he's in the mood he can be a lot of fun. Anyway, he was approved for residency in the October meeting, so obviously everyone thought they could get along with him." Her tone was defensive, as if wondering why her friends had not protected her against her choice. "They all like him. He seems to get along best with Tommy Chesler," she added.

"What about Vaun? How did he act toward her? Did she vote for him?"

"I don't remember anyone not voting for him—wait a minute, she wasn't here, I think. It was the Harvest Meeting, and she wasn't here, she had to go to New York, I think it was. How did he act toward her?" she repeated. She chewed on her lip and fixed her shiny eyes on a part of the carpet, and sobbed a small laugh.

"I thought he was jealous of her. She was my friend, before he came here. My old man took off about six months before she came, you see, and then she built her house, and we were neighbors, and she admired my needlework and weaving and helped me with the colors and the designs and—she was my friend, you know? And I thought he was jealous, though he never said anything. I thought it was funny, cute in a way, that he'd be jealous, but I didn't want to bother him, so mostly I'd see her when he was away, or when I was up working in the garden. She let me use her sunny hillside for vegetables, you know, so we could use our open space for the ponies. Tony was never nasty about her, he'd just quietly go out the back if she came to the house, or look away if we met her on the Road. Nothing obvious or rude, you understand. I thought he was just being nice to me, not wanting to break up my friendship with her, but if what Paul says is true, if he is this Andy Lewis, then I suppose he wanted to avoid being recognized by her." Her voice dragged to a halt, and her face looked drawn and haggard.

"But he transported some paintings for her."

"Yes, four or five times. She knew he had a truck, and she asked him once about a year and a half ago when Tyler's was broken down and she was desperate to get them off to some show."

"Did he pack them up for her, too?"

"No, Vaun had Tommy Chesler help her. They built these big crates, one for each painting, and Tommy'd help Tony load them. A couple of times Tommy went with him to the airport, but Tommy doesn't much like cities."

"Did Vaun go?"

"No."

"Tell me about when Tony was away. Did he go regularly? What was he doing? Do you know where he went?"

"Earning money, doing odd jobs in town or over the hill. Never anything regular, just a day here and there or overnight. Never more than four days in a row. It worked out to about two or three days a week, I suppose, just to keep us in spending money. It wasn't regular. Sometimes his friends would leave a message with Tyler telling him there'd be work on a certain day, other times he'd just go."

"Do you know the names of any of those friends?"

"There was a Tim who left messages sometimes, and another guy in San Jose named Carl, but I don't remember ever hearing their last names. Tyler or Anna might know."

"I'll ask them. You can't think of anywhere he might go, any favorite places?"

"San Jose, I guess. We went there, once. He took me to a bar. I don't like bars, but he thought I might enjoy it. It had a funny name, like a joke. Gold something. Gold girl? No, that's right, Golden Grill. Stupid pun. On one wall they have an enormous painting of a naked blond woman tied to a barbecue. Disgusting, really." She suddenly noticed the identical expression on the faces of her three listeners, the sort of expression an Olympic archer makes when he hits the bull's-eye in the final round. "Did that help any?"

"My dear Angie, you have given us much food for thought, almost as nourishing as your onion soup. I thank you, profoundly."

The matchbook found near the body of Samantha Donaldson had come from a bar in San Jose called the Golden Grill.

Angie could tell them little more. She did not know what he'd been wearing, how much money he had, or whether or not he'd taken a gun, but she said he was a good shot with both rifle and pistol. A quick check showed his truck in the shed and no other vehicles missing. Hawkin sent Trujillo up with Angie to try to find out what her husband had taken with him, and told him to have the nurse, Terry Allen, stay with Angie for a while and then to go and pick what brains he could find in Tommy Chesler's head for any possible leads. Tyler he sent out front, requesting that he obfuscate matters as much as possible in the eyes of the media while Hawkin and Kate made their escape.

The uniformed policewoman in Vaun's room was tall and formidable and blocked the doorway most effectively until she was satisfied with their credentials. She left them alone in the room.

It was the first time Kate had seen Vaun since early Saturday. Her face was slack, her lips were slightly parted, her skin was almost as white as her pillow but for the red mouth and the dark smudges under her eyes. The intense contrasts of white and black and red gave her the aloof, other-worldly beauty of a geisha. Kate would have thought her dead but for the monitor.

Hawkin grunted and left after a minute, but Kate lingered. She was struck with the irrational wish to see Vaun's hands, but they were under the covers and she hesitated to touch her. Finally she left, and the policewoman returned to the room.

Dr. Tanaka's office held five people. Hawkin stood at the window looking down at the entrance parking lot. Kate sat with a notebook. Dr. Tanaka himself wore a neat blue suit and spoke with great precision. The other two doctors wore white jackets over their clothing, and the woman, whose name was Gardner, had a stethoscope in her pocket, an obvious sign of low status, Kate thought in amusement. Hawkin turned back to the room.

"So, to put it in English," he said, "it's too early to know what's going on."

"That is an oversimplification, but in essence, true. Her symptoms and her brain waves are neither those of a coma nor of catatonia, but they have characteristics of both. Until we know more, all we can do is continue to support the bodily functions."

"Then, Dr. Tanaka, I do not envy you and your hospital the next few days. The press has arrived."

An undignified scramble for the window ensued, the telephone rang, and Hawkin stalked off with Kate close behind. He sent her off to warn Vaun's guard and call in the hospital security for reinforcements while he went to close himself in with a telephone. Within hours the world would know that Eva Vaughn lay in this small hospital. He no longer had any time to wait. When Kate returned he handed her a slip of paper.

"You will meet this plane tonight."

"He's coming, then? Dr. Bruckner?"

"I gave him no choice. You go home now and sleep for a few hours. It's going to be a long night."

22

The plane from Chicago was late. Kate spent the time in an all-night cafeteria at San Francisco International's north terminal, drinking bad coffee and fighting her way into an introduction to the theory of art that she had taken from Lee's shelves at midnight. At two o'clock she went for a walk through the other-worldly halls, and found herself in a display of the work of local artists. She long contemplated two pieces, one a battered briefcase that was actually made out of clay, the other a massive and highly realistic section of adobe wall formed entirely out of styrofoam and leather. She finally decided that any intended symbolism was beyond her ability to decipher, thrust the book into her shoulder bag, and retreated into the cafeteria for more coffee (Was it actually made of hot stewed twigs? Was the artificial creamer formed entirely of styrofoam?) and the evening paper. Eva Vaughn was on the front page, and Kate tortured herself by reading every word.

The plane touched down at 3:15, and a few minutes later Kate planted herself firmly in the flow of dazed passengers, watching for the self-described "little fellow with a brown briefcase." (Presumably made of actual leather.) A likely candidate appeared, and she spoke vaguely in the direction of the short, foreign-looking man with the gray goatee, spotless white shirt, and bow tie.

"Dr. Bruckner?"

But it was the surprisingly young-looking man next to him who stopped in front of her and held out his hand.

"Yes I know I don't look like a psychiatrist," he said rapidly, "and yes I know you didn't expect me to be so young, but then if you're 'one of our inspectors name of Martinelli' I wasn't expecting you either, so we're even."

He had an unidentifiably eastern nasal voice and a crooked grin, and his hair was too long and he needed a shave, and he was indeed a little man, barely taller than Kate, and she laughed and took his hand, which surprised her with the calluses of a laborer.

"Casey Martinelli, and Al may have forgotten to tell you I was a she or he may have been aiming at the truly liberated attitude of not noticing or he may have had some obscure reason of his own. At any rate, I'm glad to meet you, and thank you for coming."

"I would have come tomorrow even if you people hadn't called, as soon as I read the morning paper. No, no luggage, just this. I hope you haven't been up all night to meet me."

"Oh, no, I set my alarm clock for midnight. That's my car, over there." She had to scurry to keep up with him, for despite the bulky case he bounced off the balls of his feet in an energetic stride. She pegged him for a handball player.

"Do the police always park under No Parking signs?" he asked curiously as she reached past him to unlock his door.

"Only when we know that the person on duty won't have it towed. Inconvenient, that. Do you want your case in the back? No? Okay."

Kate buckled herself in and settled down for a nice fast drive on a nearly deserted freeway. As they passed the Bufano statue, Bruckner stretched until his joints cracked and then slumped down in the seat with a little sigh of pleasure.

"Hard flight?" she asked.

"Flying is the pits. A surefire way to produce long-term symptoms of hostility towards humankind. Particularly its younger generation," he said sourly.

"I take it you didn't get much sleep. Well, there's no need to make conversation now, if you want to close your eyes."

"I'll sleep later. First of all, cards on the table. Your Inspector Hawkin said that Vaun is no longer under suspicion of committing those murders. Is that true, or did he just want to manipulate me into coming out to treat her? It's difficult to tell, over the telephone."

"Wouldn't you have come in either case?"

"No." Kate glanced over at him. "I said I would have come out, but only to see her and her family. I'm not going to bring Vaun back to life just for you people to lock her up. If that's the choice, you can let me out now and I'll make my own arrangements."

"I thought you were her friend. They say she'll die if she's left like this."

"That's her choice. She'd die anyway, if she was imprisoned again. It would be deliberate cruelty, and I'll have nothing to do with it. Vaun isn't my client, my patient. She's a beloved friend, and I refuse to interfere in her life that way merely for the convenience of the police."

Kate, hardened cop that she was, found it difficult not to be shocked. She cleared her throat.

"Yes. Well, you don't need to worry, it's obvious now that she's a victim, not a perpetrator." She gave him a synopsis of the last few days, ending with what they knew of Andy Lewis/Tony Dodson. He made no comment for several miles.

"Yes," he said finally. "I know about Andy. We worked on that for a long time, Vaun and I."

"What—" she began, then realized that he would undoubtedly refuse to talk about Vaun's revelations during therapy, and changed it to, "Is all this possible? I mean, it seems such an unlikely scenario, even to us—some lunatic who goes to such elaborate lengths to make life hell for a woman he resents, then tries to kill her, and all without giving himself away."

"Oh yes, it's quite possible. And, from what I know of Andy Lewis, through Vaun, you're probably looking at the right man."

"I wish I could understand it." Kate heard the plaintive undertone in her voice and hastened to modify it. "I mean, I've been a cop for six years now, and God knows I've seen what people can do to each other. But this one, it makes even a torture-murder look straightforward. I just can't get a handle on it, can't imagine his motives."

"The mind of someone like Andy Lewis is not finally comprehensible to a normal, sane human being. You can trace patterns, even analyze the labyrinth enough to plot its development, but motives and sequences are very slippery things, even at the best of times."

"But if he's so abnormal, why didn't we see him earlier?"

"Because he's very good at keeping up the front. When you track him down you'll probably find all kinds of criminal, even pathological, behavior, but until you pry up the lid, all will look normal. Actually, I would venture a theory that had

189

it not been for Vaun, it would have remained at that. He would never have taken to murdering children, or not for many years at any rate."

"You mean Vaun set him off?"

"Triggered him, yes. She must never suspect this, by the way."

"No. Oh, God no. You don't mean she did anything deliberately, I take it."

"As innocent as one chemical reacting with another. No, that's not a good analogy, because in a reaction both chemicals are changed, and in this case Vaun remains Vaun. Vaun doesn't need to do anything deliberately to change people's lives. Perhaps a better image is that of a black hole, one of those things the astronomers love to speculate about, so massive they influence the motions of everything around them in space, so immensely powerful that even light particles can't escape, so that they cannot even be seen except by inference, by reading the erratic movements of nearby planets and stars. Vaun passes by, utterly tied up with her own inner workings, and people begin to wobble. Tommy Chesler makes adult friends for the first time in his life. John Tyler gets serious. Angie Dodson looks at her hobbies and sees a mature art form. Andy Lewis is nudged from criminality to pathology. A psychiatrist in Chicago tears his thinning hair out and finds himself practicing a style of psychotherapy unknown to modern science, and damned if it doesn't work. God only knows what effect she's having on a couple of unsuspecting homicide detectives from the big city," he laughed. "And none of it deliberate. Vaun is as passive and as powerful as a force of nature. Her only deliberate actions are on canvas, and even then she would insist that there's no choice, only the recognition of what's needed next. Someday Vaun may be forced into action. I can't imagine what would do it—certainly not a threat to herself; perhaps to protect someone she loved—but I can imagine that the results would be spectacular. Or perhaps catastrophic."

Bruckner talked with the enthusiasm of a man finally permitted to speak about something that has long fascinated him, and Kate was not certain what was required of her in the role of coenthusiast.

"You sound like you've given this a great deal of

thought." She settled for a cheap therapist's tell-me-more noise. He caught her uncertainty and laughed happily.

"Said she, dubiously. Yes, Vaun is the sort of person one tends to think about. My wife wants me to work up a paper on the 'triggering personality' concept, but I can't see that it would do much good. After all, you can't very well treat the innocent trigger, even if the explosive personality blames him, or her. And it's hardly a new idea, after all. Do you know *Othello?*"

"Er. . . ."

"Iago is a nasty, sly, traitorous character, but even he needs his self-respect. To justify to himself the enormity of his own evil, he blames his victim Cassio for it, saying, 'He hath a daily beauty in his life that makes me ugly.' Count on it, when you find Andy, he'll blame Vaun."

"He's proving a slippery character to find."

"If you're patient, he'll come to you. Not turn himself in, I don't mean that, but he'll come. He won't be able to help himself, not now. It's gone too far. However. Enough of Andy Lewis and black holes, and chemical reactions. Metaphors and analogies are the curse of cheap psychotherapy. Tell me about Vaun. How she is."

"Vaun? No change, they say, over and over."

"I don't want that 'they' way. I know what 'they' say, endlessly. How do *you* think she looks?" he pressed.

"I don't know how she looks. She's unconscious. She looks like someone who got run over by an overdose, is how she looks. I'm no doctor."

"Good, I don't want a doctor's eyes, I want your eyes. In one word, don't stop to think about it, how does she look?"

"Dead. Dead is how she looks. I'm sorry, you're her friend, but you did ask."

"Yes, I did, didn't I?" He sighed. "All right, tell me about her. What kind of room do they have her in? Who comes in contact with her, and how do they touch her? And what do they smell like?" He spoke as if unaware of the lunacy of his words, and Kate looked closely to see if he was serious before she began hesitantly to answer him. He made short notes by the light of the glove compartment in a small note-book that he pulled from his jacket pocket, and asked more

191

questions. Then, abruptly, he flipped the glove compartment shut and leaned back.

"Right, that'll do for now. I'll need a few things—any chance of getting someone started on them at this hour?"

Kate reached for the car phone, got the hospital exchange, asked for the extension of the room Hawkin had said he would be using. He answered on the second ring.

"Hawkin."

"Sorry to wake you Al, but Dr. Bruckner has a list of things he's going to need, and it might save some time if he has them there when we get in."

"Go ahead."

She handed the instrument to her passenger, who first asked about Vaun; listened; asked about her pulse rate; told Hawkin not to bother, it wasn't that important; and asked if he had a pen. He read from his notebook: a cassette player; some roses, any color so long as they had a smell; a bristle hairbrush; some dark orange velvet; a patchwork quilt—perhaps one made by Angie Dodson?—a large pad of artist's watercolor paper; a can of turpentine; Vaun's most recent painting; and finally, complete privacy and quiet in Vaun's wing.

"That means no voices in the hall, no rattling trays, no televisions, telephones, or clacking heels. Yes, I know they'll raise holy hell, but get it done. Yes, that's all for the moment. The orange velvet may have to wait until the shops open—I'll need a couple of yards. Right, see you soon."

A smile played across Kate's lips at the thought of Hawkin following this younger man's emphatic orders and sending out for patchwork quilts and velvet at five o'clock in the morning. Bruckner's matter-of-factness was daunting—did he not consider that extraordinary list just the least bit odd? She glanced over and saw that he was studying his hands, lost in thought, slightly ill-looking in the green dashboard lights.

"Do you mind my asking what you have in mind?" she asked him. His head came up and his teeth gleamed white at her.

"My dear Watson, can you not deduce my purpose from my requirements?"

"Sensory stimulation of some kind, but some of the things seem a bit—arcane."

"Eye of newt and wing of bat," he cackled, and continued in a more normal voice. "All those things have strong personal associations for Vaun. Some of them I know from working with her in the prison—I know some of the passwords that worked before."

"So you wouldn't ask for these things for just anyone in Vaun's state?"

"Oh, God, no," he laughed. "What I'm going to do for Vaun bears very little resemblance to any sort of proper psychiatric treatment, even my more experimental approach. That's one of the reasons I insisted on complete privacy—the good Dr. Tanaka would be shocked out of his shoes by my irresponsibility. I go as a friend, masquerading as a doctor. And you are not to repeat that to anyone."

"But what—I'm sorry, you probably get tired of explaining yourself to amateurs."

"That's quite all right. You want to know what I'm going to do to make her notice those things, right?"

"She is unconscious, after all."

"Ah, but there you get into the amazing subtlety of the human mind. I suppose I ought to qualify all this by saying that I am working under the assumption that Vaun's current state is analogous to the state she was in when I first met her. Until I see her I can't know for certain, but her symptoms and vital signs are nearly identical. How much psychological theory do you know?"

"I took some classes in psychology at the university. I don't know if you'd call it theory, it was more nuts-and-bolts stuff. Rats and such."

"Well, then I hope you'll assume that what I'm going to tell you is generally accepted among my colleagues, instead of being on the outer fringes of experimentally verifiable hypotheses. I'm not going to tell you otherwise, because I'm right, and it is the truth."

His voice was archly self-mocking with an undertone of dead seriousness, and Kate smiled.

"Another question: Have you ever spent much time around a small baby?"

"A baby?" Kate was surprised. "Not really. I have a nephew and I've changed his diapers, but not much more."

"Then you may not have seen the way a very small baby can choose to block out the world when the stimuli become oppressive. Newborns in a hospital nursery, for example, can sleep despite the most appalling noise, not because, as some people insist, they're too undeveloped to hear it, but because the noise and the light and the cold, dry air and their hunger for their mothers and the strangeness of it all just overloads the circuits and the switches blow, and the whole system shuts down. That is not a technical explanation, by the way," he added with pious precision. "Severely traumatized or neglected children do the same thing sometimes, to an extreme. Even if their bodies are strong and healthy, they'll just curl up in a corner and die, unless something interrupts the process." Kate nodded with feeling, as the memory of a tiny blond girl from her first week as a policewoman came to her, a child dead not of malnutrition or abuse but from the starvation of human contact. "That is what Vaun is doing. She is not, strictly speaking, comatose. She is closer to the state we label catatonia, although normally—if 'normal' is not a contradiction in terms—catatonia is a temporary state into which a schizophrenic person retreats and comes out again within hours or, at the most, days. Normally.

"Vaun, however, is not schizophrenic. She is an immensely sensitive artist who spends a good part of every day flaying herself and laying her lifeblood out on canvas for the world to gawk at. She maintains in her life the most tenuous of equilibriums, balanced between the world's pain and her own self-preservation, for the sake of the vision and the power she can find there, and only there, hanging on the very edge of the precipice.

"Since December she has felt herself slipping. When the first body was discovered her past suddenly rose up to haunt her. The second one nearly drove her from Tyler's Road. The only thing that kept her there was sheer willpower. I have never known a person with as powerful, as one-track, as unshakable a will as Vaun's. She has carried through under loads that would crush most of us flat, but now that will has turned itself toward death. It's killing her. The growing fear of the last months, followed by the trauma of the overdose,

194

has knocked her off her tightrope, and all her power is now taking her away from the world, away from pain, into peace.

"I nearly lost her fifteen years ago. I was volunteering some time at the prison when I first saw her. She was completely withdrawn, curled fetally when they brought her out of the solitary cell. I waited in all my confident textbook knowledge for her to emerge, and a day passed, and two days, and four, and suddenly I realized that in spite of the IV her signs were weakening and she was slipping away. I worked my guts out for days, then, trying to find a way to get in, a key, some way to intervene in her chosen path. It was her paintings, of course, that made me do it. I'd go home and I wouldn't be able to sleep thinking of her paintings and of what I could do to restore them to the world. I learned more in my first two weeks with her than I had in all of my student days, and in fact my life since then has been largely an exploration of what she taught me. In my ignorance I nearly lost her, and God damn it, I'm not going to lose her now."

He was silent for a long moment, then laughed quietly.

"Have I answered your question?"

"Sensory stimulation."

"Of a highly specific, personalized variety. Do you know, it was only four or five years ago that I discovered why the smell of roses caused such a powerful reaction in her. She had come out to visit us—my wife and me—during the summer, and I found her in the garden one afternoon, tears streaming down her face, sobbing and laughing and shaking her head. She was sitting next to a couple of rose-bushes my wife had planted, and she remembered: there was a faint smell of roses in the prison's solitary-confinement cells. Some quirk of the ventilation system brought it in from the warden's garden. For most people roses would be no more than a pleasant smell. For her the fragrance was the outside world, air and sun, while she lay curling up into a fetal ball choosing to die. We are nearly there, I think? To the hospital?"

"Twenty minutes."

"If you don't mind, I'll spend the time putting my thoughts together. I need to clear my mind before I see her."

"Certainly."

Kate called Hawkin and reported their progress, and

drove into early dawn with a much-removed Bruckner, past the few stubborn press vehicles, their occupants distracted by a conveniently timed emergence by Trujillo, and up to the laundry entrance. Hawkin met them, and they wound their way through the silent, antiseptic halls to the wing that housed Vaun. The guard slipped out past them as they entered the room. Bruckner walked slowly up to the high bed and stood looking down at the sleeping woman. After a long minute he sighed, almost a groan, and with great gentleness put out two fingers to lift a lock of hair from Vaun's pale forehead, tucking it back with the others.

"My little sweetheart," he whispered. "What have they done to you?"

23

Kate collapsed for several hours in an adjoining room, and woke to find that the painting of the agonized woman, the intricate patchwork quilt from Vaun's bed, and a length of burnt-orange velvet had been delivered during the morning to the hallway outside Vaun's door. The guard sat next to them and rose when she saw Kate. Low music came from inside the room.

"Morning, Lucy. It is still morning, isn't it?"

"Barely. You want some coffee?"

"I'll get some in a minute. Anything happening?"

"Just this stuff arrived. Inspector Hawkin said nobody but you could go in, and the shrink hasn't been out, so I just left them here."

"Have you heard from him? Hawkin, I mean? Or Trujillo?"

"No, I've just been sitting here listening to golden oldies coming through the door and wishing I hadn't drunk so much coffee this morning."

"You haven't had a break? You go ahead, I'll stay here until you get back."

When the woman returned, Kate went for coffee and a

stale roll, retrieved some clothes from her car, had a shower, and returned just as Lucy was going off duty. Her replacement was a massive Hispanic man whose movements were slow, except for those of his eyes. Kate introduced himself and made sure he knew that he was not to enter the room if he could possibly avoid it, and then very quietly. She then let herself in with only a faint click.

The first thing she noticed was the bright drawing taped to the wall above the light. Teddy's effort, no doubt. Paul McCartney was singing about blackbirds. The bed's inhabitant lay as before, limp and remote. Her hair had been heavily brushed. The perfume from the roses on the bedside table rose above the pervasive medicinal smell of a hospital room, two dozen incongruously perfect scarlet blooms hacked off and stuck into an institutional mayonnaise jar with patches of the label still clinging. Next to the jar were several items that Bruckner must have brought with him: a flat box of jumbo-sized crayons, the kind designed for pudgy little hands, a package of Conté crayons, and one of charcoal sticks. Kate wondered if he was planning on some kind of sleep-drawing with the unconscious woman and wished she could be witness to it.

Bruckner was sitting on the edge of the bed, bent forward in close scrutiny of Vaun's right hand, which lay curled up on her chest. He looked around when Kate came in, winced, stood up slowly, and eased his back. He was wearing a drooping bud in the lapel of his corduroy jacket. His hair stood on end, his five o'clock shadow was verging on an early beard, and when he came over to Kate he brought the mustiness of stale sweat. They both kept their voices very low.

"How is it going?" she asked him.

"Too early yet to know. Hawkin said you'd be able to help me today?"

"I haven't heard any different. What do you want me to do?"

"Relieve me for a couple of hours. I've got to shave, and I should talk to Tanaka and go through her records so I look professional."

"There's a shower in number seventeen," she suggested.

"I am looking forward to using it." He dug a crumpled shirt and a zip bag from his briefcase, and handed Kate two cassettes. "Put these on next, and brush her hair. Don't talk to her, and try to keep out of her line of sight. And watch her."

So for two hours Kate listened to half-remembered songs by Judy Collins and Bob Dylan and Joan Baez and Simon and Garfunkel, and brushed firmly until the black curls lay flat against the head and pillow, and held her breath at several imagined movements and once at a faint noise that she decided must have come from the tape player. At the end of the hypnotic time, she was startled at the careless shock of the door being thrown open and Bruckner carrying in the canvas. He propped it on a chair against the wall facing the bed, and as she looked at it Kate realized that it had no signature. Bruckner came back with the glowing velvet and the quilt, and closed the door. She got up from the bed and went to whisper that there was no change, but his eyes swept over Vaun and the monitor that he had reattached to her, and grinned.

"Oh, yes there is. Look at her color, and her pulse rate."

Kate looked more closely, but could see no variation in the skin. The luminous numbers on the monitor had read between 55 and 58 before, and now read 59, hardly a note-worthy increase, she thought. It blinked to 60, then back to 59, and stayed there.

"No movement, though?"

"I thought a couple of times, but it's kind of like staring at a spot on a blank wall: It starts to jump after a while."

He nodded, tossed the velvet on the chair, and shook out the quilt to spread over the bed. He picked up Vaun's loose right hand and something fell out onto the folds of the bed, a small black something that brought an intake of breath and a look of slow, intense satisfaction to his face. He turned the flaccid hand over, plucked something from the furled fingers, and laid the hand down again on the bed, patting it affec-tionately. He walked around the bed to Kate and held out his hand. On his palm lay two short lengths of a charcoal stick. Kate picked them up and looked curiously at him.

"She broke it," he explained. "She felt it, knew what it was, and tightened up on it enough to snap it."

"And that makes you happy."

"That makes me very happy indeed. I'll need you again in two or three hours. Will you be here?"

"All day and tonight, so far as I know. Shall I come back in two hours?"

"Make it three. If I want you before that I'll ask Cesar or whoever's on duty to find you."

So Kate waited. She ate an overcooked lunch in the hospital cafeteria, ducked a reporter by diving into the kitchen and emerging from the back door in a white coat, talked to Hawkin when he called from San Jose, found someone to remove the stitches from the healed cuts in her back, and felt generally useless. In two hours and fifty minutes she went back to the room, and Bruckner told her what to do. She thought he was crazy, but she did it: she stood next to the unconscious woman (*did* her face seem less waxen?) telling her in slow, emphatic tones the outline of their investigation. She dwelt on Angie's concern for Vaun but not on her need for comfort; she told of Tony Dodson/Andy Lewis and his assumed guilt, though she did not say that he was missing; and finally she stressed that the police were aware and satisfied that Vaun was a victim, not a suspect, as much a victim as Tina Merrill, Amanda Bloom, and Samantha Donaldson. Then she went away, and fidgeted, and talked on the telephone to Lee and to Hawkin, and slept fitfully in a hospital bed on the other side of the wall from Vaun's.

The next morning Vaun's pulse rate was 62, and she had broken another charcoal stick and a Conté crayon.

It was a dreadful day, that Thursday. Bruckner called her in twice to repeat her story to the senseless figure on the bed and then sent her away. She couldn't go home, because he wanted her close and Hawkin had turned her over to him. She couldn't leave the hospital without trailing a conglomeration of loud people with flashbulbs and microphones. Tanaka and his assistants began to stop by and stare at the door with pointed questions, which they all knew she couldn't answer. Hawkin and Trujillo disappeared to direct the hunt for Andy Lewis. She felt closed in, forgotten, pushed to one side, bloated from the cafeteria food and the lack of exercise, and altogether gloomy about the future of the case and about her future as a detective.

At ten o'clock that night Vaun's pulse rate was 63. She had not moved. There was now a thick orange crayon in her hand. Her picture rose up at the foot of her bed, arrogant, demanding, unfinished. Bruckner subsisted on coffee and looked drawn, nearly as pale as his patient. His voice was hoarse. Kate went to bed to the whisper of music through the wall, and woke to silence. It was dark outside.

Vaun's guard paced up and down in the hallway, nervously fingering the clasp on his holster and eyeing the door, so dead silent after all these many hours. Kate met his glance, hesitated, and reached for the door handle.

The magnificent painting, what was left of it, leaned drunkenly against the wall. The canvas was sliced in two places, and the soft paint remained only in chunks and smears; the image had disappeared. A palette knife gleamed on the floor, its edges clotted darkly. Kate took two rapid steps inside, and the bed came into view.

The wires from the monitor lay in a tangle on the floor. The machine had been turned off. The tape player sat in silence on top of it. The IV bag dripped patiently into its tube and onto a growing puddle on the linoleum. Gerry Bruckner lay asleep on the bed, in socks and jeans and shirtsleeves, his right arm under the head of Vaun Adams, his left arm around her shoulders. She lay almost invisible, turned toward him under the patchwork quilt that covered the hospital blankets, her curls buried against his chest, completely within the circle of his arms. Rose petals covered the small table and spilled onto the floor, and their final perfume mixed with the fumes of turpentine and filled the room, driving out any smell of illness. Kate padded silently in and turned off the IV, and closed the door carefully behind her when she left. She stood in the hall feeling the stupid grin on her face.

"Is everything okay?" asked the anxious guard.

"I think it will be, but look, nobody is to go in there. If the nurse wants to change the IV drip, tell her it's been disconnected, she doesn't need to do anything. Nobody is to go in," she repeated, "not Tanaka, not the head of the hospital, not the President himself. Nobody. If you need me, have me beeped."

She went off humming to wake Hawkin with the first good news in many days.

Bruckner looked empty, Kate thought. It was late morning, and he had come out to talk with her and Hawkin. The psychiatrist slumped into the armchair, head lolling against the back, hands limp over the chair's arms, only his eyes moving. He looked like someone recovering from a long fever, pale, exhausted, and very grateful. His athletic bounce was gone, and he was speaking to Hawkin in a slow voice several tones lower than normal.

"I should have been back today. I can stretch it to Sunday, but I have to be there at nine o'clock Monday morning. I haven't told her yet, because she's in such a fragile state, but we must decide very soon who's going to take my place."

"Tanaka? Or one of his people?" asked Hawkin.

"It doesn't need to be a doctor. In fact, from her point of view it might be better if it weren't. She needs a friend, to protect her until she can grow some skin back."

"Someone from Tyler's Road?"

"She has three friends there: Angie Dodson, Tommy Chesler, and Tyler. I can't see Tommy coping, somehow. Angie would be ideal, but I don't know how she's dealing with her husband's role in it, and we don't want a weepy, guilt-ridden woman near Vaun. Tyler—I don't know. An ex-lover might be uncomfortable, and he's got too much on his hands as it is."

"You have somebody in mind?"

"What about Casey?"

Hawkin did not seem in the least surprised, but Kate jumped up from her chair and stared at the two men.

"No!"

"C'mon, Casey," Hawkin reassured. "She's going to need a bodyguard anyway until we get our hands on Lewis. You've done that kind of work before. You've been on this case from the beginning, and though normally you'd be too high a rank for straight guard work, she's an important lady and Lewis is without a doubt still after her."

"Al, this could drag on for weeks. Months!"

"I don't think so. If it does we'll make other arrangements. I want you to do this, Casey. I could order you," he pointed out. She saw nothing in his face but the decision, and she sighed.

"All right, then, two weeks. I'll babysit her for two weeks, that's all."

"That'll get us started anyway."

"Not here, though," said Bruckner firmly.

"No, not here," Hawkin reassured him. "Someplace quiet and safe."

"Good."

"When will she be able to talk to us? We have to get a statement from her."

"She's asleep now. I think she'll sleep for some time. Tonight, maybe? She'll eat and the nurse wants to bathe her, so about eight? But it'll have to be short."

"Twenty minutes okay?"

"That should be fine." Bruckner closed his eyes for a moment, took a deep breath, and pushed himself to his feet. "Now for the good Dr. Tanaka and writing up what I did with Vaun so that it doesn't sound like absolute quackery." He laid his hand lightly on Kate's shoulder as he went by. "Thank you, Casey."

When they were alone Hawkin went to stand by the window and light a cigarette. He smoked it and looked out between the blinds, and Kate pushed herself deeper into her chair and watched him warily.

"I've become very suspicious of your cigarettes, Al," she said finally. "I told you I'd babysit her. What else do you want?"

He turned around, surprised, and looked down at the thing in his hand, smiled sheepishly, and went across to the chair opposite Kate.

"The problem is what to do next. We can't very well send Vaun home and trust that Lewis will go away and play elsewhere. I can't very well go to the captain and say, 'Well, awfully sorry we don't have your man, but I sincerely doubt he'll try anything like it again, for a while anyway.' We're stuck unless we can track him down or flush him out."

"You want to use Vaun for bait," Kate said flatly.

"You have any other ideas?"

"She's in no shape for it, mentally or physically. Bruckner would have a fit."

"He won't know. She's a big girl, it's her decision. In ten days she'll be on her feet and Lewis will be relaxing, convinced he's shaken us, and starting to sniff out ways to get back at her."

"You're so sure about him?"

"Yes." Hard, flat certainty.

"All right, you're the boss. So what is it you're going to try and wheedle out of me?"

"You live on Russian Hill, don't you?"

The room was suddenly very cold, and a hand was at her throat.

"Al, no."

"You don't? I could have sworn—"

"Yes, I live there, but no. It's not my house, you can't ask it of me."

"A quiet, residential area with private houses, trees, dead-end streets. Looks vulnerable, but the sort of place you can plaster with eyes and ears—"

"No."

"Casey—"

"It is not my house, Al. No."

"Where, then? My place? One bedroom, bald and open, a busy street, neighbors three feet away on both sides."

"A hotel."

"Oh, well, hey, how about putting her in the county jail, with a string of crumbs leading to her and a piece of twine tied to the door to slam it shut behind him? For Christ's sake, Casey, he's not stupid. Anything unnatural and he'll sit tight and wait for six months, a year. He's capable of it. It's got to be natural, as natural as having her go to the home of a friendly police officer to recuperate and be half-heartedly watched over, because the police don't really think he'll try again."

"How would he find her? I'm not exactly listed in the phone book."

"A judicious press leak, perhaps?"

"Oh, God, Al!" There was real pain in her voice, and he relented.

"Not your address, just a couple of vague hints."

"Al, no, please don't ask me to do this."

Hawkin did not answer. He looked at the precarious ash on his cigarette and reached for the decorative ashtray on the table. He concentrated on the ash for a moment longer, took a final draw on the stub, and proceeded to grind it out methodically, like an apothecary working a mortar and pestle. His face was without expression, and when he spoke it was in the manner of a recitation of facts.

"You are right, the house does not belong to you. The house you live in is owned by one Leonora Cooper, Ph.D., a practicing psychotherapist who specializes in art and artists, particularly among members of the gay community. She was at Cal the same time you were. You have rented a room in her house for the last twenty-one months. That is all I need to know about your home life." His hard blue eyes came up and drilled into her wide brown ones. "All I need to know," he repeated, "unless and until your home life begins to interfere with your work. Is that understood, Martinelli?"

"Understood, sir," she said. Her voice was even, but he was beginning to know her well enough to see the effort of control in her jaws and hands.

"Good. This is not an order, I have no right to do that, but I would like you to ask your housemate Lee if she would be willing to move into a hotel for a couple of weeks, at our expense, of course, to give this a try."

"She won't go."

"You'll ask?"

"All right, God damn it, yes, I'll ask. But she won't go."

She wouldn't. Kate knew without thinking that there was no way Lee would go while the painter of *Strawberry Fields* was under her roof.

She also knew that Hawkin was right, that the best trap for Lewis was one that looked like no trap. She looked up at him, and caught on his face the same expression she'd seen in the parking lot outside the restaurant—approval, sympathy, and an odd element of pride. It was gone in an instant, and he stood up.

"The last few days have put you behind, so I told Trujillo he was to be available for you today. He'll bring you up to date, not that there's that much to tell. I'm going up to Tyler's Road to have a chat with Tommy and a look 'round at Angie's but I'll be back by six. Feel like going to dinner? My treat. I'll even drive."

"Sounds great," she lied. Her appetite had been ground out by the hospital air, and she doubted she would feel like eating.

"Trujillo recommended a place."

She made an effort.

"Tofu enchiladas?"

The flash of his grin made the effort worthwhile.

"A first rate Italian place, he swears. I was hoping for some edible veal. Six o'clock, then? To be back by eight?"

"I'll be ready."

He walked to the door and paused with his hand on the knob.

"Thank you, Casey." He pulled the door open, and the sounds of the hospital drifted in.

"Al?" He looked back at her. "My friends call me Kate."

24

Shortly before six Hawkin reappeared and swept Kate out by one of the lesser exits. He was in a strangely ebullient mood and hummed some vaguely familiar tune that she thought might be Bach or Beethoven, whom she tended to confuse, and ground the gears in Trujillo's sports car. They were seated in a quiet corner, draped with napkins the size of small tablecloths, and presented with three-foot-tall menus, a wine list the thickness of a novel, and a waiter who identified himself as Phil, who for the next three minutes proceeded to rattle off the day's specialties before he vanished into the gloom. Hawkin looked at Kate, and his lips twitched.

"Did you get that, Martinelli?"

"Something about pasta, and fish, I think."

"Right, I'll have the veal parmigiana."

The antipasto was good and they were hungry, Kate to her surprise, Hawkin because he loved to eat. The salad was

205

served before the entrée (chilled forks, a pepper grinder the length of Phil's arm), and Kate could stand it no longer.

"All right, Al, give. You've been clucking like a mother hen. What's up? You haven't found Lewis—you'd have told me that."

"No, not yet. But I've got the last pieces of the puzzle now. It's a nice, smooth picture, and I'm very glad to have that much."

"Your talk with Tommy Chesler this afternoon? It was successful?"

"The talk, plus a bit of honest-to-God, old-fashioned, snooping-about type detecting. I found a copy of this— behind a hidden panel, can you believe it?—in some shelves in Lewis's cabin. Angie's cabin."

"This" was an issue of *Time* magazine from the previous summer. The copy Hawkin laid on the table was stamped with the name of the local library, and had a date-due card clipped inside the cover. The other was undoubtedly in the police lab.

"Look at page seventy-two," he said, and stretched across to steal the candles from two neighboring tables so she could see.

It was the article on Eva Vaughn, the mysterious genius of the brush (as a caption read). The left-hand page showed three of her paintings, all from the New York show. The right-hand page held *Strawberry Fields* and the beginning of the article, which continued on page seventy-four with a discussion of the revival of art as psychological revelation and social criticism. A jazzy three-color bar graph, the bars represented by stylized brushes, illustrated the phenomenal rise in prices brought by works of living artists.

Hawkin reached across and flipped the page back to the beginning, then tapped one of the three reproductions, which showed two very small, grubby, naked children squatting on a dirt road, heads together, studying something on the ground between them. One of them looked vaguely familiar, and after a moment Kate realized it was Flower Underwood's little hellion who had dismantled pens and sprayed her with milk while she had tried to interview the mother.

"Tommy Chesler helped her crate this one up last June. In August this article came out, but Tommy didn't see it until

October, up in Tyler's room. He stole the magazine—took me twenty minutes to convince him I wasn't going to arrest him—and kept it in his shack next to his bed. Three or four weeks later—he wasn't sure about the date, but it was before Thanksgiving and after the first rain, which for your information was from the twelfth to the fifteenth of November—his buddy Dodson saw it lying there, and Tommy, who was just bursting to tell somebody about his role in getting that picture into *Time,* told him all."

"And within two weeks the Jamesons were burgled and Tina Merrill was dead."

"Yes, indeed. He can move fast when he wants, but then we knew that already, didn't we? So you see the nice clear portrait of a two-bit punk who can't stand it when someone gets the better of him. As a child he kills dogs and cats when he's angry with the owners, and he ends up with getting the preacher's only daughter pregnant and then beating her up. He goes away for two years, I think to Mexico—his only decent grades when he went back to school were in Spanish—learning God knows what tricks and having himself tattooed along the way.

"For some reason, boredom probably, he decides to go back to Mama for a while and puts himself into a small-town high school to strut around. Where he meets Vaun. Little Vaunie, who falls for his charm and his recreational poisons until she decides she's had enough and three weeks later very mysteriously murders a child she's fond of."

"I wouldn't want to have to go to the D.A. with only that in my hand," Kate said unhappily, and saw the last of the day's ebullience fade from Hawkin's face.

"Couldn't you just see it in court? 'So, Inspector Hawkin, you would have the jury believe that Andrew Lewis let himself in through the back door of a house, strangled a strange child, undressed her, and arranged her body to look like it did in a painting, all to get back at the child's babysitter who had hurt his pride?' "

"But you think that's what happened."

He was saved from the immediate need to answer by the arrival of Phil with their entrées. The waiter arranged their plates and hovered over them until Hawkin glared at him and he slunk off, hurt. They each had taken several hungry

207

mouthfuls before Hawkin answered her question, obliquely.

"I came across a study recently. It said that as many as a half a percent of all suspects charged with violent crimes are wrongly convicted. I can't believe that, but even if you reduce it by a factor of one hundred, that still leaves eight or ten every year.

"And you think Vaun Adams is one of those."

He sighed. "I'm afraid I do."

Both of them concentrated on the food for a while, although their pleasure was dulled. It was hard not to take a failure of the judicial system as a personal failure.

"So," Kate prompted.

"So Vaun goes through a mockery of a trial, is sent to prison, gets out, travels, ends up on Tyler's Road. He may have known she was here, or he may have come across her at the 'Faire' entirely by accident, but however it happened he found her there three years ago, and when she didn't recognize him because of the beard and the years and the hell she'd been through, he decided to stick around.

"It took him a few hours, but he found Angie that day, a simple, abandoned woman with a small child. She was charmed—God, I'm beginning to hate that word! And in no time at all there he was, living next door, unrecognized, to a woman he'd sent to prison. The one thing that strikes me as odd is that he stuck around Vaun for two years without doing much of anything, other than going off every few days to do some kind of work in the Bay Area. Probably something illegal."

"Tyler's Road would be very inconvenient, but plenty far enough from San Jose to make him feel safe."

"Maybe. At any rate, he plays this little game, living half a mile away, transporting her paintings—already crated—for her, but keeping away from her so her artist's eyes don't see who's under the beard. Until November, when all-trusting Tommy Chesler tells him that he helped box up the painting shown on page 72 of *Time* magazine, and Lewis realizes that little Vaunie isn't just making a few dollars out of her canvases, she's an internationally recognized artist whose paintings bring in five and six figures. It may have been the money that got to him, and the thought that if eighteen years before he'd played his cards right, he would now be in charge of that income. Maybe it was just the sheer effrontery of the woman, to become such a stunning success despite his efforts to crush her. Either way, his knack for a clever revenge comes into play, and he works out a way of first driving her around the bend, then destroying her reputation, and finally killing her, making it look like suicide."

Kate pulled the magazine back beside her plate, and with her left hand began to turn over its pages. She remembered it now. This article, like the one she had waded through in the glossy art magazine, was also bipartisan, divided into a pro and con. A reflection, no doubt, of the ambiguous attitude of the art world at large toward Eva Vaughn. A few phrases caught her eye, the names of Vermeer and Rembrandt again, and Berthe Morisot.

She glanced at the final paragraphs. The pro writer ended with:

In the thirteenth century the painter Cimabue happened across a young and untrained peasant boy sitting by the road drawing remarkable sheep on a stone. The child's name was Giotto. He went on to surpass his master, and it was his reworking of Gothic forms to include drama and human emotions that paved the way for the Renaissance and changed the face of European art forever. Now in the late twentieth century we have, appropriately enough, a woman, Eva Vaughn, coming to bring form and formalism back to abstract emotionalism. She has brought craft and the human heart back, in forms we thought to be drained empty, and even the most jaded are forced to see classical Realism with new eyes. Giotto's revolution came at the right time. It remains to be seen whether the vessel refilled by Ms. Vaughn can contain her.

On the other hand:

It is impossible to deny the sheer raw talent in these pictures. It is, however, a pity that such power has not been turned to saying something new, instead of a cautious, deliberate reworking of threadbare forms. Paul Klee once said that the more horrific the world, the more abstract its art. If we may apply that theory to the individual, when faced with the style of Eva Vaughn, one can only assume that the artist has led a very sheltered life indeed.

"Sheltered," Kate snorted.

"Ironic, isn't it? The rest of the article wasn't bad, but to end by quoting a man who obviously has no sense of history, and cap it off with a logical fallacy—I wonder if the writer'll be embarrassed when this thing breaks."

"It will break, won't it? It'll all be in print before the week is out."

"Bound to be. No more coffee, thanks." This last was to the waiter, who returned bearing a discreet little tray with two chocolate mints and the bill. It had been an unimaginative menu but a satisfying dinner, and after his preliminary burst of eloquence Phil had left them alone. Hawkin peeled several crushed bills apart and dropped them in the neighborhood of the tray, and looked at his watch.

"Quarter to eight. Hope she's awake. I'd like to sleep in my own bed tonight."

Vaun was drowsing on her pillows after the effort of a meal and bath, but her eyes snapped open when the two detectives walked in. Gerry Bruckner was sitting at the small corner table hunched over a neat stack of typescript with a pen in his hand. A fresh vase of roses, pink and yellow, glowed on the table next to him.

Kate was stunned at the change in the woman. She had been beautiful before, but now she was alive. The muscles of her gaunt face did not move as she watched them come toward her, glancing at Hawkin and then studying, absorbing, Kate; but her eyes, her startling blue eyes, brimmed over with life, filled to overflowing with vitality and awareness and the beauty of being alive.

"Thank you," she said to Kate. Her voice was husky but clear, and the force of the life behind those eyes made Kate want to turn away even as they held her and made her smile foolishly in response. There was nothing to be said to that, and eventually—in ten minutes? ten seconds?—Vaun re-

210

leased her and turned her gaze at Hawkin, who withstood it little better than Kate had.

Gerry Bruckner broke it, finally, when he came up to the bed and adjusted her pillows and rested his hand lightly on her head. She smiled at him, lovingly, and Hawkin cleared his throat.

"Are you feeling up to giving us a statement now, Miss Adams?"

"Of course," she said. Kate took out her notebook and dutifully recorded the details of what had very nearly been the last day of Vaun Adams's life.

There was nothing there. Yes, she had noticed a peculiar taste in the whiskey, but then she'd felt as if she was coming down with a cold, and that always made things taste odd. And yes, the heavy-duty antihistamines she'd taken had probably compounded the effects of drug and whiskey. No, she did not take chloral hydrate. She was a hypochondriac, sure, but drew the line at sleeping pills. No, she'd seen nothing out of place when she returned from her walk. No, she had not realized that Tony Dodson was Andy Lewis, but yes, she supposed it was possible, and that could account for the frisson of apprehension she occasionally experienced when coming on him unawares. She would have to think about it. No, she had not noticed that the painting of the young Andy Lewis had disappeared, but it had been in her studio at Uncle Red's farm in August, she was certain of that. No, she had done nothing very out of the ordinary that Friday, deliberately so, that being the only way to keep the fear at bay. The storm had helped distract her, and she spent the afternoon clearing up some branches, talking to various neighbors about their damage. Yes, she had seen Angie, but not Tony. And finally, yes, she had talked it over with Gerry, and though she did not wish to, she was willing to cooperate by being, in her words, the goat tethered out for the tiger. She looked to be on the verge of saying something else but changed her mind as the whole situation seemed suddenly to be more than she could deal with and exhaustion flooded in.

They left, with Bruckner speaking soothing words and stroking her clean hair, and drove home and slept in their own beds that night. Neither of them, incidentally, slept alone.

211

25

Kate had first set eyes on Leonora Cooper nine years before in a vast lecture hall at the University of California, Berkeley. Kate was nineteen, beginning her sophomore year, closed into this inadequately ventilated space with several hundred other budding psychologists on a drowsy October afternoon, the fourth lecture of the term. A new figure walked up to the lectern, a tall, slim young woman with an unruly mop of yellow hair, awkward knees, and an air of quiet confidence as she stood beneath the cynical gaze of nearly a thousand eyes, eyes that had long since learned to view T.A.'s with misgiving.

This one, however, was something different. For two hours she held those hundreds of sleepy freshmen and sophomores—made them laugh, respond, made them like her. She even made them learn something. She was less than five years from them in age—three years older than Kate—but she possessed a maturity and scope of vision most of them would never know. She took three more lectures during the quarter, and each time it was the same: the back rows of sleepers sat up, newspapers were put away, the constant undercurrent of whispers and coughs died down. Her passion for the workings of the human mind ruled them.

In the winter quarter Kate arranged to be in the section led by Lee Cooper, by the simple expedient of bribing the graduate student who was responsible for assigning students to T.A.'s. It was the best ten dollars Kate had ever spent.

The first week of the spring quarter came, a quarter in which Kate had no psychology course, and on a brilliant April morning she tapped on the door of the tiny cubicle that was Lee's office and asked if her former instructor would like to join her for a picnic up above campus. She would, and they did, and by June they were friends.

During Kate's junior year their friendship deepened, and for the first time in her life Kate found herself telling someone about her problems, her questions, her life. In the course of the year Kate had three tumultuous relationships with men, and Lee listened as the affairs first blossomed, and then became rocky, and finally fell apart in rage and pain. In the miserable cold of a wet January, Kate's kid sister was killed by a drunk driver, and when Kate returned after the funeral, stunned and unseeing, Lee talked gently and fed her tea and toast and walked with her to lectures.

Kate's senior year was also Lee's last year in her Ph.D. program. They were both extremely busy, Kate sweating her finals and Lee writing her dissertation. Over the Christmas break Kate told her family that she had decided to join the police force and spent the next days devising snappy answers to the questions repeated by person after person. Why do you want to be a cop? To see if I can clean up some of the dirt in the world. But isn't it dangerous? No more so than driving on a rainy January afternoon. At the end of it she escaped to Berkeley and went to tell Lee she'd made her decision. Lee simply nodded and said she thought it a good idea, and what did Kate think of the Bergman film down on University Avenue tonight?

During those last months the relationship between the two women developed some odd areas of tension and restraint, though Kate was not sure why. She thought it might be that the end was near, when the sheltered world of the university would throw them in separate directions, and they were preparing themselves for the wrench. Kate also had a relatively stable relationship with a man and for the first time began to think about living together, even marriage. She wondered occasionally about Lee, who had a hundred friends for every one of Kate's, who hugged and touched men and women alike, but who never, as far as Kate knew, had a lover. She even asked Lee about it once, late one candle-lit night, but Lee had smiled easily, shrugged, and said that she was just too busy.

Graduation was in June. The following day Kate was in her room in the house she shared with five others, putting her last bits and pieces into cardboard boxes, when a single tap came on the closed door. She opened it, and there stood Lee, hair wilder than ever, shirt wrinkled, face tight, her pupils dilated hugely.

"Lee! Or should I say, Dr. Cooper? I'm glad you came by.

I was going to hunt you down later to say good-bye. Sit down. Are you okay? You want some coffee or something? There's still pans and food in the kitchen. Sit down."

"No, I won't. I'm leaving tonight for New York. I decided to take that residency."

"Oh. Two years." Kate looked dumbly at the book in her hand, and she turned to arrange it with great precision inside a box of others. "I'm happy for you. I thought—I admit I was hoping you'd take the job in Palo Alto." Her hands felt cold and sweaty, and she wiped them along the sides of her jeans, then straightened and turned back to Lee. "So. I guess it's good-bye."

Lee's green eyes were nearly black and seemed only inches from Kate's. "I hope not," she said finally, and then, shockingly, she took a step towards Kate, seized Kate's head between her hands, and kissed her hard, full on the lips. When she loosed her hands, Kate jerked back a step as if she'd been held by an electrical current, and Lee turned and disappeared rapidly in a clatter of feet on the uncarpeted stairs and a slam of the front door. Kate made no move to follow her but stood for several minutes staring blindly at the open door before mechanically reaching for the remainder of her undergraduate life and packing it away into its boxes.

The stable relationship died a bitter death, and Lee was not there. Kate did not write to her about it but answered Lee's letters briefly. She graduated from the academy, made her first arrests, began painfully to construct the essential armor of distance that looks like callous indifference but which enables the cop to preserve a humanity in the face of dead bodies and abused children and the bestial inhumanity of greed.

The only problem was that the armor began to prove more and more difficult to shed. She slept with a number of men but found it difficult to rouse much interest in the proceedings unless they'd both been drinking and edged into argument. At odd moments, in bed before sleep, on patrol, doing paperwork, she would taste Lee's mouth on hers, and it never failed to bring a brief spasm of ache and a flood of repugnance. She took to running long miles that fall, and it helped. She settled in for the long haul.

Thirty months after graduation two things happened to

tumble Kate from the tenuous security she had built. The first was a letter from Lee. The second was the night when she nearly murdered a man.

The letter arrived a few days before Christmas, just before Kate left for night shift. It was Lee's first letter in months. Kate looked at the familiar scrawl and the New York cancellation, and put it unopened on the table next to the front door. It was still there when she came in early the next morning, and there waiting when she woke up at noon. She made coffee and sat in her bathrobe at the tiny table in her incongruously cheery kitchen and pulled it open. In its entirety, it read:

My dear Kate,
New York was going nowhere. The people in Palo Alto offered again and I accepted. I start immediately, on the 23rd. I won't call you, but if you could bear it, I would be grateful if you would allow me to make you a picnic lunch.

Lee

It gave her new address and a telephone number, and Kate reread it until the sour stench of boiling coffee brought her to her senses. She dumped the coffee out into the sink and started again, and pushed the memory of Lee's last sentence away as she left for work. She did not call, and the letter sat in a drawer, waiting.

It waited until the middle of January. Kate was in a patrol car, her partner driving, just after midnight on a night of cold drizzle, in one of the nastier parts of town. A faint tinkle of breaking glass sent the car accelerating forward into the next block. Two young men sprinted away from the store window pursued by the skidding patrol car, around the block and down an alley. Her partner slammed on the brakes and Kate was out in an instant, shouting for them to stop. One of them slowed and threw his hands up, but the other whirled around with a glinting black ugly thing in his hand that flashed and shot out a window far overhead, and in the same movement he let the gun go skittering across the filthy concrete and his hands went up and he began to shriek not to shoot, not to shoot, not to shoot. Kate lay sprawled with her sights on his

215

chest and her finger aching, needing, lusting to put just that much more pressure on the bit of metal underneath it, and it took all her will to block the rush of desire to end it all, as if she herself were the target rather than this blubbering, shaking boy whose cheap leather jacket filled her vision. It was not until her partner had the cuffs on the kid that the wave began to subside, and as she lowered her suddenly heavy gun she felt herself began to shake, shamefully, uncontrollably. A cup of scalding coffee at the station didn't help, and her partner, an older man she'd worked with before, and liked, told her to go home early.

A hot bath turned her skin scarlet, but not until she finished the second big gin (a drink she hated, but it was the only alcohol in the house—one of her men had left it) did the shakes turn to occasional shivers. She did not sleep, though. Every time she closed her eyes she saw the dark leather disintegrate in an explosion of blood, so she turned the heat up high and wrapped herself in a blanket, and watched the late/early movies and the farm reports and the morning news with the sound off, and at a more reasonable hour, slightly drunk, called Lee. She answered at the third ring.

"Cooper." When Kate did not respond, Lee's voice sharpened. "Hello? This is Doctor Cooper's office."

"Lee?"

"Yes, this is Lee Cooper."

"Lee, this is Kate." There was no response, so she added, "Kate Martinelli."

"You don't have to tell me your last name; there's only one Kate. You did get my letter, then. I rather hoped I hadn't mailed it. I was . . . not myself . . . when I wrote it."

"Can I come and see you?" Kate said abruptly.

"I would like very much to see you, Kate. When?"

"Now?"

"Now? I was just on my way out the door."

"You're leaving for work?"

"This is my office number. I'm on my way to the hospital to see a client. I'll be there most of the morning."

"Can't it wait?" Kate bit back her desperation. "I mean . . ."

216

"I can't put it off till tomorrow. He's dying and may not be there tomorrow. I can be back by eleven o'clock."

"Give me the address." Lee did so, and Kate wrote it down. "See you at eleven, then."

"I'm—. Thank you for calling."

"I love you, Lee."

The silence at the other end was so complete that eventually Kate thought Lee had hung up, and she said in a question, "Lee?"

"Yes. Eleven o'clock. Good-bye, Kate." Then the line did go dead.

And that was it. When Kate walked through the door of Lee's ridiculously oversized office, and Lee looked across the desk at her with hope and fear and doubt jostling one another in her green eyes, all of Kate's prepared speeches fled from her, all her own doubts and demands dropped away, and the two strong, competent professional women stared hopelessly at each other across the room, mouths empty and hands fluttering in aborted little gestures, until Lee rose from her leather chair and picked her way around the large desk as if she were walking a balance beam. She stopped in front of Kate, and Kate took the final step, and they folded into each other's arms like two storm-ravaged sailors coming blessedly into home port.

Completely, profoundly, body and mind and spirit, Kate fell into love with Lee Cooper—or rather, acknowledged the love that she had so long denied. She was amazed at the ease of the thing, almost like, she thought one day driving home to Lee, getting to the end of a puzzle and finding you'd been given the wrong pieces and then finding the right ones, and it all falls smoothly, naturally into place. With Lee it was, from the first day, so very natural, so right, skipping all the stages of flirting and the fawning erotic tension of new couples and moving easily into the feel of a long-established, successful marriage.

Life, too, seemed to slip into a remarkably smooth patch, in that way things have sometimes of imitating internal states. Kate transferred sideways into a niche in San Jose, worked her way up the ladder, attended classes, passed exams, shooting hard for promotion into the investigative division. Lee began to make a name for herself; flew to conferences and workshops, with increasing frequency as a guest speaker; discovered in herself the ability to work with terminal patients which, in combination with her training and interest in the arts, steered her straight into the gay community's epidemic. It was emotionally grueling work, and at least once a month Lee let herself into their apartment with swollen eyes and smeared makeup. But it was needed work, and she could do it.

Then two years ago Lee's mother died. Kate had never met her, and so far as she knew Lee had not seen or talked with the old woman since being thrown out in disgrace at the age of eighteen. Mrs. Cooper did not approve of lesbians. It came therefore as a considerable surprise to everyone when her will revealed that she not only had never actually disinherited her daughter but had gone so far as to leave her the house she had lived in for thirty years, a house, moreover, that was not only valuable in and of itself but was located on perhaps the most desirable acres in San Francisco. Russian Hill overlooks the financial district, the port of San Francisco (the tourist port, not the heavy cargo area), the two bridges, and the sweep of the Bay around the eastern tip of the peninsula. Cable car bells drift up from three sides, fog horns from the fourth. North Beach and Chinatown are an easy walk (downhill, at any rate) and Fisherman's Wharf a slightly longer one. The view alone was worth a million dollars. Real estate agents had fought for the listing, and Lee's future was tinted a nice shade of rose.

"Don't you want to see the place before it goes on the market?" Lee asked Kate one Saturday morning in April.

"Lee, I don't want anything to do with your mother or her house. She was an awful woman; she treated you like a dog that piddled on the carpets. I think you deserve every penny you can get out of her estate, but I don't want any more personal contact with her than the dollars in your bank account."

"She's gone from the house. Completely gone, with the last of her furniture. I think, just as a building, you really should see it. It's an amazing place. There's only a handful like it in the city. It was built by Willis Polk just before the

218

turn of the century. In another fifty years they'll want to make it into a museum. Come with me. Please?"

It was obviously important to Lee, so Kate packed away her feelings of indignation and went with her, and that afternoon she fell in love for a second time. It was a strong house, solid and honest, not overpowering in the way showy architects strive for but as a capable and supporting friend is strong. Lee showed her through the house, reviewing all the work that needed to be done, bemoaning its state of disrepair, and gradually falling silent, so that when they both drifted across the stripped and bare living room to stand at the panoramic window, no words had been said for about five minutes. Finally Kate tore her eyes from the view and concentrated on the mockingbird perched in the neighbor's large tree.

"Damn it, Lee, you did this deliberately. We couldn't possibly afford to live here. Why did you bring me here?"

"My income would cover the taxes and insurance," she said mildly.

"And we'd eat off mine? That's a lot of beans and rice, honey."

"We can change our minds any time. There'll always be a market for this kind of house."

"And move where? How the hell could you live in an apartment after living here? Be like eating cat food when you were used to caviar."

"But you'll do it? You don't mind if we try?"

"It's completely crazy," said Kate despairingly, and Lee kissed her.

It was crazy, and it was hard—hour upon hour of backbreaking, unfamiliar, filthy labor with hammer and crowbar, Skil saw and belt sander; making heartbreaking mistakes, learning new skills, working long hours of overtime to pay for this mad venture; tedious commutes for Kate, who could not shift jobs as easily as Lee; fights over bills and burst pipes.

The one great blessing, disguised though it was at first, was that it left them neither time nor money for a social life, and the cloud that had threatened from the horizon, that in fact had blackened the skies and thrown several ominous drops on them, had retreated somewhat, become an uneasily ignored factor in their lives.

Kate would not come out. She told Lee the very first day, in Lee's office in Palo Alto, and Lee, flushed and alive with the incomprehensible return to life of a dream that had begun to degenerate into mere fantasy, and believing that in this, too, Kate would change her mind, acquiesced. She had Kate; she would not risk losing her by insisting that they go public. Time would bring it.

Time had not. What had begun as a mild irritation had grown to an open sore, threatening to infect the entire relationship. The month before Lee's mother died it had flared up when Lee invited two of her colleagues home for dinner and over coffee had casually revealed that she and Kate were not just housemates. The guests left an hour later. Kate turned on Lee in a fury.

"How dare you! You promised me, you gave me your word that you wouldn't say anything about us to anybody. You probably brag about it at the clinic, 'how I overcame my lover's scruples.' Lee, how *could* you!"

"Oh, Kate, this isn't 1950, for God's sake. It's not even 1970. Your coming out might be a five-minute wonder in a very small circle, but that's all."

"No, Lee, that's not all, not by a long shot. We move in different worlds, you and I, and I can't take the risk. I'm a cop, Lee. A woman cop. If we came out, how long do you suppose it'd be before the papers managed to let slip the juicy tidbit that Officer K. C. Martinelli is one of the leather brigade? How long before the looks and remarks start, before I start drawing all the real hard-core shit jobs, before I'm on a call and someone refuses to deal with me because I'm that lez in the department and I might have AIDS? How long before some mama flips out when I try to ask her daughter some questions about the bastard that's raped her, because mama doesn't want that dyke cop feeling up her daughter?"

"You're being ridiculous, Kate. Paranoid. Look, if this were Saudi Arabia, or Texas, or L.A. even, I could understand, but here, in the Bay Area? Now? It's not news that there are gays in the department. Nobody gives a damn."

"*I* give a damn," Kate shouted. "It's none of their goddamn business if I'm straight or bent or twisted in a circle."

"You're ashamed of it. You've always felt it shameful, but Kate, you've got to face it, or it'll tear you to—"

220

"I'm not ashamed of it!" Kate bellowed furiously, and then abruptly, without warning, her fury deflated, and she looked at her lover in a despair that came from the depths of her fatigue. "I'm not ashamed," she said quietly. "It's just too precious, Lee, to allow strangers to poke their fingers into it. Yes, I'd love to go to your club with you, go to the coffee-houses, kiss you in public, but I just can't risk it. You tell me that my refusal to breathe the fresh air is stifling us both, but I know, as sure as I'm sitting here, that coming out would be the end of it. I'm not strong enough, Lee. I'm just not strong enough."

Lee let it go that night, angry at herself for handling the confrontation so badly. It was out in the open now, though, and Lee knew that Kate's refusal fully to accept herself chipped at the foundations of their relationship and cut them off from the very community where they might find strength. She could not let it lie, and two days later, on a Friday night before two days off for them both, she approached the problem again. Kate was ready for her, and blew up.

The battle lasted until Sunday night, when Kate packed a bag and left the house, saying that she had to sleep or she would be dangerous on duty. She stayed away all week. Lee went through the motions of therapy with her clients for two days, and halfway through Wednesday realized that it was impossible. She went home to think.

It took her three days before she could see the truth, three days and nights before she was sure of her facts and could analyze the situation as she would a case. By Saturday night she had to admit it: Kate's mania for privacy, her phobia of self-revelation, would have to be the basic premise of any future life together.

Subject's job, she told herself as if dictating a case history, Subject's job is one which brings Subject into constant proximity with the worst in humanity: pimps who sell children as prostitutes; men who sell drugs to melt brains; large and angry men with various weapons; drunks who stink and vomit on their rescuers; bodies dead a week in August, smelling so awful the wagon men wait outside. Subject puts her body and her mind on the line daily, in exchange for which she is allowed to be a part of one of the most powerful brotherhoods there is, men and a few women who are united in the inhuman demands made on them, a secret society in which superiority is recognized and rewarded, where the bickering and back-biting inherent in any family structure does not weaken the mystique that—give it credit—had sustained Subject for two years until she had been brought up short by the ugly, inevitable end product of distancing herself from the rest of humanity. It is the most public and visible of jobs, with the most stringently demanding code for its members. Is it not understandable that Subject refuses to risk an action that threatens to leave her without support, leave her outside the fraternity? Further, is it not understandable that Subject, to avoid being completely consumed by the demands of her job and the unwritten demands of her brothers and sisters on the force (a telling appellation), guards her true self, her private life, with such ferocity?

So. If Kate remains a cop, she will continue to guard herself, by giving herself a nickname, by not socializing with other cops, by keeping her home life a hermetically sealed secret. The question was, then, could Lee survive in a vacuum?

Another day alone, and she had decided that living with Kate was worth the suffocation. It might not always be, and Kate would change, given time, but for now, it would have to do.

She telephoned Kate at her hotel, they had a brief conversation, and Kate was home in forty minutes. Patiently, Lee set out to change Kate. Stubbornly, Kate would be moved a fraction of a pace at a time. The house came to them then, took up all their time and most of their energy, and despite the shakiness of that one cornerstone in their lives, a strength grew in them, supported them, drew them on.

They were happy. Against all odds, two troubled people had found their place and worked hard to preserve it.

They had never had an overnight guest before. Kate's job, the more vulnerable, had never intruded before. Outsiders had never entered the heart of the home. And now, they were being invaded.

THREE

THE
CITY

At birth our death is sealed,
and our end is consequent
upon our beginning.
—Marcus Manilus, *Astronomics*

———

Nobody ever notices postmen somehow . . . ; yet they have passions
like other men, and even carry large bags
where a small corpse can be stowed quite easily.
—G. K. Chesterton, "The Invisible Man"

26

At five minutes before four o'clock Monday morning Kate's car reached the top of Russian Hill and rounded the last corner before home. With considerable relief she poked her finger at the button for the garage door opener and saw the light spill into the darkness as the door rose slowly to accept them. Her passenger's eyes flew open with the sharp turn and the abrupt drop from street level, and when the door had rumbled shut she slowly sat up and looked around in the sudden, still silence.

"Home." Kate smiled at her. "You wait here for a minute." Kate got out and did a quick check of the garage—in the storage closet, in the back of Lee's sleek almost-new convertible, under the stairs. She then slid home the bolt on the garage door and went to open Vaun's side.

"We'll get you settled and I'll come back for your things."

"I can carry one," Vaun protested.

"Best not." Kate, hands empty, led the way up the stairs. She punched the code into the alarm panel at the top,

225

opened the lock with her key, and reached up immediately to still the little bell the door set to ringing as it opened. She bolted the door behind them, flipped the inside alarm switch back on, and turned to Vaun.

"I'll introduce you to the alarm system tomorrow. Can I get you anything to eat or drink?"

"I'd like a glass of water."

Kate led her down the short hallway to the kitchen. Lights were on all over the house, as she'd told Lee to leave them, and she went across and filled a glass with spring water and added two ice cubes before she realized that Vaun was not behind her. She walked rapidly into the living room and found Vaun with the curtains pushed back, the magical sweep of the north Bay spread out in front of her. The night was clear, and every point of light from Sausalito to Berkeley sparkled. Alcatraz looked like a child's toy at their feet, but Kate pulled the curtains together in Vaun's face.

"Please don't stand in front of a window with the inside lights on. It makes me nervous. Here's your water." Vaun looked like a startled deer, and Kate knew she had been overreacting. "I'm sorry, I didn't mean to snap at you, but it's one of the rules of the game. After I've checked the doors and windows we can turn off the lights, if you like, and you can look to your heart's content. You've got the same view upstairs," she added, "and higher up, though there are fewer windows."

Vaun said nothing, just nodded, and drank thirstily.

"I'll give you a quick tour so you'll know what kind of place you're sleeping in, and then take you up. Okay? This, as you can see, is the living room. If you get the urge there's a television set and VCR behind those cabinet doors." The room was the full width of the house, more than fifty feet, with high walls of virgin redwood and natural hessian and a magnificent expanse of oak floor inset with a complex geometrical border of cherry, birch, and teak. It was divided informally by a hodgepodge of mismatched furniture, a beautiful rosewood dining table with a dozen odd chairs at one end, pale sofas and chairs at the other, two inexpensive Tibetan carpets in rose and light blue and white, a number of large and healthy plants, and an enormous metal sculptural form bristling with a hundred delicate pointed bowls, each

226

one supported by a tiny, perfect human figure. Vaun went over to it and eyed it curiously, and Kate laughed.

"That's one of Lee's treasures. It's a sort of oil-lamp candelabra, from South India. Each of the bowls is filled with oil and has a wick stuck into it."

"Do you use it?"

"We lit it once, but either we had the wrong kind of oil or else it needs to be outside, because it smoked to high heaven and covered everything with black smuts."

"And we slipped on patches of oil for a week afterwards," came a voice from behind them. Lee stood in the doorway, wearing a long, thick white terrycloth bathrobe, her hands deep in the pockets. The tangle of her hair spoke of the pillow, and an angry red smudge on the bridge of her nose showed that she'd fallen asleep with her reading glasses on again.

"I'm sorry we woke you, Lee," Kate said, and made introductions.

"You didn't wake me," she said, and looked at Vaun to add, "I'm often up early."

"Lee, would you finish giving her the five-cent tour while I run her things upstairs?"

"Glad to."

Kate followed Lee's easy monologue with her mind while working the alarms, stilling the bell, and carrying the bags up from the garage to the recently furnished guest room. She then checked every window and door, every closet, and (feeling slightly foolish) under every bed, before joining the two in Lee's consulting rooms.

The suite of rooms where Lee saw her clients shared a front door with the rest of the house, but was entered by a door immediately inside the main entrance. The rooms were self-contained, with a toilet and even a small refrigerator and hot plate.

The first room was a large, informal artist's studio–cum–study, with a desk and two armchairs in one corner and an old sofa and some overstuffed chairs in another. Three easels, a high work table, a sink, and storage cupboards took up the rest of the room. In the cupboards were paper, canvas boards, watercolors, acrylics and oils, big tubs of clay, glazes, dozens of brushes, and myriad other supplies that

227

might be called for by a client putting shape to an image from the depths of his or her mind. It was a comfortable, purposeful space, but the next room, the smaller sand-tray room, was Lee's pride and joy. Kate followed the sound of voices back into it.

She had not been in the room in two weeks, and she was struck anew at the enchantment of the place. Three solid walls of narrow shelves held hundreds, thousands of tiny figurines. There were ballerinas and sorcerers, kings and swans and rock stars, horses, dragons, bats, trees, and snakes. One long shelf held two entire armies, one tin with knights and horses, the other modern khaki. Tea sets, tiaras, and teddy bears, the walls for a castle and a gingerbread dollhouse and a suburban tract house, thumb-sized street signs, creatures mythical and pedestrian, men, women, children, babies, a tiny iconic crucifix and an ancient carved fertility goddess, a porcelain bathtub, cars, planes, a horse-drawn plow and a perfect, one-inch-long pair of snowshoes. There were even the makings for a flood and a volcanic eruption at hand, when destruction was called for. Vaun was standing next to the taller of the two sand-tray tables, drifting her hand absently through the silken white sand and concentrating on Lee's words.

"—exactly right. That's why I start nonartists out in the other room, and ask them to try the paints or a collage or a sculpture. But of course, an artist is used to forming things into a visual expression, and it's not as likely to be therapeutic as the sand trays are. Here, where all the objects are already available, not waiting for manipulation, the unconscious is freed from aesthetic decisions and judgments and can just get on with telling its story through the choice and arrangement of figures and objects. The statement the final arrangement on the tray makes can be very revealing."

"Revealing to you?"

"Both to me and to the client. When they have finished, I usually come in and ask questions and comment, and I often leave it up for a while to study it, though I do have a couple of clients who do one by themselves and then put it away unless they have a question. If I know the person well enough to be sure he can handle it, I encourage it. It's all therapy."

"Speaking of which," Kate interrupted gently, "do you

think this is the best treatment for someone just released from a hospital bed?"

Vaun did look tired, despite the short sleep she had had in the car, and followed Kate meekly up the stairs, past Lee's room on the left and Kate's on the right, to the large airy room at the end of the hallway, the one with no nearby trees, no sturdy drainpipes, no balcony, and windows that framed an incomparable view of the world. Lee had put roses on the dresser, delicate, tightly furled buds of a silvery lavender color.

"Bathroom," said Kate, opening a door and shutting it. "Television," doing the same with a cabinet. "Alarm button," handing Vaun a looped cord on which hung a small black square with an indented button. "It's not waterproof, but other than in the bath wear it every minute or keep it nearby. Push it and I'll be here in ten seconds. That's my room there, if you need anything during the night. Lee's is on the other side. If you want a book, the door at the other end is what we grandly call the library."

"Does Lee really get up at this time, or was she being polite?"

"Lee keeps even weirder hours than I do. A couple of weeks ago she spent several nights at the hospital until about this time, but when she goes to bed at a normal hour, she gets up early, yes. She doesn't sleep much. Don't worry about Lee, don't worry about me. You are welcome here." To her own surprise, she realized that she meant it.

"Thank you, Casey."

"Kate. Call me Kate, please?"

"Yes. Thank you, Kate. Good night."

"Keep the button near you, and don't open the windows until I rig a way to override the alarm. And turn off the lights if you open the curtains. Please."

Vaun looked suddenly fragile, and she sat on the bed. "Oh, Casey. Kate. Really, I don't think I can go through with it. Let me go home and—"

"Oh, God. Gerry Bruckner said you'd feel like this. Please, Vaun, just turn off your brain for a few hours. You're tired and unwell and easily discouraged, that's all. Tomorrow the sun will shine. Even in San Francisco. Yes?" Lee would have reached out and touched Vaun, to soothe them both, but Kate did not.

"All right, yes, you're right. Al Hawkin is coming?"

"For lunch. Good night."

"Thank you, Kate. Good night."

Kate slept lightly, every fiber aware of the woman who slept down the hall. She woke several times, at the short rattle of a cup in the kitchen, a door opening, once a short cry of words, Vaun's dreaming voice. The doorbell woke her finally, and she lifted her head to listen to Lee's footsteps as she went to answer it. The clock by the bed said it was ten forty-two. Hawkin's voice came up the stairs, and she relaxed, lay back and stretched hard, and in a minute got up to put on her clothes and go down to greet him.

The burr of the coffee grinder pulled her down the hallway, and she found Hawkin ensconced at the little table eyeing Lee's back with an expression of uncertainty and slight distaste. Lee was wearing one of her typical eclectic outfits, in this case baggy, paint-encrusted trousers made of Guatemalan cloth, a long-sleeved blouse of smoky plum raw silk, the sleeves rolled up, a pair of moccasins Kate had bought her in the Berkeley days from a Telegraph Avenue vendor, a starched white apron Lee's grandmother had made, and a pencil holding back the knot in her hair. Nothing to inspire distaste. Perhaps the pencil?

At her entrance Hawkin's face was immediately amiable and workmanlike.

"Morning, Kate. No problems last night?" She had been given an escort to the door and had talked to Hawkin after Vaun went to bed, so he meant after that.

"Good morning, Al, Lee. You mean this morning, not last night. No. no problems."

There had been on Saturday, though, and perhaps that was the source of the look of distaste. Hawkin had come to the house to meet Lee and explain to her why she should leave, and Lee listened attentively and then, when he had finished, told him in the politest of terms that he was a damned fool if he thought she would, and why on earth should the official police assume total responsibility for a

230

human resource like Vaun? The two of them had circled each other warily for the better part of an hour, two fencers testing each other's psychic foil in feints and flurries, never quite committing themselves to outright combat.

Suddenly Hawkin had stood up and gone out the front door. After a minute a car trunk slammed and he came back in with a familiar armload: Mrs. Jameson's old curtain wrapped around Vaun's paintings. He undid the parcel on the dining table, set them up along the wall, and with a sweep of his hand turned to Lee.

"So. You're an expert. You tell me what sort of a person painted these."

Lee's eyes were filled with the wonder of them, and with an air of tossing her sword into the corner she went over to the paintings and knelt down and touched them. She studied Red Jameson and his sweating son and the innocent temptress and the painful young/old girl in the mirror and the slouching young man. After a long time she stood back and ran her fingers through her hair. Her eyes on the canvases, she spoke absently.

"What was it you wanted to know?"

"I want to know what kind of person did these."

"A woman with the eyes of a witch and the hands of an angel." She was talking to herself, and Hawkin gave a bark of derisive laughter.

"Is that what they're teaching in the psych department at Cal these days? Don't burden me with so much technical jargon, please, Dr. Cooper."

Lee flushed in anger, and swung around to face him.

"What particular aspect of the artist's personality interests you? An analysis of the change in her sexual state over the time these cover? The degree of psychosis exhibited? Perhaps a Freudian statement regarding her relationship with her parents?"

"I want to know if she could have committed murder."

"Anyone can commit murder, given a strong enough motivation. You should know that."

They glared at each other, and a faint smell as of burning hair reached Kate's nostrils. Hawkin spoke again, precisely, through clenched teeth.

"In your professional opinion, *Doctor* Cooper, could the

231

person who did these paintings have committed the cold-blooded murder of a child, under the possible influence of a flashback from a previous dose of LSD?"

Lee pulled her eyes back to the row of images and seemed to draw up a barrier as she collected her thoughts, eyes narrowed.

"In my professional opinion, no. I am not an expert diagnostician, but I would have thought that this woman would be more likely to commit a devastating murder of someone's self-image on canvas than she would an actual, physical murder, particularly of an innocent. As for the LSD, it's an unpredictable drug, especially the street kind, but I have participated in sessions of LSD therapy and studied its long-term effects, and I'd say that kind of violent 'flashback' would be extremely unlikely. But as I say, I'm no expert. I could give you some names, if you like, of people to see."

"Who would you suggest?"

She reeled off half a dozen names. "Those are Bay Area people, of course. There's a man in Los Angeles—"

"No, that'll do. I've seen all of them except for Kohlberg. She's in France." He started to gather the paintings together and wrap them in Becky Jameson's old curtain. Lee watched, and handed him the last one reluctantly.

"What did the experts say?" Kate asked.

"Pretty much the same thing." He tucked the thick bundle under his arm, paused, then shook his head in frustration, and left.

Kate had felt a sudden rush of exhaustion when he had gone, but Lee had seemed in great good spirits, and burst into snatches of song at odd moments during the rest of the day.

She was in the same aggressively cheerful mood now, Kate could tell, from the line of her back and the rapid, dramatic sweeps of the knife on the cutting board. She was using her self-assurance as a weapon, and Hawkin could only sit sourly and wait for his chance. He turned deliberately to Kate, fished a manila envelope from inside his jacket, and handed it to her.

She pressed open the metal wings and slid four glossy black-and-white photographs and three drawings out onto the tablecloth. Hawkin reached over and arranged them in

232

two lines like some arcane variety of solitaire. She picked up the first photograph and looked closely at the young face, its mouth open in a shout. It had obviously been cropped from a group action shot, with a shoulder across one corner and a leg in the foreground wearing tight white leggings and a cleated shoe.

"Coach Shapiro's?" she asked.

"Finally. The photographer did a good job on those."

She concentrated on the other three prints, which showed the same face touched up first to show middle age, then with a moustache added, and finally with a full beard. She puzzled over this last one.

"It doesn't look quite right," she said finally. "I only saw him for a minute, but the nose was different, and the shape of the eyebrows."

"Well done, considering the circumstances. Angie and Tyler agree with you. Susan took the photograph and worked it into the drawing she did last week, and came up with those," he said, pointing. Susan Chin had also done a good job. The drawing with the beard was the man Kate had seen at Vaun's house ten days before. Susan had then removed the beard and left the moustache, using the jawbones of the high school picture, and finally shaven him clean.

"That's him. He must have had a nose job, and something done to his eyebrows."

"We also know who Tony Dodson is. Or was."

"It's not just a false ID then?" She was surprised.

"Apparently not. There was a man named Anthony Dodson who worked with Lewis, and even resembled him quite a bit: same hair color, eyes, height, only fifteen or twenty pounds heavier. Lewis went north after high school, spent some time in Seattle, then got a job in Alaska on the pipeline. He met Dodson there, they became friends, spent several weekends in Anchorage. After a few months the two of them went off for a week in Seattle and didn't show up for work again. Lewis wrote a letter to say they'd both got jobs in New Orleans, they were sick of the cold, that their clothes and equipment should be given away, so long. Nothing more is heard of Andy Lewis—nothing—but Tony Dodson, who was from Montana originally, gets a driver's license in Nevada two months later."

233

"And the photo?"

"Is the same man who went to high school as Andy Lewis, given that the photograph on the license is lousy, he's ten years older and has had facial surgery."

Food began to move from stove to table to plates—avocado and mushroom omelet and hot buttery toast and orange juice fresh from the machine on the sink and mugs of thick coffee. Kate took a mouthful of the hot liquid and swirled it around her teeth, feeling the distinctive bite of the Yemen Mocha. She raised a mental eyebrow at this but didn't comment. Lee would not like it pointed out that a special effort was being made at this meal.

The cook sat down with a cup but no plate and picked up the original photograph. Several hundred calories later Kate looked over at her.

"You're not eating?"

"I had something a while ago. I thought I'd wait and keep Vaun company."

"That picture bothers you," Kate noted. Hawkin glanced up sharply and then looked more closely at Lee, whose face revealed nothing other than a slight curiosity.

"It does. I was just wondering if it would bother me if I didn't know who it was. It reminds me of someone I knew when I was in New York. Not one of my clients, though I'd seen him around the clinic. One day he told his therapist that he'd been beating up drunks, just for the fun of it, and one of them had died. She was really upset after he left, but managed to finish out the day. That night he waited for her and followed her home and killed her. He later said he'd decided it was unwise to have told her, but she'd already reported him to the police, and they were waiting for him when he got home. He didn't actually look anything like this," she waved the picture. "Maybe around the eyes." She gazed at it for another long moment, then with a slight shudder put it away from her. When she looked up it was directly into Hawkin's eyes, no swordplay now.

"As a therapist I am required to deny the possibility of such a thing as innate evil. There are reasons why people become twisted. As a human being, however, I recognize its presence. This man Lewis must be stopped. I believe that my

234

being here might help you catch him. If I see that I am in the way, I will leave. Immediately."

It was not put as an offer, a compromise, but Hawkin chose to take it as such. The two women waited as he finished his toast, placed his fork and knife across his plate, took a swallow of coffee. When he spoke it was to Kate.

"All right. I am still very unhappy about having a civilian involved, and if I thought for a minute there was a chance Lewis would get into the house, I'd scrap it now. Yes, it will look more normal to have Lee in the house. Yes, Lee will help with Vaun, and yes, it will, in theory, free up your eyes to have Lee looking after Vaun. I have to trust you on that, that you won't be distracted by Lee. And I have to trust you," he jabbed a finger at Lee, "to watch for that, and get out fast if she's looking out for you instead of Vaun. I don't like trusting too many people at once, but if we go with this it'll be your show," back to Kate, "and your judgment. If you decide to put your friend here at risk, knowing Lewis, then we'll go ahead with it. If not, or if I'm not satisfied with the safeguards, we make other arrangements. Agreed?"

Kate took a deep breath, and committed herself.

"Agreed."

"Fine. We start with this." He took an object from his pocket similar to the button that Kate had given Vaun, and slapped it onto the table in front of Lee. "You will wear this at all times. You push it, and across the street we know something's wrong. If you take it off, I pull Vaun out of the house."

Lee smiled sweetly at him and stood her ground.

"I rather doubt you'd have any legal basis for moving her around the countryside if she preferred to stay with me, but I shall be happy to cooperate with any reasonable request."

Kate busied herself with more coffee while Hawkin glowered and Lee smiled like a steel rose. Finally his lips twitched.

"Dr. Cooper. It would bring me considerable reassurance as to the safety of all in this house if I knew that you were carrying that alarm button with you at all hours of the day and night."

"I do understand, Inspector Hawkin, and I will be most happy to comply. More coffee?"

"Your coffee, my dear young lady, has been one of the

few bright spots of the last two weeks, but I think I'll have to refuse a fourth cup and make an appearance at work. I thank you also for breakfast."

He stood up, and Kate followed him to the door.

"Al, I think Vaun was wanting to see you."

"I have to be in San Jose ten minutes ago. I'll stop back this evening."

"Come for dinner."

"Oh, no, I—"

"Please."

"All right, I'd enjoy that. If the traffic's bad it'll be after seven."

"I'll plan for eight. I should warn you, you won't get food like you just had. I'm a lousy cook." He smiled. "Will you see the Donaldsons?"

"I'm afraid so." He sighed. "How many different ways are there to say, 'Trust me, we're working on it,' when she wants to know everything that's going on? I can't blame her, but it doesn't make things any easier."

"Glad it's you and not me," she said frankly, and did the alarm business to let him out. Neither of them looked at the house across and two down, whose upper floor was temporarily occupied by various men and machines. She watched him climb into his car, closed the door, and went to talk to Lee about dinner. As she had expected, Lee insisted on cooking.

That evening Vaun's photograph was on the front page of the paper. Some enterprising amateur with a powerful lens had caught her staring longingly out of her hospital window, looking for all the world like a prisoner in a cell. It was a very clear picture.

Over hot-and-sour soup, beef in black bean sauce, snow peas with shiitake mushrooms, and fried rice, they hammered out the plans for the next few days. Or rather, Hawkin and Kate hammered, Lee commented and made suggestions, and Vaun picked at her food. She kept glancing at the folded newspa-

236

per on the side table, with the expression of a person fingering a bruise.

In the end, sitting in front of the fire, they decided that it would have to be Saturday. By then Vaun would be more rested, physically and mentally, Lewis would be feeling safe and anxious to resume, and besides, it would make the Sunday papers.

"I've made preliminary arrangements with a man on the *News* staff, who's willing to go along with it in exchange for an exclusive and an interview with you," he said to Vaun, who winced. "It will, I'm afraid, mean more photographs, and your privacy all shot to hell. I'm sorry."

"After this afternoon's paper, there's not going to be much of it left anyway. It's a miracle I've managed to get away with it as long as I have."

"We may find Lewis before that, remember. Every cop in California has seen his picture by now." His offer of encouragement sounded thin, and Vaun shook her head.

"No, now be honest, Alonzo Hawkin. If you picked him up tonight, what could you possibly charge him with? I'm no expert, but it sounds to me like you have nothing at all that you could take to a jury. Isn't that right?"

"Vaun, that isn't really our responsibility."

"Of course it isn't, but there isn't much point in arresting somebody if you then have to let him go for lack of any evidence. Don't worry, I do understand what I am to do. There's no point in putting out bait if the tiger doesn't come far enough to make his intent clear, isn't that it? I shall sit and wait for him to come for me, don't worry," she repeated, but none of the other three liked what was in her face, and in each of them a special gnaw of concern started up.

"I want your promise . . ." Hawkin began, and Vaun laughed, a bleak, brittle sound.

"No, I'm not about to 'do something foolish,' as they say. I will cooperate, I will do what you tell me to do. Four lovely little human beings have lost their lives on account of me, on account of this gift of mine. It must come to an end."

There was a cold, dead undertone in her words. Lee started to speak, and stopped. Hawkin cleared his throat.

"So, we're agreed. On Saturday morning you set off for some public place like Golden Gate Park or Fisherman's

Wharf, accompanied by these two and a number of other plainclothes along the way. The three of you are photographed by our pet reporter and his cameraman, and you will appear the following morning on the front page of the Sunday paper. We'll give it three or four days, and if he hasn't appeared by then, we'll do it again. You think you'll be up to it? Vaun?"

She pulled herself back from some distant and unpleasant place and focused on Hawkin.

"Yes, yes, whatever you want. I'm sorry, I was just thinking of those three sets of parents. I wonder if they can bring themselves to read the papers anymore. I wonder what impression my smiling face eating a crab cocktail at Fisherman's Wharf will make on them. I would like to speak with them, when this is all over."

"I think it would do them a lot of good," said Lee. "But it might be very hard on you."

"What does that matter, now?"

"Well," Hawkin broke in, "first there's the minor matter of getting this all over. I suggest that a good night's sleep might help. 'Night, all, and thank you, Lee, for yet another ambrosial feast. Are you wearing your button?"

"I am." She pulled it up from inside her shirt, and dropped it back down.

"Good." He caught himself. "Thank you." He touched Vaun's shoulder lightly in passing, though she seemed not to notice or indeed to notice that he was leaving. Kate stood when he left but allowed Lee to run him through the alarms and waited for the thoughts beneath the black curls to surface. It took several minutes, and Lee was standing in the doorway behind Vaun, also waiting, before Vaun finally spoke.

"You saw that last painting I did, didn't you, Kate?"

"The one with the woman and the child?"

"Yes. You saw it in the studio that day. Gerry had someone bring it to the hospital." Its terrible beauty had been gouged and shredded beyond recognition, and Hawkin had personally seen it put into the hospital incinerator. "That was Mrs. Brand, Jemma's mother. Her face stayed with me for eighteen years, how she looked that night when she realized Jemma was dead. I started to dream about her again, last

December, and I finally had to paint her. It was one of the most . . . difficult paintings I ever did," she said with a terrible calm. "Possibly one of the best. And now it's gone."

"Perhaps—" Kate stopped. She heard the thoughtless insult of what she was about to say but plunged on regardless. "Perhaps you'll do the painting again, one day."

"Oh, no," Vaun looked up at them, with the gentle acceptance of finality in her face. "I said it must come to an end, and it shall. I will not paint again."

27

It was a terrifying week. Vaun drifted through the house like a lost soul, her hands in her pockets. She slept a great deal during the day, although her light was often on in the night. She watched the television, sitting down to whatever channel it was tuned to, game shows, old movies, British dramas indiscriminately, and would get up and wander off upstairs at times that made it obvious that she was completely unaware of the machinations of the plot. Only a cartoon would hold her interest until it was broken by a commercial.

She did not go into Lee's therapy rooms.

She ate automatically what was put on her plate, took part in conversations when she was addressed directly, seemed relaxed and good-humored about the necessary inconveniences. She even made a shy joke about being held prisoner for her own good.

Lee recognized it as one of the stages her terminally ill patients would go through on the way to the grave, and she grieved and she understood and she fought it with all her determination and skill, to absolutely no effect.

To Kate it was like watching an intelligent wild thing calmly gnaw off a trapped foot.

On Tuesday John Tyler came to the house. Kate was not quite sure how he had talked Hawkin into it, but he came in an unmarked SFPD car in the afternoon, still in ironed jeans and soft shoes but with a linen jacket as his nod to the formality of the city. No tie. His attitude too was more formal, and he drank a cup of coffee with the three women before following Vaun up the stairs to her room. They remained there all afternoon, their voices an occasional rhythm overhead, and when Tyler came down at dusk he was alone. He came to the door of the kitchen where Kate and Lee were talking as Lee stirred a pot. Lee saw him first.

"John, would you like some dinner? Just soup, almost ready."

"I have to go soon. I told Anna I'd be home."

"A glass of wine first?"

"That would be nice, thanks." Kate got up and poured them each a glass.

"I'm glad you came," Lee said. "She's feeling lost, and far from home."

"I don't think that's anything new for Vaun," he said mildly. "She feels far from home in her own house. Vaun is one of the saddest ladies I know, and where she is or who's with her doesn't make much difference."

"Oh, surely not. She has friends."

"Vaun has friends, but as far as I know the only one to really touch her has been Gerry Bruckner, and he's too central to her to be called a mere 'friend.' "

"I met Gerry. I'd like to meet Angie, too. How is she?"

"Angie is the same, only more so. This latest has not helped her self-esteem any, as you can imagine. 'A woman with worn hands and a hopeful heart,' Anna called her in one of her more poetic moods. And she teams up with a woman whose hands are now still and whose heart is without hope. Somebody better kill that bastard," he spat out. "I'd do it myself, I think, given the chance."

"You knew, didn't you?" Kate asked suddenly. "That Vaun was imprisoned for murdering a child?"

"Um. Well, yes, in fact, I did."

"And you allowed her to move in."

"I didn't think she'd done it. No, that's not strong enough: I knew she couldn't have done it."

"And in December, when Tina Merrill was found? Weren't

you just the least bit worried that you knew who had killed her, and after her the others?"

"No. I should have told you, that first day you came, but I couldn't bring myself to cause her grief for nothing. And I knew she had not done it. And I was right."

But not about Tony Dodson, Kate thought, and did not say.

"You mustn't tell the press, or anyone else for that matter, that she is completely innocent. Not yet." She tried to sound stern.

"I don't talk about it at all. I find that's usually best."

He stayed another twenty minutes, and left in the police car.

It was, for the women in the house, a truly terrifying week.

Knowing that she was far from the center of action made the week even harder for Kate. It was given out, when anyone asked, that her injuries were keeping her away from duty but in truth she would have preferred to bleed to death rather than miss this part of the case.

For it was now that the solid groundwork for an eventual prosecution was being laid, the jigsaw answers to all the questions locked into a tight, smooth picture for the District Attorney. Who? Andrew C. Lewis, alias Tony Dodson. What? Murder, of a peculiarly cold-blooded and thus inexplicable sort, murder not as an end, but as a means of building an elaborate and creative revenge. When? Could he be placed, by witnesses or evidence, near the relevant sites at the right times? Where? Now that was a good one. Where was Lewis on the days in question? Where did he go when he went 'to work'? Where were the clothes and lunchbags and backpacks of the three girls? And most important, where was Lewis now? And finally, how? How did he get to the children, how did he spirit them away, how did he avoid attracting attention?

For all that week Kate had to live with the knowledge that the case was being investigated without her, and that knowledge made it hard to stay cheerful and calm and alert. Vaun drifted; Lee went out to clients in the hospitals or the hospices; Kate fretted and phoned for updates a dozen times a day; and Hawkin and Trujillo set out to get some answers.

For the past week Trujillo, ill-shaven, dressed in grimy black pants, hideous shoes with pointed toes, and a leather jacket that he had come to loathe, sat at the bar of the Golden Grill beneath the glowing skin of the woman on the barbecue and drank himself into an irritated ulcer. He got to know the regulars, he got to know that several of the regulars who were friends with the man they knew as "Tony Andrews" had been very scarce recently, and finally he got to know a flabby, pasty-looking kid with acne who appeared for the first time on Tuesday afternoon and who knew "Tony" well enough to have seen where he lived when he was in town.

The flabby kid knew little more than that. He was a hanger-on and had not actually been to "Tony's" apartment but had only seen him come out of the place one morning, climb into his truck, and drive off. Trujillo invited the kid out of the bar, found the apartment house, and contacted Hawkin, and before too long they moved in with a large, heavily armed escort and a search warrant in Hawkin's jacket pocket.

The apartment was empty. The resident manager produced a key and let them into Andy Lewis's third persona.

It was a large apartment, furnished in tasteless luxury, up to and including a vast round bed with satin sheets and a well-stocked, padded leather wet bar in the living room. The prints of Andy Lewis/Tony Dodson/Tony Andrews were all over. Two other prints brought up the names of men with records for narcotics dealing. There was a canister of high-grade marijuana in the closet, a tin of hashish on a shelf, about fifty thousand dollars' worth of heroin tightly packaged for the street in colorful balloons, and all the attendant paraphernalia. Later the lab was to find considerable cocaine dust in the carpets and furniture. There was one loaded shotgun in the coat closet near the door, a second one in the bedroom closet, and two loose forty-five-caliber bullets and traces of gun oil in the drawer of the bedside table.

The clothes in the bedroom's oversized walk-in closet were clothes of two different men, though they were all the

242

same size and all had the same dark hairs and black-brown beard hairs in them. To the left everything was arranged on wooden hangers: silk shirts, wool suits that made Trujillo whistle, a neatly filled stack of shallow shelves holding hand-made Italian shoes. The clothing verged on the flashy, and Hawkin reflected that some of them must have looked a bit incongruous on a man with long hair and a full beard. On the right hung his Tyler's Road clothes: old work jeans, worn flannel shirts, and denims, all on metal hangers with the paper of dry cleaners on them. An odd assortment of scuffed and grease-impregnated boots and tennis shoes lay in a tumble on the floor underneath.

There was also a painting.

It protruded slightly from behind the shoe shelves, and the frayed canvas at its back edges caught Hawkin's eye. He pushed past Trujillo (who was still dressed as a bar rat and was fingering lapels enviously) and drew the canvas out to carry it into the light. At the window he turned it around, and there was Andy Lewis, just as Red Jameson had described him, half naked, slightly sweaty, a small sardonic smile on his lips, the narrow back of the chair thrusting up like some phallic structure under his chin, the dragon coiled on his upper arm.

Hawkin's tired blue eyes traveled over the glossy sur-face, searching for the painting's depths, and because he was looking for them, he found them. Most of Vaun's better paint-ings had something behind the surface image, a hidden meaning that emerged only for the patient eye, and this was one of her very best. Red had not studied this one, Hawkin mused, had been too put off by the obvious surface meaning, or he would not have worried about his niece.

It was a caricature. Skillful, amazingly subtle for a teen-aged artist, but it was a caricature. At first view it was the portrait of a young man with whom the artist was both in love and in lust. Gradually, however, the slight exaggerations asserted themselves, and soon Hawkin knew that she was not painting how she felt looking at Andy Lewis but rather how Andy Lewis imagined women in general felt looking at him. It was dated April.

Trujillo heard him laugh and emerged from the closet to

243

come and look over his shoulder. He made an appreciative noise in his throat.

"Wish some lady would see me that way," he commented.

"Do you?" Hawkin asked. A bustle in the hallway outside indicated the arrival of the prints and photograph crew, and he handed Trujillo the painting. "I want you to study this closely for a few minutes, and then tell me what you think. Be careful of it," he added. "It's worth more than you make in a year."

Ten minutes later he came back and found a confused and troubled Trujillo sitting in a chair staring at the image of the young Lewis. He looked up at Hawkin.

"But, it's . . . it's cruel, isn't it? She's laughing at him. Making fun of him."

Even Trujillo had seen it, then, given time and a hint. How long had it taken Andy Lewis to see the derision in it? Had it taken him, perhaps, until the month after it was painted? Had Vaun told him what she had really painted, when she broke up with him? Had Jemima Louise died because of this painting? And, indirectly, Tina Merrill and Amanda Bloom and Samantha Donaldson, and very nearly Vaun herself?

Suddenly Lee Cooper's words came back to him: Vaun was "more likely to commit a devastating murder of someone's self-image on canvas. . . ." This painting was her weapon, the victim as yet quite unaware that the murderous blow had been struck. Hawkin could see that anyone knowing Lewis, and truly seeing this portrait, would never take the man seriously again. It spoke volumes about Lewis's methods that he had not killed Vaun outright when he first realized what she had done. To Lewis, mere death was not sufficient revenge: hell must come first.

The apartment and its surroundings yielded no other immediately satisfying piece of evidence. The telephone answering machine gave out one succinct message: a man's bass voice said, "Tony? This is Dan. We could use a hand if you're free." There was no way of telling when the message had been left, but the state of the refrigerator indicated it had been some days since anyone had been in residence, and as the day wore on the neighbors interviewed confirmed that the last anyone had seen of him was before the big storm.

There were no papers, no address books or scribbled telephone numbers, no letters in the mailbox addressed to anyone other than Occupant. The neighbors could describe only a few of his numerous guests, and the only vehicle any of them had seen him with was the old pickup currently sitting in Tyler's metal shed.

That evening, Wednesday, Hawkin and Trujillo returned to the apartment house to catch the residents who had not been in during the day. It was tedious work, with little added to their meager store of information, until they rang the bell of number fifty-two. It was after nine o'clock, but the door was answered by a child of about ten or eleven with glossy black hair and a mouth full of braces, dressed in fuchsia-colored thermal pants and an oversized Minnie Mouse T-shirt. She peered at them gravely beneath the chain.

"Good evening, miss," said Hawkin. "I wonder if I might speak to your mother or father?"

"I do not know how I would produce my father," she said with considerable precision and an air of suffering fools, "but my mother may be available. May I tell her who's calling?"

Hawkin identified himself and Trujillo to the child, who looked unimpressed. She started to open her mouth when she was interrupted by a woman's voice from behind her.

"Who is it, Jules?"

The child stepped around so Hawkin could see her profile, which in another eight or ten years would be devastating.

"They claim," she said, "to be policemen. I was about to ask them for some identification."

"That is a very sensible idea, miss," said Hawkin firmly in an effort to retain some sort of control. He pulled his ID out of his pocket for the forty-seventh time that day and flipped it open for the benefit of the eyes, on two levels now, that peered through the gap. The door shut, the chain rattled, and the door opened again to reveal the paradigm on which the future devastatrix was modeled.

Ten pounds of gleaming blue-black hair balanced precariously on top of an oval face with brown in its genes and,

245

intriguingly, golden-green eyes surrounded by eyelids that had been shaped somewhere in Asia. Damp tendrils curled gently around the collar of an ancient bathrobe like one that Hawkin's grandfather used to wear, of a particularly gruesome shade of purple, mercifully faded. She had bare feet and heavy horn-rim glasses of the sort Cary Grant might have removed to reveal a secretary of hitherto unseen beauty, and Hawkin was very glad that he was standing in front of Trujillo because he knew that his own face would reveal nothing, despite his immediate and intense awareness that beneath the robe, the rest of her was every bit as bare as her feet. Trujillo might take a moment to regain control of his face.

"Good evening, Ms. Cameron," he said coolly. "Sorry to bother you. We're trying to find some information on one of your neighbors, and wonder if you might be able to help us?"

"Certainly. Come in." She stood back and waved them into a room so utterly ordinary it might have come from a catalog of motel furniture, onto which had been strewn a solid layer of books, covering every flat surface—heavy books with dark leather bindings and titles in gold, gothic letters, in a number of languages. She gathered a few together to clear the second pair of the quartet of metal and vinyl chairs at the Formica table, then stacked the tomes onto the table and sat looking over them. She was not a short woman but looked small beneath the hair, within the robe, and behind the books.

"I'm afraid I won't be able to help much," she said. She had a sweet, low voice, and not so much an accent as a careful precision and rhythm to her speech. "We've only been here since January, and I'm so rarely home, I haven't had a chance to get to know my neighbors."

A voice came from the sofa, accompanied by one foot waving in the air. Hawkin had all but forgotten the younger generation of this incredible race of genius-goddesses.

"My mother was recently appointed to the chair of medieval German literature at the university," said the voice, and then volunteered, "I am going to practice criminal law." Hawkin blanched at the thought of such a defense lawyer and hoped he would be retired before she came on the scene. Her head appeared over the back of the chintz. "Which neighbor?"

"Mr. Tony Andrews, in number thirty-four." He dragged his attention back to the mother. "He's been missing for some days, and his family is beginning to worry."

The daughter snorted derisively.

"So they sent two high-ranking officers out to look for a missing person?"

"Jules," her mother began.

"Oh Mother, the police don't do things that way, and besides, I've seen them both on the news. They're working on that case of the little girls and the artist."

The mother turned a look on Hawkin that made him feel like a student who had been caught in a bit of plagiarism.

"Is this true?" she asked.

"We do work on more than one case at once, sometimes," Hawkin said, trying for sternness, but it sounded weak even to his own ears. He pulled himself together. "Mr. Andrews. Do you know him?"

"No, I don't think—"

"Yes, Mother, we met him last month, don't you remember? The day you were giving a paper in San Francisco and couldn't get the car started."

"Oh, yes, him. I had forgotten his name. Nice man."

"He was not," said Jules sternly.

"Well, I thought—"

"Pardon me, miss," interrupted Trujillo. "Why did you think he was not nice?"

For a moment the child was at an obviously uncharacteristic loss for words. She quickly mustered her forces, but her answer was given with a chin raised in half-defiant embarrassment.

"I don't have a reason, not really. Nothing concrete, I mean. It was simply an impression. I did not like the way he looked at my mother. It was," she paused to choose a word. "It was speculative, without the earthy immediacy with which most men react to her."

(Earthy immediacy? thought Hawkin, uncomfortably aware of the earthiness of his own first reaction to the woman. Where does this kid come from?)

"Jules!" her mother scolded. "You sound like a bad romance novel."

"I thought it was a good phrase," her daughter protested.

"It is inappropriate."

"But accurate." Accuracy was obviously the ultimate consideration in Jules Cameron's life and, judging by the capitulation of her mother, it was a family trait.

"Was that the only reason?" Hawkin interjected, before the conversation deteriorated into semantics. "The way he looked at your mother?"

"I also found his physical appearance, his untrimmed beard and dirty hands, didn't go with the clothes he was wearing. They seemed almost to belong to a different man entirely, although they fit him well. He helped us with the car," she concluded, as if to a panel of jurors, "but he was not a nice man."

"I see," said Hawkin, trying to. He spoke halfway between the two women. (Women?) "Did he say anything to you, about where he was going, friends, anything like that?" To his relief the mother picked up the story.

"He saw I was having trouble with the car. Jules and I were looking into the motor trying to find a loose wire or something obvious when he walked by and saw us. He rummaged around for a few minutes—"

"It was the alternator lead, as I told her," Jules put in.

"—although I said he mustn't get his suit dirty. He said not to worry, he was a mechanic and it would only take a minute, and it did—he got it going right away."

"He told you he was a mechanic?" asked Hawkin.

"That's what he said. I offered to pay him, but he laughed, a nice laugh—"

"It wasn't," growled the sofa.

"—and said I should keep my money and buy my little girl a doll."

(Ah.)

"Can you believe it?" exclaimed the insulted party. "Can anyone be so sexist and archaic in this day and age?"

Trujillo was looking from fond mother to indignant daughter with a stunned expression, his mouth gaping slightly.

248

"Did you see how he left? His car?" Hawkin asked.

"No. Did you, Jules?"

"Yes. There was a man waiting for him on the street, in a red Grand Prix. I remember thinking the name of the car was funny because he so obviously considered himself a big prize."

"Beg your pardon, Miss?" said Trujillo, who was trying to write all this down. She looked at him pityingly.

"Grand Prix. A pun?" She sighed. "Grand Prix is French for 'big prize'."

"Oh. Right."

"It must've been his car, too, because the other man moved over into the passenger seat to let him drive."

"I don't suppose you noticed the license plate number," said Hawkin, knowing that if she had, she'd have given it to them right off.

She looked abashed. "I knew you would ask me that. No, I didn't. All I remember is that it wasn't personalized—I did look for that, I remember—and that it was fairly new."

"Was that the only time you saw him?"

"Yes," said Jules.

"No," said her mother, and looked at her daughter apologetically. "I saw him a couple of weeks ago. It must have been a Tuesday night, because I was coming in from my late class. He was just going out as I came in, so I said hello and thanked him again. He said he was glad to help. That was all."

"Which Tuesday was this?"

"Not last week. The week before, a couple of days before the storm."

The day after Samantha Donaldson was killed. Hawkin stared for a long minute at a book spine with a title he couldn't begin to pronounce, and thought. And thought. When he finally looked up the woman was looking amused.

"Sorry," he said.

"I do it all the time." She smiled, and his middle-aged heart turned over, and he wanted to stay seated at this horrid plastic table forever.

"What was he wearing?" It was nearly a random question.

"Something old, blue jeans and a dark jacket over a work

249

shirt of some kind. Plaid, I think. Red plaid. It looked better on him than the suit did. More appropriate."

"How did he seem to you?"

"Cheerful. Excited, almost. He looked tired as well, though."

"Do you think he killed that little girl?" breathed Jules, looking curious and doubtful and more than a bit scared. Hawkin turned from her to her mother, who just looked scared. He took out his card and wrote a number on it.

"Ms. Cameron, if you, or your daughter, see the man Andrews at any time, do not allow yourself to be alone with him, and call this number as soon as you can. He may no longer have a beard." He showed them the drawings. "I would also appreciate it if you would not talk with your friends or neighbors about this conversation, not for a few days. It could jeopardize the investigation and put people in danger." He fixed Jules with a hard eye, and she put her chin up.

"I don't gossip," she said with dignity.

"I didn't think you would," he said, and stood up to go. At the door he stopped and looked down at the child and thought of poor, confused Amy up on Tyler's Road.

"So you want to go into law?" he asked.

"It's one option," she agreed.

"Would you like to see a trial some day, meet the judge, talk to the lawyers?"

"I would, very much." From the gleam in her eye he might have been offering Disneyland.

"When this case is over, if I can work a free day, we'll see what we can do."

Trujillo stared at him as if he were crazy; Jules looked at him as if he were God; Jules's mother looked him over as if he were a distinct possibility.

In the elevator Trujillo watched the numbers change with great concentration, and they had stepped out of the box and onto the ground floor before he could no longer contain himself.

"Did you really have to ask the kid to go to court with you? I mean, God, the mother, and it's probably the only way to get to her, through the kid, but still. Can you imagine her cross-examining you?" The thought was one to give him nightmares, obviously.

"I thought she was cute."

Trujillo looked incredulous. "Cute like a cobra, you mean."

"Not so bad. And look at it this way, I may convert her to aiming for the D.A.'s office. We could use a few of those on our side, don't you think?"

Trujillo just shook his head and muttered something under his breath. It sounded like "earthy immediacy."

Hawkin let him conduct the last three interviews of the evening, which were short, uninformative, and extraordinarily dull.

28

Thursday involved sending people out to trudge through every garage, gas station, and body shop in that part of San Jose, with no luck. Friday they widened their search, with little hope, but within the hour one of the San Jose men found the garage. Hawkin and Trujillo were there in twenty minutes.

It was a big, sprawling work shed filled with men and cars and noise. The owner, Dan Whittier, was a giant with a huge belly and no hips, whose greasy black trousers threatened to descend with every step. He recognized "Tony Andrews" from the drawing, a guy who came in occasionally to help when they were rushed. First met him about a year ago, at a bar. Yes, it might have been the Golden Grill; he went in there sometimes. No, he didn't think anyone introduced them, just got to talking. No, he hadn't seen him for a couple of weeks. Yes, he'd tried to reach him, left a message on the answering machine like usual, but he never showed up. It had happened before; no problem, the work got done eventually. The number? Yeah, it was here, next to the phone.

It was the number of the apartment.

Trujillo asked a few more questions until it was obvious that to this man, Tony was a nice guy, an adequate mechanic who helped out occasionally in exchange for being able to use the facilities during off hours to work on his own cars. Offhand, nobody could remember any of his cars except in the vaguest of terms—a pickup, a red Grand Prix, a couple of old Dodges—but no paperwork had been kept on any of them.

Frustrated, they left, and looked back, and then came the little break that was to earn Trujillo his promotion. Among the many cars, trucks, and vans sitting inside the chain-link fence of the storage yard were two U.S. Government mail-delivery vehicles, the boxy white ones used for streetside delivery. Trujillo walked around the unmarked car to the driver's side and then paused and looked thoughtfully back over the car roof toward the storage yard.

"Have you ever noticed," he said slowly, "how people don't remember seeing things like mail vans? They're nearly invisible."

Hawkin stared at him, then stared at the two innocent white delivery trucks, and was one step ahead of him when they went back through Dan Whittier's door.

Dan Whittier was surprised and a bit annoyed at seeing them again, and followed them back into his office. Yes, they had Post Office vehicles here from time to time. Not regularly, just when the government's regular mechanics were swamped. Oh, yes, those they kept close records of. What dates were they interested in? Trujillo gave him the three dates. The first one would be from last year's books, Whittier told them, which weren't here now, but the second and third dates were very clear: yes, there was a mail van in during both those times, had come in two working days before in both cases, and yes, Andrews had worked on them, and yes, Andrews had taken them out for road tests, and come to think of it the last time, yes, he had been gone a long time, four or five hours, something wrong with the fuses, and yes, Trujillo was welcome to the license numbers if it would allow Dan to get back to his cars.

Several telephone calls later a police team laid claim to the two vehicles. The one that had been into the shop back in January had since been thoroughly cleaned; the one that

252

had been in on the day Samantha Donaldson had disappeared had not been and gave forth several very nice latent prints of Andrew Lewis, from places one would not normally expect an engine mechanic to lay his hand, places where a man might brace himself, say, when lifting an awkward weight from the back. More materially there were several hairs, which proved later to make as close to a match with hairs from Samantha Donaldson's head as modern forensic science could judge, and finally a small snag of blue knitting wool that was microscopically identical to the remainder of the ball in the knitting basket of Samantha's grandmother.

The postal van, the apartment, the Lewis/Dodson/Andrews tie, the rough partial print on Samantha's neck—Hawkin had a case that was air-tight.

All he lacked was Lewis himself.

Lee's dinner that Friday was the closest she ever came to failure, and it first amazed and then amused Kate to see Lee bothered out of all proportion. Kate didn't show her feelings, though, and dutifully protested as the tight-lipped cook scraped the fallen soufflé into the garbage and reassured her that carrot soup, chewy multigrain rolls, a cold marinated vegetable salad, and raspberry-walnut torte were quite enough to keep them from starvation. Normally Lee would have shrugged and served the soufflé flat, but it seemed as if the uneasy peace between Lee and Al Hawkin allowed for no sign of weakness.

However, several glasses of an excellent Pinot Noir smoothed things over, and by the end of the meal even Lee had relaxed. She shooed them off to the fireplace with a tray of coffee while she did a preliminary cleanup, and Kate put some sticks together and produced a merry blaze that added to the *gemütlichkeit*.

Hawkin sat with Vaun at opposite ends of the long linen-covered sofa and propped his feet up on a stool with the attitude of a man resting from a heavy burden. He perched his cup and saucer on his stomach and closed his eyes. Vaun pulled one leg up under her and considered him, head tipped to one side. Kate drank her coffee and wondered what the artist's eyes were seeing, the effects of late hours and human

253

ugliness that his job had carved into his face, the bone sheathed in muscle, the skull beneath the skin. She looked from him to her, and abruptly, disconcertingly, she knew that Vaun was looking at this man Hawkin not as an artist, but as a woman, with interest. The thought so surprised her that she put her cup down with a rattle and broke the tableau.

Hawkin opened his eyes and looked at her, and she had the uncomfortable feeling that he had followed her thoughts, impossible as it might be. Vaun uncurled to lean forward and fill her cup from the carafe on the table, and paused to look questioningly at Hawkin, who held out his cup to her. She poured, looked the same question at Kate, who shook her head, and they all settled back as Lee came in and took the chair between Vaun and Kate.

Twenty minutes of light conversation followed, Hawkin's entertaining story of a rock star and his current and equally famous lady friend who found themselves tumbling out the front door of the poshest hotel in town, stark naked and screaming obscenities to the amusement of passersby and the horror of the management. Hawkin told a good story. Even Vaun laughed and showed a faint flush of color in her cheeks, though whether it was from the wine or from Hawkin's story, or from his presence, Kate could not be sure.

As the laughter of his audience faded, before there could be any anticipation of what he was going to say, Hawkin put down his cup and turned to Vaun.

"It's decision time," he said, and before they could tense up, continued, "let me go over what we've got, first," and he told them of the week's findings. Kate had heard it before and had passed on abridged versions, but Hawkin laid it out in a clear series of interrelated steps, ending with Dan Whittier's garage. He waited for a moment to let it all settle in and then sat forward, elbows on knees, and studied his palms and interlinked fingers as he continued.

"When we made this plan for a publicized outing, we had almost nothing on Lewis, and the purpose of drawing him to Vaun was as much to incriminate him as it was actually to lay hands on him. That situation has changed. It will take several days for the full lab results, but I think that mail truck will provide enough evidence to nail him.

"How, then, do we take him? He could be in Mexico, but

254

I don't think so. I think he's in the Bay Area. If we took the place apart, plastered the newspapers and the notice boards with the drawings, we'd probably find him. I'd like to do it that way. There's a very good chance we'd have him in two or three days."

"And the other chance?" Vaun smiled, but he was not looking at her.

"The other chance is that we miss him or that he's already out of the area and will go to ground when he hears there's a manhunt out for him. Which leaves you in an extremely difficult position." Now he looked at her, with a sad, lopsided smile. Kate had told him that Vaun intended to paint no more, and it had hurt him, she knew him well enough now to see, although he had said nothing. "You could probably afford to hire a bodyguard, but I don't imagine you'd care for that much, not for any length of time."

"No."

"Now, I wouldn't normally ask someone else's advice on this kind of thing, but in this case I need your cooperation, and I want to know how you feel about it. Do we continue with the idea of a trap, or do we drop it and hunt him down?"

Vaun did not hesitate.

"I would like to go on with it."

"Somehow I thought you would." He grinned at her, then became brisk. "Right, tomorrow you three go out and wander around, pose for a couple of pictures and answer some questions from our pet reporter, come back here in the afternoon. Meanwhile, Trujillo or one of his people will bring that gorgeous car of yours up from Tyler's and leave it down the street with its cover on. Sunday there's a nice article and photograph of Vaun, and in the article two pointer arrows for Lewis to follow: first, that you're staying in the Russian Hill area with a couple of friends, and second, that you'll be meeting with reporters at an unspecified place on Tuesday morning. That will give Lewis two options, either to wander around the neighborhood with several hundred others, all of whom hope to catch a glimpse of you, until he recognizes the shape of your car, or to call the paper to find out where you'll be meeting with the reporters on Tuesday morning. We'll set up a trace on any such call, and if we don't get lucky, we'll wait for him to show his head Tuesday morning. If none of the three brings him to us, on Wednesday we'll go after him. What's wrong?"

"Nothing's wrong," said Vaun, "it sounds fine. It's just . . . it's so difficult to tie all this together with Andy."

"He's a bastard, Vaun," said Hawkin in a hard voice. "He's a monster inside a man's body, a creature who thinks nothing of strangling cats and dogs and little girls and sending other people to prison and into madness, so long as he has his revenge."

"Oh, God, I know, I know. You have to stop him—*we* have to stop him. You have to remember, though, he was my first lover, and to a part of me he'll always be that. For heaven's sake, Al, don't look so worried. I won't go all sentimental on you. I'll do what needs doing."

"Are you sure? It's not too late to back out."

"I am sure."

He studied her face for some hint of the future, and sighed.

"All right. I just need a word from you to get the machinery moving. Where do you want to go tomorrow?"

Lee cleared her throat. "There's a lovely show of Postimpressionists at the Legion of Honor, if you haven't seen it," she suggested. "Or some gorgeous Tibetan sculptures at—"

Vaun set her cup down with a crack and stood up, thrust her hands into her pockets, moved over to stand at the gap in the curtain and peer with one eye out at the city spilling down at her feet.

"I couldn't do that," she said lightly. "I could never look a Cézanne in the face again if I performed this farce in his presence. No, some place that can't be spoiled." She turned to face them, an odd expression around her gaunt eyes and mouth, an expression that in another, less invariably serious face might have been read as deadpan humor. She met Hawkin's eyes and jerked her head slightly to indicate the curtain behind her.

"I think, if you don't mind, I would like to go to Alcatraz."

29

After Hawkin left they dispersed upstairs, each to her separate room. Kate stripped and put on her warm robe, and went to run herself a long, hot bath. She had not slept well in many days, partly because of the omnipresent responsibility down the hall, but mostly because she did not like to sleep alone. She was tired, and edgy, and unhappy because she was not in top form and tomorrow would need her full attention. She ran the bath very hot, soaked until it cooled, and then half drained and filled it again with hot water until she felt rather boiled. She then took a rough washcloth and methodically scrubbed every reachable inch, and shampooed her hair three times, and shaved her legs. She then turned the shower to almost straight hot, and when her skin was numb with the heat she flipped it to cold and screamed silently for a count of ten. She turned it off and leaned against the tiles in relief for a moment before reaching for her towel.

She dried her hair, did her nails, cut her toenails, brushed and flossed her teeth, put on her bathrobe again, and went down the dim, carpeted hallway to her room. The heat and the water had emptied her, and she felt hollow, and more at peace than she had for many days. She could sleep now.

At the end of the hall a flickering light showed under Vaun's door, and the low mutter of the television. Kate stopped outside Lee's closed door and saw from the blue-white light under its edge that the reading light was on. She heard the sound of a page turning, and a minute later the tap tap tap of a pencil on the oversized artist's board that Lee used as a desk in bed, and a grumble as she complained to the author about whatever article she was reading. Kate smiled, reached out for the doorknob, and then slowly let her hand fall away.

In her own room she exchanged the robe for an oversized T-shirt and a pair of soft running shorts, in case of nocturnal emergencies, and crawled into her bed. Sleep came to her quickly and pulled her down into a place that was thick and black and heavy and dreamless.

Hours later a small sound broke sleep's hold on her and she struggled up from the depths, automatically fumbling for the gun on the table next to her as the door whispered open across the carpeting. She had the sights trained on the gap before she was yet awake, and Lee's outline stepped into them.

"Oh, Christ, hon," Kate blurted out. "Don't do that to me." She put the gun carefully on the table and sat up. "What's wrong?" she whispered.

"Nothing's wrong." The door closed and Lee moved surely through the dark room. "Move over."

"Lee, what are you doing? We agreed—"

"I didn't agree, you told me, and now I've decided you were wrong. Move over."

"Look, sweetheart, Vaun's just down the hallway and I promised Al—"

"You and Al didn't talk about our sleeping arrangements, and Vaun couldn't give a damn."

"But what if she—"

"If she comes in during the night she'll figure we're sleeping together. I don't think there's much that can surprise that lady."

"Aren't you going to let me finish a sen—"

"No. Shut up."

Kate shut up and moved over, and during the time that followed she made a considerable effort to maintain an awareness of the world outside the door, but there were moments when she would not have heard Andy Lewis come through the house if he'd been wearing cleated boots and sleigh bells.

Some time later Kate lay limp and purring, and spoke into Lee's shoulder.

"What was all that hostility about?"

"What hostility?" Lee said drowsily.

" 'What hostility?' I like that. And what have you done with your beeper?"

"On the table next to your damned gun. And I wasn't

258

hostile, I was healthily sublimating my hostility into a libidinous outburst. If you'd been Jack Zuckerman I would have been hostile."

"I'm glad I'm not Jack Zuckerman. I'm always glad I'm not Jack Zuckerman. Who is Jack Zuckerman?"

"He wrote an attack in the *Psychotherapeutic Journal* on that article I did for them last month. A brilliant piece of writing. His, I mean. Nasty, snide, but slippery, nothing to respond to. Leaves the reader with the distinct impression that Lee Cooper is a well-meaning amateur who would be better off leaving people's heads to the big boys like himself who know what they're doing."

"Remind me to thank him for giving you some hostility to sublimate."

"Oh, he'd like that. He has a special place in his heart for me, because he knows that his ex-wife told me all the more sordid details of their relationship when she was working herself up to leave him, and he hates knowing that I know. He also thinks that I convinced her to make the break."

"Did you?" Kate was not interested, but she enjoyed lying on Lee's shoulder and listening to her talk.

"Of course not. I didn't have to. Look," she said abruptly, "what are we going to do about Vaun?"

"Well, I was sort of hoping to help keep her from getting killed," said Kate mildly.

"Yes, but after that?" Kate smiled to herself at Lee's casual dismissal of obstacles and wished she were as sure of the outcome as Lee seemed to be.

"All right, I'll go for it. What *are* we going to do about Vaun?"

"I'll have to talk with Gerry Bruckner again, see if he's come up with anything." Lee was lying staring up at the gray square of ceiling, and had her arm been free she would have been tapping her teeth with a pencil eraser. "Maybe she should go to him for a while."

"If she wants to," Kate added, even more mildly. Lee laughed.

"I'm doing a Hawkin, aren't I? Go here, go there, do this. I do know one thing that might help her, and that would be if you would allow her to be your friend instead of doing your armadillo routine."

259

"My what?"

"Don't get all huffy, you know what I mean. Two people in the last couple of weeks have held out a hand to you in friendship, and with both of them you pretend not to see it and curl into a well-armored ball. First Hawkin, and now Vaun. Both of them would be good friends for you."

"I thought you didn't like Hawkin," said Kate, sidestepping.

"Like doesn't enter into it. I respect him. I trust him."

"Really?" That surprised Kate.

"Oh, yes. He may be hard on you, but he won't hurt you. But I do think that if you allowed Vaun to make you her friend, it would do her a lot of good. Probably more good than anything Gerry Bruckner or I could do for her. Professionally, anyway."

"All right. When the next few days are over, I promise to be less armadilloish. Armadilloid? Can I go back to sleep now? It's been lovely, but unlike some people in the room I don't function well on four hours a night."

"Shall I stay?"

"Yes. Yes." Kate molded herself up against Lee, but it was like trying to relax beside a quivering spring.

"What's wrong, sweet Lee? Jack the Sugarman?"

"Partly that, yes. He's right, you know."

"No."

"Yes, he is. I was overreaching myself in that article, trying to say something about theory without the foundations to hold it steady. Since I came back from New York I've been concentrating on therapy, on helping people keep their lives together. I don't regret it—it's important work, and I've learned so much."

"But."

"Yes. 'But.' I told you that I've been having nightmares about being eaten. I don't know how much longer I can go on without giving some attention to myself. What I've learned is too one-sided. I have to take it and work with it, test it, build on it, or else make up my mind to dump it and stick to straight day-to-day therapy. That's what Jack was saying, in his own sweet way, and he's right."

"You want to leave San Francisco?"

"Not without you. Never without you. And not perma-

260

nently. A year, maybe. Gerry Bruckner invited me to his place for a couple of months; then I'd like to spend three or four months in New York, maybe six months in Zurich."

"I'd have to quit my job."

"A leave of absence?" Lee suggested. "But look, love, this is a lousy time to bring it up, and I'm sorry. We'll talk about it another day. Go to sleep."

"You said it was partly that. What else?"

"Nothing specific, just nerves. What the next few days are going to bring."

So, Kate thought, she's not so casual and confident after all.

"I think you should go away for a few days, until it's finished."

"I won't do that. You know I won't leave. It's just that waiting and uncertainty are difficult."

"Are you scared?"

Lee did not answer.

"It isn't right that you should be in this. You don't have the training or the background for it. I'm going to tell Hawkin to move Vaun out of here."

"No! No, Kate, you can't do that; you must not. Yes, I'm frightened, but not for myself. Why would Andy Lewis want to hurt me? No, it's you. I'm often frightened for you, you know, when you're off at night or when you go all silent about a case and I know it's coming to a head. It's the cop's wife syndrome, that's all. I worry about you, but you must not change the way you do your job because of me. Please?"

"I still think you should go away for the next few days, until it's over."

"Not just yet. Vaun needs me. I'll be okay. But, you be careful, promise me that."

"Dear heart, with all the people who will be watching the house, we're safer than we would be driving to San Jose."

"Promise me."

Kate wondered at the urgency in Lee's voice, and relented.

"I promise. When this is over I'm going to make them give me a week off and you can have someone else see your clients, and we'll go somewhere. Baja? Go lie on the beach for a week and drink margaritas? And listen to some overweight mariachi band singing about doves?"

"And play with the parrot fish and get sunburned. Yes, I'd like that. I love you, Kate. Thank you."

"For what?"

"For bribing that Todd kid to get into my teaching section at Cal. For calling me one nasty gray morning in Palo Alto. For loving me."

They lay together in the dark, Lee's hand on Kate's hair, smoothing it gently. She felt Kate relax, and heard her breathing slow, until finally Kate gave a twitch and slipped back into sleep.

Two hours later Kate was awakened again, by a small noise and a change in Lee. It was still as black dark as the city ever is.

"What—?"

"Shh!" Lee hissed, and Kate heard then the sound of a door closing and the nearly inaudible but somehow distinctive movement of Vaun coming down the hall and going down the stairs.

"What time is it?" Kate whispered.

"Just after four."

"I'd better go see what she wants," said Kate. She started to throw off the covers, but Lee stopped her.

"Let her go. If she needs something she'll ask, but give her a bit of rein. I'll get up in a while and make myself a cup of tea, if she wants to talk. Go back to sleep."

Kate got up and put her T-shirt and shorts back on and went down the hall to the toilet. The hall light was on downstairs, but no sound came up. Well, she couldn't get out without Kate's knowing it, and Lee was right to say she shouldn't hound the poor woman's steps. Maybe she wanted to watch a video. Kate went back to bed and eventually to sleep. Lee got up a while later, made herself tea, and took it into the living room. There was no sign of Vaun, which meant she was in the therapy rooms.

At six-thirty Lee was still curled up on the sofa, with a journal and a cup of coffee now, when she heard Vaun come out of the rooms, go into the kitchen and pour herself some coffee, and then start up the stairs. Lee looked up from her reading.

"Do you want to talk about it?" she called softly.

The footsteps stopped, and after a long minute they turned and Vaun came to the door.

"Good morning, Lee. No, I don't think so. There's no need, really." She looked as if she hadn't slept in days, but calm. "I left it there. You can put it away, if you like." She had done a sand tray, then.

"Do you want me to put it away before anyone else sees it?"

"It doesn't matter."

"You're dreading today, aren't you?" Lee asked, careful to keep any sympathy out of her voice.

"Wouldn't you?" Vaun's voice was also matter-of-fact.

"You won't be alone."

Vaun smiled, a slow and affectionate smile.

"There is that, yes. It makes it almost bearable." She looked at the half-empty cup in her hand. "I'll go have a shower, I think. A bracing shower might help." She drained the cup and went to put it in the sink, then came back to look at Lee.

"You're very good, you know. I've met a lot of therapists, and other than Gerry Bruckner, you're the best I've met at getting down to business."

Lee was surprised and didn't know quite how to respond. Vaun nodded anyway, as if she had, and went up to shower.

At seven o'clock Lee went up the stairs with two fresh cups of coffee. Kate was awake, her eyes puffed with sleep. Lee put one of the mugs on the table for her and sat on the edge of the bed.

"I'm glad you didn't try to shoot me again this morning."

"I heard you coming. Last night you were sneaking." She wrapped her body around Lee, reached for the coffee, and sighed contentedly. "Al Hawkin was right. You can make coffee like nobody else I know."

"Vaun did a sand tray this morning. That's where she was going when she got up."

"Did she now?" Kate glanced at the closed door and lowered her voice. "Can you tell me about it?"

"She said she didn't mind. It was odd. Sad. Powerful. Extraordinarily lonely. You know how most people use the sand as the foundation for the story, a stage setting built up into hills or valleys or abstract lines and shapes—something to set off the figures and hold them upright? Well, in hers the sand was the main character. She used the larger tray, dampened the sand and smoothed it into a perfect round bowl all the way up to the top edge, nearly exposing the wood on the bottom. It looked like a circular wave about to collapse in on itself, or an animal trap, or some kind of carnivorous earth formation. This perfect wide sweep of sand mounting up on all sides, and in the middle, the exact middle, the small stub of an orange crayon."

30

Alcatraz is a rock. It is a bare, ugly, pale, oversized rock dropped down into the water off the San Francisco peninsula like an inadequate dot atop an upside-down exclamation mark. Had the rock been closer to the mouth of the Golden Gate it would have been dynamited as a hazard to shipping, or perhaps been used as the foothold for another bridge, a very different bridge from the dramatic orange spiderweb so beloved of tourists.

However, the rock was not actually a hazard. It was too small, too barren, too far from the mainland to be useful, yet too large, too close, too tantalizing to ignore. It was—it is—a jutting, bald pile, where seagulls nest and a foghorn groans, that commands an incomparable view of one of the world's few beautiful cities and the sweep of bay and hills into which it has been set.

So they built a prison there.

As a place to torment the most incorrigible of men, its

choice was brilliant: ugly walls, no privileges, nothing to do but think of the surrounding barrier of water and the unreachable beauty and renowned freedom of "Frisco." It took its first military prisoner in 1861; it transferred its last federal one in 1963; it sat vacant; it was taken over by Indian rights activists, who shivered nobly in the fog and burned down some buildings. When they left, the parks department took over, and it is now, until such a day as it is made into a gambling resort or amusement park, a place of crumbling walls and tourists with earphones following the prerecorded tour through the cell blocks, their faces preoccupied as they contemplate the room where Al Capone ate his corn flakes; the closet where Robert Stroud, the Birdman of Leavenworth, lived; and the scorches and holes in the cement walls where the great escape attempt failed.

Vaun's day out was choreographed with minute attention to detail. At no time would there be fewer than three plainclothes watchers on hand. The goal was to show Vaun in public, to the reporter Tom Grimes and to any of his colleagues who might show up, and then to spirit her away. If all went according to plan, by tomorrow noon Andy Lewis would know that Vaun was well, was free to take a day sightseeing with friends, was in San Francisco, and planned on talking to reporters on Tuesday.

Lee drove, to leave Kate's hands and eyes free, and a couple of motorcycles followed them discreetly all the way. She pulled into a parking spot on the street that a moment before had been blocked off by orange traffic cones. Kate put money in the meter and then opened Vaun's door. Lee came around and, with Vaun between them, they strolled casually to the ticket booth. A young couple with their arms around each other fell in behind, their eyes hidden behind black sunglasses, and gave a close semblance of romantic interest as they eyed the other boarding passengers.

Lee led, as prearranged, through the cabin and up to the top deck, which had benches and open sides. The intertwined couple stayed below, but after a minute an interracial one appeared up the stairs. The hard-looking black man in the slick leathers and impenetrable sunglasses and the harder-looking pale blond woman, also poured into leathers, attracted glances, but nobody would look at them long enough to remember their faces, and apart, in normal clothes, they would be unrecognizable. As he turned to sit down, Bob Fischer eased the twin mirrors down his nose with a long forefinger, winked at Kate, and pushed them back into place before sitting and taking possession of nearly seven feet of bench with his outstretched arms. The blond woman, who was the only person in the department to make Kate feel tall, was an expert in one of the more obscure varieties of martial arts. She looked like an anorectic heroin addict.

It was a glorious day, San Francisco at her spring finest. The smattering of off-season tourists along Fisherman's Wharf looked stunned at their fortune, having expected fog or rain, but the rains were nearly over for the year, and fog is a summer resident. The sky was intensely blue and clear, with an occasional crisp white cloud to cast a shadow across water and buildings for contrast. A fresh breeze raised white-caps, but the sun warmed the bones even on the top deck. Berkeley looked about ten feet away, Mt. Tamalpais was at her most maternal, and a sprinkling of triangular sails studded the blue waters where Northern California's more successful computer wizards and drug importers took a day at play.

Kate casually appraised their fellow passengers while Lee nattered on to Vaun about a boat trip she'd taken as a child. Kate had always envied Lee her ability to enjoy life even when the future held something unpleasant, whether the threat was the oral defense of her dissertation or the approaching death of one of her clients. Today Lee's pleasure in the day and the outing and the company was if anything sharpened by her awareness of the incongruity of the reason for the trip, and her pleasure was contagious. At least, Vaun seemed to be finding it so, and Kate made an effort to relax physically so as not to disturb the two of them. Nobody had recognized Vaun yet, and if someone hadn't done so by the time the group broke up on the island, it would be up to Bob Fischer to plant the suggestion in the mind of some passenger bound for shore. Meanwhile, she would do all she could to encourage Vaun to enjoy her moment of fresh air and freedom. God knew she'd had few enough of them lately, and would have no more for some time.

266

Lee was now telling Vaun about the Native American occupation of the island, a year and a half at the end of the sixties. Kate listened with half an ear. The boat was cast off and began to reverse out of the pier, and as it cleared and started its turn, a small movement near the ticket booth caught her eye. Half a dozen permed and rinsed tourist types were staring up at them, one woman's outflung arm pointing at Vaun, whose tipped head and intently listening face were full in the sun. The boat pulled away from the mooring, and Kate glanced to see if Bob had noticed. He nodded at her over a blond head. She sat back and sighed. Poor Vaun. Her public would soon alert the media. The day had begun.

They would have perhaps an hour on Alcatraz before anyone caught up with them, and Kate decided not to tell Vaun. She dug an extra pair of sunglasses out of her purse and gave them to Vaun, who put them on absently.

They disembarked, heard the ranger's lecture, bought postcards, and set off up the hill, the two couples at their heels. Through the tunnel, past the rusting, glass-enclosed guard tower, they zigzagged along beside the long-empty homes of the guards and their families, the anonymous chapel, the burnt shell of the warden's house. A handful of spring flowers waved among sparse weeds, the few hardy survivers of some gardener's suburban dream. Dirt had been transported from the mainland in the last century, back when Alcatraz was a cannon-ringed garrison defending the entrance to the goldfields. The soil was laboriously brought in with an eye to absorbing the explosive power of incoming cannonballs; what remains now grows spindly weeds.

At the island's peak they entered the prison itself, and the cold dampness of it shut off the sun behind them, although it occasionally worked its way in through dirty, high windows. They wandered along the rows of cells, into the barbershop and out to the exercise yard. It was like being inside an immense concrete and steel machine that had been turned off but not yet completely dismantled. Only a few of the more extraneous decorations had been stripped away, with the essential prison unaffected. If this were a volcano, Kate thought, looking up into the tiers of cells and walkways, it would be classified as dormant rather than extinct. It felt distant, but watchful. She wondered how it was affecting

Vaun, and whether the ex-inmate might hesitate at coming too close to the cells, but she did not. She even walked into one and ran her fingertips over the walls, where for thirty years the cell's occupants had leaned against the concrete and worn it smooth with their rough shirts. She would not, however, go near the dark, solid holes of the solitary confinement cells.

Finally they stood in the mess hall, where the last day's breakfast menu was still mounted on the wall for the tourists to photograph. Long windows on either side let in the light, and from one side stretched out the view of San Francisco that tantalized and taunted. Lee and Vaun stood there, heads together, Lee talking still, Vaun absorbing and reflecting Lee's vivacity.

"—fed them a bit too much, kept them a bit too warm, gave them very little exercise, and of course no visitors, no privacy, either physical or mental, no goal, no change in the routine. It turned men who were accustomed to action and power into soggy cabbages. They thrived at other prisons, but this place broke them. Look at Al Capone, for ex—"

Lee's voice was cut off by a sharp, nasal exclamation from the doorway.

"There she is, I told you, it's Eva Vaughn!"

Kate had seen her coming and moved in front of the two women, who whirled around at the voice. Bob Fischer and his partner stood apart on the other side of the room, looking mildly interested at the disturbance. Kate took Vaun's arm and propelled her firmly out past the group of chattering gawkers. The central figure, the woman Kate had seen at the pier, raised her voice and turned to follow but was pulled to a sudden and unexpected halt by her elbow, upon which a very large and utterly immovable hand was laid. Her face looked up, and up, into the smiling teeth and invisible eyes of Bob Fischer.

"Pardon me, ma'am, I couldn't help overhearing, but could you tell me please who you thought that was?"

His words were faultlessly polite; his stance and dress were definitely, well, big; and the thumb and forefinger grasping her arm were like a clamp. She looked into her own face staring down from his glasses, and quailed.

"I, well, Eva Vaughn, the painter, you know, down on that

Road, the little girls. . . ." Her voice drifted off as she realized that her quarry was rapidly getting away from her. She plucked at his fingers with nervous little jabs and looked desperately over her shoulder. Her husband hugged his big video camera bag to his chest and began to protest weakly. The other three ladies and two men in the group faded back a step or two and eyed each other as their leader explained valiantly about artists and pictures and maybe an autograph, for her granddaughter, who was such a clever little artist herself, you know?

After several minutes of this Bob bared his teeth hugely and loosed his clamp.

"Oh, yeah, I see, the artist, she was in the paper, I remember. You remember, Lily, down on that Road where they kept finding them little girls?"

The pale woman nodded and dropped her purse, and by the time the last errant lipstick had been rounded up by the gallant gentleman from Schenectady, Kate had called ahead on her walkie-talkie to have the boat held for them and had taken two precipitous shortcuts across the Road. The pursuers never had a chance.

Kate hustled her two charges aboard, followed closely by the other "couple" who had dawdled behind Bob and the pale "Lily" during the morning, and by a solitary older Japanese man who had been sitting on a bench at the landing with a booklet on the history of San Francisco until Kate had spoken into her radio. Kate shoved Vaun into a corner seat as the door swung shut behind them. Ropes were cast off, the engines began to work, and they were well away by the time the cluster of art lovers burst from the tunnel and slowed to a disappointed walk. She smiled grimly and turned to the man with the history booklet.

"Hello, Inspector Kitagawa. Is Tom Grimes waiting for us, then?"

"Oh, indeed, with about five hundred others."

"What!"

"Word got out," he said laconically.

"We won't be able to land, then."

"It's all right, half the department is there, too. Hawkin has a car there; he wants you to take your ladies right into it. If we let her stop to talk there'll be a riot, so he's arranged to meet Grimes later. Somebody'll take care of your car, if you'll give me the keys."

She unhooked Lee's ignition key from her ring, gave it to him, and stood up.

"I'd better go talk to the captain or the pilot or whatever he is and let him know what's going on."

"He knows."

Half of San Francisco knew, it appeared. Every tourist from Ghirardelli Square to Pier 39 must have heard, and added their numbers to the professional voyeurs. An alarmingly narrow line had been cleared by the uniformed police, a gauntlet of lenses and microphones to be run. Kate looked at Vaun to see how she was taking it and saw the same face she had met all those days ago: achingly beautiful, pale as death, and without the slightest expression or hint of life within. Vaun's hand reached up and removed the sunglasses, folded them, handed them to Kate. Even without them there was no sign of her thoughts about the chaos before them.

"Are you going to be okay?" Kate asked her.

"Probably never again," she replied calmly.

The boat bumped into the berth. Ropes were made fast, the door opened, and the gangway stretched out towards the crowd, and Vaun stepped out to meet her fate.

She walked slowly through the mayhem of shouted questions and outthrust microphones and the swell of clicking and whirring cameras, looking only at the equipment-laden belt of the chunky policeman who led their small procession through the crowd. She seemed completely oblivious to the uproar, looked only like a woman preoccupied with a minor personal problem, and allowed herself to be guided to the waiting police car and pushed in. Hawkin was there, and while Lee and Kate got in on either side of Vaun in the back seat he raised a bored and authoritative voice to inform the assembled media of their opportunity Tuesday to ask all the questions they might want, but not until then, sorry, no more comments, and with that he climbed into the front next to the driver and off they drove.

The driver spent the next few minutes shaking off several pursuing cars and vans while Kate gave Hawkin an account of the trip onto Alcatraz, Vaun stared unseeing through the front window, and Lee touched Vaun's hand

270

lightly and watched her. The driver was good, and in ten minutes they were on the freeway going south, free of followers.

They drove for twenty minutes to a huge, anonymous motel three hundred yards from the freeway, went directly to room 1046, and ordered a room service lunch. Vaun asked for tea. The food arrived, and on its heels came Tom Grimes and his photographer.

"You weren't followed?" Hawkin asked him at the door.

"I wasn't followed, Al, don't bust a gusset. Is she here?"

"You can have fifteen minutes," Hawkin growled, and let him in.

Hawkin and Kate stood and munched; Lee picked at a sandwich and watched over Vaun like a mother dog with a litter of one; the cameraman squinted over his cigarette and filled the anonymous room with equipment and harsh white light. Grimes set a small tape recorder on the table in front of Vaun, who sat at the center of it all in a plastic chair, feet together, hands in her lap, as calm as a royal personage on her way to the block. She answered his questions as if she were reading them from a page; she was impersonal, non-committal, but honest.

She told him that yes, she was Eva Vaughn, and also Siobhan Adams, that yes, she was the Siobhan Adams who had been convicted of murder, and no, she had not committed these recent murders, had in fact nearly been murdered herself. Who did them, then, and why was she involved? She could not comment on that question, not until the police investigation had been completed. Grimes had not expected an answer, and he went on. How long had she been living on Tyler's Road? Almost five years. No, her neighbors had not known who she was, either as artist or as murderess. Yes, she painted there. Yes, some of them appeared in her paintings.

On and on, human interest questions for the most part, as Grimes could fill in the rest for himself. Through it all Vaun maintained an air of polite disinterest, until nearly the end. Hawkin had just stuck his head out the door to signal the driver that they were nearly ready, and the photographer was packing up his lenses and paraphernalia.

"A last question, Miss Vaughn," said Grimes, casting

about in desperation for a quote with some zing to it. "I'm curious about your name change. Did you have any reason for choosing the name Eva Vaughn?"

This unexpected question caught Vaun's attention, and for the first time she seemed to look at him.

"Adam and Eve were the same person, weren't they? Two halves of a whole. It wasn't really a name change at all."

"Are you a religious person, then?" Grimes tried not to sound surprised, as if Vaun was about to declare herself a born-again believer, and at that she fixed the full gaze of her remarkable eyes upon him and smiled gently.

"Not church-religious, no. But a person who has been through what I have is not apt to find such thoughts . . . without interest."

The camera flashed a final time, and in three minutes they were back on the freeway, going north. The driver went off on the second exit, drove east for a few miles, and joined the other northbound freeway. Hawkin nodded and eased his neck. No followers.

Kate leaned forward in her seat, and Hawkin half twisted to talk with her.

"There were television people in that lot at the pier," she noted. "How much do you suppose they'll put on tonight?"

"They're sure to have something. Saturdays are always slow."

"Anyway, Lee and I will stay inside from now on, as there's sure to be people wandering up and down the street. Hopefully it'll be a couple of days before one of the neighbors squeals on us. Lee has to go out tomorrow afternoon to see one of her clients at the hospice, and she has two people coming to the house, one tonight and one Monday night, that she really doesn't want to put off. The rest she's cancelled. Is that okay?"

"Let the guys across the street know exactly who they are and when they're coming, so they don't get nervous. There's no point in locking yourselves off entirely, so long as—" He stopped with a look of astonishment, and Kate jerked around to look at Vaun.

She had broken, at last. Her eyes were shut and her mouth open in a little mewling o, and she was trembling. Her hands came up to cover her face, and she twisted toward

272

Lee, who held out her arms, and Vaun went blindly into them and curled up as best she could, with her head in Lee's lap, and with Lee's arms and upper body bent fiercely around her. She huddled there all the way home, and Lee rocked her and murmured to her. The others sat silent with their thoughts.

Vaun spent the rest of the afternoon upstairs. Lee cooked, making croissants from scratch and an elaborate *salade niçoise* with fourteen separate marinated ingredients that took her several hours and filled the kitchen with pans, and might have been iceberg lettuce with bottled dressing for all any of them tasted it. Kate prowled the house until her nerves were jangling, and finally disappeared into the basement to pedal the exercise bicycle for an hour. She came up dripping and had a glass of wine, showered and had another glass, and watched the local news, including the amateur videotape of the backs of three blurred women, after which she felt like having several more glasses but did not.

When the news was over Lee went upstairs with a glass of whiskey, which she made Vaun drink, and then came back and set out the dinner, which they all picked at. Finally she took the food away and went to make coffee. Kate and Vaun cleared the table, but to Kate's surprise Vaun, instead of retreating upstairs, went to sit on the sofa. Kate obligingly laid and lit a fire and wondered if Vaun just wanted company. She fetched the coffee tray and poured them each a cup.

"Do you feel like a game of chess, or checkers? Backgammon?" she offered.

"No, thanks. I'd like to tell you something, you and Lee. Something about myself."

The hum and swish of the dishwasher started up in the kitchen, and Lee came in for her coffee. Vaun rattled her cup onto the table and got up to make a silent circuit of the room, touching things. When she got back to the sofa she folded herself up into it and simply started talking. For the next two and a half hours she talked and talked, as if she had prepared it all in advance, as if she never intended to stop.

273

31

"I cannot remember a time when my hands were not making a drawing," Vaun started. "My very earliest memory is of a birthday party, when I was two—I have a photograph that my aunt sent me four or five years ago, and it has the date on it. One of my presents was a box of those thick children's crayons and a big pad of paper. I remember vividly the sensation of pulling open the top of the box, and there was this beguiling row of eight perfect, smooth, brightly colored truncated cones, lying snugly in the cardboard. They had the most exciting smell I'd ever known. I took one out of the box—the orange one—and I made this slow, curving line on the pad. There were all these other presents sitting piled around me, but I wouldn't even look at them, I was so fascinated with the way the crayon tip made this sharp line and the flat bottom made a cobwebby wide rough line, and how I could make a heavy line of brighter orange when I pushed hard, and the way it looked when I scribbled it over and over in one place. I can still see it, my fat little hand clenched around that magical orange stick, and the thrill of it, the incredible excitement of watching those lines appear on that clean, white paper.

"My poor mother, she must have looked back on that day with loathing. Everything she hated, everything she feared, there it was, welling up in her sweet, curly-haired, two-year-old daughter."

Vaun smiled crookedly and leaned forward to refill her cup. She put down the pot and poured a dollop of cream into the black liquid, where it billowed up thickly to the surface. She watched intently the color change, her mind far away.

"My mother was born in Paris, just after the First World War. Her father considered himself an artist, but he had absolutely no talent, other than for latching on to real artists and drinking their wine. He and my grandmother weren't married, but she put up with him until the winter of 1925, when my mother, who was about six, nearly died of pneumonia from living in an unheated attic. Grandmother decided to emigrate to California, so when he was out at a weekend party in the country she gathered up all the presents he'd been given, or helped himself to, including several respectable canvases, sold them, and bought passage for herself and my mother to New York. It took five years to work her way to San Francisco, but they made it eventually. She married when my mother was twelve, and had two more children, Red and another daughter who died young, but she never let up on her first child and drilled into her the unrelenting image of an artist as someone who steals, drinks, and is willing to allow his own daughter to die of neglect in his self-absorption.

"In due course my mother married a man who was as far from the art world as she could get. He was an accountant. He rarely drank, his parents lived in the same house they'd bought when they were first married, and he hadn't been inside an art gallery or museum since high school. Utterly stable, unimaginative, twelve years older than my mother, completely devoted to her, and, I think, somewhat awed by her sharp mind and beauty. A good man, and if he wasn't exactly what my mother needed, he was certainly what she wanted. The snapshots he took of her in those early years show a happy woman. Until my second birthday. They didn't have any other children, though as far as I know there was no physical problem. And I never had another big birthday party—she was probably afraid of having someone give me a set of paints or something.

"Of course, at the time I knew nothing of her background, why she so furiously hated my obsession with drawing. I was probably too young, even if she'd tried to tell me, but she never did try. It was only recently, about five years ago, that I finally pieced it together."

"And how did you feel about it?" Lee asked curiously.

"Vastly relieved. When I was young I thought it was my fault, and that my inability to control myself led to their deaths. Later I put it onto her, and it seemed to me that she was a sick, jealous woman. After I dug out the truth and learned about her parents, I felt a tremendous relief. It wasn't my fault, it wasn't even her fault. It was inevitable, perhaps; certainly acceptable.

275

"I wonder too if her phobia didn't drive me more deeply into it. It would have been there anyway, but perhaps a more gentle, natural talent. As it was, her continual attempts to distract me, find other interests, pull me away from my crayons and pencils served only to make me more completely single-minded. I wasn't interested in toys; I didn't want to play with other kids; I just wanted to draw. Before I was four, the lower half of the house walls were a disaster, and nobody could put down a piece of paper or a pen without my making off with it. I can remember having a screaming tantrum one day when she tried to get me past the crayons in the grocery store. It must have been one unending nightmare.

"When I started going to nursery school, at about four, at first the teachers were overjoyed with this little kid who could do the most amazingly mature drawings. After a few weeks, though, they got very tired of fighting to drag me out into the playground, or sit and listen to a story, or do all the things normal, well-balanced kids do. That's when I started going to a psychiatrist.

"I must have gone through a dozen of them in the next couple of years. The earlier ones were mostly women, and looking back I think that at first they all figured that I just needed a firm hand and an understanding ear. When that made no difference they'd begin to suggest that perhaps they should be treating Mother instead, and soon I'd go off to another one.

"When I was about five, maybe six, they began to be men, rather than women, and older, and more serious. I remember asking my mother once why some of them had framed pictures on their walls that had only writing on them, and she explained about diplomas and the like.

"Finally, when I was seven, we met Dr. Hofstetter. He had a whole wall of framed diplomas and letters in his waiting room, and I was intrigued with the pattern of the black frames against the white paper and the beige wall. Four of them had red seals, beautiful symmetrical sunbursts that leapt out from the wall, the color of blood.

"I spent several months with Dr. Hofstetter, talking about what I liked to draw and looking at books, and finally he must have decided that radical therapy was needed, because one afternoon my father took me out to a movie—it was the beginning of summer vacation—and when we came home there was not a single writing instrument in the entire house. No crayons; no paint; no pens, pencils, or chalk. I was furious. They had to use tranquilizers to get me to sleep that night. The next morning I poured my porridge onto the table and drew in it, so my mother started to feed me by spoon. If I went outside I'd use a stick in the dirt, so I stayed in. I made patterns with soap on the bathroom tiles, so I wasn't allowed to bathe myself.

"I stood it for five days. I just couldn't understand why they were doing it to me. It was like being told not to breathe. I felt like I was going to explode, and finally on the sixth day I wouldn't get out of bed, wouldn't eat or drink, and wet myself. Mother bundled me off to the shrink, who tried to explain that it was for my own good. I just sat there, staring straight ahead, not really hearing his voice, and finally he gave up and led me out to the waiting room while he and my mother went into his office. I could hear their voices, hers very upset, and his receptionist in the next room typing and making telephone calls while I sat there in the stuffed chair and looked at the pattern of the frames on his wall, and the red sunbursts.

"As I sat there, alone in the world with those seals, they began to bother me. They were wrongly arranged, out of balance, and the more I studied them, my mother's voice rising and falling in the background, the more they bothered me. It needed another spot of red, just up there, on the upper right, above the sofa, and I reached in the pocket of my coat for my crayons, but of course they weren't there, and I thought of going in and finding something in the secretary's desk, but I knew she would stop me, and there was that unbalanced arrangement of red seals waiting for me to do something about it, and I had to do something—I couldn't stand it, sitting there with those lopsided marks dragging at the wall—so I did the only thing I could think of, which was to stand up on the sofa and bite my finger, and use that."

She paused in the deathly silence and looked down at her hand, and rubbed her thumb across the pale scar that curved across the pad of her right index finger.

"That was the end of psychiatrists for a long time. My father came into my room that night, with a paper bag. He sat on the side of my bed and he opened the bag and took out one of those giant boxes of sixty-four crayons, with silver and gold and copper, and a real artist's pad, thick, textured paper. He put them on my bedside table and he crumpled the bag into a twist and he started talking to me. He told me that artists needed wide experience to do their art properly, that anyone who never looked up from the paper soon had nothing to draw. Therefore he would make a deal with me. I could draw and paint for one half hour before school in the morning, for two hours in the afternoon, and for one hour after dinner if I would agree to pay attention in class, play outside at recess time, read, and do my homework. If I agreed to this, and if I stuck to it, I could begin to have lessons on the weekends. He was a very wise man, but he was not very well and was totally intimidated by my mother most of the time. His compromise stuck, and that was how I lived for the next six years, until they were killed."

Vaun looked at the flickering fire for a long moment and shook her head.

"My poor mother," she said again. "If she had lived . . . But I would be a different person, not Eva Vaughn at all. They died when I was thirteen, in a stupid boating accident—the man at the helm was just drunk enough to make a mistake. I went to live with Red and Becky, my mother's normal half-brother and his normal wife and two nice, normal kids, aged nine and eleven. They were totally unprepared for someone like me dropping into their life—smack into puberty, terrified at losing my security, and filled with anger at my parents and a guilt that I couldn't express, awkward and ugly physically, and saddled with this all-consuming obsession that nobody could understand and I couldn't even begin to talk about. I moved three hundred miles away to a small farming town, into a school with overworked teachers, kids who'd never even known an adult artist before, much less a weird kid their own age—and, of course, no more weekend lessons.

"They tried, my aunt and uncle, they really did, but they didn't even know where to begin. I bullied them into giving me a shed to paint in, and before long I just lived out there. I tried, too, when I thought about it. I took over a number of jobs around the place to make myself less of a burden. When I was sixteen I began to babysit around the community, to earn money for my supplies. I built a box to hold my paints and small canvases, and I was happy to cover a kitchen table with newspapers and work until the parents got home.

"For about six months I was happy, really happy. I had money for paint, my aunt and uncle had decided hands off until I was old enough to leave, school was easy enough to be undemanding, and the local librarian was very good at finding me books on art theory and reproductions to study. At seventeen I began to think about going to college. My grades were decent, there was a small settlement left from my parents' death to get me started, and I was putting together a portfolio that I thought was not too bad. With my uncle's approval I sent in applications to three universities.

"It was an exciting time. I was in my last year of what I thought of as exile, and I could see that my work was good, that I had a future waiting for me. These were the early seventies, and even in rural areas the times were exhilarating. Then in December of my senior year two things happened: I slept with a young man, a couple of years older than I was, and he introduced me to drugs. Andy Lewis. It was part of the whole package, you know. If you looked like 'one of those hippies,' it meant you did drugs, so I did. For six months I did, mostly grass, but twice LSD. The first time was in December.

"The acid was interesting. It changed the way I saw colors and intensified the vibrations of different colors, the glow everything gives off. Not only while I was under the influence but for a couple of weeks until it faded back to normality. And in the middle of March when Andy offered me another tab, I took it.

"It was bad. I don't know why it was so different from the first time, but I just went insane. A little while after I swallowed the stuff I was sitting and looking down at my hands. There was a faint smear of red paint on my finger, near the scar, and as I watched it suddenly started smoldering and bubbling and eating into my finger and exposing the bone, which turned into a white bristle brush—" She broke off and looked up sheepishly. "There's no need to go over all the bizarre details, but in the end what happened was that my fingers turned into brushes and when I looked at one of the guys there—not Andy, I don't remember him being there, it was one of the kids who used to hang around—I saw paint pumping through his body, pulsing, every color, brilliant and iridescent. I was trying to get at the paint in his throat when the police arrived, and after I attempted to throttle several other people, they hauled me off to the hospital and filled me with some kind of heavy-duty tranquilizers. It was a lot of excitement for our little town, as you might imagine.

"By the next morning I was okay—sick and covered with bruises, but my fingers were flesh and blood again. They let me go home later, and the following day I was carrying a pan full of hot soup across the kitchen and felt my fingers turn to wood and dropped the pan. I had half a dozen relapses—sometimes I'd see paint pulsing in one of my cousins—but gradually it tapered off in frequency and intensity. I swore I'd never touch anything again, and bit by bit my family began to relax.

"In the first week of May I received a letter from one of the universities, the one I badly wanted to go to, saying that if I wished to send some samples from my portfolio I would be considered for a freshman scholarship in the fall. I went through the stuff I'd been doing, and somehow it didn't look as good as I'd thought it had. The next day I laid it all out, and I was appalled. I'd done nothing but crap since January. There was not one piece that wasn't sloppy and careless, and what was worse, it was all false, pretentious, shallow. Typical druggie stuff. I flushed the various leaves and tablets down the toilet and that afternoon told Andy to take a jump and got to work.

"As I said, that was early May. Just before my eighteenth birthday." She paused and wiped the palms of her hands on her knees. "Could I have a drink? Yes, that would be fine. Thank you.

"Early May. In mid-May Mrs. Brand called and asked me to babysit. She was a neighbor I'd worked for before. Some of my regulars didn't ask me much that spring—word gets around in a small town, and I wasn't exactly discreet. Well, this was their anniversary, and I think my aunt reassured her that I was okay. I needed the money, so I took my paint box and went along at about eight o'clock.

"They had two kids, a boy of fifteen, who had some kind of a play rehearsal at school that night, so he couldn't babysit, and yes, a little brown-haired girl, aged six. Jemima, but we all called her Jemma. She was in bed when I got there, but I went in to let her know I was there, and when I checked again at eight-thirty she was asleep.

"The son came in a bit before ten, had something to eat, and flirted a little, or tried to, but I was deeply into this piece that was going so well, the first solid, honest thing in a long time. I nodded my head a few times until he took the hint and went off to bed. The parents got home a few minutes before midnight, and I started packing away my box. When the mother went in to check on the kids, the girl was dead. Lying on the floor. Strangled. Naked."

Vaun looked curiously at her hands, which were trembling. "I haven't told anyone this story in fifteen years.

"I just stood there in the corner of the kitchen for the next hour, totally stunned. The doctor and police came, then more police, detectives, and then somebody thought to look at my painting.

"Have you ever had a leech on you? No? It's the most desperately revolting feeling, to find this horrible, slimy, slow-moving thing attached to your skin, sucking away at you. That's exactly how the policemen looked at me after seeing the canvas. I saw that look a lot in the next few months.

"That painting convicted me. Oh, there were a lot of other things, of course, from my history of psychiatric treatment to my use of LSD and what I'd done in March, which came out early on. But the painting clinched it. If I'd had a decent lawyer I might have tried to plead insanity, but as it was, the painting stood there for all to see, evidence that I was a coldhearted and ruthless murderer, a mad, artistic, murdering cuckoo in their nest.

"You see, what I'd been working on was a picture of Jemma as I'd actually seen her the week before. I had been out walking, thinking about what I wanted to do for the scholarship portfolio, when Jemma appeared. She didn't see me. She'd obviously been down in the pond catching pollywogs, which she wasn't supposed to do, and had her dress and underpants off so she wouldn't get mud on them, and she looked so amazing, like some pale wood sprite, totally at ease with her nakedness. She spotted a butterfly and dropped her

281

clothes to go racing up the hill after it, and at the top of the hill the new green grass was so soft looking, you could just see her decide to roll in it. I knew I'd have to tell her that she mustn't do that any more, for her own protection, but for a few minutes I just enjoyed the sight of this nature child. At the end of it she just lay there, all alone in the universe, head back in the grass, looking at the clouds, and I knew I had my main piece for the portfolio. The colors were perfect, the position technically challenging, and there was this subtle innocent exuberance that I knew I could capture. And I did. It was a good, solid painting, one of the best I'd ever done, and it sent me to prison for ten years because she was found in exactly that position, arms sprawled, head back, and naked.

"I know now that the whole trial was a farce. There wasn't enough money for a proper lawyer, so I had a public defender, who was a total incompetent, but what did I know? I couldn't imagine those twelve people would actually believe the prosecuter's accusations, they seemed so utterly absurd. Once when he was going on and on about Timothy Leary and the hippie movement being anti-Church and the painting being a crucifixion scene because Jemma's father was a deacon in the local church, I actually laughed, it was so ridiculous. That was a big mistake, I realized later, but by then the verdict was in.

"The first few months in prison were pretty hellish, but after that things calmed down. They let me paint for a few hours every day, and my aunt sent endless supplies of pastels and Conté crayons and paper. I learned to walk very quietly around certain inmates, and I made a lot of flattering drawings. That was my first taste of prostitution." Her smile was gentle, and ugly.

"I had been in for just short of three years when there was a riot at some low-security prison in the Midwest, and all of a sudden the press was full of stories about how prisoners were being coddled instead of punished, and the law-and-order people grabbed onto us. Our prison had a reputation of being more humane than some, which I suppose was why I was sent there, because of my age. Some newspaper decided to run an exposé of the place, as an example, and the powers-that-be were forced to crack down on us. I learned all

282

that afterwards. The first thing I knew about it was when my painting privileges were taken away. Two days later there was a sweep through the cells and all my supplies disappeared. It was like when I was seven, only now I had no parents who I knew, underneath the confusion, loved me. Now I had nothing.

"And you know the funny thing? The relief was tremendous. I had carried the burden of this gift since I was two years old, and it had ruined my whole world. Now it was all over, it had been taken away from me, and I had no control any more, none whatsoever. I felt as if I were floating, and I could let go. So I did. At first they thought I was, as they called it, 'being difficult,' instigating a hunger strike I suppose, and they slapped me into solitary confinement. When they came to get me out, I was catatonic.

"The rest of it you've seen in my records, I'm sure. I used to wonder what would have happened to me if Gerry Bruckner hadn't decided to volunteer one afternoon a week at the prison, or if he'd been an ignoramus about art, or if the prison's warden and governing board had been less cooperative. What if, what if. . . . So many opportunities for that little game in a life like mine, aren't there? What if he hadn't thought to put a crayon in my hand, and what if two years later he hadn't had a good friend with a gallery in New York, and what if the pieces hadn't sold so well, and what if he hadn't been willing to fight for me. . . .

"I owe him my life. I dedicated the show to him, last year, the one you saw." She drained the glass, her third, and set it carefully on the table. "He is the only person I've ever fully, wholeheartedly loved. And I've never even slept with him." She smiled at Kate, a crooked smile that touched her eyes. "Except, I suppose, that night at the hospital last week. God, I'm so tired. Will I ever feel rested again? And now I'm half drunk as well. I think I'll take my dreary self off to bed before I begin to weep crocodile tears on this nice sofa."

"May I ask you something?" Kate interrupted.

"Only one thing? Must be something of a record for a detective, only one question."

"Two somethings, then, but one of them I have no business asking, and you're welcome to tell me that."

"All right."

"Why didn't you make an appeal?"

"I—I didn't think there'd be much point. The jury was only out for a few hours before they returned the verdict, and the lawyer—"

"Come on," Kate chided. "You're far from stupid, and you certainly had plenty of time to think about it. Why didn't you appeal?"

Vaun sighed and looked faintly embarrassed.

"Because by then I wasn't sure that I hadn't done it. I only took acid twice, but it's strange stuff, like stirring your brains with a spoon. Even after the first time I had half a dozen flashbacks. Like hiccoughs of the brain. Things would shift, somehow, and go unreal for a few seconds, or minutes. And the second time, after I'd tried to strangle two or three people. . . . Well, even during the trial I began to wonder if maybe I actually had done it while I was having a flashback or hiccough or whatever you want to call it, and it scared me. The whole thing scared me, the thought of having to go through all those leech-looks all over again. I crawled into prison and pulled it around me like a shell, and I found that it wasn't as awful as I'd thought it would be. When my uncle came to visit me he offered to begin an appeal, but I could see what it would do to him, and I think he was relieved when I told him that I couldn't see much point. It was easier to forget it, to just get on and deal with what was in front of me. That sounds so feeble now, so stupid, but—in some ways I was a very young eighteen."

Kate looked dubious, Lee waited, and Vaun fiddled with a small seashell from the table while something struggled to push its way to the surface. She opened her mouth, changed her mind, started again, and the third time got it out.

"And I . . . There was also the fact that I was guilty, if not of killing Jemma then of enough other things to make me feel that prison was the place for me. I know," she said, though Lee had not actually spoken, "Gerry and I spent a lot of time on free-floating guilt complexes. At the time, though, it seemed . . . appropriate, that I should be locked away from society." She put down the shell and seemed to push the subject away. "What was your other question?"

"You don't have to tell me—"

"I didn't have to tell you the other one either."

"True. And I'm glad to see that your ego has recovered."
She grinned at Vaun, who grinned back. "It's curiosity. Why
Andy Lewis? What did you see in him?"

"A lot of things. He was very attractive, sexy, dark and
dangerous, aloof. He exuded an aura of secret power. And he
was an outsider, but by choice, rather than being left out.
That was a feeling I craved, that self-assurance. Together we
could look down on everyone else. I felt chosen, powerful,
unafraid—even pretty, for those few months. With Andy, the
whole mess of my life made a kind of sense."

"But it didn't last."

"No, it didn't last. I couldn't paint, with Andy. There was
no room for it around him, I couldn't pull away from him far
enough to paint. It was tearing me apart, and when I realized
that my work was becoming crap because of it, I had to
choose, and I chose my brushes."

"What did he do when you told him?"

"That was frightening. It was a Saturday, and Red and
Becky had taken the kids to town. I was in my studio trying
to sketch in a canvas when he came by. I was preoccupied
with what I was doing and disturbed by my realization that
I had five months of garbage to make up for, and so I was
abrupt with him—I just told him I couldn't go on, it was over,
and went on sketching. When I turned around a minute later,
he was still sitting on the bed, but he was so angry, so furious,
it stunned me. His eyes . . . And he seemed to fill the whole
room. I thought—I knew—that he was going to get up and
come over and hit me, beat me up, but I couldn't move. I just
waited for I don't know how long, and then all of a sudden his
face changed and he started to smile, and it was like the smile
he had when he was going to take me to bed but different—
horrible, cruel. And he stood up, and I knew he was going to
kill me, and he came over to me and he kissed me, with his
teeth, and he said, 'If that's the way you want it, babe,' and
he went out and got on his motorcycle and roared off. And
every time I saw him after that he smiled that same way, like
some brutish little boy pulling wings off a fly."

"How long before you began to think he'd had something to do with Jemma Brand's death?"

"I wondered, even during the trial, because of a look he
gave me the first day—a satisfied, 'I told you so' kind of look.

But I decided it had to be my imagination. I couldn't believe Andy would do something so, so—pathological. He was very good to me; he could be gentle when he wanted. How could I imagine him doing such a thing? I still find it difficult." Sagging now with fatigue she looked at Kate. "Have I answered your questions?"

"Yes, thank you," said Kate, and she thought, which still leaves a hundred others, but not tonight.

Vaun rose like an old woman, and stood studying them. "It occurs to me that I haven't thanked you for all that you've done for me. Not that any thanks could be adequate."

"It has been a great joy," said Lee simply.

"I agree," said Kate. "I'll be sorry when it's over, though I won't be sorry when it ends." She listened to her words, and scratched her head. "I think I need some coffee. Want some?"

"No thanks," said Vaun. "I just want to crawl into bed."

"Lee?"

"Yes, thanks. Make a whole pot, why don't you. Jon, my client, will probably want a cup. Maybe I should turn on the lights in the front rooms—he'll be here in a few minutes." She moved off down the hallway and Kate turned toward the kitchen. Vaun started up the stairs, and then stopped and turned back to follow Kate.

"All that talking," she explained as she reached for a glass. "I'm thirsty." She scooped some ice cubes into the glass, the bottle of spring water gurgled, and she drank gratefully.

Kate measured the beans into the grinder and switched it on just as the doorbell sounded. She turned off the grinder.

"I'll get it," Lee called. She sounded distracted, and Kate wondered how closely she would listen to the problems of Jon Samson, né Schwartz. Kate turned back to the coffee, and a sudden anxiety struck her. She moved quickly past Vaun towards the door.

"Don't forget to—" she started to warn Lee, but she was too late, and it was too late, for when she reached the hall Lee's hand had already released the bolt, and in the slow motion of horror Kate saw the door explode inward, sending Lee staggering back against the wall, and the figure that stepped in looked for an instant like Lee's client with his snug trousers and neatly clipped moustache, but it was not Jon

Samson, it was Andy Lewis, Andy Lewis with a .45 automatic in his right hand, Andy Lewis with the eyes and stance of a pit bull zeroing in on his victim, Andy Lewis looking past Kate to where Vaun stood waiting.

32

Kate's first frozen thought was that he was smaller than she remembered, shorter perhaps than Vaun, certainly more compact and concentrated than the hairy mountain man she had seen at Vaun's door.

His eyes and the gun stayed rock steady on Vaun where she stood behind Kate's right shoulder, not moving a millimeter as his left hand pushed the door shut, found the bolt, slid it home. For the space of five heartbeats nobody moved, or breathed, until finally his lips curled.

"Hello, Vaunie."

The quiet, sure menace in his voice washed like ice through Kate's veins and sent her mind yammering like a mad monkey against the bars of its cage, screaming at her to run, fly, dive for cover, leap for the drawer three feet away and get her hands on the gun there *because that is the voice of a goddamned poisonous snake of a crazy man, Kate!* But other than one all-over jerk of her muscles she stayed quite still and watched the hand on the gun.

At his words Lee, staring horrified from where she had fetched up against the wall, shifted her gaze from the gun to his face, but Vaun seemed not to see the gun or hear the menace. Neither of them made a move to touch the forgotten alarm buttons they wore. At his greeting she seemed to relax, and Kate heard her exhale in what sounded like a happy little sigh.

"Hello, Andy." Her voice was calm, even warm, a simple greeting at the mildly surprising appearance of an old friend. His smile deepened and Kate saw the face that Vaun had described when he walked out of her studio three weeks before Jemma Brand had died—amused, cruel, and utterly sure of himself.

"Good of you all to wait up for me like this. Damn stupid time for an appointment with a shrink, but I couldn't very well change it, could I?"

"What—" Lee shrank back under the stab of his eyes, but the gun did not waver, and she pushed the words out. "What happened to Jon?"

To Kate's surprise he laughed, a hearty sound, full of amusement, incongruous from a tidy man with murder in his eyes.

"I used some of his own toys on him. He'll be all right, unless he struggles too much. In fact, he's probably having a fine time, all trussed up like a pig. And speaking of which," he said, and looked at Kate, all his humor instantly gone, "you'll have a gun. Where is it?"

"Upstairs," she lied automatically. There was a chance that in moving them around he would leave himself vulnerable for an instant. He studied her, eyes narrowed, and seemed to hear her thoughts, for he smiled again, as if at the feeble efforts of a child.

"No, it isn't. Well it doesn't matter, so long as it's not on you." He ran his eyes over her T-shirt and jeans, which could hardly conceal a penknife, much less a police revolver. "Still, I'd better have a check. Vaun, you come on out into the hall. That's right, by that table. And you, next to her." He nodded curtly to Lee, who obeyed. "Now you, come here, hands against the wall. Get your feet further back. That's better." Kate felt a sudden sharp pressure against her spine, and he spoke past her. "Now, if you two don't want your cop friend to have a big hole in her, you'll stay very still."

Kate braced herself, but the search was impersonal, if thorough. In a minute he stood back, satisfied, and looked down the hallway toward the opening and the expanse of drapery.

"That's the living room?" he asked Vaun, and she nodded. "Right. You first, Vaunie, then you. Now you, cop."

Vaun turned smoothly to the door, the glass of ice water still tinkling gently in her hand. Lee followed with a curiously old-maidish stance, her hands clasped together between her breasts, hunched over in feeble defense or fear or cold. Kate

288

moved down the hall, feeling the tingle in her back where the cold metal of the gun had pressed, and took great care not to stumble. She did not glance at what Lewis had referred to as a table, a decorative Indian apothecary's chest with a telephone and address book on top and her own familiar gun yearning from the top right-hand drawer, as useless to her as if it were on the bottom of the Bay. With a wrench she pulled her mind off the gun and off regrets and demanded that it get to work.

In the living room she moved directly to the first sofa and sat with her back to the dining area. Lewis hesitated, his instincts against allowing her any choice or independent move, but he studied the room and realized that there was no place she could have hidden a gun and that her position would put him with his back in the corner, away from the room's only internal entrance, the long windows, tightly draped, and two small, high windows that obviously looked into nothing but the neighbor's trees. He subsided, told Lee to take the other sofa and sat Vaun in the chair between them, facing the fireplace. Good, thought Kate. Now to get him talking.

"How did you find her?" she asked, and was pleased to hear just the right shade of querulous amazement in her voice.

Lewis preened. "It wasn't that difficult. I had a friend pretend to be a newsman willing to pay a lot, even for rumors. He found an orderly who said Vaun was being released to a therapist who specialized in artists. I figured it would be either here or in Berkeley, and since the police here were in on the case, I started here. I went into the kinds of bars and coffeehouses that artists go to, in the Haight and Polk and south of Market to begin with, and everywhere I went I talked about crazy artists and that woman down on Tyler's Road." Here he paused and reached out to run the tip of his left forefinger along Vaun's ear. She did not react. "Took me about eighty gallons of coffee and a hundred and fifty beers, but I finally got lucky—a tight-ass little jerk in a silk shirt practically drooling to tell me all about how he knew the policewoman who'd been on the TV down on Tyler's Road, oh yeah, knew her personally, well, no, not well, you know, but he'd once seen her, with a lady shrink who'd come to the

289

hospital to see an artist friend of his who was dying a year or so back, lady shrink name of Cooper. That was noon on Wednesday. Took me until midnight to track down one of Dr. Cooper's regulars, and when I found out when his next scheduled appointment was, I just arranged that he'd be too, uh, tied up to keep it. And here I am."

"Can I ask you something that puzzled us? Inspector Hawkin and me, that is?" Kate continued, not giving him a chance to find his own topic of conversation. He looked irritated, then nodded magnanimously.

"The names. You are Andrew Lewis?" She made it a question, hinting uncertainty. "Without the beard . . . Where did you get the name Dodson?" She held her breath, playing for time, skirting the revelation of how much they knew about Lewis and Dodson, hoping he might relax into scorn at their ignorance but not wanting to give him the impression of incompetence—that could only arouse his suspicions. Keep him talking, keep him relaxed. However, she was startled at his response.

"You know my middle name?"

"Uh, no. There was an initial. . . ."

"It's Carroll."

"Carol?"

"Two r's, two l's, like in Lewis Carroll. You know his real name?"

"I don't think—"

"Dodgson. The Reverend Charles L. Dodgson. With a g. So when I came across someone who looked like me, with a name so close, well, I just had to be him, didn't I?" He was grinning, daring Kate to ask what had happened to the real Dodson, but that was not the direction she wanted to go in, not yet. She desperately cast around for another topic.

"Where did you go during that two years you took off from high school? Inspector Hawkin thought it was Mexico, but I—"

"All right, enough crap. I don't have all night."

"What do you want, Andy?" Vaun's even voice distracted Lewis, almost, but not quite—enough for Kate to tense up in preparation, for what she did not know. He stood looking down at Vaun speculatively. She met his eyes, waiting.

290

"What do I want?" he said to himself. "What did I ever want? I loved you, and you treated me like shit."

"You never loved me," she chided him gently.

"No? Maybe you're right. I did nearly kill you, you know, when you told me you'd rather paint than be with me."

"Yes, I know that. But what you did was worse, wasn't it?"

She gave him her knowledge and the pain of those years in her voice and face, and he went very still. After a moment he looked at Kate, but she had ready a slightly puzzled expression to hide her fear and fury. Damn the woman, what was she playing at? Surely she could see that the very worst thing for all of them would be to push Lewis into a corner, to let him know how trapped he was. He looked back at Vaun, warily, reassessing her.

"What I did."

"What are you going to do now, Andy?" she asked him, and Kate felt like screaming at her not to push him into any action, stretch it out, give Hawkin a chance, but Vaun would not look at her, and Lee sat frozen.

"I'll tell you what I thought of doing," he said absently, and Kate knew then that all was lost. "I thought of knocking off these two and making it look like you did it. You'd never get out in just nine years after that. I could still do it."

"No, Andy. They know everything."

" 'Everything'? Oh, right."

"They do. Tommy's *Time* magazine. Drugs in your apartment in San Jose. That garage. Your fingerprints and some hairs from one of the children in the postal van. They'd never think I had anything to do with killing anyone."

Madness, thought Kate, this is madness speaking, she probably thinks he'll shoot her first and give us a chance, but it's impossible, I've got to stop her. But Kate couldn't think of a way that wouldn't set him off, so she prayed for Hawkin and readied herself for an unavoidable, futile lunge from the depths of the sofa.

The cruel smile crept back onto his lips, and Lee made a faint sound of protest as his left hand went down onto Vaun's head, gently playing with her curls, caressing the back of her head and cupping the nape of her neck, dipping his forefinger under the collar of her shirt. And then he froze.

Slowly his hand came back up, the cord between his first two fingers, and Vaun's alarm button emerged from the front of her shirt. He looked at it, and at Vaun, who sat through his touch and his discovery with unmoving aloofness, looking up at him. He twisted his hand around the cord and brought it up, and up, until the black line was biting into Vaun's pale throat. She watched him as her hands came up and plucked without passion at the cord. For the first time the gun moved away from Kate, but abruptly the clasp broke. Vaun jerked back into her seat, and Lewis took a sharp recovery step back and stood with the thing dangling from his hand.

And this is the Andy Lewis that that preacher's daughter saw just before being beaten to a pulp, thought Kate. His skin was dark with fury, his hand trembling with this evidence that he, Andy Lewis, might have been tricked, trapped, thwarted, outsmarted. He brought his eyes up to Kate, looked at her shirt, dismissed her, turned to Lee.

"You. Let me see."

She looked to Kate for direction, but Kate could only nod. Slowly, slowly Lee's hands went up to the back of her neck, and slowly she pulled her own black cord over her blonde curls, and then she held the button out to him.

He stared at the small device swinging from Lee's fingers, his eyes narrowing in disbelief.

"You pushed it, didn't you? When we were coming down the hallway, you were all bent over. You had your hands on it, didn't you? Oh, Christ, you stupid bitch, you're going to be very sorry you did that."

"Mr. Lewis," Kate began in the calm and reasonable voice demanded both by training and by good sense, "I'm afraid you'll find there are police all around the house. However, I should point out that as of this moment we have nothing on you, in spite of what Vaun just said. With a good lawyer—"

"Shut up!" he snarled, and jammed his gun into Lee's hair. Kate froze.

"I don't care what evidence you have," he said. "I've got hostages. I'll get away, you won't risk losing 'Eva Vaughn,' now will you? I'll get away. But I don't need *you*. Three hostages is too many, and a cop doesn't count anyway."

"Andy," Vaun said quietly, "don't hurt her. Tie her up if

you like, but let her go. If you do, I'll go with you. If you kill either of them, you'll have to kill me too."

His head turned to her, his face screwed up as if he were about to spit, or to cry, and indeed the answer he spat out climbed rapidly into a shriek.

"You? You think I care what I do to you? I should have killed you years ago. All of this happened because of you, you goddamned bitch. I should have wrung *your* neck that night. I should have poked your cold little eyes out."

His rage poured out onto Vaun, and still Kate sat, knowing he was about to explode, knowing he would see her move, knowing that in a matter of seconds time would have run out and she would have to make her hopeless bid for their lives. Lee might reach him—she was out of his sight—but Lee sat, still clutching the button, stunned by his sheer animal fury.

Vaun, though. Vaun the passive, Vaun the mirror, Vaun the observer and chronicler of the world's torments, Vaun was meeting him, shaking herself free almost visibly from the restraints of a lifetime, caught up in a rising bubble of exhilarating, intoxicating, liberating rage. Her face was alive, furious, unrecognizable, her pale cheeks flushed with passion, her pale eyes glittering like a pair of blue diamonds, every bit as hard and as cutting. She threw back her head and called her death to her in the vast relief of one final clash, all bars off, no quarter given, all her confusion and torment coming to a single focus on this, her lover, her enemy, her death. She rose up to meet him, took one step back, and stood braced to hurl her words at him.

"Yes, Andy, you should have. But you didn't, did you? And everything I've done in the last fifteen years, everything I've painted, has been thanks to you. Thanks to you, Andy. These hands," she held them up and shook them in his face, "these hands have changed the way people see the world, thanks to you—"

"You'll never paint again!" he shrieked at her, and the heavy gun jerked slightly toward her, and then all three of them could see his mind reassert itself and take control of the hand's movement. He looked at her in astonishment and began to laugh, the madness and hysteria all the way up to the surface now.

"You think I'm going to kill you, you stupid bitch? That's what you want, isn't it? But I'm not going to make it that easy for you. You're going to wish you were dead—it'll make being locked up for ten years seem like a fairy tale because you're going to live knowing what your precious painting did, you're going to have to live knowing that because of your precious fucking painting people died, that those hands you're so proud of might as well have been around those skinny soft little throats and on this gun, and you're going to have to live knowing that precious little Jemma and Tina and Amanda who tried to bite me, the little bitch, and what's the other one's name? Samantha and now your good friends Lee and Casey, all of them died because of your precious fucking painting hands, and even if your hands can hold a brush when I'm finished with you, all you'll be able to paint is blood and death, and you did it all, you did it, Vaunie, it was you."

And he turned then and many things happened simultaneously, as his gun lowered onto Lee and Vaun cried out and Kate finally made her move, diving low for his knees, and the high upper window blossomed in glittering fragments into the room and two guns went off. Then there was blood like paint spattered across the room and there was death and there was the sound of two women groaning in deep and eternal agony, and then came the sound of more smashing glass and the absurdly unnecessary flat buzz of the breached house alarm, and then running feet and shouts and the wail of distant sirens, and Hawkin pulling Kate off Lee and muffling his partner's choking groans in the hollow of his shoulder, and the sirens louder now and the sudden silent chasm as both house alarm and siren shut off, and the calm rush of the ambulance men, and Hawkin holding Kate back—and then Lee was gone, and it was over, over, it was over.

294

EPILOGUE

THE
ROAD

Works of art are always products of having been in danger,
of having gone to the very end.
—Rainer Maria Rilke, *letter*

———

There was also a nun, a Prioress . . .
and thereon hung a brooch of gold full sheen,
On which there was first writ a crowned 'A,'
And after Amor vincit omnia.
—Geoffrey Chaucer, *Canterbury Tales,* Prologue

33

Tyler's Road was a very different place in the June sunshine. Even the redwoods through which Kate had run that disgustingly wet night seemed more benevolent. The roses along the fence were a glory of color, the rusty shed roof had disappeared beneath an expanse of green, and brilliant flags flew from every fence post, each printed with a helm, a lute, or a quill and proclaiming the boundaries of the Medieval Midsummer's Night Faire.

There were still a few press vans, Kate was amused to see, although they were vastly outnumbered by the buses, bugs, pickups, vans, station wagons, and just plain cars of the participants, which even at this early hour lined both sides of the narrow road for nearly a mile on either side of the Barn. She parked her own car at the suggestion of a long-haired boy in jester's motley and began to walk toward the sounds and, soon, the smells of Tyler's Barn. There was a steady flow of long-haired, bearded, long-skirted types whose costumes ranged from monastic robes to gowns that

297

would have seemed modern in Marie Antoinette's France, with a scattering of self-conscious families in shorts and cameras. She herself was dressed in proper period style, thanks to the bullying of one of Lee's clients—but as a young man, in tunic and lightweight leggings. No ruffs or farthingales for her, thank you.

As she neared the entrance gate she fished out from the leather pouch at her belt the pass that had come in the mail and handed it to the gatekeeper, a vaguely familiar woman in rustic brown who stamped her hand with something that was either an octopus or a musical instrument. Behind the woman stood a mountainous figure in green tunic and leggings, leaning on a rough staff the size of a young tree, a walkie-talkie grumbling from his hip. She looked at him more carefully, and at last knew him by the earring.

"Mark Detweiler?"

He looked at her with uncertainty.

"Kate Martinelli. Casey?" she suggested.

"Casey Martinelli!" he boomed, and crushed her hand in his. "Good to see you. I wouldn't have recognized you in a million years. How've you been?" And then his face changed as he remembered, and still booming he continued, "I was so sorry to hear about your friend, we all were. Is there—"

She interrupted quickly, not wanting to hear it.

"Thanks, no, I'm fine, have you any idea where Tyler is, or Vaun Adams?"

He looked furtively to either side and bent down to whisper in her ear.

"Vaun was around. She's helping Amy with the cart rides, or maybe doing faces, I'm not sure which. Tyler's around." He waved vaguely into the multicolored swirl of humanity. Kate thanked him and began to turn away, but was stopped by his booming voice. "Tell you who I did see, though," and he waited.

"Who?" she obliged.

"Your partner." Seeing her confused look, he repeated it. "Your partner. Al Hawkin."

"Al's here?" She was surprised. This didn't seem his sort of show, but then, maybe he was here for reasons similar to hers.

"Got here about half an hour ago, with the most gorgeous wench—oh, sorry, we're not supposed to call them wenches this year. What was it now?" He scratched his grizzled head in thought, pushing the feathered cap awry. "Oh, right. Buxom ladies, we're supposed to say. Anyway, she's a looker. They went towards the food tents—see the white ones?"

She thanked him again and set off, aiming well downhill from the blazing white canvas from which all the smells were drifting. She wasn't sure she wanted to see him, not quite yet. Later in the day perhaps, after she had talked with Vaun.

Inevitably, perverse fate decreed that the first familiar face she saw was that of Al Hawkin, dressed in twentieth-century open-necked shirt and tan cotton trousers, standing by himself across a clearing and listening to a quartet of three recorders and a viola da gamba. She had not seen him for nearly two months, since the night he had come to the house with the intention, she had realized only recently, of apologizing for his failure to send the marksman up the neighbor's tree in time to save Lee's spine. Kate had been in no state to receive him or his guilt, being on the edge of exhaustion and frantic with worry over yet another infection that was trying to carry off what was left of Lee, and had thrown him out with scathing, bitter words.

Those words hung in front of her now and she hesitated, tempted to duck back behind the tent, but was stopped by the absurdity of it. He saw her then, half raised a hand in greeting, and waited until he saw her start toward him before moving from his post. They met halfway.

"Hello, Al," she said with originality.

"Kate," he answered. "How are you?"

"I am well," she said, and was vaguely surprised to find that she meant it.

"And Lee?"

"You saw her a couple of weeks ago, I think?"

"Ten days ago. She was due to be discharged the following day. How is it going?"

"She's much happier at home, sleeping well. And she seems to be doing better just generally."

"Changes?" He was as sharply perceptive as ever and picked up the nuance of hope in her voice.

"The doctors say they aren't sure, but you know doctors. She says there's some feeling in her right foot, and the other day she moved it in reflex."

"Oh, Kate. That is good news. I'm very glad to hear it."

The sincerity behind the hackneyed phrases stung her eyes, and she looked away at the musicians. Some people were beginning a dance.

"Al, I'm sorry about how I acted when you came to see me. I didn't mean it, I hope you know that."

"I do. I chose a poor time to come. Forget it. I'll come to see her sometime, shall I?"

"She'd like that."

"Tell her I said hello, and that I'm glad to hear she's doing better."

"She's sure she'll be jogging by Christmas. Of course, she never jogged before—I don't know what her hurry is."

He smiled at her, hearing what lay behind her feeble joke.

"Buy you a beer?"

"A bit early for me."

"You have to get into the medieval spirit. They drank it all day—no coffee, can you imagine? and no tea other than herbs that they drank as medicine—and got a large part of their vitamin and caloric intake from beer. Why, do you know, court records show that the lady's servants—the women, mind you—were each issued something like three gallons a day?"

"Must have been a jolly castle." She wondered at this arcane expertise.

"With busy toilets. Speaking of which, I wonder where Jani could be? Oh well, she'll find us."

And so saying he casually draped an arm across Kate's shoulders, and she was so astonished she could only lean into him as they meandered downhill and joined the line for paper cups (printed with a wood-grain design) of surprisingly decent dark beer.

They found a quiet corner atop a pile of large wooden crates and sat looking at the pulsating, growing crowd of medieval merrymakers. The beer went down well as they sat in the shade on an already hot morning with the taste of dust on their tongues. Kate swallowed and gave herself over to relaxation, feeling small pockets of unrealized tension give way. It was the first alcohol she'd had since what she thought of in capitals as The Night. To drink would have been an act of cowardice, until now.

She didn't realize she had sighed until Hawkin turned to her.

"I almost didn't come," she said, as if in explanation.

"I was a little surprised to see you," he agreed.

"Some of Lee's clients are with her today. Jon Samson, as a matter of fact—one of her most devoted. Silly to call them clients, I suppose. If anything, they're the therapists, both physio- and psycho-."

"Friends, maybe."

"Friends. Yes. I don't know what I would have done without them."

"Are you coming back, Kate?" he asked abruptly.

"You know, until ten minutes ago I wasn't sure."

"And?"

"Yes. Yes, I do believe I'm coming back."

"Good." He nodded and drained his cup. "Good. How soon?"

"I'll have to arrange care for Lee." He waited. "Jon offered to move in for a while, to take over the front rooms. I'd have to get in a bed, arrange a relief schedule for him." Hawkin waited. "A few days. Four. Maybe three. Why?"

"I could use you now," he said. His fingers fiddled with the waxy rim of the cup, uncurling it, and his eyes scanned the crowd, and his face gave away nothing.

"Isn't this where you start lighting a cigarette?" she said suspiciously.

"Gave them up."

"Why do you need me now?"

"I've been given the Raven Morningstar case."

"Oh, Christ, Al, give me a break!" Ms. Morningstar had been found, very much murdered, in her hotel room in the city the week before. Ms. Morningstar had a list of enemies that would fill a small telephone book. Ms. Morningstar was one of the country's most outspoken, most eloquent, most militant, most worshipped, and most vilified radical feminist lesbians.

"You might be of considerable help."

"Oh, I can imagine. You could nail me up on the doors of

the Hall of Justice and let them throw things at me while you slip out the back."

"None of them would throw things at you," he said matter-of-factly. "There is, after all, a certain amount of renown attached to a female police officer who forces her superiors to give her an extended leave in order to nurse her wounded lover, lesbian variety, and who furthermore makes noises that the departmental insurance policy should be made to include what might be termed unofficial spouses." He did look at her finally, with one eyebrow raised, to gauge her response. She stared at him, open-mouthed, for a long minute, until she felt a sensation she'd never thought to feel again. A great, round, growing balloon of laughter welled up inside her and finally burst gloriously, and she began to giggle, and laugh, more and more convulsively, until in the end she lay back on the crates and roared, tears rolling down into her hair. His growing look of alarm only made it worse, and it was some time before she could get out a coherent explanation.

"When I . . . that first day, in your office . . . you so obviously didn't want to be burdened with me—no, I understood, I was being set up in a prominent place on the case because there were kiddies involved. . . ." She realized where they were and lowered her voice. "And any case with kiddies has to have a little lady in it, and little old Casey Martinelli was that lady, there to look cute and pat the kiddies on the head. And now"—she started to laugh again—"now I'm the department's representative to the chains-and-leather dyke brigade." She wiped her eyes and blew her nose, and suddenly the laughter disintegrated and she heaved a sigh. "Ah, well, as they say: only in San Francisco."

"So when can you be there?"

"Jesus Christ, Al, you don't give up, do you? Today's Saturday. I'll be in Tuesday."

"Make it Monday."

"Nope. There's people I can't reach on the weekend—have to do it Monday morning."

"Monday afternoon, then."

"All right, damn it! Late Monday afternoon."

"I'll set a press conference for three o'clock."

"A press—you utter bastard," she swore angrily, and an

302

instant later realized that she was cursing at the man who was still her superior officer.

He swung his face around, looked directly at her, his gray-blue eyes inches from her brown ones, and grinned roguishly.

"That's what all the girls say, my dear."

A voice came from behind them, a voice low but penetrating, the voice of a woman accustomed to public speaking.

"I go away. I stand in line for one half hour with anachronistic music in my ears for the dubious privilege of using a porta-potty disguised as an eleventh-century privy. I come back to find my escort has disappeared and when I manage to track him down, I find him guzzling beer and staring into the eyes of another woman."

Despite the words, the voice did not sound troubled, and the face, when Kate hitched around to face it, was only amused.

Kate nodded seriously.

"You just can't get good escorts these days," she told the woman.

"My dear," shouted Hawkin happily, "this is Casey Martinelli. Kate, this is Jani Cameron."

"Kate," said Kate firmly, and held out her hand. Another, smaller hand waved up from behind the crates, thrust vaguely in Kate's direction. Kate stretched and shook that one too.

"And that's Jules," added Hawkin. He slithered down from their impromptu seat, swore at the splinters, and helped Kate get down undamaged.

"Jani is the world's foremost authority on medieval German literature, and Jules is going to be San Francisco's youngest D.A. You needn't worry about Kate, Jani," he added offhandedly. "She's a lesbian."

Kate buried her face in her cup, which was already empty, and so missed the woman's reaction, but when she looked back the child was examining her with considerable interest. Finally, with the academic air of someone discussing the historical development of the iota subscript, she spoke.

"Are you, in fact, a lesbian, or more properly speaking bisexual?" she began. "I was reading an article the other day that stated—"

There was a rapid dispersion of the party toward the food tents, with Jules and her mother in the rear in intent conversation (consisting of a firm low voice punctuated with several *But Mother*s) and Hawkin and Kate in front, he grinning hugely, she decidedly pink, from the beer and the sun, no doubt, but smiling gamely.

At the food tents Kate allowed herself to be steered past the Cornish pasties (beef, vegetarian, or tofu) and tempura prawns (medieval Japanese, she assumed) to the sign that advertised the dubious claims of something called "toad in the hole." It turned out to be a spicy sausage in a gummy bread surround, but when she had washed it down with another beer and followed it with strawberries in cream (poured, not whipped, and with honey, not sugar—authenticity reigned in the strawberry booth), she was content.

The three adults sat on a bench in the shade of a colorful tarpaulin while Jules stalked off to try her hand at a game suspiciously like the ancient three-cup sleight-of-hand con game. Hawkin smiled almost paternally as the child stood gazing in intense concentration at the current players, a metal-mouthed page girl amid the lords and ladies who swept up and down the avenues among the stalls of crafts, foods, and games. The three of them chatted comfortably about Tyler, festivals, minor gossip concerning the department, the development of music, and the production of beer. At the end of half an hour Kate realized that Jani was someone she could easily come to like, and furthermore she saw that Hawkin was very much in love with her. She was quiet, even aloof, in manner, but listened carefully to words and currents, and when she spoke it was precise, to the point, and, like her daughter, not always politic. She and Hawkin argued, laughed, and touched, as if old companions, and other than a twinge of pain at the thought of Lee in the mechanical bed at home, she was glad. Eventually Jani stood up, gathered her brocade skirts, and went off after her daughter, with an agreement to meet Hawkin beneath the golden banner in half an hour to watch a demonstration of swordplay.

They watched her go.

"I like her," Kate told him.

"I'm glad. She's a remarkable woman."

"And as for her daughter . . ."

He laughed. "She's something, isn't she? Poor Trujillo, he's terrified of her."

"Have you seen Vaun?"

"A number of times. I brought Jani and Jules here to meet her, on Monday, in fact. We drove up."

"Ah, yes, Monday being one of the days cars are allowed. I take it Tyler's prohibitions are back in force."

"Slightly modified. They've strung a telephone line through the trees, to Angie's place and the Riddles'."

"Sacrilege. How is she? Vaun?"

"Recovering. Fragile. Determined. She sent you the pass."

"I thought so." She watched the mob, unseeing, until the question leaped out of her. "Did he win?" Was it all in vain? Were lives shattered, was Lee crippled, were three children dead, four, so that Andrew Lewis could win his creative revenge? Did we catch him and kill him and still lose the one faint spark that might have justified it? Did he have the last word in the whole disastrous, ugly, horrifying mess? Did he win?

"No." His answer was sure. "No, he did not. She's painting again. Vaun Adams is an even greater human being than she is an artist, if that's possible. She is not going to allow him to win."

"Thank God," she said, and heard the tremble in her voice. "Lee—Lee will be glad," she added, inadequately, but his eyes said he understood.

"You'll want to see her," he said, and stood up.

"Have you any idea where she is? I saw Mark Detweiler at the entrance and he said she was here, though I'd have thought she'd be hiding out."

"She is, like the purloined letter."

In a few minutes Kate saw the sense of this cryptic statement, as Hawkin pointed her to a seated figure, clapped her on the back, said he'd call her Sunday night, and went off to find his Jani. Eva Vaughn had disguised herself as a painter—of faces. She was dressed in characteristically understated fashion—as a nun—but her face was transformed by grease-paint into the visage of a cat. Not that she had fur, ears, and

305

black whiskers drawn on, but the arched eyebrows, self-contained mouth and neat chin were decidedly feline.

She was finishing the delicate webbing that outlined huge butterfly wings covering a young woman's face, the eyes two matching dots high up on the upper wings, the nose blackened as the body. It was a most disconcerting image, like a double exposure in a piece of surrealistic cinema, for the wings trembled with the movements of the face. The woman paid and went happily off with an astounded boyfriend, and a child settled in anticipation on the stool in front of her. Vaun spoke to him for a moment, smiled a feline smile, and turned to rummage through the tubes at her side. Kate stood and watched, but suddenly Vaun glanced up. The catty smile became tentative, and she got up and went to stand before Kate. She reached out a hand to touch Kate's arm, and drew it back.

"You came, then. I so wanted to see you, but I didn't think you'd come, until I thought, maybe, this would bring you."

"I would have come."

"Would you?"

"Maybe not at first," she admitted, "but I'm here now."

"Look, just let me finish this one and then I'll shut down for the day."

The child's requested face, that of an alien monster, grew up from the chin, with eyes that bulged when he puffed out his cheeks. He tried this out in the mirror, delighted; his parents paid, and Vaun firmly shut her box and stuck it under the drapery of the nearby weaver's stall (not Angie's, Kate saw). Again she made the tentative gesture toward Kate's sleeve, and again she drew back and with her other hand waved up the hill.

"There's a tent up there for us, the residents. Let me go and take this stuff off my face."

The house-sized canvas tent, a green one this time, was set off by a low fence and signs that informed the public that this was For Residents Only. It was high up in the meadow, brushed by the low branches of the first redwoods, and the opening was on the uphill side. Kate followed Vaun into the cool, spacious interior, which was scattered with chairs, tables, mirrors, portable clothes racks, sleeping children, and

306

perhaps a dozen adults. A young man in shepherd's dress stood up at their entrance, took up his crook, and stalked toward them with an aggressive set to his shoulders. Vaun held up a pacifying hand, appropriately nunlike.

"It's okay, Larry, she's a friend."

He stopped, his petulance fading into embarrassment.

"Oh. Right. Sorry, it's just that we've had about ten people in here already snooping around, and Tyler said . . ."

"That they'd be looking for me? What did you tell them?"

"Like Tyler said, you're in New York. One of them didn't believe me, but she was pretty stoned."

"I'm sorry to give everyone the problem, but it'd be the same even if I were in New York. If you see Tyler or Anna, would you tell them I've gone up the hill and that I don't know if I'll be here for the dinner or not, but not to save me a plate. Thanks."

With a shrug and a swirl the habit came off. Vaun hung it and the veil on one of a series of chrome racks that held an odd assortment of garments, from dull homespun jerkins to a brilliant brocade cape, and dozens of empty wire hangers. The ex-nun, dressed now in shorts, sandals, and a damp T-shirt, went to a table and mirror and began rubbing cream from a large tub into her face. The feline cast to her eyes and the catty mouth disappeared beneath a scrap of cloth, and then Vaun was there, in the mirror, as Kate had seen her (was it only four months before?)—black curls, ice-blue eyes, a waiting expression.

But different. Somehow very different.

And then Vaun turned from the mirror and met her gaze evenly, and Kate knew what it was: the eyes.

Before, Vaun's eyes had been so withdrawn as to appear dead and gave away no hint of the person behind them. They were no longer uninhabited; no longer did they appear to mirror the world without influence of the person. These eyes were clear, immediate, and revealing windows leading directly into a vivid person. Whatever else Andrew Lewis had done, he had stripped from Vaun her apartness, her defense. There was no hiding now, for this woman. She stood naked.

All this in an instant, and Kate turned away, shaken. Vaun put the top on the removal cream and stood up. This time her hand made contact with Kate's arm and stayed there for a moment.

"Do you have time to come up with me, to the house?"

"I have all day."

"Let's go then."

The two women left the tent and plunged into the trees like a pair of truant schoolgirls, lifting strands of barbed wire for each other, crunching softly through the dry duff beneath the heavy branches, speaking little in the thick stillness that gradually overcame the distant fair and was then broken only by the harsh calls of jays and the occasional chained dog. It was not a long walk, those four miles, but an immensely satisfying one to Kate; and slowly, in the heat and the silence and the easy companionship, and in the awareness of her decision, she felt the last of the grinding unhappiness lift from her and felt herself not far from wholeness.

In the house Vaun waved her upstairs to the studio and went off to the kitchen for cold drinks. The house seemed like something from a distant childhood, Kate thought, dimly remembered but immensely evocative, and she climbed the stairs in mild anticipation of the tidy airiness of Vaun's work space. When she cleared the stairs she had a considerable shock.

The large room was a swirl of color, a frozen moment of intense, urgent activity. The long tables were piled precariously with pads, torn-out sheets of paper scribbled with half-finished sketches, tubes and tubs, brushes, congealed coffee cups, the stubs of ancient sandwiches, brown and mushy apple cores, two bowls with spoons and unrecognizable scum in the bottom. A length of dried orange peel trailed from one work top and disappeared into a closed drawer. Balled-up sheets of thick white paper spilled in a drift from an overflowing waste basket, and there seemed to be at least three palettes currently in use, and four easels.

And the paintings.

All around the walls, two and three deep, the paintings leaned, pulsated, reached out and grabbed the viewer and shouted. Huge paintings, in size as well as temperament—essential, stripped down, powerful faces and bodies, and more than half of them were Andy Lewis. Andy Lewis as Tony Dodson, with Angie. Andy Lewis naked in front of a mirror, meeting the viewer's eyes in the reflection and looking proud and scornful and as sinuous as the tattooed dragon writhing on his arm. Andy Lewis with a beard, looking down with aloof speculation at a child with blond braids. Andy Lewis in a cold rage, a dangerous killing animal that made the flesh creep and the eyes wince away. And finally, on an easel, Andy Lewis with a gun, mocked as a cowboy and acknowledged as a murderer.

Somehow there was a cold glass in her hand, and she realized that Vaun was standing next to her.

"You've . . . been busy," she said weakly. Vaun seemed not to hear her but stood with critical eyes on the naked Andy Lewis.

"He did love me, you know," Vaun mused. "In that he was speaking the plain truth. And he was right too in saying that I never loved him. The only man I've ever loved is doubly safe—both married and my therapist. Perhaps I am saved by my inability to love," she said in consideration, as if Kate were not in the room. "I've never understood how men, and women too, can carry on tumultuous love affairs and still paint. Affection, yes, and lust certainly. Those I understand. But not love."

"You paint it," protested Kate. Vaun glanced at her, then back at the painting.

"Not often, no. When I have, it's usually been one part of something else; loss, or threat. Although recently, I have been trying." They stood for a long minute.

"I wanted him to kill me," she said abruptly. "That night. It was crazy, but it just swept over me, a lust, like sex but stronger. When he came through your door, it seemed right. Not good, but just the only possible way for it all to end. I knew that after all those years he'd come to finish it, and I so wanted it to end, to be taken out of my hands. I wanted him to kill me," she repeated.

"I'm very glad he did not," said Kate quietly.

Vaun sighed and looked at her glass.

"Yes. I have days now when I begin to feel the same." She smiled. "Tell me about Lee."

So Kate told her about Lee, about the surgeries and the slow recovery, about Lee's mind and spirit, about their friends, about her own decision to return to the work that had nearly cost her lover's life. They sat in the hot stillness of Vaun's deck until the afternoon brought a movement of cool air from off the sea, and eventually they went back inside. Kate stopped in front of one of the canvases that was not of Andy Lewis but rather of a young girl with short brown hair and a missing front tooth.

"Jemma Brand?" she asked.

Vaun nodded, paused, and seemed to come to a decision. She tipped the picture forward and reached for the painting in back of it, and when she slid it out, Lee was in the room, Lee standing on legs that were whole and strong at the railing of the Alcatraz ferry, Lee half-turned to look over her shoulder with the laughter spilling out of her, her mouth poised for speech, her tawny hair tumbling about her face in the wind, the whole brilliant light of her blazing out of her eyes. To a stranger it would be a dazzling portrait; to Kate it sent a jolt through every nerve in her body and left her stunned and speechless.

She turned to Vaun, eyes wide and filling, mouth moving helplessly, and then she was crying against Vaun's bony shoulder, feeling the painter's strong arms around her and hearing the age-old litany of comfort.

"It's all right, Kate, it's all right now."

And though she knew that it was not all right, would never be completely all right, she felt, for the first time, that perhaps it might be.

310